Title - WRONG' UN II – 'A proper wrong 'ui
Wyatt © 2016

A CIP catalogue record for this book is available from the British Library.

Dedication

I miss my dear mother in law Patricia Rudman who is no doubt cursing me with her loving two finger salutes from above.

With respect, I also miss two of my mates, Matt Petre and Mick Field who have left the Rugby tour far too early, so see you in the sky bar later guys.

I would like to also thank the many friends from Facebook who allowed their nicknames, altered first or surnames to be added to the storyline, I hope you enjoy your parts no matter how short or long.

Next, my grateful thanks to Elaine Cappi, Lisa Rouse and Richard Baker, my voluntary editors who have been there for me throughout and to Lana Furey my illustrator, massive hugs. However, my greatest dedication is to my wife Paula who through thick and thin has put up with me these past years, a true lady who I love with all my heart, thanks Pumpkin! X

Chapter 1

1956 Texas

Texas, the Lone Star state, the second largest in the USA and it has a land mass that proudly extends to over three times the size of Great Britain. Championed as a state of Stetson wearing cowboys, cattle drives and pecan pie, it is a land that is dominated by desert, over a quarter of a million square miles of it. Born from bedrock, Texas is a place where the sun rivets the soil, a heat so intense it can sear flesh and vapour the horizon. Add to this, 'Wind Devil' dust storms, the insect infestation and the chaos of its tumbleweed, the summer of 56 was indeed a strained one.

In some parts of Texas there pumped the grind of steel rods, a ceaseless pounding, beating down, drilling deep, all of which were depriving Mother Nature of its darkest resource, oil. Each sucking at the earth with fervour and it was no surprise to see at least one oil derrick outside every small town, or even rigs within back yards and this included one such settlement called 'Chapel Hill.' There stood a home, unlike any other, it was where 'Valentine House' was built. Erected like every typical 'gloss white' wooden townhouse in the state, this house was by far the largest and truly, stood out, it was immense, pristine and at least four times the length and breadth of any other of the town's buildings.

Its girth boasted the longest teak wood veranda and, unlike all others, it stood three stories tall. On every level, ornate, stained glass windows sparkled throughout and surrounding this opulent structure lay the tended mint green lawn that sprinklers soaked daily and where flowering white gardenia overflowed fences.

Then, other than the two brand-new cars, one an estate and one a sedan, that sat idly on the driveway, to epitomise its grandeur, sweeping from the street layered in white chip marble, was its pathway. A snake like conduit from sidewalk to house that was flanked on either side by three feet high lengths of ornate, wrought ironwork. Each twisted and turned into artistically fashioned depictions of the various oil rigs that the owner possessed.

Finally, standing tall by the roadway was a 'greeting post,' consisting of thousands of tiny metal strands, each threading skyward, soldered and turned, depicting a tree. And as this stood tall, hanging from one of its many intricate branches, was a white, granite sign, lettered in gold leaf, that bore the name 'Valentine,' a name that oozed wealth.

The town itself stood on a land that had simply forgotten the old ways of farming. Farms that had previously grown clumps of white cotton that brushed the sky like snow, or the laying of pasture where Longhorn cattle once roamed. All had been swept aside by the relentless search for oil and now it was these oil pumps that stretched and emptied its metal horizon. Like so many of the other surrounding Texan towns it was built on land owned by Valentine Hill, this was his birthplace, named after the man's forefathers who'd built a small church and the house that still stood off the main square. Each a symbol to the community, of hope to achieve and a hope to aspire.

Within the home was Naomi, a pretty young woman. She too had a hope of her own, it was the hope of any recently married pregnant woman, one that she would bear her new husband, a large and healthy family.

For it was only three months prior, that Naomi had been a grocery clerk in one of the town's many local shops and it was the man himself, Valentine Hill, who had simply taken a fancy to her when he'd opened the annual summer fair.

It was only a fancy, a flirtatious whim, but soon they were married. Not a whirlwind romance, more like a dash, when the local gossips spread rumours. There was little choice for either, marry, or have the young woman give birth to bastard children.

As for Valentine, apart from being abundantly rich in 'Texas tea,' an apt name for the black oil his wealth swam in; he was older, taller, rather gaunt and plain faced. However, he would always stand out from the crowd with the bright coloured suits that he wore; suits weaved from the finest cotton and stitched in gold thread. Yes, Valentine could stand tall; an educated socialite who was known for his extravagance, he had married a woman, far beneath his stature and it was only Naomi and the local populace that really cared that this marriage should be harmony in the town's largest house.

1963

For the next few years no one in the town really knew the life that went on in the Valentine home.

Was it indeed blissful happiness for Naomi and her husband?

Well Naomi glowed, but this was usually a glow of regular bruises, in coloured variation, from mauve to black and then dark brown. It was beaten flesh that was well hidden by an array of large sunglasses, varied long sleeved tops and dresses that stopped at her ankles.

These injuries would tell their own story if ever questioned, but none were ever asked. As it was, from the birth of the children, the household no longer held lavish parties or welcomed guests and the only visitor ever allowed entry to the hallway would be the weekly grocery delivery. Valentine Hill had now forbidden all else.

Did Naomi have a choice? Well in her small-town mind, no, not really, for having given birth to two children, both a boy and a girl, each in turn had destroyed her womb.

She had a husband who told her what he expected of her and if she or the infant children ever failed him, then he would readily provide her with fists, slaps and kicks and did so telling her that she, "so deserved to be punished."

Beaten for her children's mistakes, she would take the pain without voice and when alone with thoughts of self-loathing, it was this that had her believing that there really was no option.

Naomi couldn't even seek the help of the local sheriff, Valentine owned him, like he owned all of the town who were in his employment, so the hurt, her pain, simply continued.

Then as both children grew older, they also took their beatings, the first tiny tears to the house became regular events and whenever Naomi ever tried to protect them, her beatings became twice as brutal.

Valentine would often take pleasure in his control, to taunt her pleas for mercy. "You haven't a cent to your name, you and your childless body?" In her pained mind, she accepted this torment.

It didn't help that there was little else to occupy her husband's time, the flow of oil and his wealth readily saw to his comfort and as he had tired of his wife and his children, he needed something more. Something more than his fine suits, the expensive whiskey and his regular vacations to the whore houses of Las Vegas.

It took time to figure out what it was that he actually wanted, what he needed, what he craved and it wasn't just being head of his household, he wanted more, more than his local, social status.

He knew he was born for something more than the life that existed for him, he needed recognition, not as the wife or child beater that he was, but he wanted to be seen as a man of stature and influence. So rather than accepting, as he had until then, that he was just a small voice in the second largest state of America, he decided he would do something about it.

Within weeks and a town's vote, Valentine became the town's mayor, it was an easy bribe with the sudden exit of the former and he enjoyed this first fledgling step to becoming, as he thought, revered.

It was a sudden spotlight and he revelled in this bloodless victory, so much so, that within six months and with further cash outlays and small-town promises, he became the Mayor of three other nearby towns.

Even the smallest of hamlets that didn't have a mayor, soon had one, for Mr Valentine Hill had quickly bought each on his political journey ahead.

This sudden change altered life within the family home and it was good news for Naomi. The beatings had become less frequent and it had become apparent to her that the more power and influence her husband gained elsewhere, the less he sought violence on her and the children.

Mayor Valentine Hill would steal himself away to this meeting or that hearing, the radio slots, a multitude of interviews and engagements with numerous, varied assemblies. Then there were the countless photo shoots, where opposition candidates would cynically sneer that Valentine would 'scissor open a shoebox' if it got him into the state papers.

All this accolade and jealousy rose from his God-given right to be powerful, it was his vision to represent the masses and in his every waking moment, he strove to achieve success.

Regularly he would take up his office at the Chapel Hill Town Hall, on every evening including Sundays between 6 and 8pm. He presided in his room as an open invite to his local constituents, these included those from afar. There he would hear their pledges of support, or listen to a grievance and although few stepped over the threshold, he and his secretary would be there each night.

It was also at his office where he would plan his next campaign, a campaign for the next election and the potential next target. It was his largest to date, his preparation for the Republican nomination in the Texas state election and it was to be a nomination battle that would change Naomi's life forever.

It was another pre-election evening and a hot summer's night, where just breathing would bring on perspiration. Yet again her husband Valentine wasn't at home, but was working from the town hall instead.

So, with the children safely asleep in their beds, Naomi decided to walk the two blocks from their townhouse to the Town Hall, where she hoped that she would pleasantly surprise her husband.

Long slimmed down, as if giving birth had never existed, Naomi was long bruise free and all smiles as she opened the main door and slowly ascended the two flights of marbled steps up to his office. All the time she carefully balanced the white enamel metal tray holding a small flask of hot coffee and a plate of her home-made fruit pie, a balance that was to topple when she reached and opened the office door, to the scene that she was confronted with.

Staring open mouthed in disbelief she widely stared, seeing her semi-naked husband who was, only just, wearing his half open sweat soaked shirt and 'yanked down' tight knotted tie. Her husband, her man, had just brought his young secretary to yet another climax as she lay naked, sprawled across his desk of strewn paperwork that now littered the floor. This pert breasted, young girl who, having bitten her hand to stem the screams of orgasm, this 'hussy' bitch, who now lay arching her back, pleading, "please sir," for more.

The tray fell from her grasp, Naomi was mortified, horrified, sickened. She had caught the father of their children, her husband, 'compromised' with this young secretary, ten years her junior with the longest of legs and all curves. But worst of all, although her husband was slightly embarrassed, he just looked up and told Naomi to, close the door behind her.

He actually didn't care! He simply told Naomi there and then to leave, only he was important he announced, as she turned to leave.

Only he had the money, he yelled, as she closed the door behind her.

Only he had the foresight to believe in himself, to become more than what she could ever dream of. This was screamed as she sobbed to the first step back down on the landing. When Valentine returned home, as the hour closed on midnight, he did no more than strike his wife with a blow and warned her that, "if the entanglement, were ever made public," he spate down on her, "then it would merely be a small setback towards his greatness."

That and she wouldn't be around long enough to tell anyone.

Little did Naomi realise that her husband Valentine wasn't actually going to take a chance on her telling anyone of his misdemeanour and it was within a week of tears and torment that her husband had cased and crated all of her and the children's belongings into the large estate and drove them hours away to one of his families' old properties.

They were simply spirited away by Valentine, out of Chapel Hill, out of his thoughts and out of his aspirations, to a third cousin's ranch far away.

It was hours and hours of interstate highways, then bumpy roads and dirt tracks that led them towards vast barren landscapes and it was almost an hour's drive from the last town signpost that pointed a way towards the nearest town of Ranger, Texas. It was close to dawn when they passed several minutes of broken, wooden staves and old, barbed wire fencing that led them to a large overhanging wooden gateway sign named, Hill.

It was a further short drive before Valentine braked outside the dilapidated ranch building where he turned off the engine.

It had taken Valentine over a day's drive of cold emotional feelings; all the time being shadowed by his smiling secretary who drove roughshod behind in Valentine's other car.

When Valentine finally pulled out the last of their bags, cases and food crates from both of the cars, he handed Naomi keys for the front door and shutters, a list of his instructions and a local map marked with two large X's. One X depicting the ranch she now stood at and the other positioned the town of Ranger. Only then did Naomi realise that it wasn't going to be 'living' for her and the two children, just a mere existence.

She and the children had been driven to this solitude of what was to be a tortured isolation, where her husband Valentine Hill had decided that he was rich enough to keep her there, quietly, for as long as he wanted or needed.

Chapter 2

The ranch was just a very large old building set on two levels each with a veranda. There were outbuildings behind and set back at the sides. This was all that there was amongst the barren wilderness, a wood rotting ranch, outhouses and a few large trees set away far out back. It was a place where the children's young tears were soon smothered in the dust of a car that u-turned away.

Naomi and the children were to live there alone, abandoned, forsaken, on this, an old, family ranch. No staff, no-one to help, just the three of them and Naomi joined her children's tears.

Naomi, having eventually gathered herself and opening the padlocked front door, called for her children to follow. Within the main room were sheets covering lighting and furniture, its walls were canvassed in portraits of her husband's dead ancestors. Each competed for space and each stared down disdainfully on them. Portraits of old faces, only occasionally separated by the various landscape paintings and old black and white framed survey photographs of the house and the surrounding land from varying angles.

The lighting was a mixture of gas, oil or candlelight, though there were a couple of electric sockets that gave hope to Naomi that there was a generator somewhere in existence and she silently prayed that it worked. At the back of the ranch house was a large kitchen and pantry, the contents of which were old, out of date and somewhat hazardous to health, Naomi noted that these she would clear away herself. As for the kitchen sink, it was a butler style and ceramic, one that had to be filled via an adjacent hand pump and it took her a while to pump brown water to near clear. At least the bathrooms upstairs had tap plumbing that also worked and she was fortunate to understand back boilers and fireplaces from her small apartment some years before. So at least there would be warmth and warm water, but on that first chilly night her and her scared children shared the same bed in the master bedroom.

The next day, all three set about cleaning each room in turn, first a bedroom for both son and daughter, then the kitchen, then the bathrooms, the rest would have to wait for the days and weeks to come.

That next night Naomi lay alone in bed, alone in restless sleep in that old creaking ranch, alone and in fear, as tired little children slept soundly down the corridor.

She was alone and haunted whilst she dreamt her nightmare. Only to be woken in cold shivers and sweat, physically shaking and reliving the moment when, only a couple of days before, she actually once and once only, had threatened her husband with a public divorce. It was a moment whilst packing her suitcase, that Valentine had simply reached into the bedroom drawer and pulled out a small, silver revolver and aiming it to her head, he ordered her, "Kneel!"

Having cocked back the hammer, he whispered, "you dare!"

1968

Within weeks, not months and then for years to come, if it could be 'popped, drunk, smoked or swallowed' then it was Naomi's goal to immerse her body and mind in a repeated weekend ritual of drug and alcohol abuse. She hadn't coped, she had tried and although there was a distant memory where once she thought she might have been able to secure a stable life for her children's sake, it was now just a distant blur.

Her once young-looking body was now into 'anything' to combat her daily lows as she self-abused and self-harmed in abundance. This once beautiful young lady whose long auburn hair, green eyes and the sweetest of dimpled smiles, was now sad, lonely and to all, but the small-town flings and her children, Naomi had become an outcast.

The children were now pre-teen and scarred, branded and detached. Victims of their father's want of another woman and neither child understood their mother's progressive mental decline.

Neither were schooled, their days simply filled by ritual chores, as both vied for their mother's attention and affection. It was any sense of worth they wanted, both desperate to fill the void of a missing father and a seldom present mother's love.

And if their father hadn't beat them enough, now it was mother's turn. And just like their father had done before, it was due to the failing in the smallest of chores. Cowering tears passed tea time, belt whipped till bedtime, oh how she would hit them if they didn't match her Valentine's standards. This was how Naomi now reacted when she thought of these children, she couldn't help herself, the frustration that came with these products of that bastard that had sent her to oblivion. She hated them and she loved them, she loathed herself. More often she would hug them, but push them away as just as easily, she saw sense, then no sense at all.

Naomi's only escape from reality was the small town of Ranger, it was a place she would drive to and spend all of her weekends, from Friday until Sunday afternoon.

After a quick bank visit to pick up her weekly allowance that Valentine had set up, tying the transfer of funds to that bank alone, she without the children, without a care would purchase groceries comprising of tinned and bottled everything. Then it was petrol for the car and diesel in a barrel for the generator.

After that the weekend was hers and it was regularly filled with self-indulgence and self-loathing. The alcohol, the drugs, the local college boys and the passing old men, all of these would fill her body and time.

In the first couple of months she had tried to form relationships, but the young men simply thought of her as, 'just a hangout fuck' and the elder males simply treated her as a side line to their own broken relationships, it soon became known in the Motel where she stayed, that there was a regular conveyor belt of grunted moans and a banging headboard.

Mostly Naomi didn't care, for in those sweat filled moments she would feel wanted again, in amongst that kaleidoscope of pills and a multitude of males, some of whom needlessly paid for her company.

She would have her sobering Sunday morning moments though, where awake, either alone or besides snoring flesh, this was when she would reflect on her life. When another weekend ritual was over, there she would sit quietly dressing, quietly crying and quietly she would head for the door.

But on odd occasions of clarity, she actually tried to seek inner peace by reading the motel's Gideon's bible. Whence she would look to the lord, praying silently for help and it was all types of prayer that she read. Turning the thin tissue paper, she sought anything to find an answer to her mental and moral decline. It was reading this book when she would ask to be delivered from herself, from the endless self-hate, the loneliness, her life. But she never heard a voice answer in that God-fearing state of Texas.

Naomi knew she needed someone or something though, yes 'free love' was indeed moments of pleasure to be held, used and sodomised, sometimes by one and often by more, but this had no real meaning and she hungered, frustrated, she truly wanted a reason to live.

Just a hope, perhaps? Maybe to somehow belong again, to be wanted, or simply to be liked? She didn't know exactly what she needed, other than her urgings to include the drugs and the male company that she would crave for, men that she now took as sustenance.

And it was on one of those hot summer Sunday afternoons, having showered and paid for her room, when driving from Ranger that her life would indeed take a new direction and deliver yet another life change.

It was when Naomi turned into the bend on the road, where she almost past them by and almost accelerated away from that travelling commune parked off the roadway opposite. Little did she know that in time, they would eventually, nearly all, pass, pass over and come across her in turn.

Chapter 3

Naomi quickly slowed the estate to a crawl and that's when she saw a couple of men standing on the bumper of a grey truck's hood, only then did she notice the steam rise, up toward heaven, burning hot vapour 'waved off and away' quite fervently by one of them.

Travis was the one frantically waving and coughing as he inspected the split hose that connected to the radiator. A rubber that now hissed and he was just a little fretful at the scalding water that hit the ground below.

His people had not had it easy over the last few weeks, it seemed that with each new place they visited they were told to leave within a couple of hours. It was as if by smoke signal the next towns were alerted, but more likely by phone and, of the last three towns, their local sheriffs stopped them on their approach to the outskirts, where they were turned and sent on their way.

Travis knew his commune was long overdue a decent rest, a week or so to claim social welfare payments, to preach and pick up provisions.

'Still not bad for a minister's kid from Alabama,' he thought.

It was a far cry from his younger days when he and his father, a man of God, would travel from small hick town to small nothing hamlets, where his daddy would give sermons from the back of their old camper van and where Travis would be found walking among the crowd collecting coins in an old sack cloth encouraging, "Alleluia!" Three to fifty times on each Sunday.

He had been a young boy of sixteen then, a young buck, who truly cared for his father. A daddy who was progressively ill from one ailment or more and when in the end the cancer had chewed away most of his father's body, that Christian God had left Travis alone.

Left alone in tears to bury his father, he had built up a small mound of rocks on dirt-hard ground just off the main highway. It was his daddy's final resting place, simply chosen on hearing his father's last breath and as the last rock was placed, Travis renounced God, just as God had left him.

However, he hadn't quite finished in praising the lord, it was still his only income after all. He knew he could still draw the crowds just like his pappy had done. However, he had ambition and was struck by a concept, he would prey on the homeless, the forgotten and flawed.

Travis already understood it was these people who would be easiest to convince. So many in the past had asked to join him and his father on their Christian journey. These he would turn and if possible subjugate. So, when he drove off from his dead father's grave, Travis was suddenly reborn as a guiding light to unfortunates, but with the darkest thoughts towards personal wealth.

It was only in the next town that he found two young men who were willing to follow his lead, the town after, one more male and four women. Then more followed in a mixture of personal beliefs and the Old Testament, these were now his thoughts and 'his religion.'

It was a religion where his God had specifically chosen him to become the spiritual leader and it was his 'free spirits' that he sent out amongst the crowds that collected and sometimes stole for him.

In the early days of being the new prophet, teacher and priest, Travis had no real religious direction other than profit and he now used God as God had used him and his father. He used this religion to see his belly and his pockets fill.

Travis found it easy speaking to strangers, he had done it all his young life and as the congregations swallowed his sermons it was then his immediate followers would demand money for spiritual freedom from those that listened. It was Travis who kept the 'collections' and those that travelled with him would, without fail, pass him their weekly welfare payments.

Religion was easy pickings and Travis not only had a way that would fill his wallet, but there were other Godly perks. He could gain sexual gratification from the bodies of gullible young women, by ridding the various demons, pumping them out with his weapon of hope.

'Yeah, not bad for a minister's kid,' Travis thought to himself as he glanced at Naomi approach and slowdown.

--//--

The commune's vehicles comprised of the sickly grey army truck, a couple of second-hand, old, yellow school buses and then there was a couple of cars and an ex-army motorbike.

But each of these had a large, black, hand painted logo daubed on each side that read TFS and each of these letters were held within an outer diamond shape. Naomi saw this, just as she noticed that some of the people were just standing there, mingling, some sitting and one was even playing a guitar. However, what was peculiar was that all of them were smiling.

Perhaps there were fifty or sixty or, she calculated; comprising of men, women and quite a few children and all were of various ethnicities and age.

Naomi locked the brakes of the saloon estate to an immediate halt and stopped adjacent to the hissing grey truck and Travis.

Naomi wound down her window, "Howdy guys, you need anything to fix it? There's a town and it's only a few miles or so down the highway." She pointed her thumb back over her shoulder.

On hearing her voice Travis turned himself away from under the bonnet and jumped down from the bumper.

To Naomi he appeared a young man, early twenties, fit and firm in his open buttoned red checked shirt, as he quickly walked towards the watchful Naomi. Wiping his brow, he leant forward and with his hands on his knees and smiling bright white teeth he said, "Hi there sweetness and thank you."

'Nice looking,' Naomi thought as she felt herself stare at his Athenian features, with his sweptback black hair, dark piercing eyes and large chiselled chin.

"Are you good?" She flustered a little.

"We would be, if I could take you up on your kind offer. We need tape to seal a broken hose pipe or a replacement." He answered, drawing another smile of pearly ivory.

'Very nice indeed.' Naomi thought and smiled back. "Jump in."

Travis walked round her car and sprawled the cream coloured leather bench seat across from her. Naomi turned the car around and both her and her car quietly purred their way back towards town.

At first there was a silence from the male passenger beside her that made Naomi feel a little uneasy. That was until he stirred from thought and introduced himself. "My name's Travis," he drawled.

"Naomi," she replied. It wasn't long before the commune blurred into the heat-hazed distance.

"Will a garage be open on a Sunday?" Travis asked.

Naomi smiled back towards him. "I know the garage owner personally," she told him. "He will open up for us," and gave thought that, 'Ned' had better open up his garage, she had always opened herself for him whenever his wife was out of town,' and the stranger smiled back at her.

With every mile Naomi's attraction grew, this young man was indeed a hunk of flexed muscle and on closer inspection she came to notice that on both his forearms there was an inked black tattoo, with the same TFS logo within a diamond shape and she curiously asked, "TFS, what is that?"

Travis cleared his throat and spoke from well-rehearsed lines. "It's a commune of wandering spirits, brought together to follow life's journey, bringing happiness to all," and he waved his left arm back behind them as if to encompass those that he had just left behind.

"We belong to no one, but each other, we live for each other and we are partners of no one, but each other. We follow not one singular religion, but are comforted from all religions that suit our lifestyle. So, we are every religion," he continued, "and we travel because we have no home or commitment. No commitment, but the commitment to each other, our spirits all follow the earth on which we tread."

'Wow!' Naomi thought, through the aftermath of her drink/drugged mind and embraced the idea. "That's cool."

The car's radio continued to blare out more country songs as the journey progressed and Naomi's gazed silence was ever increasing on this young man, rather him than on the road that lay ahead.

Travis was all too aware of this gaze as Naomi had to correct her steering on a number of occasions.

"Would you like me to drive?" He laughed.

"No thank you." She giggled. "I'm fine, just a little tired," and she leant back, stretching an arch in her back, where she shook her shoulder length hair, left, right and back again.

"It's nearly noon and you have only just got up." Travis teased as he leant ever more forward in his seat, staring across at her.

"How do you know?" Naomi asked.

"Well you're hardly dressed," and he again laughed and loudly, as Naomi followed his gaze and looked down at her half-buttoned blouse. Her braless chest, to near navel, was open, exposed and she realised that the desert wind that blew in from the open windows was billowing her blouse out, away from her body, revealing glimpses of her left breast and pert nipple.

"Oh my," she gasped realising her earlier 'hung over' dressing misfortune and she braked sharply to stop.

"I'm sorry." Travis apologised as the car suddenly halted, "but you are as nature intended Naomi, you are a beautiful lady."

Naomi had only managed to button one of the lower buttons as he finished the compliment and she decided to stop the refastening.

Looking back across to Travis there was a smile and an immediate blush as she replied. "Thank you'.'

Naomi again looked down to her tummy and reopened up that very same button. "Thank you," but this time in a whisper, as she looked up and forward towards the road ahead.

Naomi accelerated the car swiftly until there was the same clothing flow as before. Not another word was spoken by either during the next few minutes; Travis was again staring and Naomi's mind was filling with the thoughts of being taken and consumed by this fibrous Athenian.

Onward she drove to the occasional laughter from both as her blouse repeatedly billowed outward, revealing all of what little virtue she once had. There were quiet murmured giggles when the cotton cloth would intermittently return to her skin, only for Naomi to adjust her seating position, to lean her neck forward and down to bite on the neckline collar, lifting the blouse so it could billow again.

"Do you live in town?" Travis asked with some urgency.

"No, I live about an hour away on a ranch with my children." Naomi replied.

"Are you married?" Was the immediate next question and Naomi replied, "I am and I am not, only in name and a weekly transfer of funds to the bank in town, I haven't seen him in years, I don't wear his ring and I don't care anymore."

"Are you?" Naomi suddenly asked, noting that each of his fingers and thumbs bore at least one ring or more.

Travis was silent in the contemplation of an answer, but soon smiled as he leant across towards Naomi and unbuttoned the last two bottom buttons of her blouse. Naomi gasped as, in that second, the wind flapped her blouse completely open across her body exposing her breasts. Increasing in her breath, it tightened her nipples. Naomi now sat squirming in moistened desire, but still she remained silent as she looked back at Travis.

Her mind was pleading to be taken, but she still sought an answer as Travis reached across and brushed, caressed and gently caressed each breast in turn and, in doing, he looked into her face, "those women back there are all my wives and all those men are all their husbands."

Travis leant back and explained. "TFS, means Travis Free Spirits. Naomi do you think you are you willing to be a free spirit of mine, or just a passing moment in time?"

Naomi glanced back from Travis and stared at the highway ahead. Everything was too fast flowing for Naomi's body and mind to fully understand this concept, but again she braked quickly, steering her car off the highway over the side of the road.

Within a few bumpy seconds, the estate engine was turned off and Naomi was across, straddling this young man called Travis. Earnestly their mouths pressed tight with an entwining of tongues. All her remaining clothes were pulled free. Hands caressed, hair gripped by fingers, there was urgency as their bodies wrapped around each other's. Taking, squeezing, pulsing, to a multitude of climatic rejoices.

For it was there on that hot, sunny Sunday in Texas, on that deserted desert highway, that the seconds turned to minutes and those minutes into hours.

It was almost dark when Travis and Naomi returned to the commune of people and buses, to the stricken truck where Travis stood on the bumper and announced to all that, "Naomi was yet another Travis Free Spirit."

There were some cheers, whistles and claps of approval as each of the men and women warmly welcomed her to their fold, all hugging, some of them kissing her cheeks, others, her lips. There was acceptance and it wasn't long before the new hose and clips, given 'free gratis' by Ned, were attached and the small convey was on the move.

The night sky was darkening to a tinged mauve plume as the vehicles drove onward. It was Naomi's car, with Travis beside her that guided the way. Shepherding the flock towards the Hill's ranch homestead, a place where Travis had announced to the group, that with Naomi's blessing, they were welcome to stay.

--//--

Their mummy had never been this late home, but, with their nearest neighbour over several hours walk away and the homestead having no phone, the children simply had to wait and it was late evening when both boy and girl caught sight of the various beams of headlights that slowly bounced their way up the dirt road entrance towards their home.

A few minutes later the vehicles halted and both children ran with outstretched arms towards their mother. Hugs to remove the fear of all these strangers outside the ranch, but other than saying, "this is Travis and these people are now staying here," she was dismissive towards their frets.

Pulling their arms away from her waist she concentrated on Travis, talking and laughing as they mounted the porch steps and walking inside, her frightened children followed and so did the guests.

It was sunrise by the time the final pair of eyes closed to sleep and these eyes belonged to the spiritual leader, he lay next to Naomi in the main bedroom suite, satisfied that he had taken her a further time before she slept.

He was more than content having seen his 'Free Spirits' fed and watered. There were nearly beds for all, six bedrooms in the main house and the further disused beds in a cowboy 'bunk house' out back. That and the two empty barns outside. Naomi didn't object to moving her children in with other commune children into one bedroom just down the long corridor, Travis told her that her kids were no more special than the next and she willingly agreed

Naomi woke around midday to the sound of Travis's raised voice. It was quite vocal as it came from outside the rear of the ranch. She rose quickly and walked to the bedroom veranda where she slipped on her cotton night gown before walking outside. It was afternoon sun and her bleary eyes focussed against the sun's glare where she was able to make out her Travis standing in front of the audience of seated followers. They were about a hundred yards from the main house and partially sheltered under one of the large oak trees that grew on the property. The men, women and the children, including her own, were sitting there listening.

She couldn't clearly make out the words, but Travis was holding what looked like an inverted white cross with a large circular eye shape at its base and he was gesticulating with his arms and pointing the cross object directly towards the group who sat before him. When he would point an individual would raise both arms up, high to the sky, whilst calling out praise. Naomi realised that Travis was holding some form of sermon, she wanted to hear more, so she dressed.

Walking outside towards the group Naomi was able to make out words such as "spiritual path, wiccan belief, pagan virtue and salvation," then they were, "all blessed with benefits."

Only yards from the gathering she heard Travis now issuing orders as to what was to be done that day. "Washing," and he called out a couple of names. "Cooking duties," more names. "Wood gathering," lots of names. Next came the call, "to town," in one of the buses, "to claim benefits." He said. With this came a list of at least twenty names. Next Travis ordered. "Guard duty," and a further four names were called out.

'Guard duty though, there was no need to guard duty,' Naomi thought as she walked closer, but before she could question, Travis had noticed and smiled broadly towards her, his grin melted her thoughts.

"Lastly, children's education; Beth and Angie take the children away please." He called and, on this, two women, both pregnant, rose and gathered all the children who passed Naomi, back towards the house.

Travis was concluding and pointing an outstretched arm towards Naomi, his palms open in acceptance and called out to the sky. "We thank the gods and the demons of this earth and the all-seeing eye of nature for Naomi, our latest free spirit." The audience each turned towards Naomi and in one voice they all spoke together. "You are blessed, blessed are you."

'Thanks to you, my spirits run free." Travis announced as he beckoned his followers to rise.

It was then Naomi noticed that there were still some children present, probably 13, 14 or 15 year olds and two of those girls looked pregnant too. Naomi pointed this out to Travis when he finally approached her.

"Waifs and strays," he told her, "they have now found salvation, they are as free a spirit as you or I." He assured her.

"And did I hear you mention guard duty? Why's that?" Naomi enquired, a little perplexed.

"We have had trouble on our journey in the past," he told her, "and it is only a precaution to stop any further happenings." Before another question could be formulated he took her in his arms and kissed her passionately, sating the questions that were held in her mind.

Both then walked back with others to the main house and, where others went off on their chores, Naomi and Travis sat on the porch. It was Travis that talked as both watched the men and women working all around them and it was Travis that stood and waved off the bus that left the ranch for town.

It was only then that Naomi was drawn to tell of her past and it was her man Travis that listened intently as he held both her hands. She told of her wandering husband, the abandonment, her loss. Then the leading to drink, drugs and male company that she had fallen to. Travis never flinched, nor minded as pent up emotion ran through her tears.

Travis finally excused himself from her cries as he told Naomi that he would fetch her 'something' to calm hers down. Travis walked to the kitchen where he added powder and crushed tablets to a liquid concoction, then, within a few minutes, he returned with a glass of commune 'lemonade.'

Handing her this in one hand and a further two pills in the other she, without question, took them and swallowed. From later recollection, she then felt faint.

Naomi couldn't remember how she had found herself back in her bed, stark naked and in the darkness with Travis, but she was sure that at some point he had had his way, for she was a damp and a little sore between her legs. Slowly she tried to raise herself to her elbows, but she felt so weak and closed her eyes to the night.

Chapter 4

The next morning Travis leant over Naomi and woke her with a kiss and a smile. He was dressed and sitting on top of the bed. He told Naomi "I have run you a bath next door and there are some books for you that I want you to read." She followed his pointing finger to the wicker bedside cabinet and, as she focussed, towards the books stacked on top of each other.

"That's nice coffee as well, why thank you!" Naomi observed the steaming hot mug beside them.

"You're welcome," he said and without further ado he stood and left the bedroom and woman behind him.

Naomi leant over and took hold of the three books that were there, all quite large and thick in depth. One was on sorcery, witchcraft and the ancient spiritual arts, one was the bible and the last was titled Astrology and the Gods. She opened the sorcery book and began to read between sips. She wasn't long through the introduction before curiosity caught her.

Feeling light headed she took the three books to the bathroom and began reading again, soaking fatigue away.

She would have been quicker in the bath having dismissed the bible in an instant, however, the other two books were something quite different and she became engrossed in both, turning from one book to the other, flicking from page to chapter, amazed at the endless possibilities that the theories suggested.

Eventually she felt better and, once dressed, Naomi went downstairs where again she found the house was in full working flow. Women cleaning, others polishing and the children, including her own daughter, were oiling the wooden floors.

Naomi felt a rasping in her throat that she needed to quench, so turned to the kitchen.

The two young girls that were inside greeted her with both a smile and a kiss. Each were in their late teens and introduced themselves as 'Peri' and 'Judy.' Naturally pretty with no make-up, they offered her broth from the large cauldron that sat on the wood burning stove. Naomi gladly accepted as she couldn't recall the last time she had ate and it, "tasted wonderful," she told them.

Naomi wanted to know more about the commune and asked how the girls had come to be a "Travis free spirit" Both strangely answered in unison, "we were saved." However, when asked where they had been brought up? Peri explained that they were not allowed to tell, because their true life had only begun when they met Travis and now there was no longer any past to their lives.

Naomi thought this weird, but accepted the fact that both girls seemed happy enough as they talked about the various spirits and gods that Travis had opened their eyes too. Those same beings that had blessed them whilst being with Travis and the other commune men, but it was when Judy told her "Soon a second will be chosen for you',' a slow reckoning dawned on Naomi.

"A second, what do you mean?" Naomi questioned hesitantly.

"A second, Travis will move on, he always does and either tonight or tomorrow he will find another man to take his place in you," the girl explained.

Naomi spluttered the warm broth from her mouth. "I thought this might happen." Naomi admitted. "But I had hoped I was special," she flustered.

"We each have turns, all women are wives and each man is a husband, we are a family." Peri explained.

Naomi had heard those words before but hadn't questioned them because Travis had remained with her. Foolishly Naomi had begun to believe that she was the exception.

"Thank you." Naomi said as she left the kitchen, she was heading with one purpose, to find Travis.

Travis was nowhere to be found inside so she looked outside. It wasn't long before one of the followers, gathering wood, directed Naomi towards the ranch entrance where Travis was, apparently, 'supervising.'

It was a long walk on unsteady legs so Naomi decided to wait on the ranch's front porch. It felt like an eternity as she sat on a wooden bench with the sun crisping her skin.

Whilst waiting Naomi observed the various manual activities around her, the youngest of children being taught off in the distance and from what she could hear, they were harmonised by the feint tones of song. Others passed, some carrying wood, others fresh meat and other cleaned washing, but no Travis.

"Still securing the perimeter," one man had told her, "with his guards checking on our safety." Naomi was still more than a little uneasy about the word 'Guards.' Naomi simply didn't understand why they needed them, no one had ever ventured onto her property in those years before. Which was, by the way, okay with her, so there was 'no need for guards' she told herself.

A little later her thoughts and solitude were interrupted by the repeated loud cracks and thuds from the rear of the ranch, noises she had never heard before and so she rose to investigate. Walking towards one of the barns out rear her eyes were confronted with shock. She saw her son being instructed on how to use and fire a rifle, a tranquiliser gun that fired its needles into a large target that had been attached to the side wall. There she saw that a couple of coloured dart syringes pierced the paper cross whilst others embedded elsewhere in the old wooden structure.

Naomi took one quick breath and screamed. "No!"

Her son's morning fun was suddenly ruined.

'No more." She shouted at the bearded man who stared sternly back at her, a stare that made her take a step back on the dusty ground.

Naomi called her son over and watched as her boy handed the rifle back to the man who quickly exchanged smiles, but as the man looked back over to Naomi the smile had vanished and mummy quickly walked away with her son.

--//--

It was gone midday when Naomi saw her car driving up to the main house, she noticed that it was Travis who was driving and that he had two of the other men in the car with him.

As the estate pulled over beside the house Naomi walked to the side of the porch and called out to Travis. Naomi called his name, but all three men looked straight at her. It was then she saw that one held a scoped rifle whilst the other held a large handgun, similar to something that she had seen in old cowboy films.

Naomi immediately recollected her husband and his threat with a gun, her body began to buckle under the realisation of facing even more guns. She caught hold of the large window-frame ledge for support.

Travis quickly walked to her and, jumping up onto the porch, he soon held her. The other two just walked away, laughing, towards the rear of the ranch, out of sight, towards the outbuildings where she had just found her son.

"Hey baby, are you okay?" Travis asked as he held both arms gently.

"I don't like guns, I don't like them at al." Naomi cried a reply and as soon as she said this she caught a glimpse of Travis' waistband where the butt handle of a pistol protruded, black as night, dark as death.

Travis held her tight, "you want to be safe, don't you?" he asked her.

"I don't want guns here Travis, they frighten me." Naomi pleaded.

Quickly Travis looked over his shoulder and all around in search of a follower, he suddenly noticed Kate.

"Kate," he called out with urgency and she hurried over.

Kate was quickly introduced and Travis asked her to explain to Naomi how she had been beaten, 'for just being different.'

All three sat on the porch benches, for the next half hour Kate poured her heart out as to how she had gladly joined the free spirits. However, there was one occasion, when going into a town from their encampment nearby, when she was there simply to buy groceries, that she was attacked. She told a story about a couple of drunken local men who had taken their turns in punching her body, slapping her face and kicking her along the ground, just because they didn't like 'hippy strangers.'

As Kate spoke of the blows she received, her grip of Naomi's hand grew tighter, "it's the grip they held," she told her.

The town's sheriff did nothing, even though she had been hospitalised for a couple of weeks and then, when she was discharged, the 'Travis Free Spirits' were moved on by that very same sheriff with one of his deputies, one of the men that had beaten her.

The tearful story, once told, soon turned to smiles, as Kate began to thank Naomi for her new-found happiness in feeling safe at her ranch, 'feeling free.'

Kate hugged Naomi as if she was squeezing happiness into her host and suddenly, with that, she left both to continue her chores.

Naomi looked at Travis readying herself for her next question, "so am I to be shared?" She needed the right answer.

"Only if you want, only if you desire and if you do, you choose the woman or man, not I." he responded.

"A woman?" Naomi spoke as she thought and that thought hadn't even occurred to her as an option. Well that wasn't for her and, "no thank you," she told him.

Travis then divulged, "Listen, in about an hour we will be holding a small prayer meeting. A ceremony for all to welcome you as one of the free spirits, where you will be celebrated as a saviour, you will learn more about us then." With that Travis lent in close to Naomi and kissed her passionately. Though upset she responded in kind.

Eventually they drew breath, Travis whispered his love as they cuddled and the gun in his waistband? He dropped that under the bench where they sat and with that out of sight, Naomi began to feel far more comfortable, the first comfort that she had felt since waking.

Travis changed the subject and talked about the heavenly guides, the stars of direction and the various spells of enchantment that enhanced each earthly life. He spoke of the various religions and that, "they couldn't all be right!"

"Each must be flawed, surely, where they seek out to harm those that aren't followers." And this, as an example, was where Naomi agreed.

Finally, he spoke of the true love that he held for her and all the love of other 'free spirits' and Naomi was again submerged in his smiles, his charm and his kisses with each minute that passed.

The hour had flown and Travis asked Naomi to make her way to the large tree for the daily gathering saying that he would join her presently. Naomi walked to the tree, still slightly unsteady, but eventually she sat under the coolness of shadows from branches and leaves.

As she sat she saw Travis walk out from the ranch house ringing a large brass bell. He rang this in one hand and in the other he held the 'white cross and circle' that Naomi had seen him wave the day before. She sat back smiling as she watched him stride out towards her and following in ones, twos or as group, the commune gathered, including the children.

Within minutes all sat as Travis stood under the tree, it was sparse shadowed earth where Travis led the singing, he was accompanied by two guitarists and a tambourine girl. There were songs about invisible spirits, love and his religion, all quite catchy tunes, but it was apparent that only she and a couple of others didn't know the words.

Naomi looked at her two children, they seemed happy enough as they smiled broadly in the tight group of children that were surrounded by women and Naomi suddenly realised that she hadn't even spoken to her daughter since the commune's arrival and felt a little sad for not doing so.

As the final song finished Travis' sermon began. Naomi, just like the others, was mesmerised by his smiles, his passion and the clarity in the passages on a notepad from which he spoke.

He made mention of 'life and the resurrection in Phoenix' and he spoke of the various journeys that had been taken by his free spirits. He preached of 'the Sphinx and the conversion of shapes from any creature, such as the snake.'

It was all quite strange to Naomi, but every so often he would point the white cross/circle at an individual and would scream, "Do you believe?"

The answer would always be shouted in return. "Yes, I believe."

"All of you, do you believe in me?" he would cry out on lifting his arms to the sky, all would hail back. "Yes, we believe!"

Naomi found herself caught up in the euphoria and also called out her affirmation to Travis, she would clap as the others clapped and would whoop as others yelled and this went on for easily an hour.

Travis finally announced the sermon was closing with, 'The welcome ceremony' and there he asked Naomi, her two children and three mid-teenage youngsters, one boy and two girls, to stand.

Naomi recognised one of the girls as local to the area, a girl that would also visit Ranger at a weekend with her father.

All six received gifts from the commune and each commune member, in turn, walked forward and presented a small gift to each. There were flowers, flowered weeds, handmade cards and locks of hair. Naomi lost count of the times she had to say, "thank you'.'

Travis himself gave a gift of a charmed necklace that he hung around each neck. Once this was done Travis asked the six to remain standing whilst the kitchen girls approached with bowls of broth to drink down in one gulp and each tried their best to do so.

Chapter 5

Naomi woke with a start, again there was darkness, but even so her eyes tried to focus, to look upon and again find her Travis who lay down beside her. He was there, but so were the memories of a dream that broke her sleep.

Those fantasies that had woken her in such fright and anguish, were they true?

Hazy recollections of being carried away from the tree, hands holding her high, by eight or so men, carried upstairs, but not to her room but the children's bedroom where she was stripped, laid and taken. Was it dreaming or reality? When did she lose her consciousness?

These men, each one, were from the group that had carried her, they had stripped her bare and she had been passed from one to the other, amongst the grunts, sweat and smiles of these pleasured strangers.

The worst of the dream, 'please be a dream,' was when she had noticed that most of the youngest children looked on. All of them no older than about ten years of age. As she gazed in all directions, each child was laughing and cheering with each thrust, but not her children, they weren't there.

Naomi tried to calm her waking terror and raise herself once more, but strangely, even the heaviness of her breath held her tight to the mattress and with a sideways glance, she looked on her man and tried to convince herself to dispel those vivid thoughts.

It was he that had taken her that night and filled her body, not others, she tried to reassure herself and as for her children, they were fine, she convinced the doubt, they were simply sleeping down the corridor.

Chapter 6

When Naomi woke she found Travis had gone, but he had left a note on the bedside cabinet, 'Bath and books next door,' and on the note, was a smiley face too with three xxx and she smiled.

Climbing out of bed wasn't easy, she felt so weak, drained and breathless, but slowly, so slowly, she wrapped her bath robe around herself and edged her way along the corridor to the adjacent bathroom. With each step she sought support, holding or leaning into anything that would hold her frame on that short journey and it was another long soak, as she gathered her strength, where the time melted away.

Laying there she turned to the spell book pages and it was a soak that was long enough to engulf herself into the various methods and thought processes of ancient rituals and their modern equivalents. As she added more bath salts Naomi found particular interest in the chapters on voodoo and, with her husband in mind, his suffering. She gladly washed away any recollection of her dream from the night before and it was the knock on the bathroom door that brought Naomi back to reality.

"Your lunch is getting cold so I have put it in your bedroom," the voice called out. Naomi recognised it as Peri and called back out after her. "Thank you."

The soak had done Naomi some good and she felt a little stronger as she walked steadier, aided by the dado rail and leaning into the corridor wall, finally gripping the door handle as she returned to her bedroom.

Once inside she noticed that the veranda doors were now wide open and that there was a table and seat outside. On the table, to match the midday heat, was a bowl of hot broth. There was also some bread on a plate and a long cool iced drink, so she dragged herself over to eat.

The broth and homemade bread tasted divine and the only interruption between spoon slurps of happiness was the odd wave or call of "hi" or "hey" as commune members walked by below her.

Emptying the bowl, she took to the ice glass of what she thought was lemonade, it was cold, a little bitter, but refreshing and her tongue was electrified, then, so was her mouth. As her cheeks began to sag, so did her head, it didn't taste of lemonade anymore and again she felt weak.

Her neck rolled, her body was a lead weight where only occasionally could she raise a hand to her sun burnt head. She didn't feel the pain though, she didn't feel anything, nor did she recollect that night when Travis, with help, carried her from the veranda, down the corridor to children's bedroom.

There she was laid out and unrobed as the two women teachers slowly undressed her, naked and open she lay, slowly encircled by all of the children, including her own.

Naomi was tumbling down a hill of bright purple snap dragons, where in her hallucinogenic state she was oblivious to the pinprick injection that the teachers now gave her, into the dorsal vein of her right foot.

Naomi's children quietly stared at their mother's flesh as the off-white fluid was syringed into her. It wasn't a stare of recognition, or fear, just emptiness, for they too were having dreams of their own.

As the liquid filled Naomi's veins, Travis left her side, he left the room in the hands of one of the female teachers. As he did so, the three men that had helped him carry Naomi to the room, these eager men who had waited patiently outside, entered. It was their turn to show the children the enjoyment in being a free spirit.

The next day Naomi again woke in her bed. Travis had woken her dulled senses to a quiet, "Good morning," as he held a glass of 'lemonade' to her lips he raised her head to drink. Then it was only seconds before she was cradled by a bed of doves that floated above a wind breezed cornfield.

That day passed, then another, perhaps even more; Naomi was mentally undone, but perhaps her spirit was now free?

The little memories she did have from the actual weeks that passed since she last saw her children, were the smallest of memories. She recalled being fed, she occasionally remembered mumbling complaint that she wanted to rise and she couldn't remember her smile.

There were some 'flashbacks' though, where she'd wake to the voice of Travis preaching to her from the bedroom veranda and she could also hear muffled 'whoops of joy' raised by an unseen audience. She also relived the memories of being regularly carried to her bath, of being washed by a mixture of both male and female hands, many with penetrating fingers. Then there was the realisation that come day or night she had been regularly laid out, naked on top of her bed and taken, not only by Travis, but by numerous men and some women. Writhing, forcing their way on top of her to their own sexual gratification. Lastly, she knew that some of the older boys too had had their fill of her and still she couldn't remember her smile.

--//--

"No more lemonade." Naomi whispered quietly, as Travis raised her head once more from the pillows. "I am free. But please, no more lemonade, I am yours, I am everyone's, but please no more lemonade." Travis nodded, kissing her forehead he lowered her back to the pillow to sleep.

That afternoon Naomi awoke to her son sitting at the side of her bed, he was softly singing one of the commune songs that he had learnt word for word. He smiled at his mummy when she opened her eyes and his mummy smiled back.

"Are you alright?" He asked softly, "mummy are you okay?" Her boy asked again as he looked at her anxiously.

"I feel so weak." Naomi replied.

"Oh, that will be the journey," he replied. "Yes, the journey," he confirmed to himself.

"The journey?" Naomi whispered, still trying to gather sensibility.

"Your spirit journey mummy." her son said, "Sister and I were the same, weak until free." Her son spoke quite clearly, he didn't mention his sister's name though, perhaps these were rehearsed words, Naomi thought.

"Preacher Travis is nice, isn't he?" her boy explained, as he continued to stroke mummy's hand and again Naomi smiled.

"He has let me talk to you today as a special gift, because by law I am not allowed to talk to you until tomorrow," he said.

"Tomorrow?" Naomi questioned.

"My birthday silly," he laughed.

"I am thirteen tomorrow and will no longer be a child, I will be an adult like you mummy, free to choose, rather than be chosen, free forever, isn't it fantastic?" He smiled the broadest of smiles towards his mother. Naomi was a little startled and questioning herself as to why Travis had chosen this age to be his age to manhood, but there was no time for her opinion, there was a knock at the door.

It was her daughter who called to come in and, after asking after her mummy, she too sat on the bed but opposite her brother and Naomi watched in silence as both children looked towards each other.

Naomi took note of the gaze that her daughter had for her son and immediately realised it was more than sibling affection, it was the same gaze and open smile of that she herself had pouted for Travis, the mother shuddered.

Naomi didn't question though, she couldn't, she didn't want to think what she was actually thinking, but the way her children smiled upon each other, as they held each other's hands across her bed. No, all Naomi wanted to do was close her eyes to what her mind was telling her. Her emotions were tugging away once more at what was left of her sanity and the seconds passed in silence, until she drew breath. Opening her tear stained eye lashes, she quietly asked her children to leave.

That night Naomi was able to gather herself slowly and managed to wedge a bedroom chair under the bedroom door handle. She knew this would prevent the door from being opened and she was shaking from head to foot as she did so. Each movement wracked pain in her body but she needed time to prepare herself for Travis. She knew what she wanted and she told herself, as she would tell others who might come 'knocking,' that she would only open the door for Travis; she wanted no other, but him.

Naomi needn't have bothered though, no one came to her door and if she had thought about it with any sense she would have noticed that she had left the veranda doors open anyway. Anyone from a nearby bedroom could have just simply walked along and in, but her drug abused mind couldn't carry that thought.

Instead she sat at the dressing table mirror, it was an age before her make-up was applied. Blushed rouge masking her shame and though brushing her hair through also took time, it didn't untangle her mind as to what was happening to her and on returning to bed, in and out of consciousness, she waited.

The hours passed, Naomi occasionally stirred to the voices in the corridor, to the people walking in and around the ranch, but there was no knock at the door. Travis was obviously freeing another one's spirit, so Naomi turned to the books on her bedside cabinet and with instant clarity The Bible was thrown across the room. The wondrous almighty wasn't listening to her. There was no saviour for Naomi, so she sought salvation from the other two publications.

Naomi found it hard to focus though, her drugged filled mind was rejecting the long comprehension, some words mingled, others jumbled and a few fell from the pages, perhaps tomorrow, she thought.

Chapter 7

1969

Tomorrow came and went as her body still sought inner strength and it wasn't until the morning of the day after that Naomi was roused, gently woken by Travis with a smile and hot coffee.

Naomi found herself sodden, the bed sheets were awash from her own perspiration. It was the reaction to the drugs that now left her body and, hopefully, her mind, she thought.

However, as Travis stood over Naomi she was more interested in his words than the onset of recovery, waking to words of how pretty she was and how in love he was with her and that this day was theirs to enjoy together.

"C'mon get dressed my angel, I have run you a bath," he told her and, as the naked Naomi sat up, she immediately realised that she wasn't in her bedroom, but that of her daughter's old room.

She raised a sheet to cover herself and Travis, realising her confusion, laughed out loud telling her, "the children are long gone, it's just us."

Naomi remembered nothing as she looked about the empty room, of sheets, blankets and mattresses. She immediately questioned, "why am I not in my bedroom?"

Travis replied in good cheer, "it was your boy's birthday yesterday and he asked to sleep in your room last night. I knew you wouldn't mind." He told her.

Naomi was numbed, sick and she gagged on the coffee. She did mind, she had lost a day and her son had apparently 'chosen.'

Naomi excused herself, gathered the sheet around her, left Travis and took what was a long slow walk down the corridor.

Approaching her bedroom door her tears soon streamed her vision, she could hear the moans of her daughter and the grunts of her son as she partially opened the door. In her bedroom, she saw the writhing sheets and her daughter's red hair ribbon tied to a corner post. Naomi closed the door, there was nothing to say, she was simply in shock as she walked passed to the adjacent bathroom.

Naomi laid in that bath for an hour, its warmth was now chilled and she continued to cry between each drip from the brass taps. She listened out at the wall between her and her bedroom, but heard nothing more as she examined the new and old finger mark bruising that covered most of her legs, hips and shoulders.

With a knock at the bathroom door Naomi suddenly roused from her anguish, it was a call, "Are you alright?" It was Travis.

"I need something, I'm in pain," she cried in despair.

"I will make you one of my special drinks," he replied, as the footsteps walked away.

However, it was less than a minute before there was a banging on the bathroom door, there was urgency in the voice of Travis, for he had run back and was demanding, "Get dressed quickly the Police are outside!"

Chapter 8

Since the film release of "Cool Hand Luke" in the 1960's there was a certain amount of guarantee that if you were stopped by any form of authority in America you would be facing a mirrored reflection of sunglasses, Deputy Dawson was no exception.

He had been ordered to the ranch by his boss, the local town sheriff, he had been told in no uncertain terms. "Check it out, find out what's going on over there."

One of the commune's eldest men, was a regular visitor to the town cells when he visited Ranger and on almost every occasion the man was 'liquored up' by 3 in the afternoon, singing by 5 and mumbling weird stories by 9. But it was only recently that the Sheriff had paid more attention to his stories and deciphering some of the slurs, the sheriff became even more concerned when he found out where he was staying.

Alarmed in fact, because the recently appointed State Senator was a friend of the sheriff's department and the sheriff was being paid 'more than a little extra by the state' to ensure that nothing damaging would happen at the Ranch that could affect Valentine Hill's public image.

Consequently, the sheriff didn't hesitate in sending the ever-eager young Dawson to patrol and ask questions within.

And so, Dawson stood, leaning up against his patrol car cruiser, about a hundred yards from the main house, looking towards those that looked towards him whilst he imagined his life as the new town's sheriff instead of his boss.

Dawson stretched back and observed, he was wearing one of his many pairs of reflector sunglasses, a pair for every day of the week. He was watching the children singing under a large tree, songs led by two women, one on guitar, the other a tambourine. Then there was the throng of people milling or lazing about the ranch and that was when he saw the scantily robed senator's wife slowly walking towards him, led by the arm of a man that was holding her tight.

Dawson was courteous, "Ma'am," and he tipped his peaked cap of authority towards her as they stopped within feet. Naomi immediately recognised Dawson, this time with his clothes on, unlike the times that they'd had in the town's motel.

With pleasantries exchanged, Dawson explained his reasons for being present.

Travis was his usual smiles and sweetness as he explained his and the presence of his commune. He cuddled Naomi to stand upright and just that little bit tighter.

Naomi was quick to respond by putting her arm around the back of Travis's waist, in doing she felt her forearm brush over a small revolver in the rear waistband of Travis' jeans. Nerves jangling, Naomi physically jerked, the side arm had been covered over by his loose hanging shirt, 'but why was he still carrying a gun?' she thought.

"Are you alright?" Dawson asked.

Naomi emphasised that nothing was wrong and when Dawson asked her again if she was ill she explained the obvious shudder as having suffered, "a touch of the heat."

"All was well," and "no harm done," Naomi insisted and changed the subject by offering the officer a drink.

Well as Dawson had travelled out so far to see her, he smiled and duly accepted.

The three of them walked up to the ranch together and in doing so Travis asked a passing woman to serve drinks for their guest.

"Three bottles of pop on ice." Travis ordered and within minutes all three sat on the porch sipping from ice cold bottles that were served from a rarely used ice filled champagne bucket.

Everyone that walked passed them whilst doing their chores exchanged welcomes with the visiting deputy, even two of the youngest children were sent over by one of the teachers, each carrying a posy of wild flowers and handed them to the Deputy. By the time Dawson left the property, he had succumbed to those well-rehearsed, orchestrated manoeuvres by Travis and the commune, each working their charm and, although Naomi was quiet whilst Travis talked for both, Dawson put her silence down to her recent illness.

Three hours later Dawson explained to the Sheriff that he was content with what he had seen and as such, in turn, so was his hesitant Sheriff.

The sheriff wanted to keep on the good side of the State Senator who was paying him well for his bi-monthly phone updates and when next calling him in his new home of Austin, Texas; the sheriff now used a little discretion. He masked his words carefully, calling the commune "a couple of visitors who had only stayed a short while," and indeed he promised to continue the patrols.

There was never a mention of that old man again, the regular visitor to the cells. Travis had kept his word, no longer did the drunk come to town and this was indeed true; the man was never seen again after Dawson's visit and no one in the commune dare comment on his sudden disappearance.

Travis and Naomi had stayed sat on the porch, where and they had waved a goodbye to Dawson, as the cruiser turned to dust in the distance. Naomi was handed the drink that she'd asked for that morning, she hadn't dare ask about the gun that Travis had carried. Instead her only thoughts were that of her 'lost children.'

The fact that Travis was concealing a gun simply made her swallow huge gulps of that bitter sweet solution. Gulps that later were to glaze another commune ceremony and although she was able to watch the proceedings, her tongue failed to speak. Naomi felt the carrying of her numbed body, but she couldn't act when held high in the ritual and the commune watched, as she helplessly did, as her right forearm was then tattooed with a small TFS within a diamond shape.

Later that night, there was a blurred copulation with Travis and three other men and all this mixed with the thoughts of seeing her two children smile with happiness as both were tattooed likewise. Her daughter in a new dress, but the same hair ribbon and both son and daughter held hands, their arms, their bodies and all this tormented Naomi as the filth fuelled memories carried her to the next day.

Not only the next day, but the next week and for the next few months, hers was a daily ritual. Naomi would resign herself to waking up in bed with yet another man or woman or both, this was just a lottery, just like the 'lemonade,' the pills and any other drug that she ingested, whenever she could, wherever it was, just to fade the misery within.

Naomi was the lady of the ranch, but this held no authority, Travis and his gunmen held sway, not her, though she had no chores and between the usual 'fixes,' she would spend time in her room and read from the books. Even the bible was occasionally glimpsed at as she tried to absorb as much knowledge that her daily drug fuelled mind would allow.

Then from those three original books that Travis had given her, she soon found more to read. The commune had books on translated Muslim, Sikh and Hindu preaching's, books on potions, books on sacrifice and offerings and then there were pamphlets and periodicals that described anything from pagans to poisons.

When bored and able to stand, Naomi would help out the ladies in the kitchen. There were always ingredients and herbal remedies in the pantry and Naomi was welcome to try.

Peri, a 'struck off' nurse by profession, had been caught years previously, by her hospital employer, serving the patients in her care, her interpretations of natural remedies mixed in with morphine and was only discovered because one of her potions had caused a patient to have half of their stomach removed.

However, both Peri and Judy were great cooks and helped Naomi explore the variations of plants and their extracts. Naomi was keen on those that survived harsh desert conditions, but mostly the weeds and flowers that were scattered around the ranch.

All three would regularly wander the land together, picking plants, roots and grasses, including the poisonous ones that the two cooks would point out.

All three would refer to books on natural well-being and the secretions from earthly produce, but this would also expand to include chapters on such subjects as snake venom that could be used as medical cures and Naomi, with purpose, was eager to learn.

Both Peri and Judy were truly skilled in the preparation of food and there was always an eagerness to disperse remedies for the sick in their quickly growing commune. Naomi enjoyed the responsibility of serving food to the commune, the exact same sized portion to all at meal time and day by day she learnt more about the various cures to sickness, she did all this whilst the contented Travis looked on.

1970

Travis had truly witnessed the rebirth of Naomi; that was what he had told the others. Her transition, her 'free spirit' was now less dependent on the drugs he provided and he was happy that she now walked among the commune, free to be taken, free from her children, free from his care. Truly, Travis was happy for her and he would often sermon his people that Naomi was, beyond question, a gift from the various gods.

He looked on her and her regeneration, her body, her ranch and he was elated with the power that ran through his veins and although Naomi was seen still motherly towards her children, brushing and cutting their hair and their nails, to him they were now young adults to do as they please and she appeared to accept that.

However, he would ensure on each evening that she was taken by drugs and taken to her bed by others and oh, how he believed his almightiness glowed.

It was her ranch that drew in more unfortunates from surrounding towns each week and it was their welfare payments that would be handed over to Travis. He even had a letter presented to the bank by Naomi where her weekly funds would be handed over to one of his men.

He was as content with her as any of his flock and it was only the occasional sporadic voice of a dissenter that Travis would hear, but he had the means and he was soon rid of those.

His cult status had grown and the cash that he held in the three strong boxes in the back of his grey lorry were almost filled to overflowing. He knew he was rich and he had decided that it would soon be time for him to morph into the identity of another. Some faceless name, perhaps a member of his flock, but Travis was ready to move on, setting a personal course of rebirth that was his spirit. Travis had decided on a home of his own, one close to the bars and beaches of Mexico.

Perhaps it was the greed of 'just a few more bucks' that had held Travis in situ a little longer than needed, or perhaps it was the multitude of new flesh that his want would plunder. However, he doubted he was under any of Naomi's various spells of entrapment that she daily mumbled whilst feeding him. How he would inwardly laugh at the meals that hid the various potions of bewitchment, his kitchen staff had told him so. Whatever it was, he couldn't be happier as time passed, overseeing the ranch as his commune grew larger.

Every day his preaching came from various religious scriptures, Pagan prophecies, Egyptian and Aztec sacrifice and whatever else he felt like 'making up' on the spur of the moment. He would always encapsulate the spirits of air, land and water and every day his sermons had such variance that he would even confuse himself, often he would be 'lost in a vision' when he tried to remember what he was talking about, but all listened and all would follow him in prayer, whether they knew the meaning or not.

The white, wooden stave of power, the inverted cross and circle below was a simple symbol made by his hand that had come from his boyhood hobby of wood carving and he had enjoyed whittling out the Egyptian hieroglyphic symbols that would represent his interpretation of the spiritual gods and the heavens. It was white because he only had white paint at the time of making it and Travis would delight in wielding this stave in his sermons. His 'all seeing' symbol of authority that had nondescript written words of warning. It was his 'bullshit interpretation' that was taught to each child in their classes each day, that along with various Bible and heathen scriptures.

That's probably why Travis decided to stay longer than he needed, he enjoyed the power as he was God!

However, for all of Travis's visions, prayers and the all-seeing stave of the gods that he and his community worshipped, he didn't accept Naomi's total obsession of him and unable to read her thoughts, he was blind as to what she was prepared to do, to have him all to herself.

Naomi had realised for some time that Travis had tired of her, as, thankfully, had most of the other men in the commune, only her son would still regularly visit her in her hallucinogenic dreams.

So, with each evening that brought less attention to her, her body, her wants, her hope, her desire, the next dawn would bring another daily grind from Naomi's pestle and mortar.

Left to her own devices, her head rarely looked up from the pages of spells and witchcraft, insanity itself had breached her mind and with ease tore into her soul.

Earliest to work each day in the kitchen, she would be found mumbling words, humming chants and grinding up new mixtures. She suckled on the variation of potions, spells and chants and in doing so had become insular. Rarely would she speak to any, other than the two cooks and her two children that she still loved so dearly

Paste was ground daily from her and her children's snipped hair, all mixed with various foliage and liquid solutions, even her nail clippings, shavings, a dab or two of faeces and perhaps an occasional squirt of urine and every time that Travis ate, he would eat from the food that Naomi had personally prepared for him.

At all costs, Naomi was desperate to win Travis back to her bed with or without his blessing.

Chapter 9

1973 Southend on Sea, England

It was the brightest, tightest vest top in the charity shop, that's what Charlie Harris' pregnant mum bought him. Just slightly faded, but buttercup yellow and it was still colourful enough to spot her eight-year-old tearaway son a mile away!

The top was as 'sharp' as his six buttons, high-waist, bell bottom trousers that billowed like sails at the ankles and could alter his direction with one quick gust. To complete his ensemble the shoes, yes, the 70's had a lot to answer for; Italian high heeled platform boots, heavy, clumsy and potential ankle breakers. These were Charlie's summer clothes, not exactly 'fit for purpose' when it came to day trips to the coast, but his mother made him wear these on each of three such trips to the muddy coastline at Southend-on-Sea, Essex.

Charlie would have much preferred a pair of his old scruffy jeans, an old rugby shirt that had belonged to his father and his only pair of scuffed up Dunlop Green Flash trainers, to run about in, but oh no, his mother would have none of it and had readily clipped his ear for complaining.

So, these were three days of summer hell that Charlie had to endure, the giggles of promenade girls and the laughter of wise old men in handkerchief knotted hats were all that he heard as he stood on the seashore next to his mother. Quite a sight in his 'rock band' clothes and what visible skin there was, was totally anointed in the whitest of cheap sun lotion.

"There you are, Charlie my boy, just like John Wayne," she told him, "handsome, strong and dignified that's what you are," and his mother would smile broadly whilst dolloping another palm full of 'Woolworths' own brand milky white lotion into his face. It was a ritual, recurring every couple of hours in the bright summer sunshine, where he would stand as still as he could whilst holding his balance on second-hand shoes.

This snow-white boy with lotion stinging his eyes, was blinded as he sought out the derision from fellow 'day-trippers.'

Charlie didn't feel handsome, he simply felt embarrassed and ugly.

Chapter 10

1977 Thief River Falls Pennington County, Minnesota, USA

Kerri had already taken enough beatings in her young teenage life, her 'snowflake' father, had beaten her for this and for that and for the 'whatever.' She was beaten for the sake of being beaten, from the man who had hated her for being born.

Kerri, who was meant to have been a 'dream come true' for her black mother, but to her father? Well he had told Kerri from a young age that she had killed her mother at birth.

Her parents weren't married, just cohabitees. He was the love of her life and she was his regular 'shag' come girlfriend. She was just too damned sexy and too good 'in the sack' to give up.

So, when he was told that if he wanted more sex than he could ever imagine, in every conceivable position, then he had to accept her unexpected pregnancy and so, begrudgingly, he did.

Kerri's early memories were pinches, then slaps and kicks, all this from her 'loving' father, called Mason by others, one of the town's highway patrolmen.

Rarely did Kerri visit the town's Doctor, to this old man, a physician well past retirement age, Kerri was a model child!

She was hardly seen during her young childhood, but when she was, her father had all manner of excuses for any noticeable bruise and from 8 years old Kerri had never visited him again, even though she was now almost 15.

However, the locals thought Kerri was a 'sick' child. On those rare visits outside her home with her father, he passed her off as a girl who had complications. Many thought probably those same complications that had killed her mother at birth.

For this was indeed a small-town community, holding its roots just north of the Mississippi river, just south of Canada and only a short distance from Thief River Falls.

The town's main sources of income were drawn from wheat farming, engineering and the attraction of angling tourism. With its one main street in and out of town and multiple side streets angled off onto others, there were tight twists to match the sharp driven winds.

It was the town's people who saw Mason as a 'model' parent, 'doing the right thing' by keeping this mixed-race child, refusing to abandon her to the local care system. Together when seen, they would be viewed as a father and daughter living life together, including the 'home schooling' her father had insisted on when the local Education Department called on their home.

Their home was unlike any other in town, it was small, grey and a little foreboding. It was a single story, box type, pre-fabrication; a mini fortress on thick wooden stilts. To the front and each side, the stilts were covered by thick layers of wood, each interlocking and bolted together. Not only were there extra locks on the front door but the vented windows all round had steel shutters that were clasped tight with padlocks.

There was no need to cover the stilts at the rear of their home as the back yard was surrounded by a brick built nine-foot-tall, barb wired wall. A wall built by Mason and a couple of his Police 'buddies' and although it was a strange sight with the barbed wire on top, normally associated with nearby farm land, when his neighbours asked Mason passed this off as being security conscious. However, though the wall was tall, it could still be easily overlooked by the larger built neighbours' homes on either side.

Against the rear wall stood her father's flat roofed tool shed and beyond that was a farmer's field that led onto others.

Within the yard, placed in the middle, was a weathered children's slide made from plastic and metal and, next to it, an adult plastic poled paddling pool.

It was a yard that would only ever be visited by Kerri, if both father and Kerri were outside together.

When young Kerri used the slide regularly, but it was now too small for her. As for the paddling pool, she would never be seen in that pool on her own and the fact that she never ventured out into the yard alone was never deemed as strange or unusual by prying eyes.

For Mason was simply seen as a lawman in that North American Town, always upstanding and reliable, a local hero who was once honoured in a town ceremony for saving a local boy from a burning car.

And, when at work, Mason was always smartly dressed in his shiny black boots, dark blue uniform and silver mirrored sunglasses. A tall stern man who would usually nod an acknowledgement to the local people when out on patrol. He had a personal passion in keeping passing hitchhikers and/or prostitutes off the streets. Yes, he was the one to call if a girl was on the streets selling herself. Not only would he drive them off, but he would sample the goods 'for free' for 'good measure.'

In short, he was thought to be thoroughly honourable for raising his sweet, shy child, a child who was never seen without her father standing beside and over her.

Outside their home none knew of Kerri's vivacious study of the bible, nor the various well-worn encyclopaedias and the history books she studied, neither did they know of her fantastic talent for sketching. Nor did they know of the regular beatings Kerri took when her father 'took to the drink' when he looked at old photographs of her mother. He would drink to her memory and drink to the burden he had carried all those years.

This weekly binge would result in both father and daughter sobbing. Mason would cry at his 'bloody mess of a life' and slap his daughter down to the ground. Kerri would cry from the pain of having her father's hand clasping her mouth whilst he punched her repeatedly in the stomach with his other.

"Why were you born and why did she die?" He would sob, she would sob, tears falling into her tears as he would force himself onto her body to beat her some more.

Kerri would have no chance of escape from this hold, she was slim, petite and 'bruised pretty.' Mason had long ago removed all the internal doors when she once tried to close the door on her father.

Over these years she had repeatedly tried talking sense to her father, where she would plead and even once threatened to take her own life, but there was no escape. Kerri would just wait, sitting on the floor in her bedroom, waiting for that final drink, waiting for the footsteps to come closer.

After the beatings came his regular cuddles of sorrow, without fail after every attack Mason had his way with words, claiming sickness in his head, memory loss, once, even cancer! And time and time again Mason would promise no more pain, then no more pain, again and again.

But it was that last brutal onslaught where Kerri's body had gasped frantically for air, followed by the post beating cuddle that made her determined to escape her home, her life.

Never before had her father wrapped his arms so tight around his daughters back, that his hands and fingers were able to squeeze her innocent chest, through her vest. Though she pleaded and tried, oh how she tried to struggle from his grip, he only squeezed tighter and writhed his groin until stiff.

That was the final straw, she had read about this and seen it on the television and she knew what he writhed for and it sickened her. This was the point of no return, she would plan and she would run. She knew she had a week before his next turn with the bottle.

The following morning, as usual, Mason left for work, "to keep the community safe," he would say and as usual he first locked the rear door and windows and then to the front and from outside he locked the large wooden front door before checking each shuttered front and side window was secure.

Kerri just stared at the kitchen table where her father had put out a filled breakfast bowl of cereal and strawberries and one of the many history books that he knew she enjoyed reading. She knew this was one of his many ways in which he showed remorse. She stared at the table, but she wasn't thinking of food or reading, just fleeing.

She couldn't just run though, she needed to plan and plan well, her father was after all, a highway patrolman and there would be scores of people all willing to help him find his daughter.

'Dammit,' she thought, no, there would be legions scouring the roads, the bus stations and countryside in search of her. Her father was even good buddies with many of the pilots at the local airport, how could she avoid the planes searching overhead?

She needed to pack light and blend in, but what to pack and with what? Then she remembered Mason's old brown rucksack that he kept in the laundry cupboard, the one she had seen him use when he used to go fishing and although it was old and tired with one buckle strap missing it could still hold some weight.

No pretty coloured clothes though; Kerri did not want to seek attention. If she did manage to escape her home, her prison, then it would be difficult enough not to be seen, especially as she had never been seen out on her own. Kerri knew the streets would not be her saviour, but the surrounding woods and fields might be her only allies.

Brown was a good colour, she decided as she looked in her wardrobe and the clothes she chose to pack were either that or black or dark shaded, all darker than her mixed skin. She had an old pair of trainers sitting in the base of the wardrobe, that were now at least a half a size too small, but she choose them as they were also black.

She packed the rucksack half full with clothes and then unpacked it, leaving those clothes and pumps together in the bottom of her wardrobe, then she returned the rucksack to where it had been.

Kerri returned to the kitchen and concentrated on a list in her head whilst she consumed the breakfast in front of her. 'Nothing should look amiss,' she told herself and a missed breakfast would look strange!

Kerri spent the rest of the morning stamping the floor of their home. Dull thud, dull thud! That was the noise as the day progressed whilst she sought out a weak spot and hours later she found herself in the corner of the bathroom by the toilet. It was below those spotless white tiles that sounded hollow.

'Of course,' she thought, 'the sewer pipe.'

The pipe she had seen under the house from her time in the back yard when she had questioned her father about it years ago. Kerri sat herself down on the toilet lid and stared at the floor around her. She had a faint recollection that her father had tiled the bathroom floor as was her father's way. He had made, built or fixed everything around their home and it was then she noticed the size of those plain white tiles, four of them were much, much smaller and each lay square on to each other, about two feet away from the toilet itself. Two smaller tiles in front of the toilet and two smaller behind, half the size of the other tiles. Kerri remembered her father liked 'screwing things tight' and she was convinced that these tiles hid screws.

Kerri chose the smaller tile in the far corner of the bathroom behind the toilet and towards the wall. She had a kitchen knife in her hand to dig out the white grouting. Fifteen minutes later she had dug out the grout but had split the small tile when levering it up from its bonding.

"Shit!" she exclaimed in a whisper as she stared at the two pieces, but, when she lifted these two pieces, below there was indeed a flat head stainless steel screw head and beside it what appeared to be the corner of a cut panelled piece of wood. She pushed the knife into the screw, it turned stiffly, anti-clockwise and began to unscrew. Then she buried the knife into that gap in the wood and levered the knife upward, there was just a slight movement indicating that it was indeed a board held in place. Kerri clenched her left hand and said "Yes." She was ecstatic as she retightened the screw.

Kerri returned to the kitchen where she returned the knife and walked back to the bathroom with a small box of white flour. Kerri replaced the broken tile and sprinkled the flour where the grout had once been and sprinkled over the tile hiding the break. Kerri finally cleared up the grout and flushed it away, 'Perfect' she thought and near perfect it was.

Her father would be home soon enough she assessed and she needed a full day, a full day where she knew her father would not be in town but out on patrol. The best day would be when he was on prisoner escort day, when the county would assist the nearest prison, riding escorts to court. That day would be the day after next. Kerri's thoughts were suddenly interrupted, she heard her father's Police cruiser pull up outside and she ran to the door to greet him.

That evening dragged slowly, as her father was still offering his apologies for beating her, but there was no mention of his sexual hardness, it was as if it never happened! And Kerri tried her very best not to show disgust.

It seemed each minute lasted an age until Kerri 'sparked an idea' and took the opportunity to 'chance her arm' asking her father for a map of the local area. She used the pretence that having spent the day reading a book on local tribal history, she now wanted to see where the natives lived and fought on a local map.

"Just for an hour," she pleaded and Mason, feeling guilty, readily agreed, going to and returning from the patrol car with a map.

Mason left her to study her books and the map in the kitchen whilst he sat, quite satisfied that he had again been forgiven, in the lounge and watched television. Her father simply thought Kerri was writing notes, not tracing an outline of roads, tracks and lakes on a piece of her artist's tracing paper. Within half an hour Kerri's, home study, was complete.

The next day after Mason had left, Kerri again packed and unpacked her rucksack, adding something, removing something, addition, subtraction, more food, less food, but her bible remained within the canvas. The day passed quickly until she was satisfied that, although she was packing light, the rucksack had to accommodate a large jar of nickels, dimes, cents and dollar notes. A jar full of what her father had given her as pocket change from his guilt, as almost all of it was handed over after a good beating.

Kerri finally looked at her packed rucksack in the bottom of her bedroom wardrobe and sobbed, she stared at that rucksack, her life and she openly wept as she unpacked it for a final time.

When her father returned from work later that night he confirmed he would be working longer the following day on the usual prisoner escorts. Towards 'lights out' Kerri kissed her father on his cheek, and said her goodbye as "goodnight" and that night she saw the dawn rise without sleep and when morning dawned Kerri couldn't help but look at her father, his every move was followed by her eyes.

She couldn't help herself! She looked at her father longing that her life could have been different, wishing that he had loved her as a father should. Then, after his breakfast, he showered and dressed, she stared at Patrolman Mason, her father, all smart, pristine and an evil lie of all that was meant to be good!

Kerri stood by the shuttered lounge window and waved goodbye to her father. She stood there for a further half hour to make sure that her father would have arrived at the Sheriff's office and started his shift.

Kerri stared at her watch, 08:30 it showed and she sprang into action. She dressed quickly into jeans, boots, top, cardigan and then her anorak. With the large kitchen knife in hand she ran to the bathroom. The first broken tile was prised up, followed by the other three small corner tiles. Each of them prised from its fixing, each of them revealing flat head screws and she knelt amongst the broken tiles as she feverishly went to work with the knife. As each screw was removed she dug the knife into the cornered gap and again the panel lifted.

Then she noticed two half tiles on either side of the toilet base, these too were levered and broke free revealing two more screws on each. Once these were unscrewed Kerri stamped the floor, jumping until the grouting split and the flooring around the toilet seat wobbled.

Kerri could only lever the panel half an inch, not enough to get her fingers underneath, so she flew to the kitchen returning with yet another knife and levered both knives into the gaps. Suddenly there was space, enough for one hand to squeeze under.

Kerri pulled up with all her might, she strained as tears formed in her eyes. Both hands were now under the panel and slowly, just slowly the panel shifted upwards until a loud 'crack' of torn wood splintered the panel that broke upward and free.

Kerri stared down the hole that was on that one side of the toilet and saw the mudded ground three feet below. The ground below that beamed a light from the back yard towards freedom. And within that instant she realised that the rucksack and her size 6 frame would easily fit in just that side of the hole and that there would be no need to prise the other panel off.

Kerri ran to her bedroom and filled the hidden rucksack from the clothes that she had laid over it. Her heart was pounding. Then to her window sill where her money jar sat, next to her bible that hid her pencil traced map. Next to the kitchen, the tins she had chosen, a tin opener, a spoon and a small paring knife and then into in the lounge. There in the lounge was the house fuse board and within, a small white torch, her rucksack was now complete.

Kerri returned to the kitchen and on a piece of paper scribbled a note on the table 'I have gone, goodbye, no longer will you touch me.' She began to cry, stifling the screams that she so wanted to yell.

Running back to the bathroom she placed the rucksack next to the hole and again she went to her bedroom. She was starting to fluster, so stopped still in her tracks, taking deep breathes in an attempt to calm herself and after three deep swallows of the room's stale air she removed her cream bed blanket and took this to the bathroom.

Down went the blanket, down went the rucksack, then head first, down went Kerri to her outstretched arms and the hard ground below. Hurriedly crawling above the dried mud beneath her, within seconds she was in her back yard where she began to believe in her freedom.

Clutching the rucksack and blanket Kerri ran to the tool shed and threw both items onto the roof, her body was now moving beyond her thought and she became angry, hearing the glass money jar shatter within the rucksack above.

Kerri quickly turned, only to glance at each neighbour's rear upper windows.

'Please no one see me,' she begged and thankfully as she ran back to the slide, she saw there was no one at the windows. Kerri pulled the slide up against the tool shed's flat roof and quickly she ran the small steps till she was able to scramble from the top rung up, over and onto to the tool shed roof.

She turned and lying flat, half hanging over the roof she leant back down and hauled the metal slide up onto the roof. She didn't know where she had found the strength from, nor did she care, she just wanted 'out.'

The slide was thrust against the rear wall and Kerri strapped the rucksack across her shoulders that now crunched with shattered slivers within. Next, she laid the blanket across the barbed wire to smother the sharp twists of barbs and it was only then that she could smell the wheat growing from the adjacent field, a smell that would for ever more be associated with her freedom!

Climbing the steps of the slide she lay across the blanket and over. Over she hung gripping the blanket, the blanket that slowly tore from the metal wall barbs and then with a gasp of air she released her grip falling those last feet to freedom.

'Thud' and Kerri hit the ground running, running as hard and as fast as her legs could take her, running, looking back, sprinting, looking back, fleeing, looking back, looking back until there was nothing to look back on. Her home, her prison, her town, had now vanished in the distant horizon behind her but she continued to run. Kerri crossed farms, fields and fencing never once looking at her surroundings, she ran on dirt tracks and paths, on she ran until she finally collapsed to her knees, totally exhausted.

It took a while to wipe away the tears of happiness, sadness and of the unknown, but as she lay on that track next to a field and felt the warmth of the sunshine above, Kerri thought herself lucky to be running as the Summer was now falling into Autumn and there would be no escape come the desolation of the bone freezing winters.

Kerri eventually dragged herself up and, taking note of her surroundings, she decided to pin point her position on her trace paper map. Within seconds she had worked out that she was indeed heading south, the direction that she wanted and only a mere two hundred yards or so from Route 59.

She was close, perhaps too close, as she could hear the passing traffic speed by and with these flatlands that led towards the large town of Fargo, the lack of contours would help any search party to look for some great distance from the highway.

Kerri decided to walk as far away from the road as she dare and continue her journey south, keeping this distant grey highway as a spec in the distance as she knew she had around 100 miles to cover until the town of Fargo and beyond.

Kerri needed answers and was planning to find these from her God. The God, of whom she had read so much about, the same God that was constantly praised on local television programmes. This Almighty who was looking over her, the one who helped her escape the clutches of her father; this 'all knowing' that now guided her southwards.

For Kerri decided she was heading towards the states known as 'The Bible Belt,' located and including all or parts of: Alabama, Arkansas, Florida, Georgia, Kansas, Kentucky, Louisiana, Mississippi, Missouri, North Carolina, Oklahoma, South Carolina and Texas.

'There must be a place amongst those where she could find happiness,' she thought.

As night descended, Kerri knew there would be no turning back, for her father would be home by now and would have been alerted to her escape.

Would 'Mason the lawman' raise the alarm?

Would there be hordes of townsfolk out searching for her as she slept that night?

Or would it be the case of, she was gone and best forgotten?

Kerri tried not to worry as she had a bigger immediate concern, she could no longer see where she was walking and as she didn't dare turn on the torch in fear of being spotted, she stopped. Totally exhausted, but with her nerves taut and on edge, she walked a few yards from the dirt path and lay amongst a cool moistened crop of sunflowers.

The next day and those that followed were days of little thought, but simple prayers for guidance? Twice Kerri drank water from two streams that she came across, but other than that she ate the cold tins of beans, cold soup, cold 'hot dogs' and its juice. Kerri walked every possible moment of daylight, but when those small planes flew above, with her fingers and toes 'crossed for luck,' she would curl to a ball until she could no longer hear the engines screaming above her.

These were now her days of freedom. It was several days until she saw the town's outskirts and when she did, not only was there a sigh of relief, but this was also followed by one of trepidation.

Chapter 11

Leah was still pondering as to her next destination looking at the Greyhound bus board for her next adventure in elder teenage life. The town of Fargo held little for her from the one-month that she had stayed there and like the Canadian girl she was, like the snows she had left two years ago, she was again 'on the drift' and just like she had dreamt of, Leah was now looking at the destination board, somewhere with a warmer climate in the good old USA.

Although Leah was educated to a decent standard she had decided against college. Her father was dead and her mother didn't care, unless it involved a whiskey bottle. So, Leah had packed a suitcase and travelled from her small home town of North Bay, Canada to the welcoming city of Toronto.

Toronto, the most populated city in Canada, with its bright lights and big city noise, this was pure excitement for a small-town girl with easy virtue, and Leah had arrived.

She found it easy enough to find jobs, simply waitressing from coffee houses to short skirted eateries and her homes were wherever it took her fancy. Sleeping around was never a problem for Leah, she enjoyed making love, she buzzed at the climax or her multiple climaxes, as she found them easy to enjoy and to her young body they were almost always tumultuous, body quivering, explosions of euphoria.

Her nights would nearly always be at the home of either a man or woman as she had numerous weekly or evening liaisons enjoying both sexes. Only occasionally would it be both at the same time and if it were a passing tourist who took her fancy, there were always plenty of Hotels and Motels where she would allow herself to be taken to.

These were rooms for Leah. Somewhere to finally close her eyes of a night. Then after a shower in the morning she would head to Union Railway station.

Structurally beautiful with its grand columns and ornate archways this was her changing room. It was where her suitcase would be released from one of the many locker holds so she could go to the washroom and change into another of her figure hugging waitress clothes and another mirrored application of make-up.

For a couple of months Leah would live like this, day to day, always with a smile and a laugh, where by night with her 'urgings' her body would participate in the many sexual pleasures from one person or another.

That was her routine until one man, a very lonely man, as she shuddered in recollection, turned her life completely around.

Andy was a divorced man in his 40's, who was a broker manager by trade, with fast earned money in his pocket, he was quick to 'have' her one night.

They had met at a disco bar, one of Leah's favourite haunts just off Queen Street, located just a short stroll from the expensive harbour area where he lived.

The evening was just typical for Leah, it was 8pm and leaving work in her black waitress dress she would ensure that it was already undone at the front by three buttons. Her blonde hair, brushed through, easily passed by her shoulders, knots tugged free from what was an earlier pinned bun. Her laced pumps were replaced with the highest of black heels and her lips pouted the deepest red smile. Waitress by day and dressed to thrill by night, just the usual for Leah.

The disco bar was buzzing and so was Andy, he was a miserable failure in marriage, but excellent at his job and, as he had secured more profit in that day than many of his competitive colleagues would earn in a month, he was out to 'set the world alight.' He sat in a U-shaped sectional booth with two of his fellow managers either side of him. The champagne flowed as did the plates of oysters, barbeque ribs and bowls of mussels laid out in front of them and the three men gorged themselves whilst staring lewdly at every single woman in the bar.

As soon as Leah entered she saw the booth was taken, more importantly she saw the full and empty champagne bottles and she deliberately sat on a bar stool yards from and directly in front of that booth.

Leah's waitress dress, already short, was hitched up even higher as she sat on the cool leather stool, revealing even more of her long slender legs that she lengthened straight to the floor and for once, since their arrival, there was silence from the men in the booth. Lust and desire had suddenly taken all three, as it had also taken any number of other men that stared at Leah from nearby.

Leah ordered a vodka tonic, 'ice and a slice,' with a little black straw. A straw that she pursed, puckered, then sucked and licked sending phallic thoughts as to possibilities to those who were mesmerised by her long legs and natural beauty. Although Andy was over twice her age he realised he had nothing to lose as he stirred in his seat.

He quickly excused himself from his two colleagues bragging to them that he was, "targeting that blonde at the bar," and he strolled purposefully towards Leah.

Although the bar was filling fast there was still just a gap to squeeze in next to her. Leah had already rebutted two attempts by eager males, one was married, but smelt of burnt burgers and the other was living at home with parents.

Andy drew close and smiled and Leah returned the smile as he stood calling the bartender over "Three bottles of champagne, your finest again," he ordered and turning to Leah he asked, "and what would you like?" adding, "my treat."

Leah smiled, "an extra glass," and Andy laughed ordering that extra glass and "two shots of Tequila." For good measure.

Leah looked down at Andy's hands and then back towards to his face, examining "No ring, that's nice" she said. Andy smiled back at this girl, this young woman. He couldn't decide, her make-up was bold, if a little overdone and he thought he could smell innocence as she pursed her lips and blew air in his face. That cool minted breath was welcomed as Andy had now become a little hot under his collared shirt and tie.

"No, no ring, no wife, no girlfriend at home, not even a cat to kick." Andy cheerfully explained and Leah laughed twirling the bottom of his tie with her fingers.

The two shots arrived and Andy passed one to Leah. "Down in one?" Andy asked.

"I always down in one," Leah simmered a smile as she swallowed the shot.

The champagne arrived and Andy sent over two of the bottles to his colleagues whilst the other was opened and remained in his grasp.

"How old are you?" Leah asked adding, "you don't look a year over thirty."

"Forty-four." Andy blurted and immediately cursed his own truth.

"Wow, you could be my daddy." Leah told him with another smile and Andy was just a little hurt, because she told the truth.

Noticing the pained expression, Leah offered, "Anyways you look so young 'Daddy O' and so hunky." Andy relaxed to her teasing charm. Leah gushed further praise as her fingers explored. "Firm muscles, nice thighs."

Pulling on his tie to draw his face closer, "you could even be my uncle, I'd like a wicked uncle, would you, could you, be a wicked Uncle to me, if I asked, so pretty, pretty please?"

Her left leg began to rub against Andy's right and he sucked in air raising his chest and broadening his shoulders as he leant forward and smiling he whispered back. "I will be your wicked uncle."

"Good." Leah's hands spread on him as she gripped the top of both his thighs. "Because I have been naughty and I need to be punished."

About an hour later Andy was opening his apartment door as Leah clung to him, caressing his body, knowing he was hard for her.

"Thanks Uncle Andy," she said as she tried to grip him some more.

"Well come in. MI Casa, Su Casa." Andy urgently exhausted his Spanish.

His penthouse apartment wasn't that big, a one bedroom, one bathroom, but the lounge was massive and the view was pretty spectacular. It was the bathroom Leah asked for.

Leah was gone a few minutes prepping her body, hopeful for the hours to come.

Her dress was now neatly folded in her shoulder bag and she applied a little more deodorant and lipstick.

Leah clutched a pack of three condoms as Andy tapped on the bathroom door.

"Hey girl, how's everything going?" He asked.

"Pretty good Uncle Andy." Leah said with a smile and Andy was smiling from the other side of the door.

"I've got some white chocolate cookie dough ice cream in the freezer, you want some?" Andy asked as thoughts of smothering Leah in it were exploding in his head.

Leah's response was immediate and laughing. "Yes please." A nice idea, she was thinking similar thoughts as she heard Andy run to the kitchen freezer.

Having retrieved the ice cream he went to the fridge for a canister of whipped cream, 'why not he thought?' and grabbing that and a dessert spoon he returned to the lounge to await Leah.

She eventually entered the lounge in just her high heels, the smallest pair of black panties and a smile, her pert young body tightened with each forward step as both Andy and tub of ice cream now melted on the black leather sofa.

Leah spotted the canister of whipped cream next to him and bending over her prey she picked it up and quickly straddled him. Andy did his best to hide his little pot belly by breathing in as she took off his tie and undid his shirt. He could feel her moist warmth, god he wanted her moist warmth.

Leah shook the can and squirted a large dollop into her mouth and purposefully allowed the cream to overflow her lips and she swallowed hard. "Ah" she murmured.

"You're gonna have some too big boy." Writhing on his groin and spraying a circle around his lips, as both laughed.

Leah moved her face closer and began to gently flick-lick the foam from his face. Andy sighed as Leah spoke. "Oh, naughty Uncle Andy, you want to make me eat alone." And with this their lips met for the first time as their tongues entwined.

They sat there holding each other, this wanton squeezing and caressing of flesh whilst they licked, kissed and sucked between spoonsful of ice cream and the spray of whipped cream. They took turns in recovering from each other's swallow as Leah continued to rock gently back and forth across Andy's lap.

He, who was already close to bursting, so concentrated on containing himself as he licked and sucked at the rivers of cream that Leah had deliberately let slide from her face to her neck to her cleavage between buoyant breasts and as he licked Leah responded with deeper sighs and dampness.

The minutes swam by in a hazy cloud of hot lips and moist sticky flesh until Leah asked "Where's the kitchen Uncle?"

Andy couldn't speak, he was on another level, a level of anticipation that left him speechless, an intoxication of this young girl that simply directed him to thumb back and point over his right shoulder. Leah unclenched her straddled ride and left Andy breathless as she headed to the closed door where Andy had pointed. Andy just sat there voiceless, solely relieved that he hadn't just climaxed.

A minute passed, perhaps two before Andy got up and followed Leah to the kitchen, when he entered it was notable, only lit by the fridge door being open. He stopped dead in his tracks. He was mesmerised as he watched this young girl fully bent over in front of him and shift from high heeled shoe to shoe, a motion that raised the little material of her black lace panties causing them to dig even tighter into her upper buttock on each side.

Watching her like that hardened Andy to a new unknown level, Leah knew he was behind her but, without taking her head out of the fridge, she giggled, "Uncle Andy have you got anything to eat?"

Andy could just utter the word, "Yes," with no thought as to if she was really hungry or not. Leah just turned and stood upright and holding in her hands cupping in prayer one of Andy's courgettes that he had bought earlier that week.

"I think this is going to be too much for me," she said as she rounded its thickness with her fingers and so smiling she replaced the vegetable back to where it belonged.

"Have you anything else?" She asked, beckoning Andy over with her outstretched arms. As Andy walked three steps towards her Leah dropped to her knees in front of him.

Andy's groin was 'bolt upright' as she started to move her hands slowly up and down his thighs. "I will find something to nibble," she giggled.

"Are you comfortable?" Andy blurted and immediately, inwardly shouted at himself for his own stupidity, but her response was to lean her head forward, nuzzling her face, pushing her lips over his trousers and around his stiffness. She cooed, "I do love an older man to take control," and held onto him tight. Both Andy's palms covered the back of her head and pressed her even closer against his erection as she whispered, "do you think I'm cute?"

'Cute, God yes.' Andy thought, but quickly questioned himself as to 'how young was she?' She was more than cute, and she must be at least the legal age, but how was Andy going to tell her that without making himself sound like a pervert or giving her the wrong impression?

"Yeah, your cute girl," he said, hoping that would answer her.

"You're really cool too," she told Andy as she nibbled, lightly biting his stiffness through his trousers.

"Can I see it?" she asked looking up at the man he could only nod in response.

Her eyes were then glued to Andy's zipper as it was slowly pulled down and as the fly spread parted, open and undone, Leah reached inside his damp pants and, gripping the hard shaft, she pulled it free. Leah's silence was finally broken as she spoke only one word. "Wow!" she said.

"You can lick it if you want to." Andy said, attempting to gain control over this young girl kneeling in front of him.

"Oh, it's so big," she said, "way bigger than any I have seen before." She lied.

Andy stood there in the kitchen fridge light, hard and proud.

"That's because you've only had boys and I'm a man," Andy said as her hand slid around his shaft. 'Her small fingers made it look so much bigger,' he thought.

Andy let out a low moan as she started moving her hand slowly up and down his cock.

"Even your moan sounds nice," she said.

Andy now gripped both of Leah's shoulders, he was now going to be in charge. "Kiss it," he told Leah and she duly obeyed. "Lick it," he ordered and she licked its length.

Reaching over and releasing one shoulder Andy stroked the side of her cheek with this hand and she looked up into his eyes.

"Go ahead, swallow me if you're that hungry," he said in anticipation of her lips opening wide on him. Leah slowly obliged, pressing her lips to the tip and holding them there.

"You're not going to try and push your penis in my mouth?" she asked coyly.

That immediate single thought that Andy had had in his head vanished in that very sentence, "No." He replied.

Gazing down and leaning herself over she moved her lips as she kissed the head and Andy felt her tongue slide over it for the first time.

"Like that?" she looked up smiling.

"Just lick it like you would a lollypop." Andy told her and she went down and did just that.

She licked the shaft of his manhood running and tongue tipping all the way from the girth to its head.

Andy groaned loudly in pleasure, "now swallow it whole like you would a lollypop," and Leah willingly obeyed.

Over the tip, over the head and along the shaft her head moved slowly forward and Andy groaned more.

Leah stopped about halfway down and Andy felt her gag a little, but she didn't pull away, she simply moved slightly back and then pushed her head forward again. She was swallowing more and more, she wasn't an innocent, she took the full measure.

Andy resisted the temptation to put his hands on the back of her head again, to bury himself entirely in her mouth and throat, but waited and after a short moment Leah pulled herself off his throbbing muscle after a quick cough and wiping her salivated lips she asked. "Am I a good girl Uncle Andy?"

"Perfect." Andy replied.

Leah pulled from the front of her knickers one of the condoms that she had hidden and biting the packet open she mouthed her lips over the rubber and over Andy's erection.

"I am ready Uncle Andy and I so want you to have me, to fill me." The young girl announced as she stood pulling the other condoms out from the front of her knickers and, handing them over, Leah slowly walked back to the sofa stating. "I want you to use them all."

Kneeling on the sofa Leah raised her butt high and as Andy stood behind her he could see the moistness through the black panties still clinging to her. However, moving the tiny scrap of material to one side Andy slowly slid a finger over her neatly trimmed cut hair producing a longing moan from her.

Andy took his time, the same slow time that Leah had spent on him in the kitchen. He started off rubbing lightly applying more and more gentle pressure which made her moan even louder, as he moved his finger to her clitoris and rubbed gently.

As the minutes passed and as Leah's moans intensified, the faster Andy rubbed. And it wasn't long before he could feel her body tightening just to the point of no return and as she became taut Andy pushed in one and then two fingers and the girl soon shuddered into orgasm and soaked his hand.

Andy was now a mountain of a man, a caveman, 'the man' and he gave her his full length and she moaned, cried and exploded time and again. The condom and champagne helped Andy hold back his climax and the sweat soaking his lips from his brow ensured he could think of something else other than his personal fulfilment, but as the alcohol wore off, his senses drove him to his peak.

Removing the condom and turning Leah around to face him he pulled her back by her hair and she arched her back upward and opened her mouth wide. Within a dozen gagging thrusts of his cock he felt his scrotum explode. So much so that he thought he could be drowning her, but she didn't pull back or choke loudly, Leah just thrust herself forward to meet his need and she gulped until the jerks slowed to a stop.

The next morning Leah woke early and smiled at the other two used condoms that lay on the bedside cabinet. She showered and dressed quickly in the bathroom and, as Andy still hadn't stirred in his sheets that they had both soaked until the early hours, she decided to close the apartment door quietly behind her.

However, Leah hadn't noticed that Andy was already awake, he had just pretended to be asleep, waiting to be 'woken' with a kiss, perhaps a chat about 'future plans' but there was none, so as soon as the apartment door was closed without a "goodbye," his eyes opened, he jumped up and quickly dressed, pumps, jeans and sweat top and he was gone!

That pretty girl was going to leave him without further plans to meet up, how dare she? Andy was having none of it! He wanted more of her, much more he told himself, he wasn't a loser and he wasn't about to lose her!

Grabbing his keys and wallet Andy was out of the apartment and followed just seconds behind the blonde aura of Leah as she swept along the streets and sidewalks of affluent apartment blocks. He tried to concentrate on keeping his distance, keeping people or obstructions between him and his prey on what was a busy commute for many.

He knew that as she hadn't woken him he was just a 'one night stand,' but there was no way he was going to let that be so, he could still smell her lust for him. He had tasted this young free spirit and he so wanted more, much more of her.

Leah never noticed Andy behind her and it never occurred to her to look back, look back on her past, to look back at Andy following her every footstep. Not once did she see him at the rail station where she went to her locker to get a change of clothes for the day ahead and then go to the nearby women's toilets and emerge, refreshed. She never noticed him stand just yards from her, not even when she walked to the café to turn up for work.

After half an hour of standing nearby, waiting, looking, observing, staring, Andy was simply anonymous amongst the passing crowd as he walked passed the café window where he saw her waitressing.

Leah's expression was laughable and Andy did just that when he saw her look back at him as he entered the café for lunch. She just stood there opened mouthed in the middle of her floor space, open just as she had opened for him that previous night, but not open in pleasure, it was open in shock!

"Surprised to see me Leah?" he called out as he walked up to her. She simply just nodded a reply.

"I'll sit here then." Andy announced and sat at the empty booth immediately next to her.

Leah just looked perplexed as he sat. "Is this an accident?" She leant over and whispered.

Andy replied "Simple fate my love, I'll have the days special my special one and a sparkling water on the side."

Leah excused herself and went to the grill and called out the order, but, not stopping, she walked away to the staff room door and closed it behind her, Leah needed a moment, in this moment of confusion, a moment to gain control of herself.

'Coincidence?' she questioned herself.

'No' her mind told her, 'not in a city this big.'

She waited a minute gathering her thoughts, 'last night was great, but today is another day,' and this was not an experience that she wanted or liked.

'He was too old,' she thought, 'and after all, it was just sex and a bed for the night.' Leah settled herself, smiled in the mirror in front of her and returned to her work.

Andy called her over time and again as he watched her outline glisten around her as she worked the greyness of the gathering midday crowd, but other than serving his meal and drink she purposefully distracted herself away with the other diners.

"See you at dinner." Andy called out as he paid at the bar counter, but Leah didn't acknowledge him from the other side of the counter, she didn't want to.

However, she did think it was a nice gesture, the $20 tip for the $5 meal that he had left on the table for her.

That was, until she noticed scribbled on the back in marker pen the word ANDY and a telephone number. Leah immediately changed this up into smaller notes and said goodbye to the number.

It was another busy day for Leah, she worked the afternoon customers with smiles and winks and she had done her best to forget about the strangeness of 'Andy' her latest conquest.

That was until 5pm when the owner, Big Al, walked over to the booth where Andy had sat that lunchtime.

Big Al by name and as nurture intended, Italian by birth, his family had moved to Canada after the Second World War where they started the café/diner and when Big Al inherited the business he would insist on tasting his three best sellers daily, homemade garlic burgers, spinach meatballs and Tuscany pie.

Big Al was a barrel of a man, with a grand smile, but the sharpest of tongues when needed and he used it on Leah when she confronted her boss, just as he placed a reserve sign on the booth table and told her it was there for her friend.

"Please don't, he is not my friend" she asked.

"Well I have $500 deposited in the till, a reserve that now tells me you and him are friends," Al retorted.

"Please, I don't want to serve him, he gives me the creeps." Leah exclaimed.

"You don't have to honey, I can find another waitress and you can find the door, your choice!" He snapped.

"But," Leah was interrupted.

"Not another word on the subject, he helps pay my bills, you don't," and Al held out the palm of silence and Leah stayed silent.

Andy and the same two work mates from the night before came to the café that evening and sat at their reserved table. All three were loud and brash and none held back when ordering. Each adding words to the menu, words and innuendo, such as a "hot dickery, spicy sausage,' and adding a, "lathering of cream cheese." This clearly told Leah that his guests knew of 'the conquest' of her and it soon became the longest two hours of her life. For every time Leah heard laughter from the booth she thought that it was her ass that was the butt of their mirth and when the other two left, Andy again settled the bill. There was another $20 tip left on the table and again his name and number was scribbled on it.

At 9pm the diner closed its doors, the last of the customers left and Leah just stood at the window peering out from the neon lights above her. Squinting her eyes, searching, seeking out another pair of eyes that maybe looked back at her through the raindrops from the darkened street outside, but she saw no-one, just passing crowds of faces on the busy city sidewalk, out there, in the wet and the cold.

Leah was the last but one to leave, she didn't fancy going out to a bar that night, she didn't fancy any company as she had had unwanted company all day, she told herself.

Big Al closed up the café/diner ushering out and leaving Leah standing alone by the locked front door as the lights went dark inside. Leah hugged her small jacket tight around her body, unsure and begging the question of herself, 'was it for warmth or a protective layer against the insecurity that she felt?'

She didn't know exactly which, but she hugged it close and her shoulder bag was held tight against her all the same. She stood outside for several minutes looking up and down the busy main street; she was again looking for eyes staring back at her and with every darkened shadow that walked towards her she worried.

Was it Andy who approached from the gloomy shadows? No, none of the shadows turned out to be him and Leah was now telling the 'silly girl' inside herself 'not to be so stupid, get out of the rain, and get a room for the night.'

Leah sighed deeply as she stepped forward, her first small steps towards the nearest hostel that she knew was only 8 blocks away, she accepted they weren't the nicest of rooms having stayed there once or twice, but it was the closest hostel and she wanted to 'lock out her world' as quickly as possible.

Leah was glad she was still wearing her 'work pumps' her footsteps were silent amongst those that walked around, behind her, or those in front on the street. Leah heard a multitude of metallic quarter tipped heels, the latest shoe accessory for both sexes and they beat like tiny tin drums with an occasional 'screech' of a foot skid as metal slid the wet sidewalk concrete.

Her pace quickened. Leah kept telling herself, 'don't look around or behind you, look down, don't look forward,' but she couldn't help herself and inwardly she kicked her stupidity as she would glance back every 50 feet or so.

She couldn't see those faces in the distance behind her, just dark figures going about their business, but it was those manly shapes that increased her pace.

One block to go, one block to go, one block and a long dark alleyway to get to the hostel door as her mind began to falter. Leah turned the alleyway and many strides in she stopped.

To catch her breath in the choking silence, to wipe a tear of cold or nerves, she didn't know which, but she now took time to compose herself.

'Silly girl' she told herself again and again. "Stand tall," she whispered as she focussed on the neon hostel sign. Not far and her padded pumps walked her forward.

There were varying degrees of darkness, just like all alleyways, and with only the faintest hint of light from adjacent buildings, she didn't see the wine bottle that she suddenly kicked on the ground. The glass piercing forward startled her brain to the acuteness of sound and she stopped in her tracks once more, this time waiting for the bottle to take its last roll and settle. Leah felt very alone as she started her next few steps and that's when she heard the faint click of a footstep behind her. Click, click, click, click, the strides matched hers as she hastened herself. 'Run girl, run!' her mind now yelled 'sprint!' and she did. The steps that led to the hostel's open front entrance were leapt in two and only when she was half in and out of the doorway did she stop, turn and look. To listen out for what was now silence in the darkness, she peered into the dark, but there was neither sight nor sound, the only thing she recognised was the turmoil in her head.

Leah's sleep was punctured with the dream of the uninvited Andy and his two friends in her diner and those footsteps in that black alleyway that became louder as they came closer, but she woke from the black when those steps were upon her and the next morning she rose later than normal.

Quickly she washed in the room's sink and towelled herself dry with the bed sheet and she made work just on time as Big Al opened at 7am. He was all smiles as customers and staff entered together. It was a good sign to the diners' popularity and it was busy from the start.

The morning flew, no Andy, lunchtime came and went, no Andy and as the early evening drew to a close, no Andy. Leah was pleased that all the seats had been filled and that a queue had formed throughout the day with still no sign of Andy and for the first time that day Leah smiled as she returned from a quick smoke break out back.

On her return, Big Al called Leah over to the counter and quickly pointed to a huge bunch of red roses laid out at the end of the serving hatch.

"The delivery man asked for you," he stated and a number of staff and customers converged on Leah as she picked up the flowers and began to read the small card she pulled out from tiniest of envelopes.

'My dream angel' and as she read out those words voices around her hushed "ah," and "that's lovely," but Big Al grounded everyone's thoughts when he announced, "put them out back in the staff room and get back to work."

Leah carried them out alright, out of the customer area, straight through the staff room and out the back where she threw the flowers and card into the rubbish dumpster out the back. She was no-one's angel and her one smile that day had disappeared.

That night Leah again only ventured out as far as the hostel, but this time she jogged the journey and when she got to the alleyway she turned on the old torch that she had 'borrowed' from the diner's tool cupboard and sprinted the now brightened path until she was inside. She never looked back once and the only noise she registered was her pounding heart. That night she dreamt that again in the darkness she shone her torch down to her feet, her feet that stamped on withering red roses that snaked the ground attempting to wrap their stems round her ankles, but they eventually all died with a crunch of petals and hisses.

The next morning Leah rose early enough to visit the rail station locker for a change of clothes and another wash in the ladies' restroom, where she chatted to other regular girls in the same routine as hers. Washing, dressing, applying make-up and gossiping, girls, mostly older than her, only one or two younger and all in various jobs, just girls seeking an existence, in search of a better life.

"Bye girls." Leah called out to replying voices as she left and returning to her locker she took her time to sort out her dirty clothes from clean realising that soon she would need a launderette, so placing those that were dirty in a plastic bag and pushing this bag into her shoulder bag she decided that the 'evening's entertainment,' was sorted.

Leah bumped and bustled through the vast throng of commuters as she left the busy rail station, a concourse where almost all, including Leah, excused themselves to others as they weaved their own individual paths.

Checking the station's clock Leah knew she had time to stroll rather than walk with purpose and she soaked in the bright sun that would occasionally break through the envelope of cloud cover and she was full of smiles as she said, "Good morning honey," to Big Al as she entered the diner.

He smiled back over the main counter. A counter that was stacked with groceries in readiness for the day's trade, but there was nothing for Leah as she checked the café post that hid amongst the vegetation and this broadened her smile.

"No news is good news" she told Big Al and she turned with a spring in her step practically skipping from table to table, ensuring each was clean and presentable for their first customers.

The doorbell tinkled a little ring as usual from the small brass bell that was attached to the front door as customer after customer busied themselves inside and every time it rang out Big Al's smile broadened.

It was mid-morning, brunch time and the diner finally slowed allowing everyone to relax from what was an incredible morning's trade. Leah was excused to stand outside in the rear alley with another of the waitresses, both smoked their filtered cigarettes. Both chatted and laughed and Leah decided she was now ready enough to enjoy herself again, 'to go out tonight' she thought, 'to hell with the laundry, everything I'm wearing is fresh on today and I deserve it,' she confirmed.

The two-hour lunchtime session came and went, Andy's reserved booth remained empty and Big Al took $100 from his reserve envelope to cover the loss of potential earnings and another $100 went that evening with no sign of Andy.

'Good!' Leah had time to think, 'his dollars would soon run out,' as she went through her routine of pouting her reflection into the staffroom mirror as the diner now closed for the evening.

"Leah, Leah," Big Al called out from the diner.

"I forgot something, are you there?" he called.

Leah was all smiles as she wiggled her return from the staff room and standing in front of Big Al she posed a classic Betty Boop with her hands on her knees, her bottom pushed up high and facially wanting, she coyly asked, "What was it Al, did you forget a pay rise?" she giggled.

"Never," he chortled at her teasing, "I forgot this package came for you." And with that he held out a small white box addressed to Leah with the diner's address. Leah's heart sank just a little, she had only ever received one item before at the diner and that was the unwanted roses, now she stood with this box in her hands.

She opened the outer package and peered inside to find another white box with black lining and this one she lifted out.

Chanel No5 Paris the black lettering pronounced.

"Wow, that must have cost a small fortune!" Big Al exclaimed and he took the perfume box from her open hand.

"I have seen the adverts girl, sugar someone really has the hots for you!" he said.

At the bottom of the transit box was a small note folded in half and then half again and Leah picked it out. Opening the note, Leah noticed it was the same style of handwriting as was on the flower delivery and this worried her, but, what she read made her weak at the knees and sick to her stomach. Leah grabbed the serving counter for support and she gasped at every word read, 'I couldn't smell any perfume on you this morning. Xxx'

On leaving the café and within the hour, Leah had washed her laundry and now sat watching a kaleidoscope of colour revolving as it dried three feet from her bench seat. Yes, she knew she had her laundry to do, however, she had been in such a good mood that day that she had wanted to go out for the night. Instead her plans all changed with that perfume and those words on the note.

Yes, it had all changed back to her original laundry plan of revolving knickers and bras, each matching the revolving thoughts in her head.

The launderette itself was quite busy for late evening, though Leah only paid occasional attention to the front door as it opened and closed to the outside world. Other than that, she just sat trying her hardest to gain her composure as she stared at her soft pinks and dark blacks. Leah's mind raced as she repeated assertions of her dominance to herself, subduing the weak thoughts in her head that now ran scared.

'Stupid girl,' she repeated and repeated, but still she sensed she was being watched. 'Stupid girl,' she retorted to the thoughts that she had been followed to the hostel. 'Stupid girl,' had Andy actually been so close to her to notice that she hadn't applied any scent that morning?

"Stupid girl" she murmured as the dryer finally clicked stop in front of her.

Gathering her underwear and four of her short black dresses that doubled as work and going out clothes she carefully folded each to avoid too many creases and gently caressed these into her shoulder bag that she would now carry at arm's length to avoid squashing her clothes against her body.

The laundrette itself was halfway to the hostel and although she was wearing her pumps for speed Leah had told herself to walk, walk slowly, walk tall and she did.

Still the thoughts of her stalker hit her mind likened to lightning bolts that flashed beware, be scared and for all her poise she was. And it wasn't long that her head now turned in every direction, walking past and seeking out the unknown in the dark and her pace once again increased.

Within minutes and outside the alleyway to the hostel she stopped dead, her head pounded, the squeeze of darkness began to crush normality as she peered into the corridor of invisible foes. The alley appeared darker than ever before and she cursed herself for returning the flashlight to the cupboard at work. Now the only guide was the neon hostel sign in the distance.

Half a pace forward, but then, half a pace back, 'Stupid girl,' she thought again and her eyes began to fill with tears as she felt ridiculous, standing in the street crying over nothing.

Slowly, so slowly the torment eased until Leah braved the torture and edged forward again, one step, two, followed by more until the busy noise of street life grew distant and quietened to a whisper. The yellow neon sign of salvation grew brighter with only 50 or so yards to go and Leah stared forward as her ears pierced the silence behind her, waiting for a 'click' of unknown heels, but none came.

30 yards and her heart was pounding African drums that filled her head.

20 yards and she never saw the hand that grabbed her bag in the dark.

"Spare some change," the black voice urged as the material of bag strap creased her skin and Leah tugged back, screaming at her confusion and she wet herself pulling free from the grubby hand that grasped her bag.

Two yanks and another scream, she pulled free and she flew those final yards to the hostel, again leaping the steps to the echo of a male voice laughing loudly behind her in the dark.

That night in her room Leah pulled the wardrobe across the door and then the bed across the wardrobe, she was two flights up from ground level and once done she finally felt safe. She used the room basin to wash herself and clean her soiled knickers and it wasn't long until the corridor noises were smothered by a deep grateful sleep.

In the morning Leah noticed there was no soap left to 'wash away her fear,' so pulling back her fortress defence she decided to return to the railway station where she could also return her clothing. Walking downstairs she approached the hostel reception to once again 'check out,' but she was surprised to see two Detectives asking questions of the staff and residents that were gathered there.

"Did you see, did you hear" the questions were somewhat stifled until Leah walked closer and it was then that she realised that a 'down and out' had been kicked near to death close to where the hand had grabbed her bag in the dark!

Leah knew nothing, heard nothing she told the officers and as she was late for work, she told them "that's it" and she left for the railway station.

Having refilled her locker, she washed and changed and all the time Leah stared into the mirror for answers, none came. Leah opened the perfume bottle and applied the No5 scent and then dashed to work, keen to observe those around her, in front of and behind her and when she arrived Big Al and the other waitresses were already busy preparing their stations. Leah said nothing other than, "sorry," to Big Al who was tapping his watch face as she was almost five minutes late.

Leah simply grabbed her cloth and lime scented disinfectant and went to work at her tables and booths. Rubbing, cleaning, and cleansing the grubbiness of vinyl seating, polishing the Formica tables and wiping away her personal anguish of what had now become her life.

By 8am the café diner was again in full swing and Leah felt a numbness as she saw Andy walk in and take a seat by the window. Then to all of Leah's protestations to Big Al standing behind the counter he told her to, "serve him or find the door."

"Good morning Leah, are you okay?" Andy asked and she nodded a reply as she stood in front of him. Then with a sharp intake of nasal breathe he smiled. "So, you like the perfume then?"

"No more please Andy," Leah asked quietly. "No more gifts, what we had was fun, but that was all it was, fun, what would you like to order? I have other customers to serve."

Andy looked across at Leah, his eyes narrowed and his lips grew thinner as he whispered. "I haven't finished wooing you yet my love, don't you realise you are mine to have and protect."

It was the way Andy then whispered, "and you need protection."

It was as if he knew of her recent alleyway struggle and with this comment, she noticed his smile, a knowing smile with raised eyebrows, this made Leah shiver.

"Coffee, ham, pancakes and two eggs, sunny side up just like your breasts." He giggled to himself and Leah walked away to fetch him his coffee.

When Leah returned Andy asked her to wait as he pulled from his jacket pocket a small gilt edged black box that he held in front of her and opening it there within, laying resplendent in beauty, a gold necklace with two small heart pendants, one inscribed 'L,' the other 'A' and he told her, "this is for you, I thought of you when I bought it and I had it inscribed, you need the finest things in your life."

'My life, my God,' Leah thought, her heart sank as she slammed the hot coffee mug down in front of him and snatching the box from his hand she closed it and dropped it onto the table. "Andy, we need to talk." Leah said, but there was no time.

"Leah, customers need serving." Big Al was screaming at her from across the floor.

"When?" Andy asked expectantly.

"Tonight?" he urged.

"Now Leah!" came another yell from behind the counter, Big Al's face was turning red with frustration.

"After work." Leah confirmed quickly, turning back towards Al who was continuing to 'plate up' various meals waiting to be served.

Within the next five minutes of flurry, serving various customers, Leah heard Andy's order waiting to be collected called out, but when she turned towards the booth with his hot plate of breakfast, the booth was empty, Andy had gone.

The rest of the day dragged and Leah was happy that this was the case, never before had she so wanted time to stand still, to put off the inevitable, but every time Leah tried to gather herself on how she was going to deal with Andy that night, another customer order got in the way of her thoughts.

Leah's last hour of work was the worst, 'would he listen to her? Would he stop this harassment?'

Why was it that every minute that now passed still fogged any clarity of mind? And with 15 minutes until closing Andy was pacing the diner sidewalk, 'as if on guard duty.'

Leah inwardly cursed the thought that she now had to confront, to overcome, it was not in her nature, she knew she would rather flee and be free of this, her current turmoil.

Leah wiped over her pumps and presented herself for inspection in the glass reflection of the diner window, but was quickly distracted by Andy tapping impatiently on the glass and as she left Andy stood at the doorway in front of her.

He was all pleasantries, compliments and smiles as he took her hand that wasn't offered and asked "Fancy a drink?" and Leah nodded, 'more than one to get her through this' she thought.

Three blocks down and two along Leah found herself facing Andy in one of her favourite bars. He had left her at a table and returning from the bar he brought over a bottle of champagne and sat there opening and proposing a toast. "To us," he declared and on those words Leah gulped the glass empty and then the next as she formulated a small speech in her mind.

Andy began talking about planning a vacation for the pair of them and was asking if she had a preference as to where she would like to go? Leah had to seize the moment and holding her palms up as 'stop signs' Leah began to speak.

She used words like. "This situation isn't right for me," and, "I'm not ready yet." Quotes of, "please don't push me," and, "what we had was nice, but I'm not ready for a relationship."

Whatever else she needed to say, she said it at length, but she spoke it quietly, gently, soothing the wound that she was opening and once she stopped, expecting an awkward silence, Andy just sat there and smiled.

He smiled and explained that she was confused with her emotions and that he could see that it was fate that had brought her to him. He simply fed her another glass of champagne. Andy told her that he had looked into larger apartments for them to share and then also offered his opinion on what clothes he thought best suited her physique. It was a one-way conversation as Leah thought of an exit plan, but still the champagne flowed and by now it was from another open bottle and Leah between short smiles, sat there in silence.

Nodding at appropriate moments, her mind was stumbling towards screaming the words "fuck off!" But after a short while that thought soon 'hazed over' as she began to slouch lower and lower in the chair, her mind, her body drifted, until her last memory was of being helped to her feet.

It was past midday when Leah next opened her eyes and she opened them in Andy's bedroom.

The sun was high in the sky as she turned her aching head and looked towards the adjacent buildings and it was in that moment her sore body told her mind that she had been used for sexual gratification. Pulling the bed sheet away from her nakedness she looked down in tears on her body as she saw both breasts and inner thighs displayed finger mark bruising and her anus was still pulsing in sodomised pain. Then she felt the trinket around her neck, her neck that now wore that gold chain with hearts, her neck was sore to touch and she gently rubbed the graze marks near her throat. She knew she had been drugged, raped and she sobbed and broke down into jerking convulsions.

It took a very long time for Leah to gather any sane thought, she felt ill, betrayed, used and abused and she had stomach cramps that matched the pain in her head as bile reached the base of her throat.

Leah gulped hard and pulled herself up from the bed, she stumbled to the bathroom and on her knees in front of the toilet Leah convulsed and vomited. Acid burnt her throat as her stomach emptied and she gagged for air as more tears flowed.

Kneeling, slumped, hanging onto the seat edge to prevent further collapse, Leah eventually gathered enough strength to rise first to her knees then to her feet, but still she gripped the seat edge for steadiness. Leah gagged again and again over the toilet, but there was nothing left but her inward spirit and Leah intended to hold on to that. She took a deep breath and raised herself up, she needed to feel clean, she needed to wake her senses and the shower in just a few steps was her closest salvation.

Leah's arms outstretched, her hands palming the ceramic white tiles as the flow of hot water soaked her body and, as she cleansed, she soon realised that the gold necklace was still around her neck. However, with one yank of her hand, it snapped free and was thrown to the shower tray, with her right foot the golden gift was manoeuvred to the plug hole where, with a flick of her big toe, it disappeared to the pipework below.

Leah was careful when she cleaned her private areas, these were sore and as she washed herself, she felt violated. It was twenty minutes or so before Leah was able to drag herself from the shower and gently dab her body dry.

Returning to the bedroom she gathered her clothes from the floor and started to dress. Looking towards the smashed mirror on the dressing table, which was 'weird' she thought, she also noticed a large A4 piece of paper, a note scrawled in black ink that read, 'Will be home by 6 my dearest, my love!' Followed by a smiley face and three kisses.

Leah was bewildered, astonished, 'what the hell was happening to her?' she freaked. Beside the note, was a large camera, a 'Polaroid Land Camera Square Shooter 2' was the decal. The type of camera where, within minutes you could release and develop your own pictures. Leah looked down to the floor beneath the dresser, three empty film boxes, spent 'Magicube' flashes and spent film backings, but there were no pictures, no pictures!

Leah was appalled and fell back to the bed, she sat in revulsion realising that she had been photographed whilst unconscious.

Truly! Andy was in a fantasy land all of his own, a fucked-up fantasy land where Leah was subservient, abused, raped and sodomised, where Leah again found herself sobbing uncontrollably, anxious despair filled her mind as she was in an overload of wretchedness.

More minutes passed before Leah steadied herself and began looking for the developed photographs, she started to look around the dressing table area, the wardrobe, the side tables, but there were none to be found. Then to the wardrobes where she threw his clothes out amongst the boxes of shoes that she emptied, still nothing and conscious that Andy couldn't be trusted to be home until 6, Leah began to ransack the room, but still nothing!

She screamed and spat out at anything and everything that didn't reveal the photographs, she punched the wardrobe doors in frustration and she toppled the dressing table over to one side.

Suddenly there was a banging knock at the apartment door. "I've called the police." A muffled voice yelled, stopping Leah in her tracks.

"Shit," she said and, 'shit' she thought, would the Police believe her?

A drifter, a carefree spirit who went from one bed to another, from one sexual partner to another, someone who had been showered with gifts and last seen in public drinking champagne with him, the man she could cry rape against?

'Never' she thought, 'hardly' she believed and 'run.' She did.

Leah, barefoot, with her pump shoes in hands, ran from the apartment block towards the direction of the diner, only occasionally stopping to catch her breath at the various road junctions and when she did, catching the stares of other pedestrians for some strange reason they would either smile or smirk.

Leah couldn't work this out at all, other than being barefoot, okay! That was all that was strange, perhaps that was it? But she didn't care, she just ran on.

It took half an hour of tired emotion where Leah's body was in agony, but eventually she had slipped on her pumps when far enough away from Andy's apartment building and the sound of oncoming Police sirens. However, she was in pain, her body ached and there was still a pounding in her head and as she walked into Al's diner.

Big Al took one look at Leah and pointing to her and then to the staff door he yelled. "Staff room!" So loudly that the business and customers fell silent. Leah hung her head in shame and snivelled tears as she walked those final few yards, knowing every customer and staff member now stared at her.

Big Al followed and within moments Leah was listening to the words, "you're sacked, collect your things, never return and goodbye!" As Big Al pulled up her left hand and placed $100 in $20 dollar bills into her palm.

"Now go!" he bellowed.

Leah said nothing, she expected nothing less, she knew she would be sacked as Big Al never took any nonsense from his staff and though she had only come to the diner to collect the few personal things she held in a staff locker, the money was a bonus.

"And best you wear my baseball cap" Big Al announced, "until you wash yourself properly'.'

"What?" Leah questioned.

"Your forehead," and Big Al pointed to it.

Leah looked over to the staff mirror and walked closer to it and there she noticed for the first time in faded bold black marker pen letters a word scribed, 'MINE.'

Leah again cried in shame. "Take my cap Leah." Big Al said, a little gently, as he went to his locker to retrieve it, "but don't come back," he added, passing it to her.

Leah took his cap and, bagging her items, she left, she left for the rail station and once there she retrieved her things from the locker and then went to the ticket office. She chose the first train out and that one headed south.

Two months and two towns later, Leah sat in yet another waiting area of yet another bus terminus, but this time it was the coach stop building in Fargo, North Dakota and Kerri followed her in.

Chapter 12

1977 Leah and Kerri

Leah noticed Kerri behind her and saw what she had seen in herself those short months before. There was a young girl who was frightened and vulnerable, frail and nervous and Leah's immediate thought was just to go over to her and give her a big hug, but she didn't, she just watched.

Leah was herself hesitant to draw any attention to herself and by going over and saying "hi," when she had just spent those last couple of months avoiding unnecessary contact so 'just in case,' she just watched.

Kerri didn't notice Leah, she was just too busy looking up and down the street, up and down, again and again, hoping that there was no-one out there looking for her. It seemed like an age before Kerri was able to pull herself away from the window and corner herself in an envelope of steel, concrete and cold people.

Looking up at the travel board of various coaches' routes travelling from the terminus, Kerri was unkempt, bedraggled, dirty and physically shaking as she wedged herself tightly against those grey walls.

Leah saw Kerri pull out various dollar bills and coins from her jacket and her rucksack and there she sat, crouching small against the wall, only to count what little she had.

Kerri made piles of coins that made single dollars and as each pile was complete Kerri would look up again to the travel board and a smaller board of special offers. Occasionally Kerri smiled as another destination was potentially purchased and it was a sweet smile Leah observed, though perhaps this girl needed something warm inside her, perhaps something reassuring and remembering the coffee stall just outside Leah walked out and purchased two, both milky, both sweet and returning to the terminus building Leah walked straight up to and over to Kerri.

"Hey girl, I got this for you." Leah offered.

"I hope you don't mind, but I thought you could do with something warm." Leah held out the plastic cup coffee to the grateful out stretched hand of Kerri.

"Thank you, God bless you." Kerri whispered back smiling away the anguish.

"Do you mind if I sit with you?" Leah asked and Kerri replied with, "Please," and offered the ground next to her.

For the next hour both sat there unnoticed by the other travellers, they had drunk their coffees, exchanged their stories and both had wiped each other's tears.

Both girls were on the run from scarring abuse and both wanted to be far away, further than they actually were. Leah did however make Kerri giggle with laughter when she told Kerri that the milk cartons didn't have her missing picture on them yet. So, there was still time to earn, beg, borrow, or steal themselves away as far as they could. On that dirty old floor both young girls made a pact that as there was no-one else, at least they had each other and would travel on together.

--//--

As the days, weeks and months followed their friendship blossomed, both would work 'cash in hand' where work could be found and these were on the various diner floors that dotted Middle America.

Both were heading south as quickly as they could afford, towards the warmer climate, away from the approaching winter. The girls would sleep wherever they could or where it was cheapest and as Leah hadn't altogether given up on men she would often allow herself to be picked up and taken to a variety of motel bedrooms.

Rooms where she would quietly, in the middle of the night, pull herself free from another man's grasp only to open the door and let Kerri in to sleep under or beside her side of the bed.

Men weren't Kerri's thing though; yes, she was approached many a time. Who wouldn't approach a beautiful curvaceous girl, so young, younger than she looked and with the prettiest of smiles, but it was the thoughts of what her father did to her that still sickened her to the point where she could hardly bear a man to even brush up against her.

No, Kerri didn't enjoy male company, but she would add to their joint income by sketching the various customers that came into the diners and she would try to sell their portrait caricatures to them as they left, for just a few cents. Hardly any refused. The management would rarely mind either, as this pretty young artist would add flair to each of the diners that they worked in.

It wasn't long before Dakota, Nebraska, Kansas and Oklahoma were mere blurred memories, dusty visions of various welcomes to this state or desert town. So many signposts with an array of bright neon colour and each with an exit that they took as they pleased.

Both girls worked so hard together, sore feet and bruised hearts, but always with a cheery smile. They would 'wave' their customers off and would welcome the dollars in, a welcome dollar, a few cents, sometimes dime tips, but it all added up and was kept in the shoulder bag that Leah carried.

Travelling between the towns and cities, the girls would either hitchhike, bus or, where possible, ride a train and it would be on these journeys that Leah would gently tease Kerri about her reading the Bible.

"Forsaking all others?" Leah would ask holding hands, playfully mocking Kerri's beliefs between earlobe nibbling that would always fluster Kerri to the point where within minutes she would have to 'give up the good fight,' and close her only book.

It wasn't that Leah didn't like the Bible, she just didn't believe in it and she found it strange that Kerri, with all that she had gone through with her father beating and abusing her, that Kerri still believed in angels and heaven and that the Love of God would protect her.

Kerri would always insist, "but my God brought you to me." Leah had no answer to that so she accepted that every now and again on a Sunday, when the girls weren't working, Kerri would wander off to a local church to sing songs and listen to sermons. Leah thought it was a bit quirky, but she guessed it was part of what made her so happy all the time.

With every new city, town or township there was always clothes to buy and with both girls being the same dress size, though Leah was slightly taller and Kerri had a more perfectly rounded figure, both girls would gladly choose the items together and would always be seen in each other's clothes.

Each would also apply the other's make up and the sweet spray of scent was shared with the nights when they would hold onto each other's cuddles and the occasional tender 'friendship' kiss before they slept.

It wasn't long before the winter came and left delivering a new spring. The sun would heat their bodies a little warmer for the hard day's work ahead, but as night followed day, as they cuddled under bed sheets, both girls realised that their love for each other was welcomed and on now on more nights than less, the girl's found contentment in each other's arms and lips.

Yes, with each new evening Leah was finding it harder and harder to find attraction in men anymore, oh there were still plenty of offers, but it was only her ever comforting, beautiful Kerri who would soothe, caress and kiss the day's worries away.

Her young partner would always be smiling when Leah would insist on just the one bed, "the cheaper room option" when they stayed in the different towns' motels and guesthouses.

Chapter 13

The girls eventually found themselves in the state of Texas, it was late springtime and they were still heading south for the summer sun and cool ocean breeze. It was in Austin, Texas where they next alighted to again earn money and on that morning, it was a bright, beautiful day.

The girls had arrived on the outskirts of the city by Greyhound bus, just after 6 AM. By 7 AM they had found a cheap, but nice, motel with hot running water and clean white sheets on the bed. Then by 8 AM they had washed, applied make up and were now wearing matching black, short, diner dresses and both in black pumps.

At 8:15am and with a skip and a giggle both girls had started walking the local streets calling in on every diner and eating establishment they could find in a radius of around fifteen blocks or so, circling out from their motel.

As 9am struck the hour on the 'Littlefield' building clock on Congress Avenue both girls now stood outside an old 'tacky,' plastic, sign written pirate restaurant called 'The Crow's Nest' and taped to its front window was an advertisement in blue felt pen, Hiring waitresses - good rate of pay.

So, both girls stood in the warming sunshine and waited patiently for over an hour, before a small balding man, short, fat and in his 50s, walked up to the front door and unlocked the chain that wrapped the large, oak, double door.

'First mate Frankie,' that was the name on the badge that he wore and asked if both could waitress? Both replied. "Yes," in unison.

Frankie simply looked the girls up and down and declared, "well you look the right size for your costumes so I guess you've got the job, come in and collect what you'll be wearing for work and then be back here by twelve midday sharp, for inspection."

Any thoughts of impropriety were soon curbed by the first mates warming smile and both girls happily agreed to enter and just ten minutes later both left carrying a large big black bin bag of clothing.

Neither of them was asked to show identity as to who they were, so the various false identity cards that they had acquired during their time together were never offered up as proof of age and the only questions 'First mate Frankie' asked was for their names and the address where they were staying.

Kerri suggested a quick coffee on the walk back to the motel and as they sat outside a coffee house nearby they took the moment to peek into the black bags.

They were quite astonished at the thigh length suede boots and realised they had to swap them over when they checked the sizes. Both girls matched with a pair of boots, half a size too big for them. Both had a scarlet-red headscarf to wear, each with a white skull and cross bones design sewn onto it and this matched the red 'off the shoulder' braless, short to thigh, plastic dress with a black cotton fishnet side trim. Then there was the front strung, black basque that was obviously used to hold the skimpy uniform in place.

Both dresses smelt stale and were clearly in need of a clean, but at least the 'heavy duty' elasticated physical education knickers and the black fishnet tights were straight out of a brand-new packet.

The girls were in fits of laughter for quite a while until they realised that the minutes till midday were slipping away so they hurried back to the motel to prepare.

Both girls sponge cleaned the plastic dresses, spraying the outside with a cheap perfume and pumping talcum powder inside to smother the plastic smell odour and they used Vaseline in an attempt to lessen the cracking noise as the plastic bent. After all that effort, they applied make-up and dressed. Both Leah and Kerri were in near hysterics as they left for work, 'pirate wenches,' off to plunder a day's wages and they couldn't stop laughing at each other and themselves, for they were sexy and skimpy and the wolf whistles they heard as they walked the few blocks put a wiggle on their bums and the broadest of smiles on their faces.

They arrived at just before noon and the First Mate presented them with their gold plastic coin name badges, and they were now 'Lookout Leah' and 'Keelhaul Kerri.' Both girls had to ask what Keelhaul meant!

The restaurant's menu had such delights as, 'starboard shellfish,' 'briny broth,' and 'the quartermaster's quarter pounders,' stupid names, but surprisingly a delight to eat and the customers kept on coming through the open doors.

Both 'Look out' and 'Keelhaul' were fairly shattered by midnight when the Crow's Nest finally sought shelter into port. The 'First mate' and indeed the owner 'Captain' who had popped in to check on his establishment, were both pleased with how the girls had worked, so everyone was happy as the girls waved good night for the evening.

The walk home though wasn't such a delight, the wolf whistles from earlier had returned, but unlike before when the girls skipped to a whistle, the surrounding darkness and leering eyes of passers-by gave the noises an eerie edge that cut the night air, there was no more skipping from the girls just a quickened pace and held hands tightly, as they headed back to the motel.

It wasn't long though before the girls could close their door to the outside world and began to smile, their giggles soon returned as they looked each other up and down.

Leah approached Kerri and started to untie her Basque as a comforting silence surrounded the girls and both gazed sweet smiles towards each other. Kerri returned the favour and it was only a matter of seconds before both girls were pulling at each other's Basques, dropping the plastic dresses to the floor.

They stood there, semi-naked with just physical education knickers, black lace tights and boots to go and there was yet another giggle as Leah pushed Kerri onto the bed and stood astride her pulling at both boots until releasing Kerri from her suede captors.

Then as Leah lay down on the bed next to Kerri lifting her left leg in the air expecting to receive the same treatment, there wasn't a pull on her boot, instead Kerri lent over towards Leah and striding across her whilst taking hold of each of Leah's wrists she lowered herself closer and as their breasts touched so the kiss came, fully on the lips.

There was an urgency within Kerri as she pushed herself down onto Leah and from closed lips she opened Leah's fully, Leah was a little surprised by this. Never once had Kerri been so intense and it was always Leah who had previously led the 'friendship' kissing and cuddles.

However, she wanted the same, she couldn't deny it and so just as urgently, Leah responded pushing her face upward to the younger girl.

Both tongues entwined as they looked intently into each other's eyes and they kissed and kissed until in time Kerri rose slightly and pulled away. Kerri cupped both sides of Leah's face in her hands and with small glistening tears in her eyes she breathed "I love you'.'

Leah smiled and nodding back, as her eyes also welled, echoing her heart. "I love you too'.'

Kerri lowered herself towards the end of the bed and urgently pulled at her girlfriend's boots, and with boots off it was only a moment when Leah arched her bottom from the sheets that Kerri stripped Leah of her remaining underwear.

Kerri returned to Leah and they laid entwined, kissing each other's lips, their cheeks their necks, their shoulders and their hands now explored the ripe tautness of each other's young breasts. Brushing, slightly squeezing and softly rubbing nipples each fully erect between fingers and thumbs.

The girl's slender legs wrapped around each other's bodies and both felt the dampness of each other's inner thighs. So, with slow exploration into wantonness, they gently nudged and rubbed each other's moistness between sighs. It was only minutes before each had shuddered to a bit lip explosion of mind, body and soul.

Moments later Kerri rose, pulling Leah up and away from the bed, towards the bathroom and once inside, Kerri pulled back the white shower curtain to reveal the walk-in shower area. Black shiny tiles against the back wall, sides and floor, each tile surrounded by grubby white grouting that clamped them close, but just like the girls, the tiles sparkled.

Kerri turned the plastic white shower head on and turned back towards Leah they once again held each other and kissed, they didn't speak, they had no need to, and each knew in their own mind what they desired.

They held each other tighter, as together they walked as one under the steaming hot spray and between kisses, during kisses and after kisses they stroked each other's skin.

Having lathered, they smothered, then again as they kissed, they washed 'the day clean away.'

With the bathroom towels provided, the girls used these to pat the other dry and again they continued to kiss, to hold each other close, as they dried each other's hair.

Vigorously rubbing the rough white cotton towels over and through their hair and once done they couldn't but help themselves to yet another embrace.

However, this time Leah couldn't help herself but take the lead. She pulled Kerri down with her to the puddled tiles and laid her out, stretched out and facing towards her, she knelt down in front of Kerri slowly parting her lover's legs open.

First to Kerri's right breast Leah nibbled, she sucked and squeezed as fingers rubbed between her legs, then to the left breast that now received equal attention and Kerri was soon gasping cries of, "oh Lord," as her eyes looked up towards heaven.

Kerri squinted between Leah and the ceiling as the ecstasy that Leah was forcing her toward made her shudder with every breath.

Quickly Leah rose herself up to reach Kerri's open mouth and their tongues circled each other's as they melted once more and then with the cheekiest of smiles Leah lowered herself further down until between her legs she placed her open mouth over and around and over in gentle licks of exploration. Kerri looked down at her lover as Leah's tongue began to flick faster and she gasped soft moans as Leah's tongue flicked between her little lips until she reached her clitoral button.

Leah laid her hands flat against Kerri's lower tummy stretched her hands upwards, tightening Kerri's skin, protruding Kerri's clitoris up and outward just that little bit more exposed.

Kerri gasped and immediately arched her back. Her arms not knowing whether to grasp Leah's hair or grip the invisible nettles that now surrounded her tingling body so she did both as her fingers danced between clenches and orchestration, her mind now unaware of anything but pleasure as Leah continued to lick.

Kerri sighed with every stroke of the tongue and moaned with every kiss that covered her moistness and as Leah's hands covered and squeezed Kerri's breasts, her fingers 'slow stroked' tweaking each nipple.

As Leah's tongue continued to lick and her open mouth now sucked at Kerri's flowing juice she heard Kerri's sweet little voice that cried out louder, "oh God yes!"

"Yes, yes, oh God yes, please God yes, yes, just yes!" were Kerri's all shuddering screams as Leah's right fingers now penetrated deeper and deeper into her and Kerri's body bucked and buckled as her virginity was fully penetrated. Kerri grabbed her lover's head as tears filled her eyes, but still she pulled Leah tighter onto her. "Do it, yes do it!" and Kerri cried screaming towards fulfilment.

Leah too was now quietly moaning as she writhed, pushing her other hands fingers into herself, thrusting her pulsating moist flesh towards her own frenzied spasm, whilst she increased her tongue and finger speed on Kerri.

Back, forth and twisting as Leah lengthened the finger protrusion and tongue flicks on Kerri. From side to side and up and down, all these combined to send electric torrents through her partner's shaking body.

The body of Kerri who was no longer a 'girl virgin' as the fingers pushed deep, but now truly a woman, no longer was she a young innocent as the tiny droplets of love juice were released amongst the endless full flowing orgasms that her body set free.

Leah didn't stop for the cries of ecstasy, but continued to repeat her invasion to another convulsing deliverance. Only between shudders would she momentarily stop to lap, suck and swallow the fluid of Kerri's climatic 'arrivals.'

Leah herself continued to writhe satisfaction on the wet floor as she squeezed, prodded and arched herself until her body too surrendered to shuddering orgasm and it was then, only then, when she opened her eyes towards her lover.

Yes, only then, did Leah survey her partner's quivering body and listened to the soft whimpers of her voice, only then did she look beyond her tummy and breasts to see that Kerri's teeth had now clamped closed on her self-bitten right hand.

Kerri also showed the lines of tears that had flowed and Leah realised that in all that had taken place, never once did Kerri try to pull away, so Leah in reassurance moved upward and laid next to her lover.

Cuddling her arms, quietening her girlfriend's whimpers with small kisses, she slowly silenced Kerri to a murmur as they finished their first journey together.

--//--

Both girls had fun at The Crow's Nest and it wasn't long before Kerri's artistic skills were recognised by The Captain, who not only allowed Kerri to sketch customers for reward, but also paid the girl good money to have her repaint the seating backdrops, walls and partitions with various Pirate scenes. However, both girls had wandering souls and it wasn't long before they hoisted the rigging of their suitcases and sailed away on yet another bland looking coach that steered them towards the south.

They had made enough money to reach the ocean, where the breeze was the coolest in the midsummer sun and they arrived on the outskirts of Houston with big smiles and big hearts.

Their first purchases were two bottles of suntan oil and four bikini sets, two black, two white all size 8, all identical in style. Then they asked the lady of the boutique where she thought the best beaches were and, from explanation, it was only a couple of bus rides away.

With excited giggles, the girls travelled about 20 miles out of Houston to an area known as Kemah, a now popular but once sleepy seaside suburb.

Once they arrived both girls fell in love with the area, not only was the high, golden sun glistening over the many beach bars and bistros, but skirting the ocean was a marina filled with expensive boats and yachts.

Inland, there were also numerous restaurants that held Kipp Avenue and the Boardwalk together and close by, were open park gardens. But it was the dark blue ocean that called to them and drew them to the soft sandy beach, both stood smiling, watching, as each wave broke.

Their gaze was lost for almost an hour, but as it was gone midday and after a small ice cream nearby followed by a dark frothy coffee, that the girls collected themselves and their cases and strolled between the various eating and drinking establishments. They sought employment together, unfortunately this time the girls couldn't find a restaurant or bar that would take them on as a pair. However, in the marina, facing an armada of glistening white yachts, they were able to find work in restaurants immediately next to each other and as both businesses had the option of alfresco dining at least the girls could call out to each other now and again.

Next the girls needed a place to stay, but what little there was in the way of available rooms were priced out of their reach, so instead they looked further inland, a local bus journey away and looking out each side they sought adverts that showed vacant rooms.

Luckily only ten minutes into the journey, on Marina Bay Drive, they saw rooms being advertised that were easily within their budget. They chose a room that at least faced the direction of the ocean if in fact they couldn't actually see it.

The last part of their first day was still theirs and so with a change of bikinis underneath their shorts and T-shirts they headed back to the beach to watch the waves break the shoreline as gulls flew over and they beamed smiles at the setting sun's rays.

The girls had finally reached the destination that they had long travelled to and they were in a relationship that neither had expected or experienced before, for the pair of them it was absolute bliss.

It was only a matter of days before the girls had settled, both worked as hard as they could and each managed to secure Mondays off.

Word soon spread of Kerri's special skill in accurately detailing a customer's portrait in less than two minutes. It was a side line of sketching that was welcomed by her employer, knowing it drew custom, it provided extra income for both.

--//--

Every day off on Monday the girls would go to the beach together and together they would call in and visit each other's restaurant for a coffee or two. In matching bikini tops and home-made jean shorts and in their eagerness to please, they would still help clear and wipe down tables when need arose.

But it was the third Monday when they had a specific purpose in visiting the marina near where they worked, as both girls had heard and wanted to watch the local news camera team that stated it was heading down to advertise the local area.

As with many of the local populace neither girl had seen a television news crew 'in action' before and they were just as curious as the gathering crowd that surrounded them. Finally, by the time the camera crew had set up and the presenter was cued for action, both Leah and Kerri found themselves edging closer to the marina water's edge as they stood four deep back in the crowd.

First one take, then another, the next lead to, take four, as the female presenter continued to fluff her lines amongst whoops, claps and whistles. It was during this last attempt that Leah's attention was drawn elsewhere.

Was that a faint cry she heard? But then a louder scream for, "help!"

Leah looked around and behind her and in the marina waters some thirty yards away she could see a vigorous splash of arms, passed by a yacht that had entered the marina.

'Someone has fallen overboard,' she thought as the yacht swept by. 'That someone can't swim,' were her immediate thoughts and these were the only thoughts as she pushed past a person behind her, flew those few short strides and dived over the wall and into 15 feet of dark, cold water.

When Leah surfaced she immediately looked for those flailing arms and saw them directly in front of her, the arm movements were slower and the cries for, "help!" were now gargled and far weaker as the cold, swallowing sharpness had begun to take its toll.

Leah swam with all her might and as her head swung violently back and forth with each stroke of front crawl she could see an old man, a very old man, at the helm of the yacht crying out for his lost love, pointing and screaming, for someone to help his drowning wife.

The marina's water was freezing, an ice cube surrounded on three sides by harsh cold concrete, but Leah knew this numbing sensation from when she swam as a child in Canadian lakes and on instinct alone, she fought off the bitter enclosure.

Slicing her way through those invisible hands of death that clutched at her, trying to hold her back and away, but with each short breath she continued. Leah was only feet away when there was no more head, no more arms, no hands, or fingers breaching the surface, the cold marina had swallowed its prey.

Just a couple more seconds was all that Leah had needed, but the reapers grasp had taken hold of the old lady's time and where there was once life there was just mere ripples

Leah reached where she thought she had last seen those sinking fingers and, shutting her eyes from the salt of the sea, she dived with one huge breath.

Leah pushed and kicked at death's icy demons and down she went further into the blind darkness of loss.

Her hands reached out but nothing was there, still her legs kicked her downward; now her brain was frantically searching for air, her body struck out once more as her mind screamed despair, but still that lady wasn't there.

Now her body was telling her that she was close to exhaustion and a potential victim herself, but again she kicked on until she could kick no more. The silence was deafening and her head was pounding 'a thousand hammers' as she opened her eyes to the salt of the stagnant water. Her vision was stung, but as she peered through the murk the sun suddenly gleamed a lighter shade toward the surface, it was then she saw her. Not five feet from her, but lifeless, as the body of the old lady floated towards her. It was if death itself was rewarding her for her efforts and returning its meal. Returning it, only to be eaten on another day, but not this day!

Leah grabbed the hand in front of her and kicked up and pushing towards the light, a light that took every last concentrated, rehashed ounce of oxygen to reach, but she got there.

Leah breached and her body swallowed the heady air around her. As her mouth and lungs gasped for more, she pulled the lifeless lady's head to the surface. It was then that Leah heard the screams and cheers of onlookers that included the television news crew that were filming an exclusive.

Many of the crowd had run down the marina and across the floating walkways and berths to get to Leah and the old lady. Within a couple of seconds men also jumped in and swam to help Leah drag the lady up and onto a wooden platform.

As Leah was pulled up by many thankful hands that grabbed her Leah sat and watched as a first-aider went to work on the old lady's chest. Pumping and pumping, the clenched fists pushed down as ambulance sirens wailed in the near distance and Leah cried as blankets wrapped round her. She had fought death and won.

A couple more minutes passed and another took over in giving first aid and this person too continued to pump the old lady's chest as more salty broth spilled from her open mouth. Then, as the ambulance noise was at its loudest, halting at the quayside, it was in that instant, against belief and amongst the numerous gasps and cheers of onlookers that the old lady choked and took her first sicken breath to recovery.

There were cries of delight including those of Leah's and it was only then that she realised that she was being kept wrapped tight by her true love Kerri, who had silently knelt down beside her, also shedding tears.

"God, you scared me." Kerri whispered in Leah's ear as both girls stood and walked back to the marina roadway, now surrounded by a thankful crowd and film crew, they looked back and saw the old lady being stretchered to the waiting ambulance.

Person after person came and shook Leah's hands, she even received kisses and embraces. All the time the local news team's camera rolled the 'live feed' having 'cut in' on a broadcast with this story of heroism.

Within moments it became clear to Leah that the camera was in her face and the lady presenter was suddenly 'firing' questions at her

"What's your name young lady?" and "how do you feel?"

"What was going through your mind?"

"Do you realise, you are a true heroine?"

Leah mumbled her answers "Leah." and "I'm fine." "Nothing, I just saw the lady."

"No not really, I'm not."

As the television lighting man came closer he suddenly shone his bright light towards Leah which made her squint and step back a little, as if curtsying away. The lady presenter put her arm around the young girl, thinking Leah was close to falling exhausted, and offered some comforting words. "There, there." she simpered.

This, though, was all for show, for no sooner had the lady presenter spoken those words than she immediately stood forward and turned her back on Leah and, directly in front of the camera she 'signed off' with a cheery smile.

Leah and Kerri walked away as, did the crowd, when the camera stopped rolling, so did the news team that returned to their truck to pack away.

However, as the ambulance drove off, there was one man, a yachtsman, who approached the girls asking for his blanket back, the one on Leah's shoulders.

"Well that's that then Leah." Kerri couldn't help but giggle a little.

"You have found fame, but you now only have me as an admirer and you didn't even get to keep a wet blanket as a souvenir!"

Leah smiled back at Kerri, reaching out her arms for a hug from her lover. When she responded, it was then that Leah really broke down and cried out loudly, it was only then that the shock of this near-death experience overtook her emotions and Kerri, quietly, held her girlfriend close, leading her away to their beach together.

Later that day the girls returned to where Leah worked and the welcome was amazing. The male manager was his happiest, full of smiles and kisses for both girls, he gave thanks to the day that Leah came to work for him.

"You are on all the television channels," he proclaimed. "And so is the front of the restaurant, thank you so much, thank you, thank you," he chorused.

Kerri was a little perplexed and asked. "All the television channels?"

"Yes, all of them, the television company must have sold out their rights," he chirped. "Click any TV channel when the news is due on and Leah features in the opening story."

It was true, all the news channels headlined the rescue and the girls sat down to a free meal and as much coffee that they could handle. As early evening approached the television 'drive time' programmes also reported the story and so, on what was a 'slow news' Monday, Leah was becoming a nationwide hit!

However, with all that had happened that day, the strength sapping rescue, the publicity and now the endless customers who wanted to shake her hands, Leah just asked Kerri if she minded that they, "go back to their room for some peace and solitude."

The next day was a bit of a blur for both girls, the restaurants along the strip were extremely busy and various news teams went into Leah's restaurant to interview the 'little gutsy girl,' that held the nation's heart.

Every word that Leah spoke was purchased through her scheming manager and, after their twelve-hour shifts, both the girls were glad that they were finished for the day.

As usual Leah would wait for Kerri outside the front door of her restaurant. Kerri would always finish work approximately ten or fifteen minutes later than her and it was while standing outside that Leah was able to relax a little and watch the marina custom slow down for the evening.

There were however a couple of dark shadowy areas that Leah deliberately avoided eye contact with people as she paced the street back and forth in front of her. The memories of Toronto still deeply scarred her mind, but when she saw Kerri skipping along the restaurant pathway towards her she was 'all smiles.'

Within a day or so and just a couple more interviews, life returned to pretty much the same. Leah had heard that the old lady was recovering well in hospital and that her husband was constantly by her side. Leah did however refuse an unscrupulous newspaper's offer that wanted to cover a follow up story and pay for Leah to visit the old lady.

Other than that, Leah noticed that her tip money from customers had substantially increased and Kerri was sketching more and more customers. Yes, life was returning to some normality for the two young girls, both worked hard and played softly, life was bliss!

Chapter 14

It was just over a week to the day from Leah's heroism, Kerri was blissfully unaware of the customer attempting to wave her over to him. Unaware as she was taking order after order from the various tables that surrounded her and he simply wasn't within her work area, that was until he rose from his table, walked over and tapped her lightly on the shoulder.

"Excuse me, is it Kerri?" he asked.

Kerri did not know the man, but answered, "Yes."

"I hear you have a reputation of drawing sketches of customers." The man enquired and Kerri nodded a confirmation.

"I also hear that you're extremely good, have you any work you could show me?" He enquired. "Only I am looking for young artists in the area to promote."

Kerri stood, spellbound, 'wow' she thought.

"Yes, I have some customers who failed to purchase and a couple of my girlfriend, they are out back, in the staff room," she informed him. As Kerri stood there smiling the man asked. "When you have a moment, could you show them to me?"

It was at least half an hour before Kerri had a chance to get to the staff room, but she needn't have worried, the man just sat at his table and smiled every time she glanced over.

Eventually Kerri took her chance between orders and the man now sat there looking at her lines and admiring her work.

"Your sketch detail, capturing the essence of femininity and the masculinity of man, is quite outstanding," he said as he surveyed the various sketches in front of him. Opening his wallet and laying out three twenty dollar bills on the table he asked her to draw him to prove that it was all 'genuinely' her work.

The man was willing to wait, he told her and wanted 'the finest detail' and of course Kerri agreed.

For the next two hours and four coffees later, whenever Kerri managed a spare moment, including a five-minute coffee break, she drew, shaded and fine lined her work until it was eventually finished.

Shown his sketch he was momentarily speechless, but he soon pursed a smile and was clearly impressed when he handed over the sixty dollars.

What was said next, she thought as strange? "Please keep the sketch and add it to your portfolio," he said. "You are extremely talented and I will have no hesitation in supporting your work." He told her.

"What does that mean exactly?" Kerri asked rather warily.

The man stood up and handed her a local gallery business card and explained that he would return with a contract, which, for decent payment, she would provide a number of pictures for him.

"Yes." With no hesitation Kerri shook his hand.

Amazed and excited, that was Kerri for the rest of the day, she couldn't wait to tell Leah this fantastic news. It looked as if it was now Kerri in the limelight and her sketches were going to be shown in an art gallery of all places!

All afternoon and evening Kerri kept looking over towards Leah's restaurant, just to wave to her, just to wave some of her excitement away, but it proved impossible for Kerri to glimpse her lover so the news would have to wait.

The last hour really 'dragged its heels,' but by the end of Kerri's shift every customer she served, the staff, the management and even the owner knew that her talent was being recognised and when she waved goodnight she not only carried, but hugged her portfolio.

Kerri ran along the path to the restaurant squealing with delight and with open arms she jumped and spun a whirling cuddle on her waiting Leah. Leah smiled surprise back at her.

Kerri blurted the news, she really couldn't contain her excitement and it was difficult for Leah to understand between being held tight, the squeals and then the jumping up and down in front of her, but eventually her garbled message was made clear and Leah announced. "This deserves a celebration drink baby doll."

"Let's go to the 'Munster club, just off the Boulevard, it should still be open."

Both girls ran and jogged as quickly as they could and within ten minutes they were closing in on the country and western music that pulsed from the small bar.

There were beads of sweat and giggles from the girls as Leah ordered two extra-large Italian wines and laughed as she told Kerri to pay for them from her new-found fame.

There were only one or two other customers nearby as they sipped wine and smouldered looks into each other's eyes in that stale, smoky atmosphere where coloured lights revolved, they held hands, sipped the wine and, when no one was looking, they kissed.

It wasn't long before Leah had ordered a bottle 'to go' as last orders were being called and twenty minutes later the girls, all smiles and giggles, clung to each other as they happily walked out onto the street in search of the nearest bus stop.

The girls were rich in love and rich in happiness and that was all that mattered as they hung and clung to each other on their walk and neither of the girls noticed the black sedan cruiser parked some 100 yards in front of them, why would they?

There was nothing special about the car as it was just a dark car amongst the many other dark cars that night time brought, nothing special, nothing, until the rounded headlights switched on and its engine fired into life.

Both Leah and Kerri were a little startled by this noise in the silence, but they weren't concerned even though the accelerator was being revved, 'gunned' and the engine shrieked its power. However, as they drew closer their footsteps shortened and their hands held each other just that little bit tighter.

Still they walked towards the twin headlights, towards the bus stop in the distance and Leah asked. "What's going on with that car?"

Time and again the accelerator pedal was being pushed repeatedly and both girls grew silent as they walked ever closer. However, it was with some relief that both girls noticed an occasional light being switched on from the near-by houses that lined the street, so they didn't feel quite so alone, but then it came.

Engine screaming, tyres, their rubber burning, stone chips pitting, and spitting debris behind and around, the dark car sped forward.

Along the yellow street lit road, it bombed towards the girls.

Both girls were scared, both were transfixed as it headed towards them, only Leah could form a small yelp in her voice as everything blackened, bar those twin headlamps.

'Eyeballs of evil,' as it screamed onward and both girls' worst fears were soon realised as the car suddenly veered off the road and onto the sidewalk directly in front of them.

Both girls stood still, 'statuesque bunny rabbits,' the pair of them, they stood in the brilliant glare as this demon on wheels hit a house letterbox sending it flying in shattered pieces.

The pistons screamed its power, the noise muffled their tearful cries and in a matter of yards, if not feet, if not inches, only then did the dark demented car suddenly veer itself back onto the street, brushing passed them, still screaming.

A plume of burnt gasoline now ruptured the air as the girls stood transfixed, but within seconds the car had gone. Disappearing, turning off in the far distance of that long straight road and as the engine noise dimmed to silence it was only then that both girls looked towards each other.

Both were shaken, both held tight to each other and they slowly took their time wiping the fear from each other's eyes and only then did the girls notice that one by one, what house lights that were on, were now being switched off.

Leah was the first to gather herself and she led Kerri along the sidewalk, holding her up in a tight cuddle as Kerri seemed to break down every few yards or so. Leah was questioning. "Why us? What the hell is going on?"

She imagined anyone from college kids, a drink driver or even a thief behind that wheel as they slowly walked onward. Leah could see the bus stop sign in the distance, yet another neon sign in the refuge of her life.

--//--

As they got off the night bus Leah so wanted their motel to be closer as she realised her girlfriend was still shivering, not from cold, but shock. It took an age, each step towards the entrance in the distance and all the time both were listening out for nearby traffic, traffic that never came close, thank God.

Just a few minutes of encouragement, of huddled cuddles and smiles and now Kerri too was finally gathering herself.

Soon they had walked through the motel car park and began to mount the steps to the first floor where their room was situated.

'Oh, how she loved her Leah,' Kerri thought climbing the stairs. Her girlfriend's inner strength was awesome and it was on the top step of the landing where Kerri turned quickly to Leah and kissed her, fully open mouthed. Leah responded with her lover's urgency and it was soon that their hands began to fumble with each other and their clothing as they began to giggle in the darkness.

But then there was light, a bright, bright light that stopped their grasped exploration, and a light that turned their heads away from each other and towards it. As they did so they heard a certain engine roar into life. It was that same car from earlier, but this time it was parked on the street, across from the motel car park entrance. Parked where they had just passed by, parked amongst the others, in the silence of the night.

The two evil eyes were full beamed towards the motel and both girls immediately took a step back as they realised that the car had been waiting for them. The engine roared as Leah pulled Kerri toward their room and, finding the room key from her purse, Leah jiggled the lock as the engine again thundered its cylinders behind them. Both hearts were pounding, racing, thumping beats with every roar, but the key was in, it clicked open and with a fast turn of the handle Leah barged the stiff door. She turned quickly and saw that Kerri was still staring out towards the car, tears were again streaming down her face and her body was shaking, no time to think she grabbed Kerri and pulled her into the room, slamming the door shut behind them.

Leah looked on as she held herself against the closed door, her heels wedged tight against the carpet floor her legs pushing back to add strength to the seal and now she watched as Kerri backed herself into the furthest corner and crouched.

Fear had simply overcome her and Leah listened out above Kerri's sobs until the car that had caught its prey now moved. This time there was no screech of tyres, just the low thud reverberation of a six-cylinder engine block as the vehicle drew alongside and passed by the motel, cruising on its 1st gear 'tick over.' Leah concentrated on listening out until she was truly satisfied that the evil had finally ebbed away and, forcing herself away from the door, she immediately ran over and sat down with Kerri. It was a night of long cuddles, unanswered questions and reassurance until both dared get changed for bed.

Chapter 15

The next morning came with bright sunshine again and again it pierced the room from the gap in the curtains. Neither girl wanted to get up to click quiet the alarm clock that rang its tiny bell on the dressing table, so both nudged and giggled until they rose to greet the new day.

As they showered and dressed for work they discussed going to the police in respect of the danger that they had been in that previous night, but there was nothing to go on, as Kerri explained, the daughter of a policeman, having had past discussions with her daddy.

No, they would just find somewhere else to live and things would go back to normal, or so they assumed and that morning the girls wore courageous smiles as they shut the motel door behind them.

All smiles, that was until Leah noticed a large envelope that had been taped up high onto their room's window.

It was marked 'Leah' so Leah broke the seal and on opening it she reached and pulled out a small square sheet of plastic.

An instamatic colour picture image, a picture of her nakedness lying sprawled out on a bed, where her eyes were partially closed and on her forehead, was the inked mark of ownership that read clearly in focus: 'MINE.'

Leah fell backwards in shock, now she realised that it wasn't some unknown freak or foe that had found them, it was Andy. The man that had stalked her, drugged, raped, buggered and abused her, now he had found her again.

Glimpsing the photograph Kerri saw the anguish and cried with her girlfriend. Leah had told her about the incident when she had fled Toronto, she hadn't hidden her past when they had 'girly' chats, but no way did she believe that it had been that horrendous.

However, now she was beginning to realise, the pain, the fear, all was clearly etched on her face and eyes that couldn't peel away from the photograph. Leah held it in front of her like a magnet to metal, that was until she finally drew breath and whispered quietly. "We are leaving and we're leaving right now."

There was no argument from Kerri, none at all, she packed her suitcase and her portfolio shoulder bag and then her handbag just as quickly as Leah had packed her belongings. Within minutes both girls were leaving the motel and heading to the bus stop.

The girls were never to return to the places of their employment and Leah was never to meet the old lady, who was at that precise time sitting quietly outside the restaurant waiting for it to open, an old lady clutching a purse full of one hundred dollar bills, just a token to thank her for saving her life.

Chapter 16

"We want to head west." Leah told the bus driver and quickly asked for the best route out of Kemah, to venture onward and beyond, as Kerri quickly wrote down the driver's instructions.

As the bus pulled away the girls made their way to the rear seats, as they had always done in the past and in between glimpses at each other, both girls' eyes were clearly focussed on what drove behind. But they could not see the dark car and it was some time before the girls both really settled into their seats and looked forward to elsewhere.

At Houston they had a choice, either route 10, a quicker but a more desolate journey close to the Mexican border, or north, on the 45 to Fort Worth and then west. The girls decided on the safer journey, a busier route with more towns and traffic, so stuffing the various bus tickets they had collected in their purses they purchased and waited.

They found that there was long transfer time and a genuine opportunity for the girls to find a policeman, but Leah just wanted to get going, to get out of there, so they spent their time drinking coffee and staring out of the windows, again looking out for the car, but neither saw it.

The journey to Fort Worth was over seven hours long with the various stops, pickups and drop-offs and it was dark when, with the last of their money, they purchased two tickets for the next coach to Phoenix Arizona and, again finding two seats at the rear of the near empty coach, they headed out on Route 20 towards Abilene and beyond.

For an hour or so the girls spotted several cars with round 'eyeball' lights, but neither girl could differentiate from what was safe and what was not as they looked behind and around.

So, Leah announced. "That's enough, let's stop looking, let's relax, it's going to be a long journey."

These were fateful words indeed, for no sooner had they begun to relax, holding hands and nudging close, then Kerri could hear a car 'gunning' its engine immediately behind.

It was the noise that both girls instantly recognised, a noise that had the girls staring anxiously into each other's face and then back over the seat headrests. To look out onto the highway behind, that dark car with the twin eyes of a demon was now giving chase no less than 50 feet behind. Unfortunately, no sooner had the girls' heads appeared above the headrests, the cars eyes went to full beam, blinding both.

Immediately the girls jumped down and turned their heads towards front where neither acknowledged the other and the beam remained beamed on them for a few more seconds until they switched off.

Still they could hear its engine repeatedly revved, but it became distant as it disappeared into a storm filled, black night.

Both girls were panic-stricken and now instinctively grabbed each other tight. It was Kerri who broke their silence.

"We have to tell the police and we have to do it now." She urged. "We don't have a choice." Leah nodded in fearful agreement.

Kerri stood and walked the aisle, passing an old lady on one side and an old man further up on the other until she finally reached the driver.

"We need to get off," Kerri explained, "but we need to find a town where there is Police or a Sheriff."

The driver, a black man who looked so old that he should have been driving an armchair rather than a big old coach, knew not to ask questions, but simply nodded instead and slowly he began to pull over.

The bus hissed its air brakes to a halt and the driver took out his route roadside map, quickly he studied until he pointed to a small dot and turned to Kerri.

"Ranger, there's a small town of Ranger nearby, I will drop you there, and it's only a short walk from the highway." He said.

The driver didn't know if the town had its own police, but he did know he wanted no trouble on his bus and he knew from past experience that where there were police there was trouble and this girl, although young and pretty, was obviously trouble.

"Twenty minutes and we will be there." He guessed. Kerri smiled her approval. Turning, she walked back down the aisle as the bus pulled away, but her smile soon disappeared as she could see in the far distance behind on that long straight highway, the tiniest pinprick of light.

Kerri didn't tell Leah though, why worry her further? Especially as she still sobbed.

Kerri held her friend close to her, her brave girlfriend who had always been strong was now in tatters and although Kerri tried to reassure in what was a dire situation, she too wept, but these were tears not for herself, but for her lover, for whom it was now all too much to deal with.

It wasn't long before the driver passed a small sign pointing towards Ranger and as he looked to his right he could see a distant light.

He called out. "Ranger, we are outside if you want to get ready miss."

Kerri roused Leah and they collected their belongings from the inner roof racking above their heads.

The bus again hissed to a halt and no sooner had they stepped off the bus, then doors quickly shut and the vehicle sped off in dust dirt, into the darkness.

"Quick, as quick as you can Leah." Young Kerry instructed, picking up a step. "We need to get to that town." And pointed towards the light.

"Yes." Leah replied, as she equalled Kerri's pace.

As the girls crossed the highway Leah became aware that Kerri wasn't looking ahead, but stared out at the road that they had just travelled.

It was then Leah noticed it too, a small distant light weaving the road and she gripped Kerri's hand.

Leah took in her immediate surroundings. "Quick in there." Leah pressed.

"Over there." Leah insisted, as she tugged at Kerri's hand.

Leah had spotted a concrete drainage tunnel just under the rise of the highway's off ramp and to it they ran.

Cowering small balls, they made themselves, as they waited and waited and it wasn't long before they heard that unmistakable engine with twin eyes of hatred speed by, no less than 50 yards from where they had sunk themselves.

"It's not stopping." Leah whispered, as the car continued onward, it wasn't stopping and the girls listened to the engine fall away to silence. It was in that silence that a form of calmness was restored.

The girls waited in that stench and grime for what seemed like an age, neither willing to push onward, neither willing to take the risk, not until there was silence.

It was maybe an hour, until their nerves calmed and it was undisturbed peace till a truck rumbled by and on that rumble the girls gathered themselves.

Quietly standing, the girls waited until that truck became distant to silent when Kerri then whispered. "Let's go."

Slowly they edged their way up through the ramp tunnel toward the other side, once they had emerged from the exit they realised that the sliver of moon that had helped guide them towards the tunnel had now gone. Instead a dark and foreboding cloud covered the sky over them and now they heard another rumble, but this was one of thunder.

As they climbed the bank all they could see was the light of the town, it was there in front of them as was a white plastic road sign claiming 'Truck-stop, food, toilets 1¾ miles.'

Both Leah and Kerri smiled at the first sign of normality, it would be their salvation knowing there would be a phone.

A long walk stretched before them. Both girls were emotionally and physically tired, it was long past midnight and each suitcase was heavy, but they increased their pace when they saw the flickering light of an occasional car or truck heading along the highway, where they had turned off, behind them.

In time, the girls came closer and they could see definition of various vehicles parked adjacent to the road, there was also a large car park that surrounded a white building and, illuminated by a streetlamp, there was another sign that told them they had half a mile to go.

As they crunched the scorched earth beneath their feet Leah agreed that she was going to explain to the Police what had happened to them both.

They explored potential scenarios regarding Police involvement and decided to quickly hide their false identities under a stack of three roadside rocks.

Eventually there was less than two hundred yards to the white building before they passed the first dormant truck out on its own. Suddenly a thunderclap and then another, even louder, and Kerri giggled out of fear.

Both girls looked at each other as they felt the first raindrop and with a bright flash of lightning tearing the clouds, the rain poured. More thunder exploded and neither girl saw the beast in the mask behind them as it wielded a club to their heads.

Chapter 17

Kerri's first recollection of thought was that of pain, a searing heat that burnt from the sun above, the bright fierceness that now flicked her eyes open. She was in immense pain. Pain all around her, but when she tried to cry out in that nerve hit agony her voice was muffled, from whatever sodden cloth filled her mouth. There was something else, another cloth that wrapped tight, gagging her face, tied off in a knot at the nape of her neck.

Kerri's eyes stared widely as she thrust that first scream. She turned her head to the left, right and down, focussing on her nakedness. Her left arm was outstretched beside her and from her bicep down to her wrist heavy gauge, steel barbed wire cut in tightly, piercing the skin, bleeding her flesh at every barb and she muffled more screams, more cries of anguish.

The wire that tore into her was wrapped around and around to the point of her forearm where there was barely any of her arm showing through and at her wrist the wire had been crimped off and crimped to yet another length of barbed wire that stretched out and staked a steel rod, driven deep into the desert mound where she lay.

Kerri tried to pull her arm, but the barbs tore more of her skin and tears soon filled her eyes. Kerri looked immediately across to the pain in her other arm, to the same barbed wire binding, to the same penetrating wire that pierced and perforated and looking beyond she saw yet another steel rod that had been struck into the ground in a similar fashion.

Kerri agonised over the pain to both hips, her hip joints that had been hammered until both had broken free and now fully extended herself open. Splayed out wide and from the top of each knee joint down to her ankles, there was the same sheathe of encased, sun heated barbed wire. A multitude of stabbing needle point pain to each of her limbs, as this thin metal cut through her flesh, deep into muscle, as fresh droplets of her blood joined the dried.

She lay there as still as she could, to avoid the pain increasing.

Oh, how Kerri tried not to move, not to breathe, but with every lungful of air she invited the pain and there, with every shudder of unknown fear, the pain simply intensified.

She tried to cry out for help, but every plea from her voice was suppressed by the oily, cloth muffler and every call for, "Leah," was subdued in that gag as she choked back the tears.

Kerri quietened and her ears turned to the noise above her head and behind her. She pulled her neck back to witness what the shuffling noise was and the chink of metal on metal.

It was then that she saw the beast.

The beast was tall in its dark leather work boots and soiled blue coveralls and the beast, it too had its voice muffled, as it growled from the hessian lace up mask with diamond patchwork eyes and as it stood before her, there was no lesser demon from hell.

This beast threw wood from a yellow, open, flat back truck and wearing its gloves it made a fire near to Kerri's prone body.

Kerri cried out for mercy, but the muffled, incoherent words that were reciprocated back to her were taunting, loud moans.

She trembled in pain and the tears that streamed her cheeks boiled.

"Leah, Leah." She cried to herself.

"Leah, Leah." She cried in her mind, as the kindling took hold and the flames lapped higher with every piece of wood that was added. Then the beast heard her moans and it looked towards Kerri, it too, mockingly, moaned in unison.

Kerri felt the left side of her body burn, her arm, her leg, her torso, each burning hotter than the early sun and still the fire lapped wider and higher.

As more planks of wood were tossed by the beast, Kerri turned her face away, she grimaced as she tried desperately to pull her left arm and leg away from the heat. She screamed as the burning metal barbs bit into her soft skin and she cried, knowing that she was now ripping her own flesh with that wire that shared the suns intensity.

Kerri heard the fire being stoked and looked back to see an iron rod protruding from the flames and as her outer layer of skin began to bubble she screamed her loudest, muffled gag before she fainted.

--//--

It was an hour or two before Kerri roused from her torment, her nostrils were filled with the smell of burnt flesh, her flesh.

Now dehydrated and in immense pain, she didn't feel the heat burning at her body anymore, so, slowly, she again looked left. She stared, tortured by her own darkened bubbled skin, as she focussed on her left arm where the barbed wire had sunk so low that there were only partial glimpses of barb above her flesh. Then she looked back, beyond, upon the black ash ground at the fire that had now been moved further away from her. Then she smelt the burnt hair or what was left of it.

Was it remorse by the beast? Never, remorse would be letting her go. Remorse would be forgiveness. But Kerri watched the beast, standing by yet another fire, drinking from a metal flask and she watched as the water spilled out over the mask.

It just stood there drinking with the fire before it and the steel rod again protruded from within it. The beast, a true vision of evil incarnation, stood just a few yards from Kerri as her eyes dimmed again into unconsciousness.

--//--

Kerri woke in sickened agony, never, never had she felt pain like this before. She looked, as the beast was knelt to the side of her left leg, and she was horrified to see the beast holding a wooden handled saw that was on its third stroke on bone, her bone. The beast grunted.

A skilful surgeon would find little difficulty, by supporting the part held with his other hand, but this was not a skilful surgeon. A skilful surgeon would not yield to find any reasonable opportunity or circumstance not to impede the motion of the instrument, but the beast held and yanked her foot on the ground as it continued with another repetitive stroke.

A proficient surgeon would note the difficulty of removal may depend upon the saw itself, when its blade is not duly stretched, the teeth not well turned alternately to the right and left, or that their points were not in good order, but this was a rusted wood saw. Its edges not sharp enough so the bone-dust may be readily thrown off to each side, but the beast's saw was old and partially blunt as it tore another stroke, as it exhaled another grunt.

Kerri screamed, pleaded. "No more!" But the beast was deaf to her screams.

A well-versed surgeon would use a saw that had teeth wider than the blade to prevent the saw being held into bone, but this one the beast used, constantly wedged and stuck fast.

Unconcerned it simply looked towards Kerri as it pulled her foot out to widen the gap and once more the young girl welcomed the darkness of her subconscious.

--//--

Kerri woke, though the excruciating pain of searing heat from what she thought was her left foot, bulged her eyes from their sockets as she looked to the heavens for salvation, as she screamed for her God's mercy.

Immediately she looked down to where her left foot once was, but instead the beast was using the glowing red iron rod on her blooded flesh and, sniggering, the beast seared the blood loss, heat sealing her ankle and Kerri screamed and screamed.

More screams, as her throat tightened, her mind was exploding in agony as the beast stood above her and grunted. She screamed again and the beast just grunted until Kerri's throat swelled in such pain that she just gargled and that was when the beast turned to the fire and stoked the iron rod.

Kerri stared at the beast as it shuffled and circled the fire and her soul simply pleaded. "Please Andy, no more." But it wasn't long before the beast returned to her, holding the saw that now also had a glow of heat red.

A surgeon would see to it that the edge of the saw should be able to cut with both edges, when the surgical saw is moved backwards or forwards, the operation would soon be expedited. The beast knew none of this, but went to work on Kerri's right foot all the same, the beast didn't know, nor did it care, when splintering her bone.

The saw, which should cut in both directions with a backward sweep of the instrument, should be regular and smooth. Kerri's body shook violently with each vigorous hacking at her bone, sinew and vein. But after an age it was done and the last had been sliced, hacked and wrenched at, until the beast finally walked back to the fire with her foot and placed her loss in a cloth sack bag.

Quickly returning it held the iron rod in its gloved hands and the beast again pushed the glowing metal repeatedly at various angles into her ankle joint. Kerri somehow found voice as her screams were only overwhelmed by the stench of burnt flesh that again filled her nostrils.

The learned surgeon should note that the movements of the saw should never be short or rapid, but every stroke of the instrument should be long, bold, and regular and without too much pressure so as to avoid the risk of an extensive splintering.

However, the beast was crudely relentless and within half an hour, a time melted within this young girl's howls, both Kerri's hands and wrists had been sawn, twisted and taken and where the removal left gaping, these wounds were again sealed with the heat fired iron.

'Why wasn't she dead?' she questioned her mystified mind, but the pain was too much for an answer.

All of those prayers to her God hadn't saved Kerri from the beast, all of her muffled pleas for mercy had been ignored and now, as she lay naked, with wracked pain all over, she was alive, but near finish. Splayed out, ripped and burnt half alive she also tormented. "Where was Leah?"

Where was her girlfriend, her saviour from this pain? As she lay there with what was left of her burnt body, in salt crusted tears, she wept.

--//--

Kerri's spirit was now totally ruptured, just as the beast had intended, and having 'brought her to heel' the beast now stood there, between Kerri and the fire and it raised itself tall with its arms outstretched in righteous glory.

Yes, oh yes! How the beast had attacked her weakness as it now took its time stroking, nuzzling each prized possession to its mouthpiece, a crudely cut hole where it suckled and sucked at fingers and toes.

A glory to the beholden, the beast had been cleansed, purified and now, a God in itself, it breathed the dry desert air and with vacant eyes from within, fixated itself on the sun's glare. A beauty only matched by its own magnificence, it knew only other gods could ever defeat it.

The beast slowly began marking letters on the ground with its boots, the beast was sated, elated on its very own transformation and now this God, just a little annoyed that it had only been witnessed by one unfortunate, however, it was still a witness even though she had yet again slipped into unconsciousness.

This God! This true God had pleasured this blessed event and now its thoughts turned to preservation. Quickly it walked to the flatbed truck where it placed the glowing rod and cloth bag of hands and feet next to the large reel drum that held what was left of the unused barbed wire. The barbed wire reel that was set against the cabin of the truck lay just opposite a rather large sack bag, a reused sack bag. Once used to feed livestock, a sack tied so tight to one end and a sack that slowly shifted and murmured.

This God returned to the fire and began to kick at the outer pieces displacing them in all directions of the desert mound around its feet. The God relentlessly kicked at the planks of wood, lessening the flame and lessening its girth and the God continued to kick and kick until all that remained was the base of red embers. It stood for a while as it smiled at the glow. The God was hypnotised until the glow dimmed, until its attention was drawn to the young girls moans and so it walked back to the girl on the ground.

It stood over her as she was trying to speak so it lent down and pulled down her gag and removed the cloth ball that was within her mouth and she whispered, "Andy, please, water."

The God stood up and reached into its pocket, pulling out and opening what was a small white piece of paper. The God showed her, her own bus ticket to Phoenix.

Then with its gloved hand its fore-finger pointed to the word Phoenix and then thumbed towards itself as if establishing its own identity. Kerri could not understand why the God gave her its name but the beast again pointed on the ticket to the word Phoenix.

Kerri nodded in confusion, she didn't realise that it was declaring that just like the Phoenix of Greek mythology it had been reborn from the ashes of flame and again Kerri whispered the word, "water."

The God did no more than take the ticket and fold it over and over again with each corner folded in on itself, it folded until it could be folded no more and no larger in size than a small calibre bullet.

The God then walked around to where Kerri's nakedness lay open and with two gloved fingers he thrust the folded ticket forward into her father's want, her lovers desire and now this God's post box.

Sending the note on its own journey, the God thought and then just in arm's reach it grabbed a slivered slice of wood ember and forcefully thrust it up further whilst Kerri pleaded undecipherable cries.

This would be the last time Kerri would look upon the once beast, the God, the mask, coveralls, boots and gloves and as she slowly closed her eyes against the pain, she thought of no one but her girlfriend as her mind hit unconsciousness again.

Kerri never saw the flat-bed truck slowly pull away, or the God remove its mask and smile broadly in the truck's mirror and she never heard it laugh as it noticed the first large black bird that had begun to slowly circle over the desert mound.

Chapter 18

It was past dusk when Kerri stirred for the last time, she woke to a tapping on her torso, a repeated tapping, a tapping that opened her eyes. She looked to her left breast to witness a flurry of dark winged feathers where the foul stench of burnt skin rose to her senses and again she felt a tapping to her burnt flesh.

Then just as suddenly, amongst the vibration, she felt a sharp nip to her tummy, a tummy that Leah would so normally kiss, but this wasn't lips of passion, this was intrusion. This was the purest of pain as the vulture dug forward and down, ripping through the crust of her charred flesh as it began devouring its meal, the meat and muscle of her threadbare life.

Chapter 19

The desert land around Fort Worth is rich in the history surrounding the old West and is best known for its truth and fabled history, involving the most feared foe of civilian settlers and US cavalryman, the native Comanche.

Known as the "Lords of the Plains," this tribe was regarded as perhaps the most dangerous of all the Indian tribes; with traditional beliefs in their creator deity, revered as the "Big Father" who was generally worshipped as the sun in the sky.

Their religion was disinterested in any political or human affairs and would entrust their destiny in supernatural visions where spirits would manifest themselves into humans, miniature people, animals or ghosts. Those gifted, who would receive these visions, were known as shamans, revered as, "power possessors" and generally known as, "medicine men or women."

These Shamans have always been held in high regard and it was that evening whilst he slept, that Joe, a direct descendant of many Comanche shamans, visualised an evil that had risen with the sun.

It was a beast, both human and animal that burned clean in flame, transforming itself into a golden bird. A bird whose screams and encircling wingspan shadowed, darkened and devoured the local, sacred land.

Conflicted, worried, too frightened to continue the vision Joe woke and, that very morning, he set off to investigate.

What Joe saw chilled him to the bone, collapsed him to his knees and would stay with him for the rest of his life. He took off his fur lined jean jacket and removed his bedroll from his pony's saddle, he covered what remained of that burnt crisp body. Only once did he note that the hands, feet and the eyes were missing, only once did he look at the corpse.

--//--

As soon as Joe had raised the alarm with the local sheriff's office and returned with him to the scene, they immediately knew that this was beyond their limited resources and called for the FBI to investigate.

By the end of the day, amidst coffee and 'smokes,' what remained of the girl had been photographed and carefully removed for post-mortem. The autopsy concluded her death was a result of exsanguination through obvious signs of trauma and the only sexual interference was that of a fluid sodden bus ticket found from a tweezer insertion into the high vagina area. That and a pendant from what remained of her neck, were her only possessions.

Subsequent investigations revealed that there were no dental records for this victim so an artist's impression from what remained were drawn and circulated within Texas. But, no matter how hard they worked the local area, no matter the amount of homes and premises they visited, the investigation petered to almost indifference when all the local girls had thankfully been accounted for.

Joe was the hardest to eliminate from the investigation and from the beginning the FBI were sceptical to believe he had simply been, 'called,' to the murder by a manifestation. So, his life was turned upside down. Questioned and questioned, four days in a cell, until his whereabouts for that previous week had been verified, confirmed and rechecked thrice over.

Then, when the next body was discovered, just four weeks later and on a dirt road, less than five miles from where Kerri had been discovered, Joe was dawn raided, arrested and again questioned until alibied. For two days he was disbelieved, threatened and ridiculed for his lack of vision into this young death.

It was another girl, just a little older, but around the same age, found naked and dumped, her hands tied together with old rope and where her mouth had been gagged, it was filled with a ball of cloth, the same cloth material that had been found near Kerri's dead body.

It was Leah and she still wore the same identical cheap chain and pendant around her neck that the girls had bought each other as gifts. This time the hands and feet weren't missing, no, there were needle marks between where her toes had formed, however these were missing along with her fingers.

Each had been pulled, ripped or cut from the stumps, where the flesh had been similarly burnt to cauterize the wounds.

As for time of death, the pathologist suggested, less than a day from when the body was found and as for the cause of death, dehydration involving kidney failure, perhaps two weeks without water, toxicology would eventually confirm this.

The excrement marks on her inner thighs suggested that she had stood whilst defecating and the loop in the rope that tied her wrists along with their deep rope burns suggested that she had been 'hooked' and held upright. It wasn't until the pathologist examined for sexual interference did they discover the same bus ticket to Phoenix, Arizona, neatly folded in on each corner and folded again until it could be folded no more.

This time in Texas the investigation had a face that could be recognised and from her previous heroics, her face was identified and from this discovery Kerri was known as her friend, but with the various false identities that the girls had shown to gain employment at different venues, it led the FBI investigation 'a merry dance,' always in circles and still no closer to their assailant.

There were other leads too, for as soon as the bus driver had been tracked down from the ticket receipts, he identified a portfolio bag of pictures that had that night been left on his bus and inside were various portraits and sketches.

It was not until three months later that Leah was truly identified, the FBI, having sent appeal posters and dental x-rays to Canada, was there confirmation from a drunk, distraught mother, who was then assisted in repatriating her daughter to a local graveyard.

Chapter 20

March 1982 Scotland

Nineteen-year-old Claire Killarney stood by the bar at the Poets Inn, just off Market Street, Aberdeen and, unsteady on her feet, she swayed just a little too much in her cream tight blouse and matching ruffed skirt.

She was cupping a hand to her ear, trying to listen to the ballad. "Have you ever been in love?" Above the loud shouts of local football supporters gearing their voices in preparation of the next day's home match against St. Mirren. Her blonde, lacquered hair was quite stiff, just like her drink and she was trying her best to hide the fact, that she was quietly drunk.

Claire was in her usual Friday night 'spot,' a position at the bar where she would normally stand with her boyfriend, Jimmy 'the squid,' so-called for his wandering 'tentacle' fingers and his family being in the merchant fisherman business.

However, as he had told his friends, Claire had been cast off, swept aside, thrown overboard, simply because his mere fumbling's were not enough for Jimmy. He wanted to 'fillet' and 'gut her' as he put it, but she had other ideas and constantly refused him her virtue.

For Claire was a true romantic, brought up on childhood books of fairy tale princes and princesses; she was looking for her knight to sweep her away to a golden castle of hushed melodies. Where, after marriage, she would lose herself in a young man's arms and lovingly embrace her new future.

She was a good Catholic girl who had watched her parents work hard for what little they owned and turning sixteen she had left her family in the nearby village of Kingswells and had come to the big city to find her destiny.

Following the discovery of North Sea oil some ten years earlier, finding work in nearby Aberdeen was easy with her typing skills and she enjoyed secretarial employment at one of the many large oil companies that was now based there.

Aberdeen was awash with oil money and where there was once a local and distinctive Lowland Scots dialect, known as Doric, now there were Norwegian, Asian and American accents, each serving the energy sector.

For the past two years Claire had commuted from home, but advancing from secretary to personal assistant she had now saved enough from her well-paid post to afford a mortgage on a small flat overlooking the coastal Esplanade, close to where she now held herself at the bar.

As Claire ordered her next drink she could smell the fish and the dirt, but it wasn't Jimmy; that reminder was bad enough, no amount of scrubbing ever made him devoid of that odour. No, in this instance it was the workmen around her, brushing up beside her, drinking and singing with the faint stench of fish guts, rubbed and bonded with the likes of 'Pagan Man' aftershave that soured their skin.

It wasn't pleasant, but Claire had no option if she wanted another drink at the tightly packed bar, so having again glanced the plastic sheet drinks menu, she chose another of the only six cocktails that the inn made badly.

"A margarita please," she shouted above the noise. She needed a tequila moment to wipe Jimmy from her mind.

"Make that two and I will pay." A distinctive voice yelled out beside her.

Claire turned to her left and focussed, with a huge smile, as she saw him for the first time, the man who had quietly without fuss, squeezed himself to the bar next to her.

He was gorgeous, handsome, even quite pretty, tall, fit and tanned and he held her gaze as she stared upward into those darkest of eyes.

"Are you okay?" He asked and Claire reddened having realised that she hadn't yet spoken, not even in thanks and she flustered words. "Yes, sorry."

His teeth were a pure gleam of whiteness and close to his chest she could smell an aromatic waft of foreign fragrance, crisp yet warming, heady and refreshing, smoked wood, but sensual, as Claire imagined strolling through the spice markets and forest floors of this world.

She was in its clasp as it was a far cry from Scotland's usual potent potions and she smiled up beyond those broad shoulders again. This man, no more than one or two years her senior, had the cutest smile and Claire was only too pleased to be held by the hand as he ushered Claire towards a now vacant space at the corner of the bar.

Swept into the corner, with her back to wall, this shining knight that stood before her filled her thoughts and focus.

Blue Levi jeans, taut around his thighs, a white Fred Perry polo shirt that defined the armour plating muscles and then those black shoes that shone like mirrors, Claire felt herself melt.

Claire supped margarita after margarita and all the time he held her hand, gently stroking his thumb across the back of her hand. Not once should she pay, this young man to her, this most handsome of men, would insist.

Claire heard words such as "oil" and "industry," but almost every sentence was lost to her as she gazed, mesmerised by his accent, smile and his eyes, where the hours melted away in the inn beyond her care.

He drew himself close to her, just as Claire had hoped, as the "last orders" bell was rung. Now there was only a hair's breadth space between them and she could feel the safety of his strength as he placed his grip on her waist and never did she realise that he hadn't edged towards her, but, it was her to him.

Claire so wanted this moment to last and when Aberdeen's Beach ballroom, still open, was mentioned she readily agreed.

Chapter 21

Friday 2 April 1982

That was the day Argentina invaded the Falklands Islands, a British territory since 1841; that was the day soldier Private Anthony Flare was arrested whilst home on leave from Cyprus.

On 14 June 1982 Argentina surrendered in a conflict that lasted 74 days, that was the same day Anthony Flare was informed that the allegations of child molestation against him had not been substantiated.

Nineteen-year-old Private Flare would not receive the South Atlantic medal awarded to those that served during that conflict, in fact on that afternoon in Colchester Military barracks, whilst he waited for transportation back to his unit, "Tony" to his friends, was about to find that his 'fumbling' with his neighbour's ten-year-old daughter would ensure he was never to receive any type of medal again.

Sat across the table from him in the secure waiting room, a room no different from the remand cell he'd spent the last few weeks in, were two men, both in pinstripe suits, one black one blue, neither gave their name to him and neither gave him a smile or greeting, the only thing that was recognisable to Tony was the waft of stale vomit and whiskey.

Already unnerved by the screams and shouts of prisoner restraint in a corridor nearby Tony sat anxiously.

"You think it's all over 'Sonny'?" 'Mr 'Black' strained his voice in a menacing, deep, Scottish accent.

This man was no older than Private Flare himself, but Mr Black's hands and face were evidently battle scarred and Tony sat there silent as he thought of more injuries under the Scotsman's Savile Row cloth.

"You think you got away with it, do you?" Mr 'Blue' joined the accusation in a well-educated voice, a voice Tony assumed more attune to public school speaking than to soldiering.

"Well you haven't, you perverted little fuck face," Mr Black gave Tony the answer and Tony remained sheepish and silent.

Mr Black opened the briefcase in front of him and read from a piece of paper that he now held high so that Private Flare would see the official notification. "You are to be sent to Northern Ireland, you are to be transferred to whatever unit is suffering the most casualties and your commanding officer will be directed to put you on point duty on every available patrol in the worst conflict areas," and with a "ha," he laughed as the private began to quiver.

"That's option one." Mr Black concluded.

"Option two," it was 'Mr Blue's' turn.

"A signed confession so that the sick bastard that you are spends the next ten years having the proverbial shite kicked out of you in here." He continued and Tony could now be seen to visibly tremble across from the two men, as silence now filled the room.

Tony looked to the floor, Tony looked to his future, both were hard, grey and bleak and after that moment's silence an answer was needed.

"Well!" Mr Black shouted thumping his fist onto the table in front of him.

"Your choice 'Sonny Jim' you fucking piece of shit, what will it be?" the Scotsman demanded.

Tony said nothing but began to hand rub tears of remorse from his welling eyes.

"I hope those Irish bastards kill you slowly and feed you your balls you evil little cunt." The Scotsman continued and Tony began to sob.

Mr Blue turned to Mr Black and ushering a well-rehearsed hand out to seize the moment he asked. "May I speak to Private Flare alone for a moment?"

Mr Black sat back in his chair and growled. "Do what you want with this sick bastard, but heed this." He turned to Tony. "I'd fucking burn you in petrol," and on that closing comment the highlander rose from his chair, tugging his buttoned jacket back into smartness, he marched quickly from the room hiding his wry smile from the pervert.

Mr Blue calculated his silence, watching Private Flare continue to hand wipe the odd tear from his face as this young soldier tried to regain his composure and when Mr Blue thought the time was right he spoke softly. "You love your country don't you Anthony?"

Tony looked up from the floor and nodded his response, then offering out a cigarette to Private Flare, Mr Blue lent forward across the table and, lighting the pale yellow 'St Moritz' gold filtered cigarette, Mr Blue whispered. "There is a third option."

Chapter 22

December 1982 London

It was past ten at night as the car horn sounded, 'beep, beep, beep,' was heard in quick succession from the mud brown coloured, Vauxhall Cavalier 2.0 L saloon that idled and purred, but the driver did not.

The heat from the car's air vents were little compensation as it struggled in the cold Christmas frost that clung to the air outside. Cooper found himself rubbing his hands vigorously together again.

"For fuck's sake." He sat there shivering and talking to himself. "I'm fucking freezing I am," and he pulled up the collar to his leather jacket, as the car radio crackled the end of yet more miserable news.

Two more minutes slowly passed by as he found himself stamping his feet on the carpeted metal floor pan beneath his seat. 'Beep, beep, beeeeeeeeeep,' Cooper hit the car horn again in that filth strewn car park in East London.

Subtlety had been overtaken by a timeframe not going to plan and Cooper was far from amused having been there, waiting. Cooper pressed down on the car's accelerator and it revved loudly as he hit the car horn once again and then finally, finally, from the flat that was nearest his car, there was a light in the hallway, a flicker on, off, on and off once more, the signal, that finally made Cooper sigh with relief.

Yet another minute passed before the door to this council maisonette opened and out stepped the young girl. So inappropriately dressed for the freezing temperatures outside, she clasped her arms tight around her white school blouse as she quickly ran in that ridiculously short black skirt towards Cooper's car and he pushed the passenger door to swing open.

"God its cold!" The young girl exclaimed as she jumped in with a vapour of cheap perfume. The girl quickly closed the door, but Cooper said nothing as he accelerated the Vauxhall quickly away, only turning the car's lights on as it left the car park.

"Have you got something for me?" the girl asked coyly and Cooper pointed down with his left hand and spoke. "Ashtray."

The girl, Maddie, lent down and opened the ashtray and taking two pink pills and a small square of blue paper from the metal container she popped them all in her mouth and swallowed.

"Maddie don't be late again for fuck sake or I will beat you, I hate being late and you're causing me no end of aggro." Cooper told her.

"Yeah, whatever." Came the curt reply.

Cooper slammed the cars brakes and once it screeched to a halt in that quiet side street, his left hand grabbed the girl by her neck and slammed her head hard into the closed passenger window.

Maddie yelped out in pain.

"I fucking mean it bitch, do you understand me?" He said and Maddie soon nodded her head quickly and cried. Cooper drove on.

Cooper's next 'port of call' was the Karan's café and kebab on Upton Park's Queens Road, just north of where West Ham Football club had regularly flirted with relegation.

It was still open. To the locals it seemed to be always open. In fact, it only closed for business once in the last two years for an employee's funeral. Inside this eatery sat another two young girls, sipping coffee, Debbie and her new friend.

Cooper had locked the car and left Maddie giggling to herself in her seat as the pills and paper acid were taking their hold and as Cooper entered Karan's café Debbie sat bolt upright and whispered, "he's here, be nice, smile sweetly, don't upset him." She said.

"Who's this?" Cooper asked abruptly as he stared down at the booth towards the new girl in her opened school shirt showing cleavage. Both these girls, like Maddie, were all dressed the same.

"This is my friend…" Debbie tried to explain.

"I am not asking you, bitch, I'm asking your mate." Cooper lent over the table and stared not a foot away from the new girl's face.

The girl gulped and, swallowing her nerves, she replied. "I'm Nikki and Debbie told me I could earn money with you."

"How old are you?" Cooper asked.

"Sixteen." Nikki lied, as Debbie glared across the table at her, kicking her new friend in the shin.

"You're too old then, I don't want you, come on Debbie we need to go." Cooper announced grabbing the girl he needed by her arm.

"No, I am fourteen, well nearly fourteen, I just said sixteen to impress you." Nikki said as Cooper pulled Debbie from her chair.

Releasing his grip, Debbie sat back in the chair as Cooper asked, "full name, date of birth and where do you live?" Nikki found herself giving her details to the man who now wrote down every detail in his large, black notebook.

"Right wait there," he said and, walking over to the shift manager, he handed over a green £1 note, receiving a telephone in exchange.

There were two short whispered conversations before the phone was returned to the manager and Cooper returned smiling. "Yes Nikki, you can come too, but let's get going, we are running late."

Cooper had two more stops to make, one was at a bus stop where another girl, Rachel, almost twelve, waited and then the last pickup outside a children's care home, where a staff member, in a flurry of cash, ushered a tired and tearful young boy in a white shirt and grey shorts into the back of the car, where he soon slumped on Debbie's lap.

Cooper made sure each had taken at least one pink tablet and a small square of blue paper before he continued his journey and, within an hour of driving, he had these quietened children who, other than school uniforms, just wore sadness.

Cooper just saw them as simple dulled faces that had no future as he held deliberately within the speed limit and journeyed on the inside lane of the A13. He knew he was running a little late, but there was no way he wanted to attract the attention of the police that regularly patrolled this busy road, but, once he turned off onto the A1012, a subsidiary road, his right foot hit the accelerator towards the small village of Chafford Hundred, Essex.

A left and two right turns later Cooper passed numerous signs stating that the surrounding land had been proposed for redevelopment, but again what did he care. Getting the children to their destination on time was the sole purpose that drove him as he sped past what few old established houses there were on the road.

'The next turning off on the left,' Cooper's mind spoke to him.

Eager and angry, 'indicate, indicate,' his mind flashed turns as Cooper took glances at his watch.

'And relax mate, you made it!' Cooper let out a deep sigh slowing his car as it passed the odd couple of houses on each side.

It was a road that ended with a long-paved drive adjacent to an old farmhouse that was signposted 'Private' and 'No Trespassers.' Cooper turned the car's lights off, slowing his car to a crawl.

Cooper's car progressed on its 'tick over' speed as he followed the drive and at the very end of this he saw the large metal gate being opened for him by shadowy figures waiting for him there. He had finally arrived with his cargo, all safe and secure.

Once past the gate, which closed behind him, Cooper knew the terrain of the slope downward, he knew to stay left at one point of a rise and veer to the right as the slope steepened beneath him. He would zigzag left, then right and finally bump over the disused quarry railway line where he looked for a space amongst the other cars to park.

Cooper applied the handbrake and turned off the engine. Then, as would always happen, the doors to his car opened and the children were pulled from the car by numerous men with large grasping hands.

Men who then helped the children walk towards the huge chalk quarry wall that stood some yards beyond the high valued cars and social care buses.

Cooper watched as each child was numbered on their right forearm with a permanent black ink pen, these children were numbered N47 and another of the men wrote the same identification N47 on a piece of A4 paper and ticketed it on the windscreen of his Cavalier. Next Cooper was handed a smaller ticket with the same number on it and was asked, "Do you know where to go?"

Cooper nodded, as he watched the children being led away, one of them was held up on either side by burly strong men in black suits where they walked towards the flickering flamed torches that were riveted against the chalk faced cliff.

Cooper could faintly hear a classical tune echoing from beyond those flames, beyond his view of the children as they turned a corner behind bracken and were out of sight. With that Cooper also turned away and walked back up the slope, stealing himself away from his thoughts of what lay ahead for those kids.

It was a few minutes later when Cooper found himself knocking on the front door of the farmhouse by the driveway. It was answered immediately by a familiar face that he recognised. It was the same man that had answered the door to him on previous occasions when attending this venue.

"How many girls, how many boys and of those how many are virgins?" Cooper was asked as he entered the hallway.

His answer was simple, "four girls, one boy and none of them are."

The man, as usual, wasn't dressed as a farmer, simply because he wasn't.

He wore a dark black suit, black tie, white shirt and he wore a signet ring, plain gold with a small red stone, a stone that perforated a three-letter inscription. The same ring that Cooper had seen on many of the men that worked these shifts, even Cooper wore one on his right hand.

He led Cooper into the kitchen and there, on the white plastic work surface, he counted out £300 for the girls at £75 each and £100 for the boy. Cooper calculated his profit at £50 per girl, £25 he would have to give to each girl and only £50 for the boy as the other half would have to be shared with the boy's care worker.

'It was good pay and not bad for someone else to have a sleepless night,' Cooper thought as he walked into the living room, where he tried to find his own personal space amongst the crush of other waiting drivers, each of whom, like him, would clock watch waiting for 3 a.m.

$$--//--$$

It was still dark when the throng of drivers left the various rooms of the farmhouse, each making their way as quietly as they could, down the long driveway and beyond the gate.

No one spoke to each other, just as no one had spoken in the house. Why would they? Each room had a television set and VHS video recorder where they watched films, to occupy their minds.

In any case, no one wanted to know each other or what each other did for a living. However, Cooper guessed, quite rightly, when he observed the gleaming shine on some of the shoes, quite a few had military backgrounds. These were the same men who would usually congregate together at these gatherings to watch recordings of old war films.

Cooper continued his walk on the downward slope and once out of any potential view from the driveway and beyond, did a couple of men, including Cooper, produce pocket torches to shine the way.

On reaching the base of the slope Cooper saw the gathering of children. Standing, crouching, sitting or lying down as they waited on that frost laden ground.

These kids were either on their own, in pairs, or in groups of three or more and Cooper counted at least five groups of eight or more children which he thought accounted for the care home and Immigration Service minibuses that were parked nearby.

"Nautical 23, N23," was called first, this wasn't the regular pattern, but Cooper had seen this happen before, the driver stepped forward and during a hushed conversation Cooper overheard that one of children of the drivers group was to remain with a client as, 'he hadn't finished with her.'

The driver then received a thick envelope that he opened and looking at the content he nodded his head. Cooper could see it was wedged full of Bank of England £20 notes and the man pulled them from the envelope and buried them in his jacket pocket where upon he returned to the group of drivers where Cooper stood.

"Nautical 1, N1," was called out and a driver walked forward to collect his goods, structure had returned. "Nautical 2, N2," was the next dispatch and so it went on, the calls and collections continued. Cooper saw that there were children of all ages and all ethnicities, some of whom, Cooper would note, spoke barely any, or no English.

Ten minutes later it was Cooper's turn to stir from the now small group of drivers that were left.

He was just one of four drivers left standing in the cold whilst others now sat waiting in their vehicles with their 'goods' and Cooper responded to his call "Nautical 47, N47."

He collected his four girls and one young boy, each one of the girls were dishevelled, shirts open and undone, their bras and knickers simply tucked into their skirts.

Both Maddie's and Nikki's mascara had run and both choked on sore throats, 'bus stop girl,' had scratches to her face and neck and Debbie was still delirious from whatever other drugs she'd been given or forced to take. The boy, however, had been dressed correctly, only his shoes were on the wrong feet.

The little lad said nothing, not even a whisper as his head hung, sunk to his chest. As Cooper raised the boy's chin still the child's eyes fixated on the ground below.

Cooper quickly ushered his group, managing to squeeze all four girls and the boy on the back seat and, ensuring the child locks were in place, he locked 'his' kids in.

Cooper knew he too then had to wait, but he stood there out in the cold. He had to wait until the various cars from Rolls Royce saloons, Daimlers and other high-value executive transport slowly made their way up the unlit dirt track slope.

These occupants had paid handsomely for their three hours of enjoyment and they rightly deserved to leave first, "a procession of opulent extravagance." Cooper said, speaking to no one but himself, as he shivered in the cold, looking at all until the last of those cars drove by.

He had focussed his mind on each car as it had passed him, each with either one or two occupants and Cooper again recognised just a few. There were a couple of known politicians, each from differing political views. In a baseball cap drove an ageing pop singer, a man whom he had heard a couple of the drivers previously nickname as "Lion," due to the amount of frenzied claw marks he would inflict on the vulnerable. Then there was an influential media mogul who had brought along two friends and there was a professional football manager with his lady, presumably his wife. Cooper didn't recognise the other one or two ladies that he saw driving off in their cars and he certainly didn't know anyone driving or being driven in those dark reflective windowed diplomatic cars that showed the licensed registration, letter D in the middle of the plate. However, such was his ability, Cooper mentally noted as many registrations and faces as he could, that was until he saw the only other person he recognised, one of the last to leave and that was usual of course, his boss.

It was a man he often called, "Sir," and a man who encouraged this work. He was alone in his car that drove slowly away. A brilliant white Jaguar saloon that glittered its chrome from the streaks of moonlight between the clouds. Neither man made eye contact as it passed.

A minute or so later, when the last of the 'rich' vehicles left the chalk quarry, Cooper got in his Vauxhall and slowly followed the convoy of minibuses and cheap cars back up the gloom of the slope. Passing the farmhouse, it took a further five minutes of slow procession before each car turned onto the T-junction and turning either left or right they disappeared into what was left of the night.

As usual Cooper was one of the last to leave so he pulled over and stopped. He turned to the back seat to check on the children. Cooper immediately told the other two girls to rouse Debbie and each girl on either side shook vigorously, asking in turn, "Are you okay, are you alright?"

Finally; finally, in whispered breath she whimpered a response, followed by a louder curt, "yes!" As the shaking continued.

Cooper relaxed and sat back in his seat, he was relieved that Debbie was now coming to her senses; he had precautions for these situations, the glove box held a pouch containing a needled syringe and a small bottle of adrenaline, but he hated giving those injections, he had only done this twice and having never been medically trained, that was two times too many.

Cooper pulled away and began the short journey back into London's East End, in the knowledge that he wouldn't be back to that farmhouse for another six months. The quarry was just one of six venues used twice each year, along with the farmhouse, that was now being bleach cleaned throughout, emptied and washed down thoroughly.

So were the once excavated and now torch lit chalk caverns that branched from the mineshaft entrance.

Caverns that had now quietened from the muffled cries of children, each were now being emptied of bedlinen from various sized mattresses and all the floors were now being swept of condoms, wine bottles, pill bottles, plastic beakers and cigar and cigarette butts.

Wherever there were flicks or droplets of blood on the floors or on walls that held wrist clasps, each were scrubbed clean using buckets and mops of bleached soap, all of this performed by the many men in black.

As for the young girl of thirteen that lay still and lifeless in one corner of a cavern whose purple tongue now flopped from the side of her open mouth, her mouth that had drawn its last breath; unable to win her battle for life from the dog choke chain necklace that had dug into her throat and all because of a drunk and somewhat overzealous participant. Her body was the last to be tidied up.

Finally, at long last, when the men were ready to leave the caverns she was without sermon simply lifted and carried away.

One man had her arms and the other her legs as they walked quietly from the entrance towards the quarry undergrowth nearby. One of the men stumbled as he crossed the disused railway track that had long ago served this quarry well, however, eventually, the two men reached a group of tree stumps that edged a sea of tall beech, oak and sycamore trees that littered this disused pit.

There a hole had already been dug and prepared, she was lowered the three feet or so until finally let go, where her body now landed with a thud.

Shovelled earth soon covered her nakedness as she lay below the natural wood markers. These moss and ivy-covered stumps of felled trees now held its secret grasp on her, just as others before her.

Soon enough there would be a small fire by the mine entrance, a wood fire littered with the debris from that evening's debauchery and as the flames burnt and melted the vile, the steel doors closed on the mine entrance, creaking once more, triple padlocked and sealing those past echoes; that vault of fear.

Chapter 23

From the T-junction, it was a repetition between focusing on the road ahead and glancing, every so often, in his rear-view mirror to check on his children splayed out on the back seat.

However, Cooper suddenly noticed that the young grey faces behind him had become tinged by faint blue and, just as suddenly, he noticed that the blue had now started to 'flash' its brilliance in the surrounding hedgerows. Cooper drove transfixed as these blue rays glowed, Hogg Lane in the eastern county of Essex, was now in a swirl of blue that beamed brighter and brighter as the light drew closer and closer to Cooper's Cavalier.

With a quick blast of a siren and bell Cooper began to apply the cars brakes, it was the police behind and he was being 'pulled over,' for inspection.

Cooper knew he had to pre-empt any possible problem, so as soon as his car halted he applied the handbrake and jumped out the car walking as fast as he possibly could towards the police car stopping behind.

"Good evening officer." Cooper called out politely and loudly as he approached the young policeman, who had only just managed to get out his patrol car himself.

"Can I help you at all, was I speeding?" Cooper asked abruptly as he came face-to-face with the young man, only a couple of years younger than himself.

"No just a routine check sir, a Christmas clampdown on drink drivers." The policeman explained.

"Well happy hunting." Cooper said as he forced out a deep breath from his lungs and blew it into the officer's face.

The policeman smelt bad garlic breath and stale coffee, but no alcohol and so leaning back avoiding any further foul breath he asked. "Have you identification sir?"

"Yes." Cooper replied and reaching behind into his back pocket of his tweed cloth trousers he produced a small black wallet and flapped it open.

Cooper held it up to the officer's face and it did indeed identify Cooper.

Cooper's face and his name on one side and on the other side of the wallet was a small black plastic card banded top and bottom in a red horizontal border, a card depicting lions either side of a portcullis, all below an ornate crown.

"My names Cooper, Special Branch and I'm on a matter of state security, so I really need to get going, if you don't mind officer." Cooper said.

Taken aback and flustered with surprise, "Oh sorry sir, no, please do, sorry I stopped you." Blurted the young patrolman and with that Cooper snapped shut his wallet closed and turned in an instant.

"Goodnight, stay safe." Cooper called back as he hurried to his car and within seconds he had re-belted his seatbelt, turned the ignition and clutched the gear into first. But, he momentarily paused as his hands reached up to the steering wheel, he paused just a moment to watch his hands stop shaking, but they didn't, so instead, he clamped his hands hard, gripping the wheel tightly as he slowly pulled away.

Cooper checked the rear-view mirror as he turned off Hogg Lane, leaving the flashing blue light behind him and stared down towards the back seat of young faces, faces still dulled by the coma of drugs.

Cooper didn't care for them; he had been tasked to pimp, control and supply on demand, to procure for the despicable whims, the loathsome fancies of others and to observe. Cooper would willingly do what was needed for the security of the Government, for the safety of the nation, Cooper, who felt like he 'walked on water' when he strolled the corridors of New Scotland Yard. All he had to note down were the various car registrations and faces that he remembered or recognised.

He had been promised promotion by his Special Branch Superintendent, his boss that had personally taken him under his wing as soon as he had arrived in SO12. Daily he found himself smiling, thinking that soon, perhaps within that year and without the exams that he had previously failed, he would become a Sergeant.

As the children stirred Cooper ordered the girls to dress themselves and he smiled as he turned on the interior light to watch the girls dress, pert breasts each one of them he thought, as they struggled for space clasping their bras and pulling up panties. Once done the light went off, Cooper had seen enough as his loin grew hard, 'they can button their shirts in the dark,' he told himself.

The first drop-off was the silent boy and Cooper only needed two 'flashes' of the car headlamps to see the scurrying arrival of the care worker that had handed the boy over.

Cooper announced the usual to the carer, "same time, same date, see you next month."

Next was 'lamp post girl' whom he paid £25, then Maddie and Debbie were each dropped off clutching their pay. Nikki was the last to be taken home, yes, she had given Cooper her address, but Cooper wanted to make sure, he wanted to see the flat, to see the squat where she had told him she lived, only then would Cooper be satisfied and hand her a share of the proceeds.

It wasn't far to the E16 Custom House 'flop' in Freemasons Road, just a five-minute drive as Nicky squirmed pensively on the rear leatherette seat, now scented with stale sex and sweat and it was still dark when they got out of the car and walked the few steps towards the block.

The corrugated sheeting was pulled back by Nikki and revealed the broken open entrance way door.

"No electricity no lifts, but it still has running water and I am on the fifth floor." Nicky explained as they entered the dark squalor.

On closing the sheeting behind, Cooper found himself being led by the hand as Nikki shuffled the way she thought best, as she kicked the odd bottle and can from her feet.

The stairwell was at the end, the blackness of the enclosed reception offered no respite and he felt that Nicky's handgrip grew tighter the further they walked.

What seemed an eternity was only a few seconds as Nicky and Cooper reached the fire door stairwell where, on opening, there was light through a broken window pane of a street light beyond and immediately letting go of Cooper's hand the girl began to climb the stairs. Followed by Cooper, he remained a few steps behind and below, as he optimised the best angle of view as this young girl's long legs and pert buttocks lifted, climbing that shrouded flight of concrete and Cooper grew harder.

The detective was a little short of breath as he reached the fifth-floor landing, but he took shallow gulps of that rancid air as he walked the last few feet to Nicky's flat door. The young girl pushed hard against the door, elongating her young slender figure, he noted, and once he had stepped inside the flat he realised that the odour, although it was stale, paled into insignificance compared to the putrefied rotten stench that had moments before engulfed the filth ridden landing.

Cooper walked past the kitchen; there were no cupboards on the walls, just a sink and drainer, where there was an open packet of biscuits and a half bottle of orange juice waiting to be consumed.

As Nikki and Cooper entered the lounge, Cooper could see through the gloom that there was no furniture other than a single mattress, no bed, and it was covered in various blankets, one of which was folded over and over again to be used as a pillow.

Cooper was satisfied that this was where she lived and that this slum was where he could get hold of Nikki and pulling out her earnings he said. "This is yours, you've earned It." holding out his hand.

Nikki took the money and his hand in one grasp and asked. "Would you mind waiting with me; that is until it gets light?"

Cooper didn't hesitate, he should have, he knew he shouldn't cross personal and business boundaries that he had set himself, but with a wife indoors more interested in keep fit classes than bedroom aerobics and, having smelt the sweet sweat aroma of this young girl that he had followed her up the stairwell, he quickly answered. "Yes."

--//--

It was an hour or so past dawn when Cooper pushed the corrugated sheeting open, he had left Nikki curled up asleep in a blanket on the mattress, where he had risen naked from her.

Cooper walked briskly under dark clouds over his head and it was only a matter of a few strides before he reached his Vauxhall saloon. He stopped and looked back up at the high-rise block of flats, mentally noting the exact flat where Nikki lived.

He got in his car and began to recall the car number plates that he had seen earlier at the quarry and those he could remember he wrote down in his black notebook for the 'security of the nation.'

Then, having completed this task, Cooper started his car. It was only when he began to drive out of the car park that he noticed the young boy on the pavement across the junction, a boy whose facial features easily resembled a 'retard.' Well that was what he thought.

Cooper simply cared to look away from this bedraggled 'local child idiot' wearing a fur lined hooded parka, a simpleton child who was dancing on the spot and, looking away as he did, Cooper drove from Freemasons Road towards central London.

Within the hour Cooper had arrived at the Broadway where New Scotland Yard, the headquarters for the Metropolitan Police stood, tall and proud and, showing his identification to the uniformed officer on guard duty, there was a quick radio check to ensure that Cooper and his Vauxhall were allowed into the underground car park.

Five minutes later Cooper had a bucket filled with soap and bleach where, if observed, he could be seen with a hard bristle brush scrubbing down the back seat and front passenger seat of his beloved works vehicle.

Cooper spent the rest of the morning on the twelfth floor completing his logs and vehicle registration checks on the Police National Computer (PNC). He wasn't shocked by some the names that flashed up on the screen in front of him, he'd seen many of them before. However, there were others that were new to him, more deviants, more perverts, from both home and abroad. At least six new potential avenues of exploitation by his superior on behalf of the Government, or names to be converted into 'sources' by the Secret Service. Cooper smiled broadly when his Superintendent woke him at his desk, to take him out for a late lunch at a nearby pub.

Chapter 24

"Good economics dear boy," his Superintendent announced, biting into his prawn salad sandwich.

"It's that simple, the government makes deals, it hands out and accepts bribes." The superintendent continued between mouthfuls of seafood and Cooper listened intently.

"We are but a small cog in the wheel of persuasion, no one really knows what anything is worth, the supply of a few tantalising items to a demanding audience at little net cost can provide this country with massive dividends." The Superintendent again explained; though it wasn't the first time Cooper had heard this speech.

Leaning forward as another sandwich over-spilled the Superintendent's open mouth, another unfortunate prawn splashed the china plate in front of him. Cooper sat quietly, listening, as his head motioned up and down just like the nodding dogs that were fashionable on cars rear seat parcel shelves.

"Cooper, you help coordinate the supply of goods that people are willing to stand in line at midnight for, well done," his boss continued, "they sample a tantalising prize, a prize that would normally be scarce to someone visiting this country. Therefore, you have to ask yourself, what is the true cost of patriotism?"

Cooper knew the reply. "Sir, it's what you are willing give up to get it," as he sipped his orange juice with ice.

"Precisely dear boy," the superintendent continued. "Johnny foreigner who comes to this country would sell his own mother for what you and others can supply when they visit and the 'powers that be' truly appreciate your dedication and hard work." Then came the broad smile.

"And if there is an unfortunate situation when a foreigner thinks he can get something for nothing, well then, the video footage works wonders when it comes to signing something like a trade agreement." The Superintendent concluded.

"Yes sir, it does," Cooper affirmed.

Although it was a conversation that both had held previously, it was an important and necessary chat that was repeated each month, so that both men took their stance together, to feel secure and trusted with each other's knowledge. His

Superintendent shook his hand once more and thanked him for the previous hard work.

Chapter 25

Later that night seven men, including the Superintendent, were found sat around a finely carved, circular, walnut table in a private room of a gentleman's club. A marbled floor building, standing three stories, just off Park Lane in central London. It was a room filled with leather seated grandeur and polished brass opulence. A room with walls filled with paintings of previous prime ministers and, a room where for the last two hours they had quaffed at succulent oysters and scallops, feasted on veal and soothed away the bitterness of eerie silence with a sweet strawberry meringue of 'Eton mess.'

Between courses, the superintendent wrote short notes, a 'wish list,' more than anything else, as did the Civil Service representatives from the Home, Foreign and Immigration Office.

Speaking as others sat silent were the other three men, two from Military Intelligence, one from the Military Police and taking orders was, 'the chairman' a 'special' assistant to the Prime Minister no less, he just nodded at appropriate moments.

Towards the end of courses, they served Artisan biscuits and cheese, a time for announcements and the Superintendent enjoyed this brief moment of recognition by his superiors. He told of the hard work that 'his man' had put in and how many more potential avenues of intelligence could potentially be harnessed from the information he had gained.

Then there was a small announcement by one member of Military Intelligence who briefly divulged the limited success of those countries' representatives who had been approached and had provided the necessary intelligence to not only keep the country safe, but to assist in Government liaisons.

Next came the announcements of the contracts that had been awarded to the country that had resulted from persuasion at 'follow-up meetings' where the various parties concerned were reminded that the exposure of depravity from those monthly parties would be harmful to their personal life and/or career.

One of the last topics discussed was stock loss, five items in the last six months. It was a pity, it was a shame, but it wasn't as if they couldn't "restock the shelves," logistically speaking, one of them muttered with indifference.

"National security, that was all that mattered," another affirmed as the group now drank vintage port.

"In the national interest," was the toast and would receive the usual 'applause' of double fingertip tapping on the polished dining table and, as the meeting drew to a close, each man lit a large Cuban cigar and all checked their diaries for the next meeting of the 'F o H' society.

Finally, one by one, each man in turn, spoke of their own department's 'wish list,' a list that the Superintendent noted through the heady smoke of clouded judgement.

Chapter 26

For month after month on the night of the 13th Cooper would work that alphabetical, overnight 'party shift,' as he so fondly called it.

Nautical had just set sail and the next party night was titled 'Oracle,' then it was 'Peach, Quiver, Royal, Surgeon,' and so the names continued. With each London home county venue only ever being used twice in one year, the dates and venues were secure.

Cooper was happy to continue his supply of young children to the rich, powerful and influential. Not only was he earning a decent wage as a Police officer, but on top of that there was overtime plus 'party' benefits. At the Universal party, later that year for instance, he too received an envelope containing £1000 cash for one of his young charges that wouldn't be returning with him that morning. Apparently one of the clients wanted the young girl for longer than a night and she had been taken away with the client before collection.

Other than that incident it was usually the same routine for Cooper; he'd find and introduce new stock on a regular basis, a care home here, a social worker there and an occasional child sleeping rough.

All could be bought, drugged and provided every month and Cooper would note with relish, the new car registrations and the new and familiar faces.

Cooper had realised that he had already supplied Nikki to at least five or six of those parties. He had done this deliberately so that, at the end of each night, he would again take her back to her fifth-floor flat and see the new dawn through with her on that blanketed mattress.

As Christmas time again approached the December Zodiac party was only a couple of days away and Cooper had been instructed by his Superintendent to supply just one child.

"Boy or girl no matter," he was told. But one who should be wearing a white sheeted toga and they were to bring with them a pillow for 'play fights' in some ill-conceived act of perverted battle, in which all of the children would have to take part.

The choice was easy for Cooper, he had decided on his favourite whim to return to the Essex quarry with her, as he too wanted some use out of her afterwards.

The day before the Zodiac party Cooper waited for Nikki to emerge from the corrugated sheeting at the base of the flats and it was roughly midday when she finally appeared. "Rough," was the word that formed on Coopers lips as Cooper saw her walking slowly towards him.

She was a little thinner than the previous month when he had last seen her, 'almost skin and bone,' his mind whispered as she stood in front of him. Cooper couldn't help but notice that the stench of the flats now clung to her.

"Nikki, you stink girl." Cooper told her bluntly as he pulled four £5 notes from his pocket.

Handing them to her he demanded. "Get yourself to a swimming pool and get showered, get yourself smelling sweet, buy some food. You and I are partying tomorrow night and I want you at your best"

Nikki looked up at Cooper and, slow to smile, she nodded.

"You need to buy a white sheet as well," he told her.

"You're gonna be a slave girl tomorrow, so do yourself a favour and make sure that sheet is big enough to cover that rotten old mattress you have upstairs."

Nikki nodded.

"Oh, and get a pillow as well." Cooper remembered and handed over another £5 note.

"Yes, I will, thank you." Nikki replied.

Raising a finger to Nikki's face Cooper spoke with purpose. "I will be here at 11p.m. tomorrow night, do not let me down!"

"I won't, I promise," and with a smirk she teased, "I will be a good girl."

At 11.15p.m. the following night Cooper was already well into his shift and was again pressing down on the Vauxhalls Cavalier's car horn, pressing and pressing hard until Nikki emerged from the flats into the car park where he had sat impatiently.

Cooper noticed that Nikki looked clean and fresh with her dark auburn hair contrasting vividly against the crisp, white cotton sheet that still showed the crease marks of recent opening that she had wrapped around herself.

'A nice sight,' Cooper thought as she strolled and twirled in the gaze of Cooper's car headlights.

"Come on we are late for fuck's sake!" He shouted out at her and her walk suddenly turned to a run. As she got in, Cooper noticed her clutching an old white pillow grubby and threadbare and she placed it on her lap.

"What the hell is that?" Cooper demanded. "That's not new, is it?"

Nikki looked down at the pillow told him. "It belongs to a friend, I've borrowed it and it's called 'Mr Fluffs.'"

Cooper laughed out loudly as he looked at the pillow where he actually saw the words 'Mr Fluffs' ink marked on it

"Well your friend is an idiot to give a name to a pillow and Christ, it smells!" Cooper realised.

"Throw it on the back seat, I don't want to smell it." And Nikki did just that.

"I have to return it to him as soon as I can." Nikki explained, "I took it from him and he doesn't know I've got it, he will be missing his pillow, so can we return it to him afterwards please?"

Cooper just laughed out loud.

--//--

In comparison to the June trip to the Essex quarry the party of "Triumph" was a quiet affair, compared to what Cooper found when he drove slowly past the farmhouse.

This time, the private drive that edged towards the slope, normally devoid of any transport, was awash with cars parked three deep on either side.

Cooper didn't deviate in pulling over himself, he continued down the drive towards the closed gate, as he had done so many times before.

Nikki didn't notice anything; Cooper had already taken the usual precautions having her swallow a tablet and paper tab before they had left on their journey.

Cooper soon passed through the now opened gate, nodding his acknowledgement to the gatekeepers as he drew level and once again he remembered the difficult zigzags of the slope to the base level of the chalk quarry.

However, when he reached the gloom of the chalk floor expanse, he actually scratched his head! Never before had he experienced this venue so full of cars, there wasn't the room for Cooper to park where he normally parked, he had to find a spot quite some distance from the quarry lake. This was some 100 metres from the torch lit chalk wall and, unlike previous parties, this time Cooper had to walk his goods to the men in black. Thankfully it was the same group of twelve or so 'black suits,' however, they seemed more interested in keeping warm, huddling next to an oil drum fire than taking care of business.

Cooper approached slowly and when close enough he called out. "We're here for Zodiac."

At that two of the huddled men turned and walked from the flaming oil drum towards Cooper and the now shivering Nikki, who held 'Mr Fluffs' close in both arms.

"You know where to go?" One of the men asked as the other took hold of Nikki.

Cooper replied. "Yes, the farmhouse." Where upon the man nodded, marked the girl's forearm Z 121 and handed Cooper a ticket.

There was the ticket for Cooper, Zodiac 121 and a piece of paper with the Z 121 for his car's windscreen. Cooper walked back to his vehicle, all the time glancing back at the 121 child, young Nikki, being led, stumbling forward, in the dark, towards the torchlight wall and the caverns beyond.

Walking back along the long, private driveway the moonlight, thankfully, was bright and Cooper mentally noted as many of the car registrations that he could before he entered the farmhouse.

The letters and digits pressed in his memory consumed any conversation that he had with the man who had granted him entry to the farmhouse and Cooper heard nothing as he was paid £150, double the usual fee for a girl.

Cooper quickly excused himself and went to the bathroom upstairs, immediately he wrote down the registrations that he had remembered. He had to write them down there and then, as there were at least double the cars that there would normally be at one of these events, so he took this small chance and sat on the toilet seat, scribbling down each one he recalled in his black notebook.

At 3 a.m. the overcrowded farmhouse filtered until empty. Cooper and the other drivers returned for their goods, again Cooper looked along the driveway, noting more car registrations, but many of the more expensive cars had already departed. This wasn't unusual in itself, but still very unusual that the driveway itself had to be used as an overspill.

When all the drivers had reached the quarry base the 'gathering' of children took place.

"Zodiac 1, Z1" and so on, as each child was brought forward in turn. Cooper noticed that by the time "Zodiac 100, Z100" had been called at least three of the drivers had received an envelope of cash rather than their charge.

Cooper had never seen the passing of so many envelopes rather than children, it was strange and more than a little concerning, especially as he couldn't see Nikki in the small crowd of children that now remained.

"Zodiac 121, Z 121" was called and Cooper stepped forward only to be met by the same man who had been handing out envelopes.

"There's £1000 in there." The man said, handing the envelope to Cooper.

"Where is the girl?" Cooper wanted to know, now aggravated by the fact that he had been looking forward to taking Nikki back to her flat with the brand-new sheet.

"She left early with a client, that's all you need to know." He was told aggressively.

So, Cooper, left with no choice, reluctantly nodded, took the money out of the envelope and, as a requirement, he handed the empty envelope back to the man and walked back to his car.

For the next few minutes Cooper stood by his car and tried to concentrate on noting the car registrations that pulled away from the chalk quarry, but he couldn't, he normally had the ability to memorise at least two dozen, but not that night, only three or four hit his memory and all because he was thinking of Nikki.

Cooper was suddenly roused from his thoughts when he was tapped on the shoulder.

"How's your kid?" It was one of the other regular drivers asking Cooper.

"What, where, who?" Cooper's mind came back to him.

"Your child fella, how's yours?" The driver enquired.

"I don't know how she is." Cooper explained. "But I've been told she is with a client of theirs." He added as he nodded his head towards the men in black suits walking towards the chalk wall.

"We'll my girl is in a pretty bad way, she's been belt whipped and is a bleeding mess," the driver announced.

"Oh, that's bad." Cooper spoke though he couldn't care less.

"Yeah, some pillow fight that was," the man continued, "my girl told me that they were all put in the main cave and told to fight each other until they could fight no more." The driver drew breath.

"Fight and swing until exhausted," he continued, "and those that stopped swinging were dragged away, punched, slapped and kicked and some, like my girl, were belt whipped."

Cooper began listening as the driver continued. "My girl's black and blue and I've got to explain her marks to her care home worker, fuck knows what I am going to say, but I know it's going to cost me more money." The driver fumed.

All Cooper could offer in response was, "well good luck with that, but I've got to go." Abruptly stopping the driver talking further by opening his car door and stepping in.

On closing the door Cooper held up his hand and, in a quick exchange of waves with the man, Cooper turned the ignition key and drove slowly away, joining the queue that left the quarry behind him.

Cooper began to ask himself, 'was Nikki okay?' At the T junction Cooper was able to accelerate away, as did his mind, it suddenly sped into overdrive. Was his girl Nikki actually okay? His mind raced. Was Nikki's outcome to be just like 'bus stop girl' when he received the £1000 at the 'Universal' party and hadn't seen the girl again since.

Before that point Cooper hadn't cared about any child disappearance, he was used to using the different kids that entered and left this trade.

'So why was Nikki any different?' He asked himself. He knew the answer, he'd tasted the goods.

The special Branch officer grew more anxious as he drove back along the A13, he didn't know why, but he needed reassurance. Get back to the young girl's squat in Custom House, perhaps find her there, 'just to make sure,' he hoped.

Twenty minutes later when Cooper turned off the A13 into Freemasons Road, much to the relief of his Vauxhall's engine whose temperature gauge had just hit red, Cooper slowed down to a halt.

This time he wasn't going to park in the car park, this time he would park just up the road before it and walk to the block of flats. Cooper stopped and quietly got out of his car.

'She may be there, she may not,' he thought as he walked around to the boot that he opened. Reaching in, he grabbed a small torch to light his way.

Cooper deliberately walked lightly, treading each step softly on the pavement until he reached the block and its car park and that's when he saw it.

Cooper couldn't help but be immediately drawn to the cream gleam of what was a Pontiac J2000 Saloon, displayed at the rear end was a diplomatic registration plate marked 'D.'

Cooper turned off his torch and stood motionless at the edge of the car park, he looked up towards where Nikki's flat was, but that, like the entire block was in darkness. Cooper listened, he listened out for the smallest of noise, but it was 4 a.m. and, other than his breath, he heard nothing but a robin sing. After noting the car's registration in his black notebook, he slowly crept, away from the street lights. Hugging the darkness of the shadows he approached to what he thought was an empty car.

No less than 12 feet away Cooper stopped, as again he listened intently for the slightest of noise emanating from the car, but there was none and so he crept forward until he could peer over the side panels to see for himself that no one was inside. Did he chance torchlight? He contemplated and with finger poised he triggered over its switch. Yes, he did.

At first there was a quick flick of the switch on and off where the beam reflected off the windows back onto him, however, he could see in the car and returning to the darkness he waited until he was satisfied that nothing stirred around him but himself.

Turning on the light, again the torchlight shone on what lay in the back seat. There he saw a pillow, not any old pillow, as he could clearly see the grubby marking 'Mr Fluffs' and on seeing that, a wave of relief washed over Cooper's mind.

'Thank God,' he thought, 'the girl was safe and back at her flat,' even though she was with another on the brand-new bed sheet!

Cooper cared little about the pair of miniature American flags that he saw lying in the foot well of the rear seat as he quietly walked back to his car and drove back towards central London.

When Cooper arrived at his office he completed the usual vehicle checks and confirmed his suspicions that the Pontiac did indeed belong to the American Embassy.

Of the other cars that he'd noted, there were four other embassies, three British company directors, a barrister, a judge, the usual and that same pop star whose details confirmed he owned more than one car.

Cooper's report was as brief as it possibly could be and that morning he would sit in the chair and wait outside his Superintendent's office to hand deliver his report personally as he arrived for work.

He did this so he could get away early, for that afternoon and for the next three weeks having booked his annual leave, he and his wife were to fly out to the winter sun for Christmas and New Year in the Canary Isles, for a well-earned rest.

It was a holiday like any other holiday where Cooper would relax in his 'budgie smuggling' speedos and glow cherry red in the sun. All the time watching his wife making the usual, alcohol fuelled, fool of herself.

Chapter 27

Two weeks later, on his return to the UK, everything was a 'rush' for Cooper, a rush to unpack and ready himself for work and, for his wife, a rush to clean and iron her way back to normality.

Back in his office there was a rush to arrange four children for the January 'Arabian' party at the next venue, the Government owned Hertfordshire Manor house.

Cooper managed his time well and connected with his 'usual people.' Two separate care workers who would each procure a boy from their sheltered homes and both were made available. Then Cooper left his office and went out into the East End, searching for two of his usual girls, one would be Nikki who he felt owed him from the last party night and the other was Maddie.

As for Nikki, well she was a 'no-show.' Cooper had waited outside her flat for most of the day, but didn't dare enter in case of being seen, so it wasn't until mid-afternoon when he decided to move on, to wait outside one of the local North Woolwich schools for the other. It wasn't long before Maddie walked up to Cooper's car. She recognised the car and driver immediately and got in the front passenger seat as any child would when do being picked up by a parent.

"Wotcha! Mister!" was Maddie's greeting, he'd never given her his name. "Where have you been? You're red." She told him. "Anyways I could do with some extra pocket money, is it the same date and time?" She asked.

"Yes Maddie, the 13th," he replied, "I will pick you up at 10 p.m., try not to be late." Cooper insisted.

"I won't be," she told him. "It's cool, I'll be ready." Maddie smiled at the man.

"Have you seen Nikki? I want her to be there too." Cooper asked.

Maddie suddenly raised an eyebrow and looked at Cooper in surprise. "Nikki, what planet have you been living on Mister?"

"What do you mean?" Cooper asked.

"Well she's dead, isn't she," her message was clear.

Somewhat shocked Cooper quickly questioned, "what, when, how?"

"Some mental kid, done her, stabbed and sliced her up in a subway, it's been in all the papers, where have you been?" Maddie asked again.

"Abroad." Cooper whispered, now smothered in thought process.

"You've missed all the fun then," she grinned before asking, "are you gonna drive me home?" But there was no response so she asked again, "well are ya, are ya gonna take me home?" She persisted.

"Fuck off, fuck off now!" Cooper yelled. And she did just that.

Cooper needed to confirm what Maddie had told him and, gathering himself, he next drove to Karan's café where Debbie would normally spend her days. Luckily for him Debbie was there and, although still upset by the loss of her friend, she confirmed everything Maddie had told him.

However, Debbie had one more thing to add, asking when he had last seen her? For it was the date of her murder, the night of the Zodiac party, found in the early hours of the 14th December! Cooper's hands began to shake visibly.

"Are you alright?" Debbie asked.

"Yes," but he was not, "so who murdered her then?" He asked.

"Well apparently it was a young boy, someone she was mates with, a kid called Ralph. The papers said it was an argument over a fucking pillow of all things and the glue sniffing cunt now denies it" Debbie told him as harsh as the reality itself.

Cooper's mind was racing as he tried to comprehend, but he couldn't think straight, all his mind would feed him was that image of 'Mr Fluffs' in the back seat of that car.

Debbie was still talking, he knew that by her lip movement, but he heard nothing, nothing for two minutes as Cooper visualised that grubby old pillow.

The next thing Cooper realised was that Debbie had grabbed his hand was shaking it "Are you sure you're right?" She asked with a smile and Cooper, snapping his mind shut, pulling his hand back, returned to the land of the living.

"The next party is on the 13th can you, do it?" Cooper asked.

Debbie was hesitant, asking. "Will you make sure I get home?" When her pimp nodded, she agreed

That evening Cooper sat motionless at his desk, just staring in front of his PNC terminal. He sat there staring at the screen displaying the registration of the Pontiac that he had seen that night outside Nikki's flat. He just couldn't understand it.

He had just walked out of his Superintendent's office having told him the facts, but his boss wasn't interested in the slightest, quoting "it was a local murder and Plaistow police Station are dealing with it, it has absolutely nothing to do with us." Those were the words his boss spoke, dispassionately.

"Under no circumstance do you tell them what you know and remember you are bound by the Official Secrets Act," those were the last words as he closed the door on leaving his office.

Cooper just sat there staring at the screen in front of him, looking for an answer that clearly wasn't there. The registration gave no name of the driver just the American Embassy address of Grosvenor Square in London and changing the last number of the registration from 6 to 7, then 8 to 9, he soon came to realise that this car was just one of the many fleet cars the Embassy owned.

Cooper told no one else and at the end of his shift he just went home, home to a wife solely absorbed in painting toenails amid partial glances towards the late news on television.

So, with no-one to talk to, to share what he knew, he immediately took himself to the bathroom where he sat on the side of the bath and opened his sheepskin jacket and, from a side pocket, Cooper produced a quarter bottle of vodka. He did something he hadn't done for years, not since his 18th birthday. He broke the seal and glugged its vile taste, he had just turned another road, but this time it was towards self-hate and oblivion.

Chapter 28

2016 France

Jules hadn't noticed the two large men in black coats that were following him that morning in Chambray-les-Tours and, why would he?

He wasn't anything special, that is, to anyone but his wife. He was just a quiet man, low paid, but happy, who simply enjoyed cleaning the walls and floors of his local hospital.

He was in his late 40s, he got to wear a white surgical coat, he wore an identity badge hung from a chain and every day he felt important.

It was Jules' job to keep the germs away and in doing so this would keep the patients healthy. Poor pay, but rich reward he thought, he liked to think of himself as the 'doctor of detergent.'

Jules would never use the staff locker to store his white coat, he would always wear it to and from work and he would have his wife wash it every Sunday prepped for the new week.

His coat would shine in starch and his identity badge twinkled in polish, both showed his importance and identified that he worked in the medical practice. Then there was his swagger to and from the hospital as he tried to add status to his employment, fair play, it usually worked. Many a stranger would believe him a doctor or surgeon with a multitude of pens protruding from his top pocket, with that clipboard he carried around, metal clipped and black plastic binding, little did anyone realise that it just contained instructions and 'tick off' boxes of the various rooms he had to clean. If ever he was approached and someone were to ask about his position, he would always reply. "I simply do my best."

Well, that day, Jules had done his best as he always did, he had completed his duties with mop, bucket and his 'trusty' circular speedy floor polisher. He was on his way home as the two men slowly approached, he never noticed them standing outside the Bakers when he purchased two small baguettes.

However, when he left the shop he had no option but to notice the pair of brutes that now stood directly in his path who stepped again in front of him when he tried to pass.

Jules was a little unnerved as both men were a clear foot taller and wider than he, but what startled him was that one said, "Jules?" And then, in broken French, the other stated. "We know where you live and we want five minutes of your time."

Jules felt uneasy, but nodded all the same, for these two men were muscular and looked strong, flanking Jules as they walked quickly towards a small café just yards from them. However, it turned out to be five minutes well spent.

The three men sat outside the front of a café and the larger of the two men ordered three coffees from the waiter who scurried off with a wave of an arm. The same big man discussed, as best he could, a proposition.

Jules knew about the big Russian under guard in one of the side rooms of the hospital, the one that had been shot whilst trying to escape the police. Why wouldn't he know, it had been the gossip for a couple of days when the prisoner was secured away in his room.

"Yes." Jules confirmed to these two men; who seemed to know anyway, that indeed he did clean his room daily.

There were wry looks all round when the other large man produced from his inside pocket, a small bulging white envelope marked 'Jules.' Handing it over, the cleaner's eyes bulged wide, as did his mouth when he lifted open the flap.

The envelope man leaned forward and whispered. "Ten thousand Euros now and the same when our friend leaves the hospital, you understand?" Jules again nodded as he gripped the envelope tight, flicking the purple 500 Euro notes with his fingers.

As discussed, every day from that day forward, at the end of his shift, Jules would stop at this café where he would meet 'the envelope carrier' who introduced himself as 'Ivan' and deliver whatever note the injured Russian, a 'Yuri Yazov,' would hand him when attending to his room.

After the note was read, there would be an acknowledgement by Ivan, with either a small tick or an X that Ivan marked on the back of Jules hand that Jules would then show to Yuri the following day.

Of course, Jules would do this, why not? He didn't think of the consequences, he was indeed important and carried this self-belief into the next morning and for those days that followed.

Jules found it easy 'palming' a piece of tightly squeezed white toilet paper from the smiling Russian as he mopped around his bed. The Police guard present; was more interested with what was on the television or reading his newspaper than to pay any notice to such a lowly cleaner.

The Russian would nod at Jules and then nod to his heavily bandaged left arm, where he'd been shot twice and he would then open his palm where, every day there would be the piece of ink marked toilet paper for Jules to take away.

Jules had opened the first tissue paper note when he had found time alone in his storeroom, but the writing was foreign, Russian, he presumed and he never bothered opening the others, he didn't understand the language.

Most days Yuri would nod and smile when Jules showed him the black mark on his hand, so there seemed to be more good news than bad. However, this middle aged, heavily scarred Russian, a bear of a man, bigger and broader than any man Jules had ever encountered, would sit up and sneer at this humble messenger if the marking wasn't to his liking. And for three days Jules showed nothing but a cross on the back of his hand. He could see the Russian's anger with whatever news it was and on one of the last days in his recovery room, the Russian eyes filled with pure hate as he passed yet another note to Jules.

Yuri had seen the marking on Jules hand and he couldn't contain himself, Yuri just yelled across at the gendarme in his room. It came as quite a shock to the guard that had been sitting there, quietly in the corner, reading his newspaper as he had always done. He now ducked the empty breakfast tray that was hurled towards him as Jules quickly ran from the room.

There was a Russian, "fuck you," and an English, "fuck you," and his best attempt at a French, "fuck you all." As Yuri sat bolt upright. Clenching his fists, he began to froth snarls at the mouth.

The guard was more than a little perplexed, wiping warm coffee and slivers of omelette from his uniform and, standing there in front of Yuri, he gestured, open palmed, the officer asked for calm. There were several minutes of raw Russian tension until Yuri finally laid himself back down on his bed, from that afternoon on there were two guards in his room.

Later that afternoon Jules handed over the piece of toilet tissue and told Ivan exactly what had occurred earlier, with the big Russian man being so angry. Jules was even more surprised when Ivan responded with a laugh and a smile; claiming in his best French. "It is good," and he again marked the back of Jules hand, but this time, with a tick.

Ivan was right, for the next morning it was all good and Jules was glad to see the big Russian smiling broadly. It was the answer he had been waiting for.

Chapter 29

London

Ernest Jones realised that the recent regulations were either 'inadequate or had not been adhered to' as he briskly walked the corridors of power back to his small office. The screams from backbenchers calling for his dismissal only moments ago still echoed in his ears.

The Education undersecretary and Member of Parliament for the past ten years, thankfully found ease at the desk in his Parliamentary office, but it wasn't long before he was soon scratching his head in total dismay.

He had returned from a question time, where amongst his peers, he had to practically admit he was totally bewildered as to the incompetence of some schools who had failed to keep, 'proper record.'

His superior was wisely 'too ill' to attend Parliament that day, so he was told, consequently, red faced and apologetic, he stood there amongst his fellow MPs clearly embarrassed in the knowledge that he had no information as to the movement and current whereabouts of school pupils who seemed to have simply disappeared from the education system.

Question after question and a list of examples that he had been unable to answer and he now cursed as he sat there sifting through the numerous copies of school registers.

He read comments, such as "moved abroad," "gone to live with grandparents" and all bar one or two schools made no mention of a forwarding address. Of those that did, not one had made any enquiry to confirm that the scribbled entries he read were correct.

"Radicalisation," was on the lips of many involved in Parliament that day. There were so many children from the ethnic minorities who were missing!

Speculation was rife. Were some forced into arranged marriages? Were some in the hands of extremists? And what of Slave labour? These were the stirrings that Ernest heard from the news reports later that evening.

However, he pondered, there was no mention, no outcry as to the numerous names of obvious white children that he had read about who had also disappeared.

What of child sexual exploitation? Why wasn't that mentioned? He questioned. Why was there no mention from others as to this possibility? He had to answer himself and surmise that those who spoke on television or who wrote in the following days' newspapers only relished in their own importance as they used such words as 'Extremists' and 'Terrorism.'

This was all now a distant memory from Ernest's fledgling career as an MP.

How he missed being on the periphery, calling out for questions to be answered, rather than being the one who now had to, disappointingly, answer. Ernest remembered one such young boy who, ten years ago, had disappeared only two streets from where he had lived in his home constituency, as he sat in his office and wrote until dawn the next day, working on potential propositions that might save his career.

So tired was he when he sat at the Terrace restaurant in Parliament, eating his way through the discounted breakfast. A place where he found himself being stared at by the early risers. He knew that 'the knives were being sharpened,' by his fellow MPs who distanced themselves from him.

He wasn't too worried though, he had worked through the night on his answers. He would claim his superior had access to those school registers and that 'truthfully,' he hadn't received any instructions on them.

He would later announce that he had taken it upon himself and written a 'mission of purpose,' to collect, record and ensure that more detailed information would be made available as to the onward movement of school pupils.

He would also propose to Parliament and ask to head an investigation 'seeking out' and, if need be, call for the sacking of those who had been responsible for past failings.

Ernest Jones MP smiled as he mopped up egg yolk with tiger bread, later he would hand-deliver his proposition to the Prime Minister's secretary, in the knowledge that the Prime Minister himself, for the sake of his own political survival, would stand up and spearhead this proposal.

Chapter 30

Gibraltar

It happened a week ago and Harris wished he could tell how his life had turned upside down and so terribly wrong.

His life as a Metropolitan Police Detective once had meaning and purpose, but that pureness had 'blown' like the wind and now all that he had left were fragments of a broken heart, as chance and fate currently swung in the favour of others, he sat there in silence.

Maya the woman he had fallen for, had left him.

Everything was silent, as he cursed his luck.

Harris' sister Lana was looking at him for answers, as they sat in the hotel dining room, whilst the morning's sun clouded over and dimmed the tinted windows that looked onto the street.

She sat quietly holding her two walking canes. She was as silent as her brother and it was her silence that helped deafen any clarity of thought from the officer.

She sat, waiting patiently, waiting to find out what her sibling chose to do next. She had been quite disturbed by her brother's recent actions. Never once had she asked for compensation, retribution or revenge on the Russian for the accident that had left her a cripple for life.

An accident which, years before, Harris' nemesis Yuri had driven at her and over her. An accident for which the courts offered no compensation as Yuri was allegedly unemployed. Now she knew that her brother had stolen brilliant cut diamonds from the same man, just to compensate her disability.

These were stones that she wanted nothing to do with, diamonds that now sat, unloved and unwanted, in her hotel safe waiting for her brother to deal with.

Harris was 'distant' as he lent forward, elbows on knees with hands gripped, clasping his head, as he tried so desperately to gather some practical thought.

He had been at his sister's hotel in Gibraltar for less than a week, a week that started in pure happiness, a week that now soured into trauma and heartache.

From the moment that Harris and Maya had arrived at Lana's hotel it had been bliss. Both Harris and Maya had been attached to each other like a couple of 'cooing doves' for almost two days whilst Lana had looked after Maya's two children and, as Harris and Maya took turns on each other, the sex soon changed to 'making love.'

However, on the third day there was complete change. It was that phone call to Maya's mobile phone. A call before dawn and one that had stirred Harris from his sleep. A phone call that rose Maya from their bed and, having quickly wrapped herself in Harris' dressing gown, she had walked out onto the balcony in whispered words of her native Russian.

That was the beginning of the end; the beginning of numerous phone calls back and forth in which Maya, 'Yuri's wife, his love,' would scurry herself away to speak on the phone. After almost three days of near constant phone calls, together with evenings of personal distance, Maya claimed not to feel well. It was three days in which Harris would see Maya smiling and giggling on the phone and, he recalls, that Maya would hang up on whenever she noticed Harris was too near.

It was the last phone call when Harris confronted her, when Maya simply claimed she was talking to family. This last phone call that left Harris perplexed and Maya withdrawn. So, Harris had decided not to question her again. He wanted her love, not her emptiness and she looked far too upset after apologising for his random accusations of, another man. However, it was too little, too late.

The next morning Harris rose late from his disturbed sleep, he woke to an empty bed and a short dash to Maya's daughters' bedroom next door revealed an empty room. No longer would Maya be around to be questioned.

Maya had fled with nothing but a suitcase stuffed with money, money that Yuri had gifted Harris and he had given her. Having checked the bedside cabinet he realised that she had left taking her and her daughters' passports.

Maya, his lover, the wife of Yuri and the mother of two beautiful daughters had left him. She had simply spirited herself and her daughters away and there wasn't even a note explaining why!

Yes, Harris sat there, silent, as he tried to understand why his heart hurt so badly. Harris tried to understand exactly what he had just lost.

Initially it had been Maya's beauty that had seized him, but it was Maya's warmth that convinced him and her voice that told him. "You are the one."

Love, Harris had been struck by it, this solitary force, not simply a lust or attraction and he was glad to accept this attachment, commitment, but now she had fled, it had all gone.

Rejection, Harris knew this feeling and he was smothered in it once more.

He had long suffered the rejection by his work colleagues who believed him guilty of a murder he didn't commit. He understood the rejection by his sister, who wanted nothing to do with the diamonds that he had stolen for her.

Questioning himself further, was Maya simply a puppet master who knew how to pull the strings that made him dance? Harris was already motivated by the crime lord Yuri who had crippled his sister. So, was Maya simply 'acting out' her love to him as reward for ridding herself of her violent, polygamist husband?

Harris was grieved, had he been entrapped and controlled with every impish smile and hard urgent kiss?

Harris also had to accept that Yuri, the Crime Lord, would have realised that he had been 'set up' and that Harris may have had a hand in bringing about his downfall.

Christ! Harris really needed time to think. The world was on his shoulders and he sat there rocking back and forth, wondering if there would be a contract on his head!

There was silence; he sat there silent, as a tag team pounded at his head, loss, fear and vulnerability, all added to the torment.

'At long last,' Lana thought, as Harris drew a deep breath and rose from his seat.

But she was disappointed as he said nothing, just looked straight through his sister to the lobby door and slowly walked past her to the reception and out of her hotel.

Taking slow steps, he shuffled down onto the road and wandered towards the inviting blue sea.

Harris was truly in conflict with himself, a shuffling car wreck, numbed and disassociated with the world around him.

He was amongst people with smiles on their faces and he couldn't understand why he felt so very angry, surrounded by darkness. So, instead of the sun and the sea, he turned and walked to the comfort of shaded side streets and back alleyways, where for hours he walked aimlessly, still trying to comprehend what was best to do next.

Harris felt humiliated, and as 'damaged goods,' he asked himself, 'Was it actually love that he had felt?'

"Was Maya perfect? No. Was Maya baggage free? No."

He just knew he wanted her back and he would eventually realise that he couldn't escape his thoughts of her, not even in his dreams.

"Harden up you stupid bastard," he continually told himself. Perhaps exile through alcohol may not be the correct step, but it would be his next step and the alcohol consuming day turned slowly to night.

--//--

At dawn, the next morning Harris found himself on the stairs to the hotel, he hadn't even made it back to his room on leaving the last bar.

That last half pint of vodka soda did it for him and he didn't even recall what bar he had left.

However, there he was; a hung-over mess who still had his wallet with cash in that he checked as he raised himself up from the stairs. He walked to one of the tables and chairs on the hotel veranda and sat for some time watching the world wake and walk past.

He sat there long enough for Lana to notice him and she hobbled out with a waiter. She brought him a large cup of coffee and with a smile she asked. "Are you alright?"

Harris looked back, smiling in assurance announcing. "I know what to do." As he zipped up the rip to his heart.

"I need to get back, I couldn't stay here even if I wanted to." Lana nodded her agreement.

Harris told her that he had to 'chance his arm' and return to London, to pretend to know nothing about Yuri and his capture in France, not until someone told him of course. Yes, he would claim he knew nothing of what had happened and get back to some form of normality, to what he did best, to solving murders.

Lana could see her brother was still pained as she leant over and kissed him on the forehead with the whispered encouragement. "Stay strong."

They sat for a while, just brother and sister, holding hands, cherishing the moment before his departure whilst one of her staff packed his bag upstairs. Within half an hour Harris had walked down to where his yacht was berthed and recovered his clothes and personal possessions, including the mobile phone that he had bought and used to contact Maya and his old boss Detective Superintendent Hemmings.

Harris turned on the phone and noticed it still held two bars of battery. There had been several missed calls, including six that he recognised, three of them that very morning from Hemmings.

'That should be enough battery life,' Harris thought, standing by the yacht wheel checking for a signal. Dialling his boss's number, he drew a deep breath as the call began to ring.

"Hello, who's this, is that you Harris?" he heard Hemmings say and, on hearing his voice, Harris immediately relaxed.

"Hi boss yeah it's me Harris, sorry I've not been available for a while, but I have had…"

Hemmings hurriedly talked over what Harris was trying to explain.

"Thank God it's you, thank God, where have you been? Where are you? Are you alright?" he was asked.

Harris was a little perplexed by this sudden concerned sign of affection, something that he had never experienced from this man before.

"Of course, I am all right boss, why, what, what's happened?" Harris questioned.

There was a silence; there were actual seconds of silence, a deafening silence as Harris pressed the mobile phone hard against his ear. Had he missed something?

"Boss?" Harris repeated, but still it took a few seconds before Hemmings eventually cleared his throat and again asked. "Where are you?"

"I'm still abroad boss, like I said I would be, I've still got a few days leave left as far as I know." Harris claimed, counting the remaining annual leave dates out in his head.

"Well you're not on leave now son," Hemmings declared. "You'd best get back as soon as you can, someone has blown up your house!"

"Oh fuck, oh my, oh shit!" Harris immediately stopped thinking out loud as he let go of the yachts wheel he'd been holding, slumping down, sitting in shock.

"What the fuck!" Harris said as he tried to come to terms with the words, "blown up." "Blown up!" Harris exclaimed. "Blown up?" Harris questioned.

There was a slight muffled giggle in Hemmings' next words, but such was his humour.

"Yes, blown up, your house and about half of the other houses either side of yours. It blew up yesterday."

Harris paused, racking his brain, as Hemmings continued. "Don't worry, no one was hurt, most of your neighbours were out at work."

"I've been blown up, I mean my house?" Harris blurted out as images of flames, flying brick and timber hurtled around his imagination.

"Yes, now gets your arse back here now! Today if you can." Hemmings ordered.

Still pummelled by visions of grey concrete, rectangular brick merging with gabled roof cladding and slate tile, all falling like shrapnel towards him, Harris brought himself back to reality and, knowing the answer, he still asked. "Was it an accident?"

"Not sure yet, an investigation has started and you're needed back here to answer some questions. So, shift your backside into gear and get back now!" Hemmings reiterated.

"Of course!" Harris said. "Yes, yes, I'm leaving now," he answered.

Harris also agreed that he would let Hemmings know the moment he landed back in the UK, but, 'like hell I will,' he told himself ending the call.

Chapter 31

Slightly traumatised by this latest news was an understatement and Harris knew he needed to get back to England immediately.

There was nothing to keep him on Gibraltar and he knew he must get back to London and if possible within the day, within the hour if he could time travel.

He knew every second, every moment in passing, even the blink of an eye could be time better spent elsewhere in covering his tracks back in England, rather than feeling sorry for himself.

He imagined that the quicker he returned, the more chance he had of avoiding the potential pain and torment that Yuri's men would inflict on him, if it was as it appeared, belief of betrayal on his part.

Harris reflected on one of the weirdest times in his Police career and gathered himself together as he reminded himself of his decision making. 'All for the greater good,' he had believed and now, again with purpose, standing on the deck of the yacht, he looked at the mobile phone. It was his only connection to Maya and, rather than noting her number, he said, "goodbye," as he threw it into the water.

Grabbing his small tattered rucksack from within one of the stowaway cupboards he opened it and counted the few thousand pounds he had held as his travel money. He locked the cabin securely and took a quick taxi ride back to the hotel.

There he packed just a few other essentials and bustled his sister to a local 'Neglected children's' charity shop where he stood and smiled as he watched her handover the heavily sealed, brown envelope containing the small fortune in diamonds.

Finally, and within half an hour he had purchased an open return ticket, 'just in case,' he told himself and hugged and kissed his little sister goodbye.

Chapter 32

France that same day

Gregor was finding a routine to this, now confined, life. He was the crux of a judicial investigation, with a French examining Judge, at the bequest of the Ministry of Justice, gathering the facts, who had ordered further investigation into this Russian witness, the man who had informed on Yuri Yazov.

Gregor was again woken to a pot of rich flavoured coffee that accompanied a plate of freshly baked croissants and, as he had done before, he sat at a table in the corner of his room where he would slice strips of fresh butter that melted on impact and all that was left was to spoon the sweet honey and eat. This was as it had been for the past couple of weeks, all delivered on a tray and when he would answer daily to two knocks on his bedroom door.

It was a door where Pierre, his personal guard, stood outside. A door that would be unlocked each morning in that old Miller's house, a Mill house that was set back in the hills South-west of Orléans, France.

Standing just one-storey, it had been built in the eighteenth century primarily as a hunting lodge, all alone in five acres of forest. 'Off the beaten track,' it was almost half a kilometre from the nearest road and no one, but the authorities, knew that this building was now inhabited.

Next Gregor showered and dressed, waiting for yet another visit from the local Judge and Chief Prosecutor. Both would be in the company of an interpreter and two further 'agent de police,' officials.

Gregor wondered if it would be another typical day where, on arrival and for hour upon hour, they would sit in the main living area, huddled around the old square oak table where Gregor would again continue to speak out against his former employer.

This same routine, with almost the same questions, with the same replies. The interrogation team always demanded more, but Gregor wouldn't tell all, that was, not unless he wanted to sit in the court alongside Yuri.

During these hours Gregor would mentally wander to the surrounding forest nearby, he so wanted to leave the house.

He was so bored with the questions and confines, instead he wanted to walk alone and actually see the birds which sung that woke him each morning.

He wanted fresh air, wind that he could actually feel, not the stagnant air that seeped into his room from a high mounted, small, open window.

But still he sat, he would have to sit with these men and talk for hours, each word interpreted and written in French, all scribed on official forms on which, at the bottom of each page, he would sign his name.

Gregor had been told to tell everything, from drug trafficking to money laundering, from human transportation to prostitution. Everything that he knew about Yuri, these men wanted to know it, but he never mentioned how high a ranking he was in Yuri's empire. He was just a courier, he had told them, just fortunate to be there when the 'Big Boss' led.

Gregor saw the smiles with every new accusation he delivered, but he didn't smile, betrayal was never a friendly face and one he had never experienced before.

Then with the sun at its highest lunch was delivered, brought in by more men in suits, all kept warm in heat retardant boxes.

Then there would be more discussion and statement taking as Gregor's memories filled yet more sheets of paper. Then at last there would be an "au revoir" all-round as these men would leave the three armed security police with Gregor left to spend another night in solitude.

Then the evening, where the guards would take turns in cooking, it was always something with pasta or something with rice and then, after the meal Gregor would be challenged to a game or two of draughts.

Next would be 'lights out' and Gregor would again be locked in his room with his skylight window, alone to think his thoughts and dream his dreams, to be fresh for the following day.

However, that very morning, would be his last in the house. Again, Pierre brought the breakfast to his room, he showered himself clean and dressed and sat waiting.

Then the officials arrived, with still more questions and again Gregor sat across the old wooden table and answered as best he could, but this time, from over 1000 yards away, he was marked in the crosshairs of a telescopic sight.

Chapter 33

London

Harris was pleased that the plane was only half filled and although he had a ticket next to some old lady he chose a window seat from those that was empty. It was a pair of vacant seats where he could stretch out and reflect. However, it was difficult for Harris to stir his mind from visions of his demolished house and those he believed responsible for it, he decided not to contemplate further.

Instead he opened his rucksack and took out the file that Mr Rupert Forrester had handed him only days before his murder. Harris thought, 'to be innocent he'd have to act innocent,' he continued where he had left off. So, in that creased brown cardboard file of report and photographs, he immersed himself in evidence and, eventually, allowed his mind to wander from his current predicament.

He again read page after page and once more Harris looked at the photographs of the dead girl, Fiona Grant-Smith. He memorised the scene. Studying each detail, he reached into his rucksack and took out his trusty, pocket, magnifying glass.

He looked at everything that the various angled photographs had to offer, her nakedness, her buckled feet that were strapped wide apart by buckles screwed into the base of her bedroom door. One of her arms was also strapped up high in a similar fashion whilst her other arm was loose, her potential self-relief and release.

Harris turned his attention the close-up photograph of her head, as it hung in the translucent plastic bag. At the front of the mouth, where her tongue sagged, there was a large lipstick circle that must have sucked to her lips as she struggled to gain her last breath, around her neck was the strapping of a man's belt.

However, upsetting these photographs must have been for her parents to view, they weren't to Harris and, with all these snapshot images of apparent sexual deviation, he was strangely drawn to and returned time and again to that image of the folded train ticket that was found on the floor in front of her bright, red, painted toenails.

The ticket was the same colour and it appeared folded in the same manner as the ticket Harris had found a just few weeks before when he had lifted the dead Mrs Forrester from the husband's car.

'The crazy thing is though,' Harris told himself, the file he was holding was of Fiona Grant-Smith, a girl in her late teens, who had allegedly died from autoerotic asphyxiation. Hung dry in rented accommodation located in Docklands East London, but this degradation and death had taken place many years before.

Luckily for Harris, the Grant-Smith's, her parents, were still alive and still resided in the UK. Both were foreign nationals from the Ukraine borders of Russia. The husband and wife were far from satisfied with the police investigation thus far. Never would their only daughter have acted in such a manner! Perversion? Not their Fiona.

Her father was a retired political official who had somehow managed to purchase a fair chunk of his homeland as a 'farewell' from his Government. Not only was that strange, but it was land that was known to be rich in mineral deposits. Suddenly, with this new 'found' wealth, he had decided to leave home with his wife and child and fly Aeroflot to Heathrow.

On landing the father was all for settling in the Midlands, all because he had seen its picturesque beauty in an inflight magazine, one where there was another article, this one, by a Mr Grant Smith who was a plaudit on the grandeur of those with double barrelled names.

So, the former Bubliks found themselves a new name and a new residence in what was a large manor house. And living happily on their small country estate, although not equal, they soon socialised with the local upper classes who would regularly visit them. Their solicitor was paid handsomely to manage their finances and when their daughter was of an age and had qualified for the City of London University, it was through this legal contact that a suitable apartment was found for their beloved Fiona.

Neither parent was keen to see their child leave such a loving home, both in the knowledge that she would soon mix with undesirables, the unemployed, the low life and indeed it was only two months before tragedy struck.

Even with their wealth and some influence the Grant-Smith's couldn't persuade the Metropolitan Police that the death was anything other than a tragic sexual accident, a four-week investigation including the post mortem results were presented to the Coroner, who directed a jury to its conclusion, 'death by misadventure.'

No. The parents wanted more. What they thought should be a thorough investigation for their daughter, not simple assumptions by the authorities and, as they were willing to pay for the privilege, there were numerous Parliamentary questions asked by their local MP.

This turned out to be a real headache for the investigating trainee detective who had been allocated the case. It was a simple case of an unfortunate death, so his superiors had told him and one that he concurred with. Although the investigation was sympathetic, there was no evidence of 'foul play.'

However, as a result of the pressure the father brought to bear; there was a further investigation, with the same conclusion. Rather than be brought before the Coroner again it was filed away where every detail was documented and every exhibit safely stored, away in the storage facility at Mandela Way, South East London.

Mandela Way, a complex of grey warehouse units that over the years Harris had frequently visited. Now on the plane home, he was 'flicking through' the numerous storage reference numbers that were still on offer to him there.

Chapter 34

"Bloody freezing." These were Harris' first words as he landed at Gatwick airport and "Christ," he was cold, as the visiting Siberian winds blew through him, waiting for the train to take him into London.

He could have afforded a black cab, he still had a few thousand 'emergency' pounds that he had kept in his rucksack from his voyage down to Gibraltar, but Harris wanted to remain anonymous, as he kept his head low. He didn't want to be recalled or observed as he made his way home on the train, then tube. He didn't ring his boss as promised, he knew he couldn't, not until he could 'tie up' loose ends and it was early evening before Harris had left the Elm Park Café.

He wanted to ensure that darkness had descended before walking every side street towards what was left of his house. Harris was confident that any investigation at his home would be carried out in the daylight hours, a day filled with various police personnel, all looking for answers, answers that he didn't have nor was he willing to share if he had them!

Harris eventually managed his way to the garages situated at the rear of his house, or, the debris of his house! He sighed with relief when he saw his garage still standing with the padlocks securing it.

Meticulously quiet, unlocking, Harris slowly lifted the pull-down door and slid in beneath. He pulled down the door behind him until it clicked shut and stood in the musty darkness. He stood and waited, waited, waited for something, anything and nothing. He waited for the slightest noise, the smallest of warnings, to match the smell of his fear and despair, but nothing came as he breathed the cold, damp air.

Harris knew where his torch would be, where he'd always left it, on the shelf. The wooden shelf, two to three steps forward and one to his right, but for the life of him he couldn't remember if there was anything on the floor that might stumble his approach.

Inch by inch, he stepped forward, his hands slowly wafting the black in front of him and, as he made his way forward, all the time, his brain pleaded, 'please don't let me hit anything.'

Finally, and with hushed jubilation his right hand, reached out, had found the shelf. The shelf. His fingers now tiptoed along before he felt the rubber banding of his old plastic torch and found the 'on' switch.

Ten minutes later Harris had completed a personal task and was now also reunited with his work phone, he closed the garage door behind him. Locking it securely he quietly walked away in the darkness, only once did he glance at the remnants of where his house had once stood and quickly, quietly, Harris moved on.

Harris had thought about going to his car which had been left outside his house, but he decided against it. It would be 'far too risky' Harris told himself. Firstly, he didn't want to be spotted and he certainly didn't want that to 'blow up' with him in it either, just in case that too had been wired to explode. Besides, he remembered, his car had been parked directly out front and would no doubt also be in a similar state to the shell of his home, either that or it would have been removed by the investigators.

Harris also contemplated turning on the mobile phone and making a couple of phone calls, but he wasn't about to ring any colleagues to see if they could put him up for the night, he wasn't that way inclined. He was independent, with little or no trust of his fellow Detectives. Besides, he didn't want to announce his arrival back in the UK yet, not just yet, he still needed time to prepare his lies!

No, the answer lay with a trusted friend, a lady who knew how to listen out for trouble, a woman who was larger-than-life and had 'more fingers than pies' in knowing the various spheres of the criminal spectrum. Yes, he decided, the landlady of the Moby Dick in Chadwell Heath, she was the answer, 'Temptress Tina,' she would find a room for him and his thoughts.

It was a sausage and chips takeaway that Harris scoffed into as he waited for the minicab at the Elm Park cab office, it was steaming hot and filling as Harris scrunched the toes in his shoes trying to abate the cold night.

Eventually the car returned for its pick up, so, wrapping what remained of his meal along with a number of no longer needed clear plastic bags that he took from his inside jacket pocket, he threw it all into a nearby bin. In only twenty minutes he reached the pub, where he cuddled his Tina and greeted her. "Hello."

It was an hour before closing, but Tina didn't move from the leather sofa where they both sat as Harris spoke. Her eyes widening between large gulps of 'house' prosecco.

"Fucking hell, fuck no." She spoke in her Sheffield accent and could be heard to giggle nervously as Harris tried out his version of the truth.

Of course, it wasn't the truth, well not the full truth, in fact far from it, but it was a story that Harris had to tell others. Harris had to test out the plausibility on, this, his version of the truth, if Tina believed it then perhaps so could others.

Harris explained that there were obvious risks by being in her presence, but when he asked. "Could you put me up for a couple of nights?"

Without hesitation Tina replied with a smile. "Of course, of course."

Closing time came and went, leaving just the two of them alone in the bar and that's when Harris asked if Tina would look after his savings in her safe. She agreed, counting out the £4000 he had handed over and, placing it in a large envelope she locked it away. Harris had already hidden the other £3000 in his imitation fur lined leather jacket. The Detective had decided that the £4000 he had entrusted with Tina was credible savings on a policeman's wage, but any more than that he knew would arouse Tina's suspicions.

That job done, Tina showed him his room, then the bathroom, she gave him the spare keys to the pub and, showing him how to operate the alarm system, a quick "cheerio," and she was gone.

Harris unpacked his rucksack, the brown cardboard file, a mobile phone and charger, toiletries, a spare pair of jeans, three shirts, two pairs of socks, a pair of deck shoes and that was it!

Oh, he knew he had buildings insurance, he had been given no option but to take that out with the mortgage he'd been offered and it was insurance that he had simply renewed by direct debit, but household insurance, 'oh bugger,' he thought, he could have made a fortune with that.

Though it didn't matter, most of the house contents, what little there was, was still in his garage anyway!

Harris always believed if he'd ever been burgled the thieves wouldn't bother themselves with the burden of taking anything away.

He was a copper who lived on his own and nothing, but the clothing he bought was ever brand-new, he never reasoned in buying new household items and he was sitting there on a single bed in a safe warm room, as he recalled when he had taken that approach. He was as a young man when he had first bought the house, he didn't go out, he couldn't afford too. The only treat was a monthly Chinese takeaway for one and, since those early sparse days, any money in his bank account was spent on going out and enjoying himself.

Harris just sighed a little sigh as he looked at the little he carried with him, even the phone that he wanted to use had no battery life.

--//--

It was gone midday before Harris finally stirred from his sleep, it had been a sleep that had disturbed him, filled with visions of brutal blows and pain, visions that Harris hoped would never come true. He awoke to sweat filled sheets.

Slowly rising he checked to see that the phone charger had worked its magic and he smiled seeing the on/off button ignite life into the small screen. He left it there as he bathed and dressed, while he listened out to the pub life that stirred just a floor below.

"Harris your phone is ringing, are you going to answer it?" It was Tina calling from the bottom of the hallway.

"Yes, yes, thank you." Harris shouted back as he heard it ring. Running to his room, with a quick glance at the screen, he recognised it was Hemmings ringing and he answered the call.

"Apologies boss." Harris first said. "I didn't get back until late last night and I didn't want to disturb you."

"Disturb me, disturb me, where the fuck are you?" Hemmings screamed down the phone.

Harris thought within a nanosecond, he didn't want to divulge where he was exactly as the police frowned upon officers staying in licensed premises, but he had to be close enough to somewhere nearby and Romford was only a couple of miles away, "Romford," he replied.

"Get to your office in Barking, I'm here now and so should you be!" The phone went dead.

Harris was a bit taken aback by the short sharp, barked order he had received, he couldn't quite put it down solely to the knowledge that Hemmings had little or no people skills.

There was something else, an edge in those few words and although there was authority in Hemmings voice, there was definitely something else, dare he say, fear.

Harris knew, from past experience, that he had attuned his ears to listen out for real, unknown or perceived fear and his boss was frightened.

It took Harris less than an hour to get to the offices at Barking and with each stop and delay on the bus and tube he visualised Hemmings becoming even more upset. It didn't help when he arrived at his murder squad office, his old office, when he was told by his Detective Inspector Jack, 'the bumbling idiot,' that he had been officially moved out.

Jack looked uncomfortable and apologised. "It wasn't down to me, you'd best check the squad team noticeboard, this will show the new room number where you are to work from."

Harris did just that, he walked down the hallway, checked where his paper name had been placed into the metal slots and it was there that he discovered that he wasn't actually allocated to any particular team. All the board showed was that he now occupied a room on his own called D3 and that his immediate superior was the new Detective Chief Superintendent in charge of all on site.

When Harris opened the door to room D3 he immediately realised that, although he had returned to his love of investigating murders, he obviously hadn't been totally accepted back with open arms. His room was nothing more than an old store cupboard with two chairs either side of a small desk. One of the chairs was occupied by Hemmings who was in whispered conversation on his mobile phone.

As the two men exchanged nods and Harris sat on the empty chair he saw next to the desk a large cardboard box with his name on it, obviously the shipped contents from his old office. Harris took note that on either side of the store room lay empty shelf stacks and on the far wall where Hemmings sat, there was nothing, not even a window to the outside world. Harris sighed as he slumped down, this wasn't the return to the murder squads that he had been expecting and when Hemmings finished his phone call there was no welcome back speech either.

"Well I got you back onto the murder squads, but the new Chief Superintendent has just arrived and apparently you are still going to be treated as the 'great unwashed.'

Harris sighed as Hemmings continued. "Unfortunately, he claims no one here is willing to trust you, however, I also know he is in the same Masonic Lodge as Detective Inspector Pete Brown, the man you helped capture, the man who is still awaiting trial for murder." Neither Harris nor Hemmings were too happy and

Harris could taste the anxiety in the Superintendent's voice. Still Harris didn't question, he just nodded in response.

"I have been told you are going to be used as a spare here Harris, you won't be a part of any single investigation, you will just be a periphery officer, used when and where needed, house-to-house, secondary scenes et cetera."

Harris nodded again, looking down to the floor at his box.

"And there's a word of warning Harris." Hemmings cautioned. "The Chief Superintendent is looking for any excuse to get rid of you, don't give him one, do what he says, when he says and try to build his trust." Harris again nodded defeat at Hemmings words.

"Believe me." Hemmings said. "This is the good news." And Harris jerked a laugh. "No, this is the good news." Hemmings urged. "The fire investigation team at your house have been unable to establish if the gas leak causing the explosion was accidental or deliberate."

Still, Harris, although perturbed by this statement, could sense something else, a fear in Hemmings voice. "Therefore, the Commissioner's office is not accepting that there may have been an attempt on your life, basically they don't have any concern about protecting you."

Harris literally felt the hairs on the back of his neck rise, but it was the last sentence that finally drew his response.

"I received a phone call last night." Hemmings said. "It came from Interpol on behalf of the French Authorities, their main witness Gregor, the informant against Yuri, was shot dead, assassinated whilst under the guard of the French Police."

"You are fucking joking me, right boss?" Harris exploded as he sat bolt upright.

"Gregor is dead, my house has blown up and everything is, 'fairy fantastic down in Dingley Dell,' according to the Commissioner's office? You are fucking joking me!" Harris tried his best to comprehend

Hemmings nodded, not once but twice.

Yuri had known all too well that pending a judicial investigation, defendants are able to have the judicial proceedings dismissed on procedural grounds. When, during the examining phase, where the evidence is weak and without witness, they tend to not reach the trial stage.

"And what about you?" Harris asked, "It's your name down as 'the handler' for Gregor the informant, you're the one that forwarded the information to the French authorities. What the fuck are they going to do about you?"

"Me?" Hemmings replied slyly. "Well you're right, because Gregor was officially my informant, just as you asked me to do, as of midnight last night I am on a paid leave of absence until I can take up my new post in a week's time."

Incredulous, Harris asked. "Where the fuck are you going?"

"Well let's see," Hemmings defended, "thanks to you I no longer have a marriage and that bit on the side you found out I was 'shagging,' she doesn't want me either." And, with ease, Hemmings calmly announced. "I've been offered a senior posting in Bermuda and I fly out as soon as."

There was silence, a long silence as Harris tried to evaluate, he had heard of such postings being available to serving British policeman, but he knew it was only the well-connected, those Masons, Catholic Guild even the 'old school tie brigade' that ever got to serve on that British Island off the east coast of the United States of America.

Harris remained silent as he bore witness to Hemmings flight and tried to gather his own thoughts as to what to do next.

It was a dead air that was finally broken by Hemmings. "I am off then, I'm gone, goodbye, au revoir and farewell." Harris saw that the bastard Hemmings was actually smiling as he spoke.

"Personally, I would run if I were you Harris." Hemmings warned as he leant over the detective and, taking and shaking the bewildered Harris' hand, he advised. "Run or think fast son, because I am in no doubt you are up shit creek without a paddle." With that he was gone and the door slammed shut behind him.

'Good riddance, Harris thought.

Chapter 35

Harris sat there for a long time. There were moments with his hands clasped on his head, there were moments where he took to scribbling notes and then there were moments where he kicked at the table legs. Kicking out at his imagined enemies. And there were plenty of moments where the unseen Harris would wipe a tear from his eyes.

'Run? Where? Run to? For fucks sake.' Harris sought answers as he desperately tried to launch himself from self-pity to regain a state of denial and potential survival.

It was obvious that Yuri would soon be a free man again, the main evidence against him had wafted away like smoke at the end of a gun barrel and he, Harris, knew he must also be suspected of being involved in Yuri's capture. Why else would his house get blown up?

"Fuck, fuck, fuck." Harris whispered as his mind began to melt until he kicked himself; he literally, deliberately, heeled his shin and kicked his other leg. He had known that all this 'shit' might happen when in those weeks before, he and Gregor had stashed drugs and explosives in Yuri's car, but had he prepared his alibi?

'Just because Gregor was dead,' Harris thought. 'Why did this change anything?'

'If anything, Gregor being dead was a distinct advantage.' Harris convinced himself as he continued to think of answers to this dire situation.

Hemmings was Gregor's 'handler' and he was buggering off, that meant that it was only Maya who also knew about Harris' involvement and she too had disappeared. Harris was alone and found himself offering up a prayer to a God that he never believed in, that Maya, one of Yuri's wives, remained long gone.

'I'm innocent.' he told himself, 'innocent, innocent!' And by God, Harris knew he had to act innocent.

--//--

Harris had eventually emptied the cardboard box with his name on and arranged his desk, all an act in, 'building up courage.'

He was to move on with his innocence and would carry on, 'as if nothing had happened,' he kept telling himself. 'Well, nothing that he knew about anyway.' And, as he took one last look at the filth strewn storeroom, he felt the disgust at the way he was being treated. He slammed the door shut on his fears on his way out.

Harris left the main building and walked out onto the surrounding industrial estate, quickly he took himself along to a small alleyway that led him to the local, raised bridge that crossed the small creek. There he knew he had good visibility all round and he knew it was a place where he couldn't be overheard.

Harris stood, circling his position as he pulled out his mobile phone and, searching the contacts list, he found the name and number he sought.

It was a phone call that Harris was dreading, but it was a phone call he needed to make if he was to survive the next few days. He also took out the piece of paper containing his scribbled notes and rang the number, he dialled Ivan, Yuri's second in command.

The call went through and Harris immediately noted that the dialling tone was an international number, the Detective wondered where Ivan might be, as the call rang dead.

Harris tried again, but it was this same result, it dialled through and rang until this time, an automated message service connected, "please leave a message after the tone."

By the time Harris rang for a third time he had formulated the message in his head, but he needn't have bothered, Ivan answered.

"Hello Ivan, how are you?" he asked. "How is Yuri? I've literally just heard the news that he's been arrested in France."

"Me? I've been on holiday sailing around the south coast."

"Missed calls, my phone? I left it at work, it's a works phone, and it doesn't belong to me, so I never take it away with me."

"So how is Yuri? Yeah, I heard he'd been shot, but he's okay? Ah good, that's good to know."

"What happened? Oh my God, really!"

"Listen Ivan, I don't know if you know, but my house blew up, yeah exploded, boom! Did I upset someone?"

"Yeah, we do need to talk, especially if you or your mates blew up my fucking house!"

"Of course, I'm fucking angry, wouldn't you be if your house blew up and you didn't know what the fuck was going on?"

"So, it had nothing to do with you?"

"Well, what about Yuri?"

"Okay, not over the phone, yeah we can meet, but not at my place, I don't fucking have one!"

"You know where I work? Yeah good, ring me whenever you get back from wherever the fuck you are."

Harris terminated the lies as he ended the call.

He stood there on the bridge and quickly rechecked the notes that he had scribbled; he purposefully made no mention of Gregor and, no, he hadn't mentioned Maya, why would he?

'Excellent.' Harris dared as he sighed relief and then with a jolt his phone rang, it was Ivan calling him back, a call Harris was expecting.

"No Ivan, I haven't heard from Gregor, I was going to call him if you hadn't answered."

"Maya, no I've not heard from her either, are they okay?"

"Oh okay, you have to go, well make sure you ring me soon."

"No, I don't know where I will be staying, I only got back last night, probably in a hotel again," he lied.

"Just ring me okay? Bye."

Harris again terminated the call, but this time and for the first time in two days he smiled. 'Operation shit creek.' he thought to himself, had just found a course to steer.

Chapter 36

It was mid-afternoon by the time Harris had decided to present himself to the new Chief Superintendent, A. Hutchings. He needed to discover for himself how disliked he was and at his door he knocked until he heard the call. "Come in."

For the next five minutes Harris listened to what his new boss expected of him.

"You will do this Arris, you will do that Arris and by Christ you will do whatever and go wherever and whenever I instruct you to do it Arris." Harris had found another who thought it cool to talk from the side of the mouth.

Then came the warnings; present, report, phone in, a tight leash, a bludgeoning. Harris was hearing from the friend of Pete Brown, the ex-inspector, the murderer and it was clear in those hate filled orders, but, at every appropriate moment, Harris simply nodded and answered. "Yes sir."

Harris already loathed this man and he knew that sooner or later, if Hutchings could have his way, 'Arris' was going to be sacked.

Harris was told to make himself available that afternoon for the fire investigation team to question him. Then, right there and then, he was told that he was on ten days leave, no pay, to sort out his current affairs.

"Any questions?" Chief A Hutchings concluded, not expecting any response, but all the same Harris looked up from the floor and asked. "Just one sir, would I be allowed to investigate..."

"No, you won't investigate anything, you are now an errand boy." Harris was stopped short as those harsh words cut across his question, leaving him nothing to say but, "Thank you for your time Sir." He closed the door behind him.

It was a short walk across the hallway to the men's toilets, Harris quickly checked that no one was in any of the cubicles before he took out his Dictaphone recording device from his inside jacket pocket. He spoke into the microphone stating the date and time and announcing whom he had just had the conversation with, before he pressed the stop button. He was preparing himself for constructive dismissal and all conversations with his new boss would have his tape recorder whirring away.

Chapter 37

The figure standing above the poor desperate young woman saw yet another tear, but this one didn't roll like the first one or two, or even the first dozen. This tear was just a small raised wave of glistening water that quickly flowed and dispersed over the already moist lines that ran to her cheeks, to her chin and beyond.

It was a trickled line of water that rippled along her flesh then dropped away to her naked body and the floor. Tears that were absorbed into the torn, scrap piece of carpet in that island of concrete that surrounded her, just beyond her cold trembling feet where she was being held up high on tip toe.

This tear had fallen as she gasped for air through the small hole of the thick masking tape that was wrapped round her mouth and, as she grasped for reality, she shook her head slowly, rhythmically, a beaten sway, uncontrollable in her fear of what had happened and petrified as to what was yet to come.

She tried so hard to look up at her arms, tightly bound, held aloft, the thin rope cutting, rasping her wrists, but there was little pain as her head filled with a heaviness of drugs and, though she tried, she couldn't quite focus on the large metal pulley in the ceiling girder that had pulled her up. Nor could she visualise where the rope had been tied off too, it simply faded into the darkness of beyond.

Why couldn't her body react, tense or move from those hands that caressed and squeezed her flesh without her permission?

She could sense her desperation, but her body was almost limp in response to the hands that groped her. Unresponsive and available to those two leather gloved hands that continued to squeeze her. Gloves that were worn by that hulk of a beast that wore a blue cloth boiler suit and pristine polished black boots. Masked in a combination of sewn sack and diamond patchwork eyes that sucked tight around the beast's head, a head that breathed hard and fast, one that grunted from within.

She closed her eyes to, once again, concentrate, to form the words. "Please no," but as she pleaded from within the confines of the masking tape all that was vocalised was an incomprehensible, slurred, mumbled fear. She closed her eyes again as her body was pushed and swung and her toes barely touched the nylon carpet until she swayed to a stop. Then, with every grasp of her flesh, her head lolled in failure and more tears formed. Slowly, but slowly, as her nakedness jerked with the pinch of every mishandled squeeze from the beast the deep grunts grew faster and louder and blackness filled her mind towards unconsciousness.

Chapter 38

Harris took a tube on the District line to his appointment in East Ham to speak to the London Fire Brigade Fire Investigation Team and the Metropolitan Police Fire Investigation Unit. However, he had no answers to give them. They in turn had theories, but were as perplexed as he was. However, when Harris asked for closure, he was told. "The investigation will continue." In no uncertain terms and, on the instructions his new Superintendent, he found out that the Counter Terrorism Command SO15 would also be showing an interest.

That was the last thing Harris wanted to hear, for he knew from his policy, like almost all policies, that 'acts of terrorism,' were not covered in his buildings insurance and Harris seethed at this, his boss' spite.

On leaving Harris contacted his bank to find out who his house was insured with, he direct debited everything, he never had the time or inclination to 'shop around' for better deals and though the bank was useful, his insurance company was not.

They were already aware of Harris' situation as his new boss had taken it upon himself to contact Lloyd's of London, the corporate body of insurance, to find out who held his policy, ['The bastard,' he thought], when they had been told of the Detective's predicament.

Harris listened to what was obviously a prepared speech, his, the most basic of policies, where there was no legal assistance and no alternative accommodation, the list went on and Harris, 'turned off,' from the negativity. Only when they asked for proof as to where he was on the day of the explosion, did Harris terminate the call.

Harris was fuming, "the fucking twats." He said out loud, looking at his inert phone. But, they had a point, 'where was he?' and he knew he'd have to cover his tracks.

Neither of the fire investigation teams had asked him where he had been the day of the explosion, all they wanted to know was how old the gas pipes were, where were they laid and had Harris left anything 'on' by mistake?

No, Harris knew he would have to cover his tracks, not only for the sake of his insurance company, but the Russians would surely want to know.

Harris took a tube ride back to Elm Park. He needed to see whether his car was still where he had left it and, if so, was it driveable? But, when he arrived, his car was gone and he could barely look at where his house had once stood. There was practically nothing left of it and not much left of the houses on either side, barring newly erected scaffolding.

In fact, most of the houses in the near vicinity had suffered some form of blast damage, some houses had windows boarded up, and one house even had a piece of Harris' beams embedded in its roof.

As for the cars parked nearby, many of the usual cars were missing, whilst others had tarpaulin wraps to cover where there were once windscreens and side windows.

Harris also noticed that no neighbour came out from their homes to meet him as he stood there all alone, alone with his mind fogged in shocked bewilderment. However, glancing up and down the street at all the damage, he could feel their presence, those various faces staring out from behind closed curtains at him, all afraid of what had happened. Harris was sickened at the thought of what might have been, but it was a, 'lucky escape,' no injured, no dead. A mere two minutes later he left the vacant plot and the road where his car once stood.

On returning to the Moby Dick he walked behind the bar and took the stairs to the first-floor bathroom and he just stared at his own reflection in the mirror. Harris tried to recognise himself, but this 6-foot frame of a shaven headed brute looked vacant, as his eyes stared back at him. His mind felt shallow, small and for once insecure. He knew he needed a good chat to himself.

Harris looked and looked into his eyes, into his thoughts and though he had nothing to stay in London for but his pride, that was in dire need of help. He couldn't run, only the guilty ran and without a doubt the Russians would conclude this and hunt him down.

'No Harris don't let the bastards grind you down,' he kept telling himself as he choked back what he thought to be tears.

'Be strong, be that bastard and, most of all, be the Detective that you are,' he urged himself. Over and over he repeated. 'Be strong,' and the tears never fell. Nor from then on, if it could be helped, 'nor would he fall.' He told himself.

--//--

The next morning Harris came down to a hearty English breakfast, Tina had cooked a huge 'fry up' for him.

'Double of everything,' filled his plate and Harris suddenly discovered his appetite, not having eaten for so long he devoured it and, three coffees later, having scanned the local classified vehicle advertisements, he made various phone calls.

Having kissed his host on either cheek he thanked her for her hospitality.

"I was never here." Harris said with a wry grin.

"Who are you?" Temptress Tina replied and both smiled as he handed back the keys to the room upstairs. As for the money, Harris asked her to keep it in the safe and she agreed. Then, going upstairs, he packed his rucksack with the few clothes and sundries he had and left.

He caught a train to Romford, where, close to the Town Hall, he visited a house and, armed with the classified paper, he haggled his first purchase of the day.

It was an old and battered White Ford transit van with double backdoors and a side door, it even a hatch door that led from the cab to the rear unit. 'Ideal,' he thought, as he realised that the rear unit was of a size that would easily hold a double size mattress and, that's what he bought next. A duvet, a couple of pillows, a gas stove, a camping kettle, coffee and mug. By midday his diesel-powered home navigated its way along the A12 towards the Essex coast.

He headed towards the marina where he had first bought the yacht 'Sofia Summer,' just those short weeks previously. On arrival, he sought out and apologised to the local harbourmaster for staying and not paying for his yacht's berth from two days earlier. The grey bearded harbourmaster was unquestioningly grateful and issued him a receipt for the £15 payment, even though he couldn't actually remember the yacht at all. It was the same problem for the other harbourmasters at the other marinas Harris visited, where he would receive receipts for progressive dates that stretched south along the Essex coastline.

Various amounts, various back-dated receipts, each within a plausible day's sail of each other and by midnight that evening Harris had crossed the Queen Elizabeth Bridge and completed half the County of Kent.

The next day was much the same, more baffled harbourmasters smiling at Harris' honesty and still more and more receipts. From Kent into Sussex and, finally, Hampshire. More marinas were visited and Harris even had the audacity to ferry himself a return trip to the Isle of Wight for even more receipts.

For the next two days Harris did little else but drive back along the same sailing route, this time he would stop at other Marinas to mislead his yacht's passage homeward. He would also note down local eateries and public houses and, every so often, he would pull over in his makeshift mobile home and write notes, formulating the multiple variations on his voyage of lies. All this, so that given 'half a chance' to explain to the Russians, he could evidence his betrayal.

That final night, having checked the receipts against the numerous marine charts that he had purchased, he made sure that all the relevant receipts were neatly folded away in his wallet. Then he made out a false bill of sale for the sale of his yacht, selling it to an indecipherable scribbled name on the day he that had returned to the UK from Spain and then, at last, unlike those previous nights in his van, he slept soundly.

--//--

Even though it was midweek and he wasn't due back into work for a couple of days, it was at 6am that Harris woke to the alarm tone on his phone. Stirring, he couldn't help but hear the rumble of trucks driving overhead on the overpass of the A406 that stood directly above the car park to the Murder Squad offices.

The detective stretched and, just for a moment, sat idle. However, it wasn't long before Harris gathered himself and dressed quickly to jog over to the gym and shower block. He shaved, showered and scented so that he would feel 'fresh' for the day ahead.

He could have gone back to the coast, to relax, to chill, but Harris knew he could do neither as he thought of the Sword of Damocles that swung above his head. No, he really had no option but to keep his mind active and, on returning to his van, he opened the glove box, took out the Grant Smith file and took this with him to his storeroom office.

Again, Harris scanned the pages and again his thoughts stirred towards the photograph that showed that folded ticket on the floor. He was convinced it was folded in the same way as that at the Forrester murder scene.

Having once more closed the file Harris found himself, 'on a mission.'

He went to the murder squad exhibits room, a mini warehouse filled to the brim, an extended secure closed area set towards the rear of the building on the ground floor. This vast block comprised of a sterile drying room where blood soaked clothes would be hung before packaging, there was also a sterile packaging area and a photographic table that directed attention towards presentation at court. But what took up the most space were the nine individual locked cages where each team kept their exhibits post and prior court. Harris walked directly to Cage 3.

Cage 3 represented Team 3 and it was Team 3 that Harris had helped before he set sail to find Maya. The double murder of Mr and Mrs Forrester, who were found in their car, where Harris had discovered that the murderer of Mr Forrester had attempted to make his part a suicide.

Harris knew where the spare key to the lock was, he knew because all spare keys were hidden there, a signed and sealed envelope precaution. It was taped, with others, to the underside of the photographic table.

Within seconds he was in the cage rummaging through the various murder scene exhibit books until he found the reference to the folded-up ticket. Box 33, Book 1, entry 179. He took several minutes of moving crated, stacked boxes around until he reached Box 33, feeling relief when he opened the box flaps and saw the bloodstained ticket that he thought had dropped from Mrs Forrester.

It was still untouched, just as he had found it on the grass when he lifted her body away from the car, an exhibit that wasn't there before he lifted her.

Harris shook his head in disgust; the ticket was still folded in on each corner and folded again and again as he had first seen it. Whoever the exhibit officer was who was now in charge of these exhibits must have just glanced at this object and simply noted it as scene debris, of no substance to the investigation. This infuriated Harris.

For many a year Harris had realised the ineptitude of some of his colleagues, for it was he who had first realised the worth of scene examination by a Detective rather than using a Uniformed Police Constable. A position of status, rather than store man, but even Detectives were blind to the obvious.

Harris knew he had to work fast as it was now approaching 7 am, when the building would start to be manned. He double gloved each hand and, with his mobile phone on camera stand-by, he began to unfold the ticket whilst it remained within the clear sealed exhibit bag.

Why not single gloved? Well he knew if he did, his fingerprint may perforate onto the sealed bag and within. There was no way he wanted his fingerprints to be connected to the ticket, so, double gloved he was, his assurance of anonymity.

With each fold turned back, black hardened blood mixed with fluid would crack from the creases and Harris would take yet another photograph. These extra creases appeared to preserve the details and, several photographs later, Harris was just a little perplexed as to the date stamped age of the train ticket. Over thirty years ago, on a single journey from Heathrow to Central London and Harris' mobile phone camera focussed in on the serial number as he clicked away.

Suddenly Harris became aware of echoed footsteps walking the long corridor towards the exhibit store. He rushed to re-fold the ticket, re-box the exhibit, close and lock Team 3's cage. He actually shuddered at the thought of being found out, but he managed to lock the cage just in time, as the exhibit store door opened and Bob walked in.

Bob, a Crime Scene Manager' (CSM), whom Harris had met and 'walked' through his first murder scene. He was all smiles when he saw Harris standing there in front of him. Harris clasped his hands tight behind his back, hidden because he was hiding the fact that still wore the gloves. Harris was nervous as he attempted such small talk, but, having exchanged pleasantries, Bob walked passed and Harris continued to turn, to hide his blue latex hands. Not until Bob turned the corner towards another cage did he return the key and flee.

Harris couldn't help himself but run down that same corridor, ripping the plastic gloves from his hands as he did so.

'Fuck that was close!' His mind told him and the pounds in his heart agreed, but, he had got away, practically unscathed. He felt sure he was safe when he drew breath and threw the gloves in a nearby bin. Little did he know that Bob had reported seeing Harris, back early from leave to Chief Superintendent Hutchings.

Later he found himself in the queue of the, 'do it yourself,' sales warehouse. It was the first building situated on the industrial road where the Murder Squad office was situated.

He bought himself a security door bolt and a crosshead screwdriver and, having returned to his cupboard, for the next half hour he was fixing this to the inside of his door.

"Sod them all." He thought, as he pulled across the latch, securing him inside.

Harris sat at his desk noting his earlier photographic captures of the train ticket, he wrote down the date, the time and the serial number that it showed and added it to the Grant-Smith file.

Placing the file in the middle of an old police magazine that had been left discarded in the storeroom, Harris was off, on his way to the storage facility at Mandela Way.

Harris decided on public transport, where he could be lost in a crowd and therefore walked from the murder squad building towards Barking station. The same route that took in a bridge leading to a council estate, a route where he noted a surreal silence. Those that worked had left for the day, those that remained, remained hidden. Then there was a pathway, a footstep and a movement behind, a presence.

Harris felt the hairs on his neck stiffen, there was someone back there, keeping pace with his, but who? Was it the Russians? Or yet another surveillance team on his back? He hoped for the latter, the lesser of two evils.

The closer he got to Barking town centre, the more he was convinced it was surveillance. He waited and backtracked, window shopped for reflections and by the time he reached the station he had 'clocked' three men and a woman who purposefully paid him no attention as they passed by. Each of them, he witnessed, held a clenched fist that no doubt hid a remote talk button that they would activate on each 'sighting.'

Harris smiled, it wasn't the Russians and as he boarded the first tube towards Central London he began a well-rehearsed routine of jumping on and off train carriages all the way to the Elephant and Castle.

Harris would ruin their day, he was confident and having been subject to an internal investigation just those few short months before, he was well practised in the art of counter-surveillance.

Harris' leather jacket was old, he'd owned it for, 'God knows,' how many years and with age it had developed small rips and tears, even to the inner lining, and it was those tears to the inner lining, near his chest, that he made two slightly larger.

His outer, left jacket pocket began to rummage as his left hand quickly dismantled his mobile phone. Removing the battery and Sim card, he slipped the phone and battery into the two large holes that freefell to the base stitching of his jacket. As for the Sim card, he slipped this into another small tear, situated on the outer right forearm. He then squeezed and prised the Sim card to the base stitching of the wrist.

'Now they wouldn't be able to triangulate his movements.' Harris smirked as he congratulated himself.

An hour later Harris was thinking. 'That poor woman,' as he giggled goodbye to her frustration. A second earlier he had leapt onto the platform just as the train doors closed shut at London Bridge. He turned back to see that woman, who he had seen twice earlier that morning, mouth the words, "fuck you," as the tube pulled away. 'Mind you, she was quite pretty,' he thought.

This latest action left Harris standing alone on the late morning platform and he didn't hesitate. Quickly the Detective ran up the escalators to the station exit and, flashing his identification to the tube worker on the gate, passed through and, after two minutes of quick sprints a left here and a right here and there, the Detective found a café for a well-deserved late breakfast.

Harris found a table tucked away out of sight of the road outside and enjoyed a small wicker basket of bacon sandwiches and 2 cups of coffee. Sometime later he emerged onto the street, happy in the knowledge that by now the surveillance team would have dissipated into the shadows to write up their notes on their 'loss.'

However, he wasn't going to take any chances and again took to the use of the backstreets and alleyways. It would be to his advantage as he made progress towards Southwark and his final destination.

--//--

As Harris arrived at the first-floor reception area he spoke to the female receptionist who asked him to wait as he hadn't an appointment.

Of course, he hadn't made an appointment, he wasn't going to leave a trail of crumbs as to his whereabouts, or to the fact he was investigating when only days before he was ordered not to.

All Harris asked was that the receptionist speak to, 'Foxy,' the manager, an old friend who would hurry things along. The lady agreed and within five minutes Harris and Foxy were smiling, exchanging pleasantries, in his backroom office. Harris knew he could trust Foxy, he had worked with him before when Harris had to remove murder scene exhibits, too large for normal vehicle transportation. Harris used this friendship and trust when asking to look at the Grant-Smith exhibits. Foxy agreed and Harris passed him the various reference numbers. The hours passed as Harris examined each and every exhibit seized from that poor girl's flat.

Harris was again double gloved whilst he examined everything; 'no way on god's earth,' did he want his fingerprints to be found on these sealed packages.

189

The first pallet box contained, 'items on her person,' and, for a while, Harris was fixated on the plastic bag that had covered her face, her death mask, on which he believed he could still see dried saliva globules where her mouth had sucked its last breath. Then there was the belt, 'definitely a man's belt,' Harris noted and, borrowing a tape measure, he followed the swirls of leather, noting the length from the buckle to the heavy crease mark on one of the eyelets. Harris calculated that it came from a possible 32-inch waist, definitely not from the victim, who was only a female dress size 6 to 8 at best.

The next pallet box contained her personal effects and clothing and Harris soon realised that everything in the young girl's wardrobe was expensive, demure and pale to match her skin tone. Chanel, Gucci and Prada labels were in all of them; even her underwear bore the same labels.

Harris also noted that the clothing had been bagged at the scene and, on checking the exhibit books stored with them, there were no remarks as to them being searched; this was something he would have to come back to, he decided.

Then there was her artwork; she was good Harris surmised, nice paintings of landscapes, fields of flowers, forests of green and blue wash sea coves, but just simply 'nice, refined,' just like her clothing and not to Harris' taste, if he had any.

The last pallet box was the, 'scene exhibits,' those items that had been found scattered around her bedroom, student-type scattering, not ransacked as her parents believed, difficult to debate, but Harris just knew. However, there was one small, plastic, sealed bag that Harris had been waiting to find, its content similar to what he had found at the Foresters car scene, it was what looked like another train ticket.

However, it wasn't just another train ticket. Yes, it had been opened up previously for examination, but the folded crease marks were near identical to those he had photographed that morning in the exhibit store at Barking.

No, this didn't cause the shivers to run through the Detective's 6ft frame, this didn't cause Harris' heart to miss a beat, the Detective's knees simply buckled beneath him when he focussed on what was now a harrowing detail. The same date, time on the same single train journey from Heathrow to Central London, only five serial number purchases from Mrs Forrester's ticket.

Harris found he couldn't breathe, he tried, he tried, but his mind wouldn't let him. His brain was still trying to realise what he had unearthed and breathing was the last thing he focussed on.

Harris just stared at the ticket and tried to process what was happening, 'so many years apart,' he kept saying to himself and yet, "what the fuck?" These were the only words he vocalised as his body suddenly screamed for air.

Harris needed to sit, no seat, the floor then and there he sat until at last he took a breath and focussed on the ticket again. This time his hands trembled so much that he couldn't read the detail, he quickly placed the ticket on the ground and again opened the file to the notes that he had written that morning and there he took in the confirmation of his discovery.

Harris made quick use of Foxy's photocopying machine and it was gone closing time at the Mandela Way storage facility when Harris finally returned to Foxy's managerial office. Treasuring the sealed bag with the Grant-Smith ticket Harris asked the manager, his friend, to keep it set aside, secure in the warehouse, safe amongst the vast quantities of money and jewellery, for this, this exhibit to Harris, was truly priceless.

As Harris left he couldn't stop looking back towards the storage facility, his heart and head were beating, both painfully fast, he didn't realise, but he was actually in shock. He needed a drink though, he needed to celebrate and he needed to try to get his, 'head around,' his discovery.

Harris walked back towards London Bridge where he had seen a pub, the Pommelers Rest, 'quite apt,' Harris thought, for he felt like a boxer who had been pummelled mercilessly against the ropes, reeling from the magnitude that he had unearthed, a link between two deaths so many years apart.

'Were there more?' He asked himself as he drank his first pint down in one open throat and arm movement. By his third pint he actually hoped there would be and on his sixth pint he had convinced himself that there must be! He was going to start looking.

It was 10 o'clock before Harris realised the time and he knew he still had a journey in front of him, so, finishing his last pint amongst the surrounding throng of revellers, he gingerly stood from the table that he had occupied for the last few hours and, concentrating, managing one step in front of the other, he walked to the exit.

Harris didn't care what the other passengers on the tube train thought of him as he sat there smiling and giggling to himself; he alone had linked two deaths, both were murders, the Fiona Grant-Smith wasn't a sexual misadventure, he was positive, but still he needed to prove it and the same murderer had struck again on Mrs Forrester, but, as for Mr Forrester, he wasn't so sure.

It was past eleven thirty as Harris entered the industrial estate towards the Barking Murder Squad offices and the last thing he remembered whilst walking the deserted pavement towards the offices and his van, was the sound of footsteps of someone behind. He had no time to react as the first volts of a stun gun, pressed against his neck, hit him, buckling him to the concrete, another zap, then another, then darkness.

Chapter 39

Harris stirred, he couldn't see and he dare not speak, but in his awareness, he realised that his head was now wrapped in layers of adhesive tape. He had no vision, wrapped, bound tight, but his nose was free to breathe and when he tried to suck air in through his mouth there must have been a small hole to do so.

'Welcome to Shit Creek,' he told himself.

He felt sure, he just knew, he was in the hands of the Russians.

He was on a chair, his body felt that, he also knew he was naked and could feel a cold porcelain rim encircling his buttocks. 'Weird,' he thought. He tried both feet in turn; both were held against their will as he pulled the hairs on his legs as he tried to raise one foot, then the other. He realised that these too had been wrapped in tape from the ankle to halfway up his shin. 'No chance of running then, he was stuck fast,' his mind told him.

Both arms were adhered on the hard-wooden armrests, again taped, securing his elbow through his wrists and, although could freely move his fingers, both his thumbs were also held against their will, again taped, he felt, but there was something else, possibly wire, possibly a cable tie that held his hands in place.

He pushed himself back against the frame of the chair and felt a velvet type material touch his skin and enclosing the inner frame, it was a material that curved in and out with studded regularity and then with his shoulder blades he was able to push into a couple of the curves and he confirmed the stud buttons. Harris finally realised what he was sitting on an antiquated commode.

'Well he wasn't dead, not yet, quite a result really.' He surmised with wry wit, but as he heard the start of a whirring noise, some kind of an industrial machine far away to his left, that echoed in his ears; spinning out those noisy decibels, he also realised that calling out for help was pointless.

Then there was the smell, air rancid with dust and dirt, old air, heavy air tainted with an odour of metal that reminded him of his engineering lessons at his old secondary school. Only his old school had wooden floors and Harris' feet were freezing from the concrete that his toes and soles rubbed against.

"I'm fucking naked, sitting on a commode, in some sort of warehouse and I'm busting for a pee, su-fucking-perb!" He growled.

Harris' bladder was full to bursting, but he wasn't going to piss, he wasn't going to let his captors know he was now conscious, no, he was going to listen as best he could. His wasn't going to be the first voice that would speak. He knew there had to be someone there, someone to start that whirring machine only moments ago, but he sat motionless and silent as a breeze, from what must have been an open window above, caused his exposed body to 'goose bump' with the cold.

Pain without warning; that was the detective's next sense, a sharp blow across the chest causing Harris to drag his feet as the chair slid backwards on its wheels.

A whimpered, "fuck you." Sounding like a ventriloquist's dummy came from the taped mouth of the detective, wincing in pain, as the tall man standing in front of the officer wielded the baseball bat once more. Witnessed by others, the Russian took another swing striking Harris' stomach.

"Fuck you and your mother." Harris coughed out in pain from the confines of the tape as yet another blow struck his chest and until the man wielding the wooden bat finally spoke, in his mother tongue, a language the detective new only too well. Yes, he was indeed in the grip of the Russians, but who?

"Ivan, Gregor, is that you?" Harris had rehearsed well and repeated those same names while he pissed into the porcelain. Then the next sickening blow, again to the stomach, but this didn't stop him urinating his excesses from the night before into the porcelain splashback and this time Harris screamed, wracked in pain, but still managed to call out the two men's names.

Still there was no answer, just a conversation between the man in front of him and those that were looking on some distance away and then another blow struck Harris across the chest and he felt the loud 'crack' in his rib cage that creased him over in agony. But then, suddenly, as quickly as the beating had started, it stopped.

Harris was in torment, in gut wrenching pain, his midriff burned as he tried not to breathe and, between his grunts, he heard the softened footsteps that walked away from him.

Harris knew, just knew, that through those internal screams of his mind he had to repeat those names and through each spasm of breath he called out to the silence. "Ivan, Gregor, why?"

For half an hour Harris sat in uncontrollable pain, he could feel that his eyes had welled in tears within the adhesive tape and it took the next half hour of short controlled breaths before most of the pain had ebbed away. It was on the hour, through the machinery noise, he heard a number of softened footsteps walking back towards him.

Harris again asked. "Ivan, Gregor, why?"

Harris suddenly realised the chair was being held in place by a number of hands, but he didn't know why until he felt a slice of something short and sharp dig into the base, right side edge of his right thumbnail and upward it sliced to its tip.

Harris fucking screamed and screamed and the commode shook as Harris' feet tried to push into concrete, push away the pain. The Russian went to the other side and dug the scalpel deeper beside the nail edge deeper into the skin and Harris' screams continued as the man pulled the scalpel up through skin, meat and sinew to the tip of Harris' thumb.

"Why?" Harris screamed as the Russian began to repeat the insertion of stainless steel scalpel on the nail base of his bloodied thumb.

"Please God why?" Harris pleaded as the Russian again tugged the scalpel through Harris' skin.

"Where is Maya?" a voice questioned. "Where is that bitch?" The voice demanded.

"How the fuck should I know?" Harris exasperated. "I haven't seen her in weeks, not since Yuri's birthday, please stop." He pleaded.

The scalpel, having done its work on both sides and bases, now pierced the tip of Harris' thumb pushing the blade length deep into the thumb and it began to slice across its width from one side to the other, Harris screeched. "Please no!" As again his body convulsed from the pain.

The blade was used in a saw-like motion until it reached the other side and Harris could feel the scalpel lifting the skin and nail upward, remaining barely attached and the pain was excruciating.

"I'm telling you I don't know where Maya is." Harris urged as the Russian produced a pair of pliers from his back pocket and, clamping down between thumb nail and skin, it squeezed a hold.

"I don't know where she is, get Yuri or Ivan or Gregor, this isn't right what you're doing." Harris pleaded, but he was stopped short.

The commode was held tight as the Russian, with a slow deliberate grip, pulled back on the nail, twisting the pliers he ripped the nail from its roots until it was finally done, the Russian held Harris' thumbnail, with flesh and root, in the palm of his hand. He walked away from the officer's tormented cries.

Harris felt the chair release from its grasp and other footsteps walked away talking and laughing to each other.

"Fuck that smarts." Harris whispered to himself, but at least he now knew it was Yuri's men that held him and not anyone else from the countless criminal enemies Harris had made over the years. 'By Jesus,' did his thumb throb!

Harris wasn't happy that he had another nineteen potential moments of excruciating pain to come, but at least he wasn't dead and, because they wanted to know where Maya was, it meant they were clueless as to her whereabouts.

Mind you, so was he, which was a plus, because he couldn't say what he didn't know and, more importantly, they were willing to communicate. This gave Harris options.

An hour later Harris was screaming obscenities at the loss of his right forefinger nail, again grabbed and held tight whilst the same Russian went to work with his scalpel and pliers. There were the same questions. "Where's Maya, where is she?"

But this time between each incision and the occasional punch to the head, Harris' only reply was, "where is Gregor, where is Ivan?" And Harris, having had this nail pulled, concluded, "I will speak to them only?"

That announcement received a large flurry of blows to his head, face and other body parts before the Russians walked away, leaving Harris coughing on his own blood.

Harris felt his head spinning over the next three hours as each nail was cut and ripped from his right hand. The nausea had filled his throat and bile could be seen dripping from the hole in his taped mouth. The Russians laughed at the fact that Harris was having to swallow his own sick in order to survive, but survive he did and on the fifth removal he refused to talk further.

'If I survive I will get all you motherfuckers.' Harris kept telling himself through the pain of breathing, as anger and adrenaline overcame his injuries.

That next hour came and went to the instant before he heard the footsteps approach and Harris braced himself in readiness for his left hand.

'Hello, what the fuck?' Was Harris' immediate thoughts as he felt his penis being lifted from his scrotum sack. He soon screamed!

"No! No! God, no!" When he realised that two metal clips now clasped his scrotum at either side and, at the end of these, an electronic shock machine. The Detective screamed his loudest when the button was pressed, just before he passed out in pain.

Harris had no idea as to what the time was when he woke, but he knew it was either night-time or a new day for the room was even colder than before and as he tried to recall reason, his mind shut out the pain that took him to unconsciousness once more.

--//--

Harris woke and found he could yawn, not only that, but he could spit out the bile that had remained between teeth and gums and he was thankful that the tape been removed from around his mouth.

'How long have I been out for?' He wondered as he now winced at the various injuries to his body and, the still remembered, burning sensation to his manhood.

Once more Harris called out, either "Ivan" or "Gregor" but not as loudly as he would have wished for, for the wound in breathing had intensified and Harris wondered what else exactly was broken within him.

He listened out for an answer, but there was no reply. Just the same familiar sound of the whirring machine, the gusting breeze from ventilation above and, just as he sighed, he could hear the same recognisable soft footsteps walking towards him.

This time the Russian held a large bucket of cold water and simply poured it over the detective to heighten his awareness, Harris was grateful and he lapped, swallowed and spat his sickness away. Wondering what was next as again the footsteps walked away.

Harris didn't have to wait long to find out, perhaps only five or ten minutes before the soft footsteps returned, walking around behind him, the Russian lent down whispering the same question, "where is Maya?"

"I'm late for work." Harris replied defiantly.

"Then I will work on you some more," the Russian replied as he began to wheel Harris across the warehouse floor.

"I will only speak to Ivan, Gregor or Yuri you fuckwit!" Harris snarled as he felt the many hands reclining the wheeled commode, his urine from the bowl beneath lapped over him, which was some relief to his burnt testicles, as the back of the chair was laid flat back on the floor.

Harris heard a flowing, a steady flow, but he didn't know what it was as the soft footed Russian walked forward with a hosepipe. Another of them knelt behind Harris' head, clamping hard against each temple, holding him in place whilst another folded an old, rag cloth in his hands and handed it to the kneeler.

Harris could smell the stains on the cloth as it was held over his nose and mouth, the strongest was that of old oil, but he had no chance to decipher the others for Harris' nose and throat was now being filled with water, a constant stream that Harris closed his throat to and close it he did for several seconds. That was until a punch to his chest opened his airway and he began to drown.

Harris could hear the words. "Where is Maya?" These was repeated over and over again, but Harris didn't have an answer; he couldn't formulate one even if he knew, his lungs were filling and his mind was emptying.

He was floating on a garden of cloud as both Maya and he lay naked next to each other, she feeding him black grapes mouth to mouth, arms, legs and their bodies entwined as they kissed.

Harris suddenly came too with a jolt, the chair had been lifted with such speed that it helped Harris force most of the water from his half-filled lungs and he choked, spluttered and sickened each painful breath through broken ribs until at last he managed a short nod of his head in recognition of the questions and coughed out each word "Ivan," "Gregor," "Yuri."

Chapter 40

Harris didn't know how long he'd been unconscious, he just knew it was some time or some days later. 'Soft shoe,' and those bastards had gone to work on Harris, repeating the drowning process at least four more times before his brain had shutdown, pushing all images and recollection to blackness.

Now he just sat there slouched, still on the commode, still in a world of agony and in immense pain, Harris pushed himself up to an angle where breathing was easier and in his mind, to a position of convincing himself that he had said nothing to the Russians.

Controlling his fear, he just sat and waited for the next onslaught to his body and brain. Still the whirring machine droned on, but he knew he was in a different part of the warehouse for the breeze was now behind him and, as Harris constantly moved his frame in order to breathe easier, there was no more attention being paid to him, no 'Soft shoe,' no nothing, just emptiness, just loneliness as Harris tried to figure what was coming next.

The hours past slowly as the fear of unknowing churned into Harris, but still they passed and still nothing, only guessing at what might well be the outcome, but again still nothing as Harris fell into a deep, welcomed sleep.

The next thing the detective knew was that his six-foot frame was, once again, being wheeled along the concrete floor towards angry Russian voices. One voice was raised above the others as it screamed foreign abuse, it was the pitch of voice that Harris recognised immediately. It was Ivan.

Harris was halted and he felt scissors cutting into the tape at the back of his head, one of the blades dug into his scalp that drew a wince from Harris and a further tirade of abuse from Ivan. Now, inwardly, Harris recognised that he had a chance.

"Harris, it is me Ivan, do not open your eyes until you can adjust the light, do you understand." Harris nodded a slowly, emphasising the trauma his body had endured.

Harris felt the taping being pulled away; relieving the pressure from his temples and forehead, pulling at eyebrow and eyelash hair it was finally peeled from him.

"Ivan." Harris spoke in one breath,

"What is it my friend?" Ivan replied.

"Kill these bastards please." he toyed and Ivan laughed.

Opening his eyes slowly, blinking focus and recognition into his pupils, Harris could see for the first time in God knows how many days, there in a chair in front of him sat Yuri's number one aide, Ivan, who drew breath on a cigarette that he offered to Harris, who declined with a shake of the head.

"Why?" Harris asked. "What the fuck?" He drew another sharp breath. "What have I done to deserve this?" he asked.

"It is simple Detective Harris, Yuri, as you would say was 'set up' and he wants answers." Ivan explained.

"Where is Maya? I don't know." Harris spoke painfully as he adjusted himself to breathe. "I have nothing to do with this." he bristled.

"Where have you been these last weeks?" Ivan questioned.

Trying to control each word with a breath. "Sailing, wallet, receipts where I stayed." Harris answered in wracked pain.

Ivan spoke short, sharp words in Russian to those that stood behind; Ivan was clearly focussing beyond the naked broken man in front of him., Harris looked up to see Ivan stand and take Harris' wallet from the man behind him.

"Receipts, where I stayed, on my yacht." Harris panted as Ivan took out a wad of various voucher type receipts showing overnight stays in overnight ports.

"Where was your phone, why did you not answer my calls?" Ivan's tone urged.

"Turned off, as always, I was on holiday, I rang you when I got back for fuck sake." Harris' breathing pained him as these words slowly drew recognition with a nod from Ivan's head.

"There is a problem Detective." Ivan announced.

"Yuri's car was found by the French police to have various bags of drugs and explosives in it and his fingerprints are on a couple of the bags." Harris nodded acknowledgement.

"You see, the bags, Yuri thinks, were like the bags of coins you gave to Yuri as a birthday present." Ivan further explained.

"The fifty gold sovereigns, in fifty plastic bags?" Harris confirmed to which Ivan nodded.

"Keys, my keys?" Harris asked, again he was trying to lean where it least pained and from scuffling behind him Harris saw the keys passed over his shoulder and handed to Ivan.

"Chunky one, the brass one." Harris said as Ivan held up the ring of keys.

"Yes, that one." Harris confirmed as Ivan held it aloft.

"It's the key to my garage behind my house, the briefcase, all fifty bags are in it." Harris just stared at Ivan, a stare of anger, of indignation, of contempt and loathing.

"Get me to a fucking hospital!" Harris demanded to Ivan, who now sat open mouthed.

Ivan stood there for a moment before he barked orders to those around him and, turning to Harris, he said, "I will be back in two hours, get yourself cleaned up." And with a pensive nod he left.

Harris began to survey his surroundings where he saw the metal lathe being switched off by one of his larger captors whilst being cut free by another. All his arm and leg hairs were ripped free as he was tugged from his bindings, quite painful, but Harris didn't wince, for by now he had experienced far worse.

He looked closely at this man, this toothless wiry Russian, a tattooed neck, wearing moccasin shoes.

'Soft shoes,' Harris stared at his face and features, a face he would never forget.

'I will find time for you.' He thought.

Harris counted that in all there were three other men in the warehouse, a building that was devoid of anything other than the metal lathe, two chairs, a small table and, of course, the commode on which he sat. He looked at the other captors; each built from Russian granite and each in turn smiling and nodding at the officer.

After speaking to each other Harris was raised from the chair and, with small tentative footsteps, he was assisted towards a small doorway beside an office door, both set aside from the main warehouse. It was a door that showed an image of a showerhead and as it was pushed open there was indeed a shower that was being turned on by one of the men for Harris.

Within seconds the room began to steam with heat and Harris was placed into the cubicle where he gripped both hands on a small chrome rail that helped him keep his balance as he soaked in the warmth.

Harris was glad when he was left alone in the shower room, he was alone to clean the cherry red and brown dried blood from each of his right fingers, his face and head, but most of all he was glad he was alone to wipe the unseen tears from his eyes.

Harris knew what Ivan would find once he had unlocked his garage as he thoughtfully recalled the night he had returned from Gibraltar:

It wasn't a bright beam that had emanated from his garage torch, it didn't need to be, the glow soon found the briefcase that Harris had sought and clicking open its catches he opened the case. It was the case that had contained 50 gold sovereigns in their own plastic bags, half Harris had subsequently used in helping Gregor frame Yuri and there was twenty-five he counted, confirming that they still remained within.

Harris had used 50 bags for 50 coins, but only used 25 of them to help fill with cocaine, C4 explosive and dozens of detonators that he and Gregor secreted in, around and under Yuri's limousine. That limousine, that Harris had organised Gregor to buy, that very same car that the French gendarmes had captured Yuri with.

Harris had wisely kept 25 of them in reserve in the briefcase, quietly congratulating himself, having remembered wise words, "never put all your eggs in one basket."

That night Harris had counted out another 25 untouched bags from the large pile he had removed from Yuri's safe and, scrunching them tight to show 'fair' usage, he simply added them to the briefcase.

Now Harris could, 'stand innocent, stand tall,' though in that shower, he could hardly stand at all.

However, having been able to plead his innocence to Ivan there was now proof of his claim. "No, not me, not I."

--//--

There was an old grubby towel that Harris used to dry himself and he did this as best he could, though bending over only increased the pain to agony when he breathed and eventually he couldn't help himself but collapse to his knees, then onto all fours.

From there he tried to pull up his jeans, he didn't care much about buttoning his shirt, but he was glad of the warmth from the fur lining that his old leather jacket brought as he gently eased it over his shoulders.

Harris pondered thoughts of escape as he wondered if he had been as clever as he had thought. But escape from what? The shower room only had a small window and even though caked in dirt he could see the iron bars covering it.

In any case, he told himself, if he had tried to escape now he wouldn't get far, he could hardly walk let alone run, no, he had given a story, a plausible deniability with a good measure of innocent abuse thrown in, he had made that bed and Harris decided that he would lie in it.

Harris coughed more bile as he opened the shower room door and, looking down, he was pleased that there was no blood within the spittle food remnants, for if there was blood it would mean that there would be a bad rupture within his body.

Harris looked up and standing there on the other side of the door in front of him was, 'Soft shoes.' He was grinning through the one or two brown stained teeth he had left in his head and he seemed to take great delight in taking the officer's hand and, 'palming,' him the five bloodied nails, their roots and skin.

Uttering three words Soft shoes spoke. "You keep, memento?" Although Harris couldn't reason his reaction, he forced a smile back towards this sick, sadistic bastard and pocketed his memento into the inside, jacket, chest pocket.

Harris was led back into the main warehouse where he saw the old wooden commode on its side, it was being hosed down and bleached and whilst this was happening, the skylight window above was now crank handled closed. Harris sat down at one of the chairs that was placed beside him and he took a lit cigarette from 'Soft shoe' and, as the Russians conversed with each other, Harris had nothing to say.

Chapter 41

"It is a nice hospital, Yuri has been here with his heart problems and you have his room." Ivan explained to Harris as they drove together away from the West Ham warehouse, from his captors, the pain. Harris, gladly, said. "Thank you."

For Ivan had indeed found the briefcase in the garage and having forced it open he had counted the fifty empty plastic bags that Harris had foretold. Ivan even examined some and on a couple, he could see the rigid emboss where the coins in the bags had been gripped. Ivan also found time to study the receipts from Harris' wallet, they looked too random not to be genuine, but still he telephoned those with numbers on them and he confirmed the billing was indeed for a yacht's overnight berth.

Finally, when returning to free Harris, the Detective had looked quite shocked when he asked where Gregor and was told. "He's dead."

Ivan had convinced himself that seizing and torturing Harris, as Yuri had ordered, had been a terrible mistake. He didn't particularly like this order in the first place as Harris had done nothing but help Yuri in the recent past. Harris had solved the kidnapping of one of Yuri's daughters and he had discovered the murderer of yet another of Yuri's daughters. What had this man received in return, a blown-up house and torture. No, Ivan was not happy with the order, but now it was time to make amends.

Having settled Harris into his room on the South Bank, overlooking the Thames, Ivan told Harris that he was returning to France to tell Yuri exactly what he had found. Ivan couldn't say, "Sorry," enough times to the pained Detective who sat upright in bed, but at least now he was tended by nurses and one of them was asking how Harris liked his steak cooked?

--//--

All afternoon Harris was examined from 'tip to toe.' After a visual examination came the scan of which the results were extremely optimistic. Five nails to his right hand removed, but each with a chance of growing back, two cracked ribs, one broken, some dehydration, multiple bruising to his mauve/black stomach and torso and, lastly, burning to the testicle region that the doctor couldn't fathom. Two needles were inserted into his arms, one a saline drip and the other attached to a pushbutton morphine box to relieve his pain, which Harris pressed repeatedly.

The doctor had been paid well to explain away those accidental injuries. "The notes I have taken, state that you fell down an open manhole in some abandoned street in south-east London and trapping your hand you eventually managed to rip your fingers free, but because of amnesia and the rib injuries even if you could move, you didn't know where to move to, is that right?"

Harris immediately went with the ruse and nodded.

"I can't remember." Harris told him, "I don't recall anything exactly, but I do need you to ring my work, my personnel department and tell them exactly what you know." The doctor agreed.

The doctor thought it strange to see this man take hold of his old grubby coat and produce various parts of a mobile phone and reassemble it to give him the number to ring, but he wrote down the number all the same and promised he'd call on leaving the room.

"One small problem though Mr Harris, the burns to your testicles?" The doctor deliberated.

"Cigarette burn sir, I did it to myself to stay awake, to call out for help. That was until that kind Russian found me." Harris suggested.

"Hmm, yes indeed." The shrewd doctor colluded. "Do you need anything?"

Harris looked up and with a sly grin he asked. "I have run out of cigarettes."

Left alone the Detective had nothing but time as he observed his surroundings. He was impressed! It was the most comfortable hospital bed he had ever been put in; even the pillows were made of goose feather, with a television on the far wall and a selection of films he could watch from a remote less than an arm's reach away.

But he made use of his time as he took hold of his phone, and, whilst noting that there were actual oil paintings on the walls, he managed to delete all phone messages and call data. Then, writing on a bedside notepad, only the essential numbers he needed, he removed any detail of the phone's history by resetting the phone to factory settings.

He looked out the window as he folded the note that contained just Ivan's phone and a couple of work numbers. Now any personal life that he'd had, had vanished, just like the various tour boats that bobbed along, eventually all would pass out of view.

He had ordered lunch from the menu in front of him and he couldn't help himself from salivating as he began to peruse the asparagus soup, quail's egg salad and beef Wellington followed by various sorbets. 'I could happily get used to this,' he thought cheerfully.

A while later there was a knock on the door and a pretty, young Eastern European nurse entered, 'white teeth, white uniform, softly spoken, very nice,' Harris stirred his imagination towards an xxx film, but it was short lived.

"You have visitors, do you feel well enough?" she asked.

"Who is it?" Harris sighed.

"A Chief Superintendent Hutchings and a lady from your Human Resources department, I don't know what that means, sorry." She told him.

Harris sat up and readied himself for the verbal onslaught and replied. "Yes."

Harris needn't have worried though, for when he first saw Hutchings he walked into his room, all red-faced and angry, but he took one look at Harris and his expression changed immediately.

"Oh my God!" He uttered. "What happened?"

Harris was surprised, this was not the greeting he was expecting and the woman from HR only glanced quickly at Harris before fixing her eyes to the lush carpet that he hadn't even trodden on yet.

Harris took a difficult breath as the woman began scribbling notes. "I don't know, I went for a walk, a long walk, thinking of work, thinking of my future," he said. Before exaggerating a wince on his next breath. "I wasn't paying attention to where I was, or where I was going and the next thing I knew I was in darkness."

"Why didn't you call for help?" His boss asked

Harris took another hard breath. "No signal, unconscious most the time, how long have I been gone?" His innocence asked.

"A couple of days, no worries, not a problem, I thought you were skiving AWOL, but looking at you." Hutchings faltered. "Is there anything we can get you?"

"I just need rest Sir, that and a phone." Harris asked.

"Not a problem, I'll get you another phone and I'll make sure Human Resources keep in contact." The lady looked up, nodded and went back to her note taking.

"Just to check on your progress and I'll make sure your next phone will have a better signal, all the best Harris, get well soon." With that Hutchings and the HR woman left his room.

"Don't forget grapes." Harris called out as the door closed.

'That was short and swift,' he thought, 'even a fart lingers longer,' and he coughed a laugh.

However, he was more than a little perplexed by his new boss' attitude. 'Only days ago, all that man could do was to scowl at him and, as for that HR woman that visited, she, 'hardly bleeding looked at him,' he thought.

Harris wanted to see what they saw and so, slowly, he rose from his bed holding his morphine box in one hand and the saline drip on a wheeled trolley in the other, he gingerly staggered to the en-suite bathroom.

It was only when he looked into the mirror that he honestly didn't recognise himself.

He was bruised black, blue, mauve and brown, swollen, with various cuts, stitches, lumps and bumps and Harris looked back at 'elephant man.'

"Jesus H Christ and Stonewall Jackson, what the fuck have they done me?" Harris was flabbergasted.

Chapter 42

The next morning Harris woke late, only to find Ivan sitting in the chair nearest the bed and eating his grapes between supping fresh coffee.

"Morning," the Russian said. "How are you feeling?" he asked.

Harris stirred slowly and, raising himself to his elbows, he pushed the morphine button. "I feel like I have been hit by a big, red bus driven by a careless fucking Russian bear." Ivan laughed, he laughed out loud.

"Yes, I doubt you would have survived the week." Ivan said, all matter of fact.

To which Harris replied. "Yeah, well thanks." He was truly thankful.

"Yuri wanted more proof," the aide informed him and Harris' eyes widened.

"Don't worry." Ivan was quick to interject. "I have had those bags in your briefcase fingerprinted by some police friends in your fingerprint branch and a couple of them actually have Yuri's fingerprints on them."

"I told you, I told you." Harris couldn't hide his relief.

"I believe you Harris, but now I have to fly back to France to convince Yuri that you are innocent, do you understand that?" He urged.

"I do." Harris replied. "But, I've also been thinking about those bags in his car with Yuri's fingerprints on them." Harris drew Ivan's attention.

"Go on." The Russian sat forward.

Pressing the morphine box again Harris continued. "I'm sure Yuri used to package sweets for underprivileged kids, to give out to the waifs and strays in the East End." Ivan tried to understand.

"Didn't he hand them to Gregor to pass these out to local care homes, schools, pubs and clubs?" Suddenly Ivan began to establish a smile.

"Yes, I'm sure I can arrange that he did this." As he began to see through Harris' words.

"Didn't Gregor begrudge Yuri's charitable work?" Harris continued. "And not only that, didn't he also want to take over his business?" Harris coerced.

"He did, he did." Ivan confirmed, as he formulated, "and I will tell Yuri and his attorney exactly that." Ivan smiled.

"That's how Yuri's fingerprints were on the bags Gregor planted in his car." Harris determined.

Ivan was nodding as he beamed. "You are right!"

Ivan admired Harris' idea and thanked him before leaving. "I will arrange those things right now." He told him and, looking at the officer, he smiled. "You rest, my friend, you rest."

Chapter 43

It took three weeks for Harris to recover, just to an extent where his face had become recognisable again and now he could move more freely, in pain, but he could move.

He hadn't heard anything from Ivan, but, 'no news was good news,' as far as Harris was concerned. His daily wandering along the corridors of what was basically a five-star hotel, had now become repetitive and somewhat boring.

Harris needed stimulation and, knowing that he had discovered a startling link between his last murder scene of Mrs Forrester and the mysterious case of Fiona Grant-Smith, his mind was urging his recovery. He had had enough by the time he emerged from the hospital entrance and, stepping out into bright sunshine, he gingerly made his way along Tooley Street towards London Bridge tube station. Carrying his canvas rucksack over one shoulder. He was thankful his captors had left it alone.

Spring was in full bloom as the hanging baskets on almost each lamppost displayed mauve and yellow. He was grateful to still be alive and he shuddered a hope that the nightmare dream of the past would subside as he journeyed his way back to Barking.

He didn't announce his return when he got back to the murder squad offices, he wasn't ready to see or speak to anyone as he sought the isolation of his van and there he waited until past 7 pm, when he knew most of the personnel would already be making their way home.

He did, however, acknowledge a couple of detectives when passing them in the corridor. A quick 'Hi' and 'Bye,' that was enough for him as he made his way to the old, storeroom office.

He sat there and noted that nothing had moved, not even an inch, but still he wondered if there was a miniature camera capturing his movements.

Harris sat at his desk and wondered what medical mental disorder he could now be suffering from to wonder such a thing? He knew his emotions were in turmoil with the constant thought that, 'the world was against him.' His 'stress bucket' was over flowing and though he knew he needed a drink, he also knew that wasn't the answer. Could he continue to bounce back from such adversity, it certainly caused him some concern. 'Get a grip man,' his mind screamed, there was no point feeling sorry for himself, but he was tired, so tired.

No, tomorrow he would lose himself in work as he had always done before and his head would simply have to 'knuckle down' and deal with whatever lay ahead. However, that night, he sent an email request to his boss asking to 'return to work on light duties' and then wrote a note to the crime scene manager, Bob, asking a small favour, this he left in an envelope under the CSM's door.

--//--

By midday the next day Harris had been seen by Hutchings and was granted light duties until fully fit. A 10 am to 6 pm shift, no overtime and, emphasised once again were the words, "absolutely no investigation work!"

His duties were to include submitting exhibits from other team's murders to the laboratories at Lambeth and he would courier whatever, whenever and wherever, that was it.

Though slightly disillusioned Harris wasn't prepared to argue his case with the man and he certainly wasn't going to 'pass on' his recent discovery so that others got the credit. No, instead he said, "thank you," and returned to his storeroom where he sat with nothing to do but wait for phone calls and 'surf the Internet' on his work PC. It was just before 6 pm that his envelope to Bob was slipped back under his door.

Harris groaned as he lent down to pick it up, but, reading the contents, he realised Bob had answered his small favour and he was now presented with two lists of London murder investigations. The first list detailed where train tickets had been notably seized as exhibits, whilst the other list was more extensive. Harris had asked after murder investigations where it described 'correspondence' or 'contents of,' both common phrases in police terminology and Harris knew these could cover any type of paperwork and, therefore, include train tickets.

He would work from the train ticket list first; a list that comprised of two parts; unsolved murders and solved murders, where it clearly stated train ticket/s and nothing else.

The second list he dreaded, knowing it would no doubt take him a year or two to complete, but at this rate he had nothing else to do. He sat at his desk studying the various reference numbers to these exhibits, mostly at Mandela Way and he was soon engrossed in the task ahead.

He also knew he wanted to meet the barrister friend of Mr Forrester where the file of Fiona Grant-Smith had originated from. He needed to know more information from this barrister, the honourable James McDermott, personal barrister to the rich and famous, as Harris speculated as to why the file had been passed from one barrister to another. Then there was Mr Forrester's murder, when a near identical ticket was found under the body of Mrs Forrester. Coincidence? Doubtful. Something in the Detective's brain rang alarm bells!

After a week of un-answered phone messages at McDermott's Chambers, Harris decided on a less subtle approach. Between 'odd jobs' on light duties Harris found time to enter the Chambers' reception area on the pretence of 'a mistake,' however, he was there long enough to note the photographs on a plaque of those employed in the building. Now he knew what the honourable gentleman looked like.

Over the next couple of weeks, in between the usual Murder Squad errands, he would find himself at either Mandela Way, sifting through the various exhibits from the first list of unsolved murder scenes where he would check every single train ticket or, when not doing that, he would be sitting outside the Law Courts' Chambers, studying those that walked past, waiting for his prey.

He knew the surveillance team were probably watching him as he watched others, but what could they prove? Nothing and his patience alone would warrant that other more serious investigations would soon take priority over Hutchings discriminate persecution.

Chapter 44

Three strikes and you 'walk,' is quite a common term in American baseball jargon. However, in London in the first week of May, Harris understood this euphemism. He was still no further forward with the hundreds of train tickets he had examined, he still hadn't heard anything from Ivan and last, but not least, the barrister was more like a fucking magician on a vanishing act than some bloke in a silver/grey wimple making speeches. But he wasn't walking away from this self-tasking, nor was he actually walking when it passed his 6pm 'book off' time. Because, for most nights, with little to do, he would be in the gym, running the tread mill for hour after hour, hitting the boxing bags or pumping weights to exhaustion.

It wasn't very sociable, but Harris didn't feel very sociable and the euphoria from one more rep, another mile or a steeper incline on the cross trainer kept a smile on his face and his anxieties at bay. So, it was work, gym and then home, the van.

The fire investigation and his insurance company still dragged their heels as his insurance broker told him, "they required an outcome of the investigation before any settlement," but, by bugger, Harris harassed them daily.

But he didn't mind too much, he could still drive to his garage and pick up another T shirt or two and swap the odd pair of jeans. He had also purchased a couple of 'luxuries' to help with his home comforts: a frying pan for bacon rolls and a small portable black and white television that ran off the van's cigarette lighter. Yes, he was warming to his 'traveller' existence.

However, it wasn't until the third week of the month that events began to change.

It was a Wednesday and he was again sitting in his storeroom waiting for a phone to ring, a call that would direct him on his next errand, as he leant back in his chair glaring at his computer screen. He had just opened a police email from Bermuda, an email that Hemmings had posted. It was titled 'wish you were here' attaching photographs of white beaches, palm trees and various girls at bars.

'What an inconsiderate, no good, devious bastard!' Harris thought as his new mobile phone suddenly began to vibrate. Well, at least Hutchings had kept his word, he now had a new phone, but he thought it wise to keep his old sim card and the administration lady hadn't noticed his 'sleight of hand' in the exchange of new for old.

It was a voice he didn't recognise, it was the barrister on the phone; now back in London from leading a prosecution case in India of all places. Harris immediately thought the man sounded very old, very tired, but he could spare five minutes, the next morning at nine.

--//--

He could tell immediately that the barrister didn't 'care much' for his dress code as he watched him approach his Chambers the next day. Harris knew that an old leather jacket, ripped jeans and T-shirt wasn't exactly what this opulent man, more used to financiers, was expecting and from that very moment Harris was treated with disdain.

"You just came on recommendation, that's all." The barrister answered dismissively.

"I hardly knew Rupert Forrester, I recall meeting him once, I think, at a Gala event." the barrister uttered.

"Have you got anywhere with your enquiries Mr Harris?" The barrister now targeted a question.

Harris immediately felt a mocking in this comment, almost as if to say, 'you look thuggish and incapable,' and, therefore, you are.

Harris was tempted to divulge, but he had no trust in the barrister and gave him the deserved answer. "No."

"I thought not." McDermott replied.

Harris gritted his teeth as he shifted uncomfortably in the leather chair that was positioned opposite the barrister, behind his huge desk.

"Are the Grant-Smith's still in this country? If so I would like an address please." Harris asked.

Tapping a pencil on his desk the barrister derived pleasure in putting Harris in his place.

"Please sir, or please your honour, that is how you address me officer." This contemptible man ordered propriety.

Harris looked at his sharp creased, silk shirt, the perfectly knotted Oxford tie, even the small red signet ring on his little finger, but, when he looked up and saw the sneer across the man's face, Harris immediately realised that he had no option but to stroke McDermott's ego.

"Please sir?" Harris asked and, though seething, minutes later he had left the Chambers with confirmation that they still resided on the borders of Leicester.

Harris really hated that pompous ass of a man, a man who knew more that he told, a man more interested in lawsuits and acquisition than justice, 'an oxygen thief' he thought and although Harris was told to bring any findings before the barrister, Harris knew the only people that really deserved an answer were the poor girl's parents.

--//--

Having stopped off for a doctor's appointment Harris returned to Barking and handed in his doctor's note, a note giving him the 'all clear' from injuries that would return him to 'full fitness' status. It was a note that Hutchings scanned once, and with no good reason, other than his own personal vindictiveness, immediately told Harris he was still on restricted duties. This again meant no official investigation work, but again Harris ensured that he had recorded every word.

So, on that afternoon, Harris found himself delivering yet more murder exhibits to the Lambeth laboratories, these originating from a couple of murders only days prior and, as he sat there waiting his turn in the queue, he was still angry from that morning's meetings. Even the bacon rolls on the 1st floor canteen left a bitter taste.

Harris drove his fleet vehicle away from Lambeth, wondering if he had time for another visit to Mandela Way, when he heard his mobile phone ring.

It was Ivan's number, he answered quickly.

"Give me a minute." He shouted at the inane object. "I will ring you back." Ending the call Harris finally found somewhere to pull over and, spotting a red public telephone box, 'just in case,' Harris told himself. It was just in case that he picked up the public phone, just in case the car or his phone had been fitted out with a recording device, just like the phones, Police vehicles and even rented vehicles that he had seen at the Stockwell depot being 'plugged for sound and vision' by those internal investigations.

No, he 'wouldn't chance his arm' and risk being recorded, so he used the payphone to call Ivan and, when he answered, Harris spoke quickly.

"The Beckton Arms pub, Canning Town, 8 pm tonight, can you make it?" He asked

Ivan answered. "Yes." Harris ended the call.

The detective made another call, then another and another, all close variations to Ivan's number. He continued to do so until the earpiece of the phone was hot to his ear and he had no change left his pocket. Each random call lasted roughly the same time, ten seconds to twenty seconds. If he was being followed and they checked the British Telecom billing from the phone box, they would have difficulty in deciphering who he had actually rung. Harris was using every counter-surveillance trick he could muster and he realised he'd either have to carry around a lot more change or buy another pre-pay phone himself.

Chapter 45

Harris had chosen the pub wisely, he knew it from old, it was one of Temptress Tina's previous tenancies and it had gained notoriety from a double shooting murder from years ago. From then on, it cast a dark cloud, the locals stayed away and through its lack of custom it began to open and close for business with regularity. With no regulars, just passing trade, anyone who entered it would be unnoticed and that night after work, leaving his 'job' mobile phone at work, he again used the tube train network to lose any potential surveillance.

When Harris arrived at the pub, he saw Ivan waiting in a corner booth, flanked on either side by two men. Neither of them Harris had seen before, that confirmed to Harris that Yuri really did have a never-ending army of men at his disposal. As the Detective took his last steps towards the booth he wondered still what fate lay ahead for him.

However, he dragged a nearby chair to the booth table and sitting, taking his rucksack off his shoulder, Harris forced a pensive smile. He needn't have worried for when he heard concern in Ivan's words. "Are you alright, what's wrong" Harris knew that the Russian actually cared a little and, if he cared, then he wasn't there to kill him.

'Phew!' Harris thought.

From his rucksack Harris pulled a box containing a newly purchased, prepaid, mobile phone, a phone that he had bought on his way back from the laboratory. Harris explained his predicament about his new boss. He told of the underlying hate that there was for him, all because he'd had helped Yuri track down the murderous Inspector Pete Brown. Ivan took down Harris' new mobile number and assured him that any future contact would be made solely on the new phone.

"Now my news." Ivan said, his smile was ever broadening as he divulged.

"Yuri really loved your idea about Gregor and the sweet bags and so does his defence team." Ivan disclosed.

He told Harris that there were now over fifty statements in Yuri's favour, some were from Yuri's men detailing that Yuri would regularly be found packaging sweets in those plastic bags for the unfortunate children of London. Not only that, but Yuri had handed some of those bags to Gregor for distribution.

Other statements described how Gregor would keep those bags as treats for himself and would scoff at Yuri's kindness. Then there were a few statements describing how Gregor was envious of Yuri's charitable work, but, most importantly, over a quarter of the statements were from dignitaries and people of standing, such as local Mayors, Members of Parliament, the odd celebrity, two Judges and a number of 'paid off' police officers, each of whom witnessed Yuri handing out sweets in that type of bag.

Harris could see the excitement on Ivan's face when Ivan explained that the French prosecutors had little or no chance of success. However, the case would still go ahead, it had to, as the Gendarmes needed to explain why they had shot Yuri.

"A massive embarrassment!" Ivan said with a smile and Harris smiled with him.

For the next half, an hour the two men talked about Yuri, his health, his wealth and the French case against him and Harris realised that Yuri would soon indeed be back in London, his London, to infect his whim on its populace.

Eventually Harris felt secure in the knowledge that he was no longer 'a target' and made his excuses to leave, he had heard enough. It was indeed a dangerous game that Harris was again involved in and he knew that he now needed time to think hard.

But on saying, "Goodbye." Ivan asked where Harris was living.

"Sleeping in my office at work." The Detective told him.

Ivan was a little taken aback.

"No, no." He said. "I will find you somewhere and ring you."

--//--

Harris had caught a bus for the journey back to Barking and alone on the top deck he sat and stared down to the ground. Through misty eyes he tried to contemplate what to do next.

He looked down at his right hand and sighed to the fact that his fingernails hadn't shown any sign of regrowth and their rawness was still tipped with deep red scars. This, to any passing glances, would embarrassingly make him look as if he had painted, red nails.

Harris reached into his inside jacket pocket and, pulling out a folded tissue, he opened it to reveal his five withered mementos.

He was intrigued at what had once been his fingernails, the blood had darkened to near black and attached to each of the nails were remnants of his shrivelled dead skin, all crusted and flaked to his touch. Harris again looked at his fingertips where he recalled the excruciating pain, it made him wince once more. Red fingertips, torn skin, blackened nails, pulled roots, red fingertips, his screams, red nails, red toenails, red toenails!

Red toenails! "Oh, my good God." Harris spoke loudly.

Harris looked down open mouthed at his nails, but he wasn't looking at those, he was looking at flashbacks in his mind and he was awestruck from the realisation of what his mind now yelled.

Red toenails, red toenails his brain exploded at the revelation that he may have found yet another link between Mrs Forrester and Fiona Grant-Smith. He knew there was something odd, out of place in the photographs that he'd seen from the file and the toenails; that was that it!

Everything about Fiona was demure, classy, rich and tasteful, the expensive fine pale coloured clothes she preferred, those that matched her skin tone and hair, but not her toenails. They didn't, not that crass, cherry red, a vulgar, tasteless choice and cheap, were they the same colour as Mrs Forrester's toenails? Oh, how he thought and hoped they were.

The bus journey took far too long and at every bus stop someone got on or off. Harris' patience was running thin. Even that day's discarded newspaper lying on the seat next to him headlining a story about a Senator Valentine Hill arriving in the UK on another trade mission paled from his mind, as all he could think of was red toenails.

"Come on, come on, get on or get off for fuck's sake." Harris thought and his right foot tapped ever increasingly when the streetlights of Barking drew nearer.

Eventually the bus braked and hissed at the bus stop where Harris stepped down to the pavement. He ran through Barking's town centre, sprinting the alleyways of council accommodation, over the bridge and into the industrial estate where his lungs began to burn, as hot as the image of cherry-red toenails.

Entering the offices and climbing to the first floor sweat dripped from his brow, but, oh how he smiled when he saw that team 3's office was still open to cleaning staff. There he saw that his old desk had been retained by the new exhibit officer and the Forester photographs were still boxed on the bookshelf behind.

He checked the scene photographs, but Sophie Forester's feet, although in shot, were some distance away from the photographer's focus. He turned to the post-mortem album and Harris noted the lady's muscle tone, a body that regularly trained, taking care of her body.

However, there was only one picture he was interested in and, for the next five minutes having pulled his trusty magnifying glass from his rucksack, he examined every pixel of her cherry-red toenails. It was the middle toe of her dainty right foot that now made Harris sit down at that desk and stare.

The detective's eyes opened wide when he realised he could see what appeared to be a fine slice of incision marks around what otherwise was a perfectly shaped, but cut down to size, false nail and Harris understood what had been missed at her post-mortem.

Harris was gutted that he hadn't noticed this before and began mentally defending himself against his own accusations, when had he ever looked at a dead person's toes? A junkie's perhaps, but, never, was the answer!

He had attended hundreds of post-mortems and never once was there the need to look at any of their toenails. All those bodies, shot, stabbed, decapitated, strangled and poisoned, none of their feet were ever an issue.

But now it was an issue and Harris, although elated at this discovery as he photocopied the digital picture, also felt shallow, he wasn't as good as he'd thought he was!

As he stood in front of the flickering bright light he recalled the post-mortem. He remembered that he only concentrated on the multiple stab wounds to her flesh where measurement upon measurement was taken and where each slice was examined in order to establish the type of weapon used. Never once did he glance at her toes as she lay lifeless, exposed, on that portable steel trolley at the Waltham Forest mortuary.

Harris went to his storeroom office and again looked at the Fiona Grant-Smith file photographs. Again, he used his magnifying glass and zoomed in on her feet, again his jaw dropped as he noticed that on the left foot of this silent witness, on the toe next to her big toe was what looked to be fine slices to her skin immediately adjacent and an identical cut down to size, false nail.

Did he really feel clever? Did he hell!

No, was the answer as he sat and realised that he was still weaving his passage through this forest of blind alleyways, but now he was convinced, more than ever before, that the murderer had fine-tuned his craft and that there must be more victims.

Chapter 46

Harris had a restless sleep in his cold van that night; his visions were filled with a tickertape parade of property reference slips and train tickets which each fell upon the lifeless bodies of young women, all stacked in a heap. A mound of putrefied bodies, maggot ridden and stacked to the sky. Over and over he twisted himself in his dreams; as contorted as the slain women that he now scrambled over. Climbing ever higher he clung to ripped, stench filled flesh, all the time calling out. "Where are you?" But as he tried to reach for each ticket that fell, it simply melted away into the skin and body of each female it touched and he woke in a sweat when those eyes opened and stared upon him.

"Fuck that for a game of soldiers." Harris spoke to himself as he sat bolt upright on waking.

"Fuck that." He repeated, for confidence and composure.

As was his daily routine, Harris took his wash bag to the gymnasium shower room and there he was able to wash his imagination away.

It was only 8 am, two hours before he officially started work, but he didn't care, he was keen to continue working his way through that first list of metropolitan murders and, until the first of the 'errand boy' phone calls, this time would be his own.

He came to realise that he had exhausted the unsolved list, so he gazed upon the various reference numbers of the solved murders and now wishing, hoping, praying that one of these train tickets would lead him to an unknown outstanding assailant who perhaps had murdered in joint enterprise.

'Excellent.' Harris thought when he was told to deliver a car that needed fingerprinting to Croydon. He knew he could easily detour to Mandela Way on his journey back. There he would be able to 'cross off' another murder or two and it was as if the 'gods of traffic' were speeding him on his way, as almost every traffic light turned green on his approach.

The journey back was just as refreshingly quick and he was at the storage facility within only two hours of leaving Barking. He had phoned Foxy ahead, as he would normally do, and on his arrival Harris was presented with yet another crate of exhibits to sift through.

Harris was starting to relish how things were falling into place, he'd only been there in the time that it took him to drink a mug of the manager's hot black coffee when he was, unbelievingly, holding himself up on the crate for support, he stared at another identical train ticket just one serial number away from the Grant-Smith murder. But he was also confused and somewhat saddened when he realised that the murder had already been solved.

'It couldn't be,' he thought as confusion filled his thoughts. But still he asked Foxy to hold that particular exhibit in the safe with the other train ticket.

Harris stared at the Crime Reference (CR) number relating to the murder, a docket that would be filed away at New Scotland Yard and, ringing the department, he requested the file be sent to his storeroom at Barking.

Harris was told that it would take a week for it to be recovered and delivered as the murder had taken place so many years ago. Harris could do nothing to expedite his request, even the promise that he would hand over a bottle of Scotch fell on deaf ears. He did, however, realise he had another option open to him when he was told of the brief synopsis over the phone. The murder had taken place in Plaistow, London Borough of Newham and with the date of the slaying and a quick phone call to the Newham Recorder, the area's local newspaper, he now found himself speeding to their offices.

It was there that one of the receptionists handed Harris a microfiche and led him to a side office. There he was able to glean the details that reported the murder to its readers.

Harris took notes, lots of notes, but where it mentioned that one man had been arrested it also stated that the police were not looking for any further suspects. Harris read this quote three times, each time in disbelief. Had the murderer been released?

--//--

That day dragged and so did the week as he continued to search through the solved murders that highlighted train tickets; all Harris could think about was the arrival of that docket.

That was until he received a phone call, on his prepay phone, from Ivan. He was back in France and full of good cheer. There wasn't any further news about Yuri's upcoming court case, but he had good news for the Detective. Ivan told Harris that Yuri had given his approval for Harris to move into Maya's home.

Harris suddenly laughed at the irony, but gladly accepted the offer. He was growing tired of his life in a van sheltering under an overpass and he remembered Maya's home with its stately elegance from when he had dropped Maya and her daughter's home to the grandeur of Emerson Park, Essex.

Maya, just one of many wives to Yuri, had helped conspire against the Russian crime lord. That slender toned, beautiful, young woman, who had since vanished from Harris and, with a coldness that he could barely admit it to himself, as she was the first woman that he had fallen in love with.

Ivan confirmed that Harris knew the address and told him where the spare keys were hidden outside, under an ornate pot at the front of the property, keys that Yuri had kept there.

Ivan also told Harris that Maya's home was in need of a little tidying as it had been ransacked when Yuri's men had searched for her and clues as to her whereabouts. Harris didn't mind, far from it, on Yuri's orders he was going to live somewhere for free.

At 6 o'clock and one second Harris had logged himself 'off duty' on his computer and headed for his van. He collected his bare essentials, clothing, wash kit and the like and, having filled his rucksack, he journeyed by tube, bus and foot to his new home.

He had decided not to take his van, it was safe where it was, besides if he was still being followed 'a loss of target' amongst the throng of travelling public was far easier to achieve than in a big white van. Ridiculously Harris felt the rise of a little snobbery, he didn't want to park his dented, rusting, home on wheels anywhere close to his new home.

He found the keys and entered the vast property, laughing at Ivan's telephone phrase, "a little tidying."

He was now a witness to the exact type of search that he had seen take place in Rupert Forrester's home when the bodies had been discovered.

Everything in every room was piled into the middle and there wasn't a computer, telephone or notebook to be found. At least Harris now had an idea as to who had been responsible for the ransacking of the Forrester home and, if correct, the Detective knew he would also want access to Rupert and Sophie's computer, anything that might lead him to Sophie's murderer.

That night, and over the next couple of evenings, Harris cleared each room in turn. Anything broken went in refuse sacks and, all bar one mattress, any 'ripped open' furnishings found a new home in the detached garage. He was left with one television that still worked and a four-seater couch to sit and laze on.

The outdoor heated swimming pool was eventually cleared of leaves and his nightly exercise regime was again reinstated. There was still plenty of food in the pantry's two fridge freezers, so he knew he wouldn't go hungry.

Harris did however have one scary moment when he was clearing the kitchen. He spotted under a glass, in one of the cabinets, an airline serviette that bore his signature, a tissue paper remnant of his past that later that night he wiped his arse with.

Chapter 47

The next weekend came and went without incident or care and for once in such a long, long time Harris and his thoughts were fairly peaceful.

Monday morning arrived and as he arrived at work he felt euphoric when he was told that the docket he had ordered had been delivered to the Murder Squad reception desk.

He told the security reception clerk that he would pick the file up later; later being long after Hutchings had gone home. It was a day like any other, go here, go there, deliver this and pick up that. He did as he was told and it wasn't until two hours after his shift was complete, when the building was deserted bar security staff, did he return to the reception desk.

The CR docket was large and bloody heavy, but Harris didn't mind as he weaved the corridors at speed carrying the 10-inch-thick brown cardboard sleeve of papers and photographs whilst scurrying quickly back to his storeroom.

Page by page he studied the file writing notes as he read and as he turned the pages the Detective became oblivious to time. The case was presented to the 'Old Bailey' criminal court as, 'young lovers, Ralph and Nikki.' Street kids who spent their time 'fixing' on any drug or substance abuse that was available to them.

Ralph was portrayed as someone who would argue over Nikki's constant waywardness towards other men that helped pay for her drugs and his glue and it was in a fit of jealousy that Ralph had stabbed his girlfriend to death in a subway underpass, the place where they would usually, 'hang out.'

There was the confession from Ralph. "I stabbed Nikki." He also confessed in court that he had said those words. Then there was Nikki's blood spray that proved beyond doubt that she had bled out onto Ralph and his clothes that gave the jury little doubt as to Ralph's guilt.

"But what of the ticket?" Asked Harris, intrigued as he read through the closing paragraphs of the case.

The only mention of its existence was of it being found during Nikki's post-mortem, but there was no mention of it playing any significant role, only that it was found and there was apparently never any mention of it in any of Ralph's interviews.

Harris sat back, taken aback, reading the Judge's directions he came to understand what the jury faced in deciding the case. There was the confession, the blood spray and the knife that killed her that had been forcibly removed from Ralph's hand when the murder was discovered. Was there really a need to delve any deeper? Apparently not.

The post-mortem photographs were quite decent in detail; and although the train ticket had only been photographed unfolded, it still bore the visible crease marks that showed that it had once been folded up and folded in on each corner, identical to the other two tickets.

Nikki had been photographed from 'top to toe' and as such there were photographs of each foot. Harris was astounded when he looked upon her right foot. Her big toe nail clearly showed that it had been ripped off but, because she was a street urchin, nothing was made of that fact. The only accounts made in the pathologist's notes was that amongst the other cherry red painted toenails, one was missing, a probable recent injury that could have happened at any time prior to her death.

It was just before dawn when Harris had written the last of his notes and he prioritised his plan of action as to what to do next. Find and visit Ralph, if he was still in prison, locate the officers who wrote down Ralph's confession and, if possible, find a way to have Nikki's underwear and internal vaginal swabs examined for DNA. A forensic avenue that never existed at the time of Nikki's murder.

Harris gleefully rubbed his hands together as he walked to his van knowing that he could manage a couple of hours sleep before work.

Chapter 48

"You must eat girl." Those words repeated and repeated in her head, but for how long had she been vacant from the outside world? Her drugged mind was so tired and her body, that now lay prone against the cold concrete floor, twitched with almost every breath. Then the firm grip on her shoulder, it tightened and violently shook her to some sense as she partially opened her eyes to the gloom of a new dawn.

The beast repeated. "You must eat girl," as he pushed himself up from on top of her body, that allowed what little light there was in that corner of the room to shine upon the dirt riddled grey floor in front of her.

She again saw the smallest pane of glass window, no larger than six inches square above her, so high above her, so distant. A window that reminded her of the basement back home where she had lived with her parents, but she knew she was far from that loving security.

Her bruised nose smelt the strong herbs, warm herbs and, slowly focusing along the ground directly in front of her, there it lay. A ceramic metal bowl, white, chipped with blue ribbing the edge. The contents, a steaming hot broth with a large wooden spoon that floated on its surface.

That small beam of light also beamed upon the beast's heavy black boots as it stood only inches away from the bowl.

The voice commanded, "you eat it or wear it!"

The words spoken were heavy in tone, it had no heart, no feelings, and no remorse. The girl painfully shuffled her bruised body forward and, half kneeling to the side of the bowl, she took the spoon in her bound, blooded hands and ladled the first spoonful to her mouth.

Hot broth that burnt.

Chapter 49

Harris had set his alarm for 9:50 and he woke in the clothes that he had worn that previous day. He didn't mind, he was all smiles and greeted all as he walked back to his storeroom, for he felt excited, elated at tracking a serial killer that no one even knew existed.

Self-tasked, his first job was to contact prisoner location and within fifteen minutes Harris was talking to London's Pentonville Prison security manager. He was able to arrange a meeting with the security officer for Ralph's wing that very evening.

As soon as the phone call finished Harris went to Hutching's office and again tape-recorded his request to be allowed to investigate murders. Again, the Detective was refused, "all good then boss," Harris said on leaving, for it was, 'all good,' as Harris had already planned his next move.

The next man he sought was Alf, a deskbound officer who could barely walk unaided from a beating that he had taken some years previously. Harris had worked with him before and found him steadfast and secure, a man that Harris would normally seek out in the canteen when he had time for lunch, where they would exchange 'problems' over their food and now, having returned to the canteen, Harris saw the cripple in his usual seat. Harris spoke whilst the man listened to what he thought was an astonishing story, towards the end he nodded in agreement and both left the table smiling.

That night, dead on 6 pm, Harris signed off on his computer again and ran to the tube station, this time he didn't have time to double back or change route, as there was an urgency to arrive at the prison on time that compelled him to rush and never look back.

He arrived, he arrived on time and was quickly taken through the grey corridors of hate. He passed stiff metal doors that opened and closed until the echoes of pain were shut from his ears. He was now face-to-face with a withered old frown that belonged to a prison guard who had risen up the ranks.

"My name's Trevor," the prison officer introduced himself and Harris took note of his pale white skin that had spent more hours of his life indoors than outside. Harris introduced himself as he was led into yet another small room, an offshoot from the wing, perhaps once a cell itself. There Harris sat on a small plastic chair that could barely hold this weight and asked the officer all manner of questions about Ralph.

"The man's mental state, for someone who is now in his forties, was still barely ten years old in much of his thought process." He was told.

The man's well-being? "Ralph had kept himself clean and tidy and was no longer a target for the sodomites that preyed on the weak."

Harris was also told about Ralph's extended sentence. A sentence to a further 9 years for having almost killed a fellow inmate whose sole aim in life behind bars had been to daily abuse the 'simpleton.'

"Ralph was a punch bag to many." Trevor admitted, but over the years he had tried his best to look after, 'the poor sod.'

Between bouts of laughter over Ralph's antics Trevor talked with genuine feeling towards this mentally retarded inmate and it took a while to convince Trevor that Harris was simply conducting background checks. However, once placated, Harris continued to make notes as he listened.

The Prison officer continued to tell stories of Ralph, revealing some of Ralph's small achievements inside, amidst the adversity, a man with a heart that only wanted, "to be loved."

Harris found the anecdotes both saddening and also quite cheerful. However, Trevor made it clear that Ralph was now institutionalised into the daily routine and Harris wondered how 'setting him free' may do him more harm than good.

Harris wasn't surprised to hear, even now, that there was still no admission of guilt from Ralph over the original charge of murdering his girlfriend Nikki.

Finally, Harris asked about visiting Ralph, under the authority of a legal visit and it was then that Harris began to understand the prison officer's concerns.

"So, you are taking over the prison visits from the other man then?" Trevor asked inquisitively.

"What other man?" This was astonishing news to Harris and the surprise in his voice reflected this.

"The Police officer who visits him once a month, pretending to be his brother." Trevor sought answers.

"Is he retiring then? Are you taking over from him? Is it still a Government secret? And if you are, who are you, a distant cousin?" Trevor asked incredulously.

Harris was dumbstruck, suddenly various warning signals flashed across his mind, but Harris mustered a whisper. "I might be."

Harris' mind was racing as he sat still for a moment.

Who was he? Who was this Police Officer? Who was this man? And what was all this bollocks about a Government secret?

But Harris wasn't going to ask, that would look too suspicious. Nevertheless, he had to find out who this other man was so Harris changed tack. "Has there been anyone else that has visited him?"

"Never on my watch, only that bloke. No-one else and I oversee most of the visits." Trevor told him.

"Are you sure?" Harris asked, needing to know more.

"Nope, only him, third Sunday every month between 2 and 4 pm." The prison officer added.

"He comes in with the public visitors so as to not look out of place and they either remain in the public visiting area or if he asks and we have enough staff, we let them use a private consultation room. I think he is due this week." Trevor added.

Harris made one more request and that was to check the details on the bookings for that week. Once Trevor had escorted Harris back to the security office Trevor held the visitor registration book open for Harris to confirm that the visit was taking place.

"See I was right, this Sunday." Trevor boasted and it was then Harris saw the name D. Cooper and a warrant number, one that was older than Harris' service record. He quickly noted the details.

Trevor asked Harris if he wished to book a visit with Ralph there and then, but the Detective declined stating, "I will check with Cooper first."

Leaving the prison Harris knew he would have to tread carefully. Who was this Cooper? And why the monthly visits? Having read the CR docket where there was no mention of relatives, it was doubtful he was Ralph's brother? What the hell was this Cooper doing? Harris was sure that he hadn't ever seen this name either on the docket. But what intrigued Harris was the quote, "Government secret," and a maze of speculation grew as he journeyed back to Barking.

Back in his storeroom Harris was right, there was no mention on the docket about Cooper. No relatives and definitely no secrets, but at least there was a way forward.

Harris turned on his computer and checked the police internal email system. There were numerous first names beginning with the initial D and the surname Cooper. Harris quickly dismissed the three women with F (female) next to their name, but none of the four men had bothered entering their first name or even registered their warrant number.

Harris was frustrated as he had nowhere to go with this, not until the weekend, he thought. As for the rest of the week there were another two murders, for which he was sent with exhibits to Lambeth and then cars to Croydon. There was also someone's brain in formaldehyde that had to be taken for a Neurology examination and, to top it all, he was handed parts from a frozen torso that he drove to Sheffield University for crystallisation examination. It was indeed a busy week, but Harris didn't mind, it brought the weekend closer.

Chapter 50

Sunday was soon upon him and the sun shone brightly as Harris walked into the visitor waiting area at Pentonville Prison. Harris watched those waiting to visit. Men on their own, men with women, women alone and those with children. Harris observed them all. Through the bustling throng of screaming children and angry young women, the non-ventilated room sweltered with every minute that passed. Harris dismissed them all, all but one that drew his close attention.

The man was older than Harris, worn out and knackered would be how Harris could best describe this man in the dishevelled grey pinstripe suit that desperately needed a press. He was approaching fifty, with a balding head and a pot belly that hung as low as his tie. As for his shoes, they were more scuffed than polished and he reminded Harris more of an ambulance chasing solicitor, than a Police officer. Another point of interest was the Sunday Telegraph that he read, oblivious to his surroundings, there sat a man of conscience who concentrated on the small print.

Suddenly, almost all rose from their seats and rushed the door to queue as the security doors opened. All, except this man and Harris, the Detective noted that the man rose slowly and strolled to be last in the queue. It was time for Harris to leave the waiting area, to breathe fresh air and wait for this man who, he was positive, was D. Cooper.

Harris walked over to a nearby cafe that gave a clear view of the prison entrance and sat at an empty window seat with a coffee. Taking a digital camera out of his rucksack, Harris waited. Two coffees, a melted cheese baguette and, an hour later, his camera snapped the first image, then another, he focussed image after image on the grey suited man as he was leaving.

Harris slammed a £20 pound note on the counter, "keep the change love." Harris called out as he ran from the café and turned to follow D. Cooper at a safe distance. Not too close to be recognised, but not too far to lose this subject.

Harris thought it might be too difficult following on his own on a Sunday, the streets were barely active, but he needn't have worried, the man never looked back, not once. The Detective followed him onto the underground system where only after a couple of tube train changes Harris was soon mounting the steps of St James's Park that led to, 'the big house' - New Scotland Yard. Harris lost any doubt that he had of who the man was, as he saw the grey suit enter the security gate, showing identification.

But there was no way Harris was going to follow him in there. Any Sunday in that place was a mausoleum so he would be easily spotted. No, he would have to wait. So, purchasing a newspaper himself, he walked to the nearby green on The Broadway SW1, where he sat reading, glancing towards his headquarters exit every moment or so.

The detective was somewhat relieved, having sat for only half an hour, when the grey suited D Cooper emerged, walking no more than 30 yards, Harris watched as he veered into the nearby public house opposite the tube station entrance. Harris could see by the numbers that smoked outside that he had a chance to lose himself in the crowd, so he decided to go in, to stand at the bar and observe.

D Cooper sat alone at a table just a few yards from Harris in the company of what looked like two whiskey chasers to one pint of ale and he drank these in quick succession. It wasn't five minutes before the man was back at the bar and ordering the same again, he returned to his seat.

'Fucking hell, he's got a problem.' Harris told himself when yet again within a few minutes, the man had 'polished off' the three further glasses and walked slowly, with purpose, towards the bar.

"Well thank God for that." Harris muttered to himself, as this time the man, checking his change, walked away from the bar with just an ale. Harris found himself fixated with D Cooper's every move and, every glance D Cooper made Harris made too. Cooper was becoming furtive, shifting around in his seat, looking around in every direction, all before he pulled out a large black notebook from his inside pocket. It became obvious to Harris that Cooper was referring to the book as he made a number of mobile phone calls.

Harris urged himself to listen above the noise of other patrons, he was curious to know if there was any importance to the calls that Cooper was making. So, he 'chanced his arm' and sat at a table behind and, with an orange juice in hand, he pretended to read his newspaper.

Harris heard three of the conversations, each to a girl whereupon Harris scribbled their names, in amongst the newspaper headlines, Kylie, Isabel and Simone. Each call sounded as if Cooper was arranging a meeting for the following week.

Harris also heard that Cooper was going to pick one of them up from a block of flats in North Woolwich, East London, a tower block that Harris knew well and, having heard the flat number, the date the 13th and also a time pickup, Harris was more than just curious, he was eager to find out more.

Harris suddenly 'buried his head' in the newspaper as Cooper rose and walked to the door. Harris rose the paper high so that if the man glanced back all he would see of Harris was the newspaper that was gripped by his burly, large hands. Harris edged out of his seat and followed to the tube station.

Cooper travelled West on the District line whilst Harris sat one carriage down. It was only a few stops before they rumbled into West Brompton Station. Harris followed off the train and again walked into the nearest public house. Again, Cooper drank hard and consistently for over three hours, as if 'on a mission' to lose the rest of his day. But eventually Cooper managed to stumble to the darkening streets outside.

Harris was glad that night was at last falling as he used the cover of alcoves and shadows to watch the unpredictability of the drunk unfold. This way and that way the man swayed and staggered, but he still kept his feet and managed to stay upright as he walked from Lillie Road towards the walkway entrance of Empress State building, a building well known for the floors that are occupied by the police service.

'Surely, he isn't going to work,' Harris thought incredulously. But the man wasn't, he walked past the building towards the rear, to the car park.

Spurred on, Harris flashed his identity to the private security man, an Asian working on minimum wage, more interested in the girly magazine that lay out in front of him than the 6-foot bald detective who quickly jogged past his outpost box.

Turning the corner Harris stood watching as Cooper walked to the far side of the car park. There he saw him open the driver's door and climb into a silver coloured Peugeot saloon.

"Jesus." Harris whispered to himself in the silence that surrounded him.

"Surely not, he's not gonna…" he said, but the man did.

Cooper turned the car ignition and the engine shuddered into life.

'What a fucking idiot!' Harris thought as he readied himself to run back towards the main road to search for a black cab that he would need if he was to follow.

Harris waited for the car to move just an inch and only an inch before he would sprint back and for some time Harris was on his 'starting blocks,' but nothing happened.

He could still hear the engine running, now it had been five minutes or so and still no movement. Harris decided to creep closer. Weaving his way around the various parked cars, he eventually found himself closer. Close enough to hear weeping and to see the man wiping tears from his eyes. Harris shook his head and wondered, 'what the hell is going on.' Harris backtracked, having decided to leave Cooper be. He would wait there hidden, out by the main road. He stood there waiting for his target to emerge either on foot or driving out onto Lillie Road as he suspected.

Ten minutes later Harris had his answer and watched as the silver Peugeot approached the car park barrier. Seeing this, Harris had no hesitation but to reach into his jacket pocket and pull out his pay-as-you-go mobile phone.

Harris dialled 999 and although he knew this man 'Cooper' had to be a policeman, he also knew he was drunk-driving and putting lives at risk. Cooper reminded him of Yuri who had driven over his sister all those years ago and Harris wasn't going to ignore this stupidity. In his best Scottish accent Harris gave false details of himself to the operator on the other end of the line, just as he spotted and flagged down a passing black cab.

Telling the cab driver to follow his direction, the cabbie agreed as Harris told him and the operator the direction of the Peugeot.

Four streets and two minutes later there were two uniformed patrol cars between the Peugeot and the black cab as the sirens and lights were turned on.

There was no high-speed chase, no pavement mounting manoeuvres, no drive through red lights, just the Peugeot pulling over and its driver being pulled from the car.

Harris ended the phone call and asked the cab driver to pull over and wait for his return. Harris left the cab and stood patiently waiting some yards away from the throng of Policemen and Cooper. Harris saw the handheld breathalyser unit turn red whereupon Cooper was arrested, handcuffed and placed into the back of an attending Police van. Harris returned to the cab and gave more directions until it reached the rear entrance of Kensington Police station, here Harris paid the full fare plus tip.

Harris was in no rush, he knew all too well the length of Police procedure and so he waited over an hour before entering the police station showing his identification.

Harris asked the front receptionist where both the Custody Suite and the Criminal Investigation Department (CID) office were located and, like on any typical Sunday night, the CID office was empty of staff and, like any CID office wall in any police station, it showed the internal telephone number of the custody suite which Harris now rang from one of the many desks.

Harris introduced himself as the 'on call' late turn Detective Inspector (DI), a Mr Hobbs who was requesting facts and figures of those currently detained, facts that the custody sergeant gladly gave to him.

In amongst the 'Joe Bloggs' burglars and 'Billy no Mates' robbers, Harris was now armed with the full name and home address of David Cooper who had just been 'booked in.' On hearing the details, DI Hobbs ended the call and Harris walked down the stairs and into the custody suite.

The custody suite was a large reinforced block towards the rear of the police station. It was quiet when he entered as Hobbs and asked for details about Cooper. Soon he established that he had just been booked in and was in a cell, awaiting an on-call doctor for a forensic medical examination, to take blood if need be after a compulsory breath test and Harris wrote notes in the presence of the custody sergeant. Then Harris asked about the other detainees and, again taking notes, Harris gave credibility as to the presence of "Mr Hobbs.'

Next, he asked for access to the prisoner property store to examine the personal and stolen items of property that had been seized and informed the sergeant that access was required to photocopy any correspondence belonging to those involved in crime.

The sergeant, who sat behind the raised desk, not adverse to the occasional 'spot check' was happy to oblige and handed Harris the keys to the suite's property store. Once inside, Harris searched through the individual boxes of property, mostly sealed in plastic bags and Harris grabbed any item that could be deemed in need of photocopying, that included the black notebook that Harris had seen Cooper with earlier.

Armed with various items Harris returned to the CID office and, for the next hour, he copied every single page of that large black notebook that he noted dated back many years. Every page and every scrap of paper that was within the notebook was copied. Harris even photocopied Cooper's warrant card and bank cards. He even photocopied his personal jewellery, including a couple of rings, an old wedding ring, just a simple plain band and the other, a red signet ring with the letters FOH inscribed, not of any importance, other than the fact that these weren't Coopers initials. Then, resealing those bags that he had cut open, he speeds signed M Hobbs and gathering everything he returned to the property store with his. "Thanks."

--//--

The next morning, when Harris woke for work, he was still tired from the night's journey home to Emerson Park. When he had got home he hadn't gone straight to bed either, he was too intrigued by the paperwork of Cooper's that he had photocopied.

The notebook had over five hundred pages that went back over thirty years, each page contained small scripted lists of car registration plate numbers. Some pages had locations showing general areas and directions, then there was tiny hand drawn maps of locations showing greater detail, some with numbered addresses in the East End of London.

There were numerous names and telephone numbers and against each name there was a highlighted £ sign and an amount. Many of these names were girls and marked £50, but some were not. However, the only thing Harris found with any regularity was a monthly, dated entry for the 13th. This would show a location, for example, a caravan site or home county residence, then there would be any amount of £ pounds amounts against the names. Harris had now understood the conversations that he had overheard on Cooper. Police Officer Cooper was nothing more than a fucking pimp who provided the flesh for his clients. Harris went to sleep sickened by this thought.

Now awake and after a quick coffee and shower he made his way to work.

The tube train journey gave him time to think and the motion of rocking back and forth helped his head nod up and down in agreement. Harris had forgotten the date of Nikki's murder so he decided to take the photocopied notes into work with him and reference the notes against her death.

He also decided that he needed to speak to Ralph; he needed to establish for himself whether he thought Ralph was indeed a murderer, or a joint murderer or even an innocent party. Harris also needed to ask if Cooper was actually a relative of Ralph.

Also pressing on his mind was the fact that the 13th of the month was later that week and could he attempt 'a follow?' Harris realised that he really needed some help, but who to turn to?

"First things first." Harris spoke loudly as he closed the storeroom door behind him and, sitting at his desk, he once again examined Ralph's CR docket. There was the date of Nikki's death, her body had been discovered in a Canning Town underpass on 14th December that sent a quick shiver of realisation down the officer's spine.

He carefully turned the photocopied pages of Cooper's notebook to the year of her death and in an instant, he saw the name, Nikki, on a number of pages that he flicked. Her name stood out as a regular, almost a favourite, as her name headed each list. For a number of months, including the party night of 13th December, the night of her death, her name was there.

Harris shook as he carefully scanned the next few pages mumbling to himself as he read, there he soon discovered that he was unable find any further mention of that poor unfortunate Nikki.

"Got you, you bastard." Harris hissed, clenching his fist, Cooper was in some way involved in that young girl's death.

Harris' first call was to Trevor at Pentonville prison and Harris pencilled himself down for several appointments, on a legal visit, for each day of that forthcoming week. He hoped against hope that he would be able to see Ralph on one of those days.

Harris also had the list of car registration numbers that had been written down by Cooper for the 13th December so, lying, requesting on behalf of Detective Chief Superintendent Hutchings, he rung the Driver and Vehicle Licensing Agency (DVLA) and asked for the registered keeper's history of each vehicle.

"What else, what else, there is something else?" Harris spoke in frustration as his mind raced, that was until eventually he loosened the grip of his fist and softly spoke the word. "Sophie."

Again, Harris visualised the dead woman's toes and there, sitting at his desk, he steered his eyes to her toenails and that one perfect toe nail. Perfect, too perfect, but just as perfect as one of the cherry-red toe nails he had seen on Fiona Grant-Smith's feet.

Harris was gutted that the Grant-Smith's had cremated their daughter, but how were they to know that when they sobbed goodbye to the coffin behind closing curtains, that they also kissed goodbye to a clue that may have led to her killer's identity.

Harris knew he had to speak to Rupert and Sophie Forester's children, both Simon and Geraldine.

'They must have some answers,' he thought.

At the very least Harris should make them aware that he was now contemplating exhuming their mother from the family grave.

However, that would have to wait, he was on restricted duties, no investigating, no overtime.

The Detective made one last phone call that morning, he rang Kensington Police Station. Harris needed to know the bail date for Cooper, the date of his first court appearance for his drink-driving offence, but Harris was speechless when the custody sergeant on the other end of his call said. "He blew under the legal requirement, he was free to go."

Harris ended the call-in silence, he was too stunned for words, even his mind couldn't realistically comprehend how Cooper had beat the machine, but he, allegedly, had.

The detective sat at his desk and finger counted what he had seen Cooper consume that day, having used up the fingers and thumbs on both hands Harris could only conclude that someone else blew into the machine for him.

Chapter 51

For those next three days Harris found himself drowning in frustration, he would clock watch the minutes slip by each day knowing, that instead of visiting Ralph, he was delivering or picking up all manner of exhibits from elsewhere.

Then Thursday came and still no joy, he had a window of opportunity and was almost at the prison gates with an hour and twenty minutes of visiting time remaining. However, he wasn't thinking straight, he was concentrating on what he was about to ask Ralph above all else when his work mobile rang and he instinctively answered it.

"Shit, bollocks, and wank!" he screamed, as the call ended. Punching the steering wheel, he threw the phone from his ear, he was required back for another delivery of exhibits and Hutchings was demanding to know where he was.

Screaming at fellow motorists and the pedestrians that crossed the road too slowly, Harris made his way back to Barking, He was ready to rip anyone's throat out with his bare hands and he would be 'smiling to boot' as he did this. To make matters worse, the next day would be Friday the 13th, party night and he wasn't prepared.

He had no means or authority to request police surveillance on Cooper, those types of requests in Met Police land had to come from the ranks of at least a Detective Inspector. No, Harris couldn't sign away authority, he was just a lowly Detective Constable, his job had always been to solve crime and make his bosses look good. His only saving grace was the fact that he hadn't seen any sign of a surveillance team tracking him for the past week or so and concluded that they must have moved on to other, more fruitful, less energetic assignments. In any case Harris had done nothing wrong for them to report on, but, 'Thank God, they were gone,' he told himself.

Harris also knew that he didn't want to advertise the fact that in the worst possible scenario he was looking at another Police officer as a potential murderer, or at the very least Cooper was pimping out children. Harris toiled with the idea of revealing his findings to his new boss, but he knew Hutchings would have no hesitation in removing him from the investigation and sack him immediately from the North and East London Murder Squads for disobeying his direct orders.

So, he tried ringing Ivan, Harris had used the Russians before for observing those that didn't want to be seen and with some success Harris recalled. But the dialling tone told him that Ivan was still abroad and he realised that, yet again, he was on his own.

Harris, without option, decided that he would use his van for the following evening. He knew where and when Cooper would be picking up 'his girls' and he also knew he needed to capture the moment on his digital camera. Going to the exhibit store equipment room, he signed for a drill.

That night Harris drove his van back to Emerson Park. Having parked on the driveway he spent the next hour drilling various small holes and after his nightly swim he returned to the van. In the back, he closed the van's doors and spent the night with his camera practising stealth shots on pedestrians that walked past the house.

--//--

Friday the 13th "what could possibly go wrong?" Harris spoke quietly as he drove his van into work that morning, a wry grin pursed on his lips.

He expected anything and everything to go wrong to be honest, but still he drove on.

Having arrived at the car park underpass he walked into the Murder Squad building only to be confronted by a young admin girl standing by the reception desk. She was holding an envelope and a large card.

"Would you care to donate and write in the card?" The young girl asked him.

"Donate for what?" Harris replied as he wondered who had died or whose birthday it was.

"A get well present for Mr Hutchings, he is ill in hospital." she told him.

"Gladly." Harris said beaming a smile. "Terminal, I hope." And placing a £5 note in front of the young girl's frown, he handed the blue note over.

Harris was handed a pen and, leaning on the counter, he wrote. "Please take your time to recover," and signed it.

'It was starting out to be a good day,' Harris thought.

Harris walked to his storeroom and waited for the inevitable phone calls, to be dispatched here and there, but none came in the first hour and none came the second. It was almost as if everyone had relaxed now that Hutchings was being drip fed in hospital.

He could also hear people laughing in the corridors beyond his door and Harris was smiling too. God how he hoped Hutchings was suffering.

As his desk clock chimed noon Harris rang Pentonville prison and confirmed his legal visit would go ahead that day and walked to the admin office where he took possession of a set of keys for one of the 'pool' cars.

Visiting hours were scheduled to take place between 2 and 4 pm and Harris was first in the queue at the security doors when he followed Trevor into a consultation room.

"Five minutes and he will be here," the prison officer explained and it was a nervous five minutes for Harris as he could only imagine what would walk through the door.

Chapter 52

Ralph was curious as to who this man was, who had stopped him from his work detail all that week just so he could visit him. However, it was his friend Trevor who had assured him that the man was a friend and that he had actually arrived that day and was waiting for him.

Ralph opened the door to the consultation room where he saw, sitting behind a desk, was a mountain of a man who stood up and offered to shake his hand.

Ralph took his hand just the way he had seen on television when he had watched other people greet each other and shook the hand in front of him. It was something he had never experienced before and he liked it. Not even his brother had shaken his hand, so he shook it once more and said. "Hello."

Ralph thought it nice of the man to hand him two packets of cigarettes, he could use those as trade and when the man handed over two packets of chewing gum Ralph was elated, "thank you, thank you, I can blow bubbles with these, would you like to see?" he asked.

The man said. "Yes." And ever so quickly Ralph opened two sleeves of chewing gum and for the next minute or so he chewed and chewed, nodding answers to the man until he formed his first bubble and it 'popped.'

"See, see, I told you I could do it." Ralph told the man and the man smiled back.

Ralph tried to recall his past, those substance addicted days. Who were the men that had taken him for money? What was Nikki like? Could he describe her? And he tried as hard as he could, to remember what happened on the night his girlfriend died, but it was all a blur.

Ralph had tried to forget the lies that the men in wigs had told about him to those people that thought he was a murderer. He told Harris that he had eventually passed out having sniffed a fresh tin of glue and that he had woken to a policeman kicking at him and a knife that had been ripped from his palm.

"It wasn't my knife, I don't own a knife and knives are sharp, you should be careful." Ralph informed Harris.

Harris sat at the desk opposite, he couldn't help but notice instantly that Ralph's physical features were that of someone with some form of mental imbalance. Then listening to Ralph, the way that he spoke, the short tale of his past and knowing his daily routine of solitary life within those thick walls that contained thousands like him, Harris felt nothing but sorrow for Ralph.

Ralph sat in amazement when Harris showed him a screen on the back of a camera and when it flickered into life, showing the images, he quietly said, "Wow."

Ralph saw pictures of his brother and he told Harris that every month he got a visit from him when he would be asked how he was.

"My brother is kind you see, he tells me he has a box called 'conscience' and he would open it and look after me with it when I am released." Ralph explained.

Harris asked Ralph to recall the night of the murder and again he told him that he knew nothing. Harris had no option but to work on the scenario that if Ralph was indeed unconscious and also innocent, then the murderer must have stood in front of Ralph when Nikki was still alive and fighting as she was stabbed to death in front of this poor unfortunate.

This had to be the only possible solution that resulted in Nikki's blood spray hitting Ralph and his clothing. As for the knife, how easy must it have been to dip the handle in glue and leave it to dry in the hand of the comatose Ralph?

"Five minutes," came the shout and a loud knock on the door made both men jump. The visit was ending, but Harris had one more task, a quick DNA elimination sample was needed and with permission he inserted two toothbrush type rods into Ralph's mouth to scrape the inside of his cheeks.

It was as the inmate was saying, "Goodbye" that Ralph thought he had made a new friend and on a final wave as he was led away down the corridor Ralph called back. "Will you say hello to my brother?"

Harris couldn't help himself, he was visualising Cooper beaten to a senseless pulp at his hands as he replied. "Indeed, I will."

On the journey, back from the prison Harris seethed at Ralph's words where 'the brother' had announced that he had a 'box of conscience.'

'How dare he fucking say that to that poor bastard,' and Harris began to dream of Cooper, sitting naked, tied to the commode.

Returning to his office, Harris had something else to concentrate on. A courier had delivered an envelope for Det Supt Hutchings care of DC Harris and a security man on reception handed him the envelope.

It was the DVLA who had sent him numerous microfiche records. Harris clutched the fistful of registered keepers, then, having borrowed a microfiche reader he returned to his storeroom.

The Detective researched all the names and addresses on his computer and soon realised that the list included a number of well-known dignitaries, some dead, but most were alive. The only difficulty he would have in tracing some of them was that the fleet cars had been registered to different Foreign Embassies based in London.

Chapter 53

It was party night and Harris was desperate to know exactly what this entailed, he was visualising vast numbers of people, a crowd where he was alone, so Harris was taking the bare essentials, removing the top drawer of his storeroom desk he ripped at the black masking tape underneath revealing his two prized brass knuckle dusters which he placed in each of his leather jacket, side pockets.

Then replacing the drawer, he placed all the various files that he had obtained, into it. Locking them securely away, happy in the knowledge that, if anything happened to him, Alf would ensure the full disclosure of his findings.

That evening after work Harris drove his van to the nearest petrol station and filled the tank to its brim. He had made a conscious decision that, not only would he photograph Cooper when he collected the girls, but he would also attempt to follow him as best he could on his own.

Harris drove to the first address in Walthamstow and parked just off the main High Street where a 16-storey block of council flats was situated. He reversed his van and parked it directly opposite the front door which gave him an excellent view from the 'peep holes' of vans rear doors.

Locking the van Harris walked over to the main entrance and to the intercom that showed the resident name of each individual flat and there was a trade button that Harris knew would only work from around 6 in the morning until midday.

He also noticed a small circular hole towards the top of the door, this he knew was a fireman's bolt lock, an entry method if ever the fire brigade were needed and they couldn't get in. Harris knew that in his rucksack he had such a cylindrical key that would open this door and, not for the first time that day, he smiled.

All he had to do now was be quiet and wait, not an easy task for someone his build when moving about in the back of a transit van. Because of this he decided to sit in the driver's seat until night arrived. It was only when he assured himself that no one could be watching that he eased the cabin's trapdoor open to move into the rear compartment.

Three hours he waited and watched and with every flash of headlight Harris hoped Cooper's Peugeot had arrived, but it wasn't until 10 pm to the second, the same time that Cooper had quoted over the phone, did he arrive at the car park and walk across Harris' view to the main entrance. Wrapped in a towel to muffle the noise Harris clicked and clicked the camera.

Harris zoomed in to focus on Cooper who had inconveniently obscured the intercom panel in front of him, but at least he had pictures of him at the door and his arm was raised high when pressing whatever number, he needed.

Cooper returned to his car and waited, as did Harris, until a young mixed-race girl, no more than fourteen years old, walked out from the flats in the shortest of skirts and a crop top that bounced pertly with every stride.

"Fucking sick bastard." Harris whispered as he saw the girl climb into the front passenger seat of the Peugeot and as soon as the car moved, so did he.

Scrambling in the darkness Harris found the trapdoor and entered the cab to watch the Peugeot's rear taillights drive off north onto the High Street. Harris followed in a crunching of gears and various degrees of sways on each tight corner taken at speed.

Cooper certainly wasn't hanging around on the journey, but at a distance Harris kept him and the young girl in sight, all the time dictating his every move onto his tape recorder. After two more pickups, each on a street corner, they continued their journey northward.

Harris followed onto the outskirts of London, towards less populated areas and the Detective wondered if Cooper had noticed the white van in his rear mirror? Harris quietly prayed that he had not.

Woodford, Buckhurst Hill and Loughton towards the M25, both vehicles had passed these signs and now there was only one vehicle cover between Cooper and Harris on the tree-lined roads as Harris grew uneasy to the fact that there may soon be no cover at all.

However, as soon as Harris saw the signpost showing the village of Theydon Bois they had to slow for traffic and joined a queue about a half a mile long. Harris could see the faint flickering of blue, emergency lights in the distance.

Fifteen minutes later, with nothing to see other than the blackened forest shrub land on either side and the blue flicker glowing brighter, Harris found himself at the Wake Arms roundabout where the traffic was now at a crawl.

One of the woodland roads, the B172, towards Theydon Bois had been closed off by what appeared to be a couple of Police cars and two vans that were angled sideways across the junction. At each end of the vehicles stood numerous Police officers and Harris could see a number of them waving the cars away from the junction. Harris looked forward towards Cooper's Peugeot only to see its indicators reflect that it was turning right at the five-point roundabout towards the blocked road.

'Where is Cooper going? He certainly wasn't heading towards the M25.' Harris questioned, but he didn't have this thought for long.

'What's this?' Harris thought as he stared straight across.

One of the policemen was waving an old green minibus full of young kids through the Police block, allowing the van to drive on. Now Cooper wanted to do likewise and indicated in the same direction. Harris watched intently as he saw that Cooper had lowered his window and, extending out his right arm in some form of fisted salute, the same Policeman also waived him through onto the closed road.

"Fuck." Harris spoke as he gripped the steering wheel in anxious frustration; the traffic Policeman just shook his head and indicated to Harris to move on by when the Detective also indicated to turn down the same road.

Harris rolled down his driver's side window and shouted. "But this is the quickest route to Theydon Bois and you let that car through."

"There's been an accident sir," the man said, "divert around," was the curt reply from the young man in an ill-fitting uniform.

"Well why did you allow that car down there?" Harris argued his point seeing the Peugeot's lights now vanishing into the distance.

The young Policeman came closer, "That was relatives of the injured, now on your way." He told Harris.

Harris' eyes looked at this young man and the cars that blocked his path and although he could see that the police cars looked genuine, the uniform on this young officer was too old, too dated, yes far too old in style for the young man who wore it. Then there was lettering on his shoulders and it showed GH, the Police code for Hackney station and they were several miles and a couple of divisions from that borough.

As another Police officer began to approach, Harris thought it best not to argue further, he didn't want to arouse suspicion and as he needed to know more he decided evasion was the answer, not confrontation.

Harris spoke a reluctant, "okay," and indicated his van to pull away.

He turned back onto the roundabout and crossed over to the opposite junction where the road took him towards the Wake Arms pub car park. The car park was emptying as it was closing time when he pulled his van to a halt.

Harris watched the chaos that the closed road was causing, but he noticed that within five minutes two other cars had also been, 'waved through,' to a fisted salute.

Harris wanted to know the reason behind this exclusive activity, he knew there wasn't an accident. Accidents wouldn't have that many police officers blocking the road. He also realised that they weren't real police officers and adrenaline began to seep into Harris' veins.

Securing each knuckle duster in place on both hands, he covered these with thick leather gloves and then, grabbing his camera from his rucksack, he locked his van and walked north on the turning just one junction prior to the B172.

He hastened along the Epping Road and having passed by a petrol station it was only then that he was confident that he was out of view of the roadblock at the roundabout that he crossed over the road. Quickly he ran into the blanket of trees, long grass and shrub that covered the area nearby and, in making unsteady progress through the bracken, he veered ever closer to the B172. He stumbled with almost every step in the half-moon darkness, but in time Harris had steered himself near-on adjacent to this road for almost a mile.

Twice he threw himself down into unseen nettle and moss, twice he cut himself on thorn bushes as cars drove past him towards Theydon Bois, but Harris took the cuts, the prickles, the mud and inconvenience, he needed to know.

On he trudged still adjacent to the road, but still he saw and heard nothing, he had been half an hour creeping in the darkness and almost blind as to what lay ahead, as tree branches creaked in the breeze and the moist cold air spat in his face. Nursing a number of scratches to his face he inwardly cursed his situation, he wasn't happy, but did he dare get closer to the road and walk the deep drainage ditch beside it? He would definitely make better progress, but he thought it best not to, if he fell, no doubt there would be a collection of discarded broken bottles for him to cut himself on. He also thought that if he walked on any plastic bottles these would 'crack' loudly and signal his approach.

No, he pushed himself onwards, arms held out in front of him to protect his face. He slogged on.

It was a while before he heard the first scream, but it was high above the wind, then followed a second, it was longer and a long way in the distance, but still a scream. Harris noted it was high pitched and in pain and he held himself, waiting for the next, but none came.

Harris picked up his pace, heading towards its direction and as he could see the road bend up ahead, about 50 yards in front of him. He also saw the start of what was a long line of cars parked on his side of the road.

Harris edged slowly closer, focusing through the darkness, looking for any sign of movement, but the cars appeared empty and Harris made his way out from the woodland and eased himself into the black ditch where he tiptoed his approach to the first car.

Broken glass shattered his third step.

"Bugger." Harris muttered.

He was annoyed that he had no option but to walk the ditch, he knew he needed to photograph each registration plate of the cars that were parked and one by one, including Cooper's Peugeot, his camera shot a digital image.

Harris tried as best he could to keep his feet on the steep incline of the ditch, but more times than not, he found himself sliding back into the filth ditch, full of rubbish and skeletal carcasses of dead animals, but he continued on his quest.

His hearing was now aware of a distant drumbeat, it pounded a constant rhythm and then there were voices, he could hear voices that sounded like native Red Indian chants.

The detective shook his head and closed his eyes in order to concentrate on what his mind was interpreting, but his ears weren't deceiving him, the air was filled with drumbeats and chanting. Harris was confused to fuck, 'what the hell was going on?' He silently questioned.

Although spurred on, Harris needed respite from the ditch as he wanted to know how far the length of cars was that he was photographing stretched. He clawed up the ditch onto the road and peered just above a car rooftop. There to his dismay, the cars rounded yet another corner and further out of view.

To the distant drum beat, to the echoed chants, Harris had taken as many photographs of car registration plates that he dared. He couldn't photograph them all for when he rounded yet another corner he was confronted with a dirt road junction that edged off on either side of the B172.

The right-side track was small and immediately led to what appeared to be a woodland car park, there weren't many cars, but it was filled with men. Many men of various ages all in various attire. However, their common denominator was that the clothing was dark, this included Cooper's, who stood to the fore. He was among the smoking throng where each could be seen to stamp their feet, grinding the cold from their bones.

On his side of the road, on the dirt track directly ahead, Harris could see another group of men and these men were identical in black suits, black ties, each built as if God had carved them from granite and Harris, quietly, photographed them all.

Neither group of men talked to any across the road, but only to each other within their own group and Harris noted that even these conversations, though inaudible above the nearby chants and beating drums, were brief and rare, it was as if each man had little in common with any other.

Harris witnessed only one small flurry of activity and that was when a small compact car arrived. That was when Harris saw the driver handover a small boy, of perhaps around twelve, to one of the men whilst another man handed the driver what looked like a ticket.

'I hope it isn't a fucking train ticket.' Harris thought to himself as the boy was held roughly by the arm and taken up the dirt track, beyond the suits and beyond Harris' sight.

For the next half hour Harris had to lay among the undergrowth, it was cold and damp and every ten seconds or so he took yet another photograph of the drivers until he was satisfied that he had focussed in on each one.

As for the men, directly in front of him, there was no way he'd be able to photograph them without being seen himself and Harris wasn't going to take that chance.

No, his next move was a commando like crawl, something he had seen in the movies, back through the long grass and tree lined undergrowth until he was far from the road. Harris was quite desperate to seek the whereabouts of the children that he assumed had been led away towards the Indian fervour and he followed the noise until it was at its loudest.

There, on the edge of a clearing, Harris was confronted with what appeared to be a red-and-white, vertical lined, striped circus tent with two large poles holding the expansive canvas structure high on either end.

Guarding the tent outside every 5 yards or so were other men in black suits, each alternated from looking towards the base of the tent to look out into the darkness where Harris hid. About 50 yards from the edge of one side of the tent, a white van, not too dissimilar to his own, was parked and, besides that there were four large industrial generators, each no doubt pumping electricity Harris surmised as he saw the leads that snaked the grass towards the huge canopy.

Harris clicked and clicked again, the data card on his camera was beginning to fill, but he crouched as low as he could beneath the thorn bush where he had positioned himself. The tent was massive and very impressive, but Harris couldn't help but focus himself on the various piles of clothes that lay in lined columns along the ground. They reminded him of War Graves as they lay in rows and by each was a small wooden stake. To each stake was tied a handwritten note that flapped in the breeze. On the closest stake, he could see a note, a scribbled letter and numbers.

It only took Harris a matter of seconds to imagine the depravity that lay out of sight in that tent that drummed its foul beat. It was the tiny shoes he saw, the smallest of football kits and the shortest of skirts all spread out in piles before him that had Harris snarling like a beast.

"Dirty scum, utter low life, filthy no good bastards!" Harris screamed inwardly, as his blood boiled in that cold damp air.

But how could he act on what he was confronted with, he was alone, so very alone and whatever those children were suffering, they had probably already suffered worse.

In pure frustration and wanton rage, Harris cried tears and was sickened every time he heard a child cry out, beyond the wails of spirit god chants. Tighter his fists gripped and squeezed the clumps of earth around him.

However, within five minutes there was silence, the beating melody of sick minds and music suddenly stopped and Harris readied himself with his camera that he angled his focus over tear sodden cheeks.

'He was going to get these sick bastards alright,' he had told himself. 'He'd make them pay, by hook or by crook,' he promised himself. Harris was 'going to see

253

them suffer.' That was what his mind voiced and there was no other thought as he watched the adults and children slowly exit the tent.

Some children could walk, some stumbled, but many were assisted, held upright by the men in black suits.

He saw up to a hundred or so children. Black, white and Asian. All wrapped in cloth sacks, some wearing feathered headwear. None had shoes and not one of them smiled, many wept, as Harris did.

Through pooled vision the detective watched as each child was checked off against a marking on their arms and then led towards their 'peg marked' clothes.

Harris watched a boy, no older than ten, who stood no more than five yards away from him. Harris could see an ink marked arm showing 'P53' and, when stripped of his sack, he saw the scratched flesh and immediately thought of Nikki 'Z121.'

Dressing was a slow process not only for this child, but for almost all of the others. Some were younger, some were older, but from what Harris could see, all of them were marked in some way. Scratch marks here, bruises there and nearly all were weeping, those that weren't, were silent, bewildered and probably drugged.

Harris took one or two photographs of the children, he couldn't manage more. He was too upset to press on, to focus. After dressing, Harris likened the scene to something like a prison camp, one by one the children were marched off down the dirt track towards the waiting cars and eager drivers who wanted to be gone.

Harris turned his attention to the gathered throng of adults that stood outside the tent. These were mostly men, some in dinner jackets and bow ties and a couple of them wore cowboy hats. Some wore their national Arabic styled clothing and although there was only a couple of women, each of these had worn trousers suits for the party. Harris calculated that the ratio of children to adult was at least one-to-one. He was furious when he noticed that a number of them were carrying their own personal whips.

Harris saw his fists flying into each of the faces in the digital images that he took as he saw them laughing and smiling to each other as they eventually strolled away down the pathway.

Harris remained still and listened to the various cars driving off nearby, but he didn't care to follow, he was captivated by the clear up operation that had begun in earnest in and around the tent site.

As each heavy wooden bench seat and table was taken from the tent, each was sprayed with what had to be either, white spirit, petrol or paraffin. Then there were four men with mops and buckets who worked the pieces of furniture, scrubbing hard on each, before moving to the next.

Every chair, every table that left the tent received the same treatment and Harris raised his eyebrows when he saw six wooden carved totem poles, each with shackles, being removed and receive the same forensic cleansing solution.

After that came the loading of these onto a large, dark, transport furniture lorry that had trundled up into the clearing. There was no lettering on the side or rear of this lorry and it didn't even have a number plate.

Harris kept low, for on various occasions torches would shine out from the clearing towards the woodland where he and the other wildlife hid. Their bright beams blanketed the pegged area where the children had undressed and dressed as the numbered stakes were removed and box loaded into the lorry.

However, the used sacks and the occasional headdress were all piled together, quite close to where Harris lay and focusing his lens he photographed not only these, but amongst them was a pair of jeans, a small coat and something else that could have been a baseball cap.

As the last was piled, another suited man emptied the liquid contents of a green metal jerry can onto the clothing, then, striking a match, the sacks and clothing were ablaze. Harris didn't have long to guess as to who had worn that oddment of clothing amongst the sacks, for his next discovery was just as chilling, just as shocking.

Four men exited the tent each carried a spade in one hand as the other held either an arm or leg of a lifeless body. Pale and insignificant to those that gripped her, the thin young girl, probably mid-teens was carried facedown into the woodlands at the back, beyond the clearing and out of view.

Harris whispered the Lord's Prayer as he held himself fast against his thoughts of retribution and he repeated the prayer again and again to hold his concentration. Harris could only imagine the suffering and the disposal that the poor young girl received.

Within minutes the four men returned and Harris clicked his camera on each, but he was eventually drawn to the man that returned to the tent time and again.

Back and forth to the white van he went and each time he was holding a small black object that he locked away in the cabin. The detective used full zoom, clicking away until he saw and realised what each of the dozen or so objects were; each was a small remote camera that had relayed their images back to the van where a small aerial protruded from its roof.

Harris understood what was going on, but he didn't want to believe his eyes, though he was so very grateful that his camera had witnessed every detail.

The last shots Harris took were as the white van drove from the clearing, it was the last to leave and there Harris lay there waiting, waiting for quiet. He needed to cross the open space and willed himself to begin his search for the dead girl that he had seen carried off into the dark.

Harris waited, his muscular frame that had tumbled, tripped, crawled and cried in the dirt, now convulsed with rage as he swore revenge. He waited. He had to be sure that none else remained and, other than the odd shiver, Harris lay motionless until surrounded by the morning dew of a new day.

Harris stirred as a cold nose brushing against his bald head, then a big long lick, followed by another. Harris stirred and heard a woman's voice calling out. "Here Sully, here Sully, good boy, come on Sully, where are you?"

Harris was startled by the early-morning brightness and quickly pushed the friendly Labrador away with his outstretched palm.

Harris quickly edged himself further back into the bracken and bush as the dog eventually responded to his owner's voice, Harris sat and quietly cursed that his adrenaline rush had eventually eased him into a deep sleep.

As the cries of, "here boy," drowned in the distance, Harris sat up, began to brush himself down as best he could, which was difficult enough with his mud-covered gloves and his soaking wet jeans. He stood and, looking down, saw that all of him was filthy, he smelt the same as he looked. He stood and waited for quiet and when it came he crossed the clearing in front of him.

Taking the same route as the four men with spades had taken and, though Harris was no Red Indian himself, even he could easily spot the trampled footsteps, the broken twigs and the hacked away branches that led him to a freshly dug mound of earth.

There Harris photographed the mudded footprints surrounding the grave before his hand dug deep into the spade flattened earth.

Several minutes passed before Harris eventually pushed his hand down to where he found the young girls cold flesh. Clearing the mudded earth, slowly, ever so slowly, he found her head and uncovered her face. Gently he wiped, brushing the soil from her features and he blew away grit from both open eyes. Lastly, pushing her tongue back into her mouth he presented the girl, in her early teens, towards his camera lens.

Chapter 54

The intermittent drips of water that occasionally rippled the calm of Harris' hot bath had no effect on his concentration. Harris was deep in thought, the same as it had been on his journey home from Theydon Bois.

'Should he have dug up the body and announced its discovery?' He questioned himself, but 'what would that have achieved other than spotlight him to the scum that he was pursuing?' he countered.

What reason did he have to be there in the first place?

And would he be allowed to investigate the murder? Of course not.

So, Harris soaked his thoughts a little longer in that freestanding bath in Maya's home and he closed his eyes to thoughts of the Russian's wife that had smiled sweetly up at him.

Once bathed Harris deliberated for the rest of the day and Sunday was much the same. His mind needed to rethink, his body needed to exercise, to swim, or go for a run, he wanted food and to drink beer.

He needed so many things, but, most of all, time for himself to reflect. He wanted to watch others with their daily lives, to re-evaluate why he was a Detective and whatever he was doing, was he doing right?

He even asked himself if there was some mystical force that tried to suppress his efforts, he wondered if he was lying to himself as he had lied to others, could he survive the evil and filth that now clung to him, perhaps infecting him?'

Those were the questions he asked himself and it wasn't until that Sunday afternoon that a stroll to a nearby park had him sit at a bench seat and, watching young children playing with loving parents, only then did he rekindle his purpose.

Chapter 55

Harris knew immediately that Hutchings was still off sick when he returned to work the following day, he walked by the windows of the administration office and there were smiling faces everywhere.

Harris didn't hesitate, he had made a list of the registration number plates from his camera and he seized the moment. Quickly Harris walked to the general noticeboard outside the office and there in front of him were layers and layers of various notices from the boss who hated his guts.

Hutchings was someone who liked the sound of his own voice and would add his signature to almost anything, from a 'do this' list, to a 'don't do' list. There was even an advert selling a child's bicycle that had Hutchings signature on, this Harris took.

Over the next half hour Harris sat, busily typing, in his storeroom office, transferring the vehicle registration notes onto headed notepaper, it was on a letter of request that he traced out the signature of A. Hutchings. Placing the letter into a green cardboard folder which he marked for the attention of Chief Supt Hutchings he took it to the admin office and discreetly placed it in the sick man's mail shelf. Next Harris returned to his storeroom and practised various voices until he found the one, the Scotsman again and, with it, he rang the admin office.

He was a courier for Chief Supt Hutchings and simply asked if the vehicle checks Mr Hutchings had asked for had been completed and if not, they would need to be ready for collection by the end of the afternoon. The young girl on the other end of the phone answered in the affirmative and Harris replaced the receiver.

Then he waited, like a giggling schoolboy. He waited an hour before returning to the admin office. There he noted that the green cardboard envelope had been removed from where he had placed it and that one of the women was referring to it as she busied herself on the Police National Computer (PNC).

Harris smiled as he called out for some assistance to which another of the girls, Susie, was only too pleased to help.

Suzie secretly had a small crush on Harris the solidly built detective with cheek filled dimples and she didn't mind searching the missing person's index with him where he was looking for any girls that had gone missing over the weekend.

"It has been a quiet weekend." Susie said, cheeks flushing in the close proximity of Harris as he lent over beside her, both glancing between smiles and the flickering computer screen.

"There's only four that have gone missing," she said, "and as far as I can see none have returned from the weekend."

'Nothing unusual in that, kid's arguments with parents, parties and the like,' Harris thought.

Suzie continued. "One is an adoption from Twickenham, one a fostered from Tottenham, then there's a family argument from Bromley and a care home girl from Barnes South-West London."

Harris now concentrated on the screen as Susie flicked from one report to the other until he saw the face he had uncovered. Harris was unsettled and asked if there was anything unusual about the care home.

Suzie told him there was nothing out of the ordinary, the home had had a number of absconders in the past and no doubt there would be more in the future.

"Just another care home," she concluded

It was just another care home in another London Borough where kids ran, disappeared, some never returned. All the same Harris casually requested the missing kid's details.

Harris wanted a printout of each so as not to raise suspicion and Suzie handed over three printed files of the girls and the boy missing from Barnes. Harris took one more look at the care home girl, a pretty youngster, forever in trouble and a girl Harris knew, would be in trouble no longer.

After thanking Suzie Harris returned to his storeroom, there he sat down and, having obtained the phone number from the directory, he telephoned the Commissioner's office at New Scotland Yard.

The staff officer on the other end of the line, a Superintendent someone or other, informed him that there was no window of opportunity to meet the Commissioner for at least three weeks. Harris after all, was just a mere Detective Constable of little importance, yet another frustration, but Harris just shrugged this away knowing that he had other phone calls to make and time to waste until the evening when the admin office would be devoid of staff.

Chapter 56

The big white van with the aerial wasn't there. The one that Harris had seen by the tent, wasn't on the driveway of that small detached cottage in Kent. The cottage, a picturesque, hanging basket, black beamed, detached building which Harris had found the vehicle was registered to.

Harris had high hopes on his short drive around the M25, but the van simply wasn't there, instead, parked out on the street, was, what appeared to be, a minicab displaying a company name. Harris again checked the PNC printout, it was the correct address, so there was nothing for Harris to do, but park with a distant view from the cottage and wait.

Harris waited all evening and still nothing, no movement, not a light on or off, nothing. At dawn Harris drove himself back to Barking and work.

For the rest of the week it was the same routine, whenever Harris wasn't sleeping at his desk he was being used as a dispatch boy and when not sleeping or on dispatch, he would spend every waking moment working on a file that he was preparing to personally present to the Commissioner.

The detective detailed that he was after a serial murderer, a murderer who had killed at least three women, one of these a girl and Harris still had only confined his investigation parameters to London.

'God knows how many others there are.' Harris thought with relish.

'I really hope there are more, not for the victim's sake,' he tried to convince himself. But more victims meant more clues and more kudos and boy, did he want to solve these murders that had spanned so many years.

The Commissioner alone would see the file first and Harris had to hope that he could be trusted.

Then there was Ralph, not merely a side line, but a man Harris believed was wrongly convicted. By chance he had found a link to a sick world of perversion and this last revelation laid heavily on the Detective's mind. He wanted to deal with it, but deal with it on a personal level.

Harris knew that almost every week there were television and newspaper reports about missing children, all swallowed up in the lure of London. For years he had heard of reports into criminal investigations that would highlight 'missing' files, some shredded revelations and the 'lost in transit' paperwork. Then 'what about the mistrials?' he considered. All those prominent figures, the clerics, the television celebrities, the pop stars, each claiming their innocence against false allegations. Harris knew too many had escaped prosecution and only sporadically was there the odd conviction, the stupid ones that had kept some personal record or trophy as a sickening reminder.

Harris had seen through his own eyes just some of the scum that must have thought little or nothing of the depraved acts that they had inflicted on the children and Harris desperately wanted retribution. So, every night he would return to the cottage and wait for the white van to appear.

It was Friday evening near dusk and Harris, though totally shattered, was alive to the adrenaline that suddenly pumped through his body when he finally saw the white van pull onto the driveway. Snatching his camera Harris quickly focussed in on the driver, it was the same man he had seen on that night of debauchery.

Click, click, click his digital camera shuttered as the man unloaded what appeared to be the same type of camera equipment that Harris had previously seen him load by that tent and, as the man closed the van, Harris left his and quietly walked up to the cottage and passed by.

Harris could see nothing, other than the flicker of an occasional light being turned on and off, he needed to get closer and it wasn't long before he found his way, skirting a well-trodden rural footpath, he approached the rear gardens at the back of the cottage and another cottage nearby. Without warning, a yapping dog halted the Detective's progress and so crouching, hiding, he waited until its owner, who was apparently fed up with the constant barks screamed at the animal, "Kya," to return indoors. Harris was becoming quite adept at dealing with foliage and sharpened bracken and he hardly made any noise, other than a soft squelch of underfoot lawn as he crept towards the illuminated rear lounge windows. There was a double door exit flanked by a large window on each side and Harris chose the side where the curtain hadn't been pulled fully across.

Harris was expecting a three-piece suite, perhaps a coffee table, or a dining table with chairs, but not the banks of television screens that covered the wall on the opposite side. No vases, no china ornaments, no pictures of loved ones, but a row of silver and black computers, at least four of them and instead of the usual display cabinets in most people's homes, there stood instead, a five-foot-high, four draw metal filing cabinet.

There was one chair, a leather and double armed office chair on wheels and this was occupied by the man who sat viewing various moving images and stills of naked men, women and children displayed on the screens.

Harris was mesmerised as he watched the various scenes flicker their images, as the man sat on his keyboard, adjusting the volume of screams and moans to all but a murmur, as he began editing a sequence of clearer enhancements on each of the adults' faces, as he pixelated out those of each child.

Harris began to realise that this was more than pure voyeurism; various keys were pressed, there was tapping on small square button boards, unlike any key board Harris had seen, and then the sliding up and down of various dials until each of the images' clarity was perfected.

Erasing shadow, tuning contrast, pitching brightness and then orchestrating the pixilation that obscured the facial pain of each child.

'Yes, a sick pervert,' Harris thought, but he wasn't sitting at the desk in front of him groaning in physical pleasure at the various children's torment. No, this man was an engineer, an artist, working the resolution of each adult image and printing the results of his work on a nearby colour copier. He also appeared to index his work, scribbling his findings onto a huge black ledger. Then there was the disc copy that he burnt and individually placed into a plastic sleeve that was then transferred to the huge filing cabinet, but why?

A long two hours passed, by now the Detective had sat down on the cold concrete patio and just looked out into the garden beyond. He didn't want to look at another sickening image, or watch this man beavering away in his office, all Harris was thinking about was, 'why?'

Harris even contemplated going back to the heated warmth of his van where he might be able to concentrate more, but when the man in the cottage suddenly cried out "Got you!" Harris jolted.

Looking up and searching in the darkness, 'had he been captured?' he thought.

"No thank God," he muttered, as he soon realised that he was alone, though he had let his guard down.

Quietly Harris rose to his numbed feet as he heard a cackled laughter from within and once more he peered into the room.

The detective's mouth dropped wide open at the face he recognised on the big banks of screens.

Not merely a German bureaucrat, but a man that was so highly ranked in their country's Government, he had become a stalwart on the Council of the European Union. Anti-British, pro-European and a man who had just recently on television; screamed for the United Kingdom to be excluded from the single market.

Harris watched as the engineer rubbed his hands with glee and, although it was past midnight, there was a telephone call of which Harris overheard a short conversation, a chat where it suddenly dawned on Harris that the man was confirming and colluding with someone, some form of extortion.

Like a sledgehammer slamming him between the eyes Harris recoiled in this revelation, a veil of blackmail; that was why. That was why there was such a performance to obtain the best visual detail and that was why Harris decided to wait.

Chapter 57

It was Saturday and Simon Forrester waited patiently for this Detective Harris to arrive at his parent's house. His weekends were precious; however, he was clinging to the hope that there was some good news regarding his parents' recent murders. As the weeks had passed, he and his sister Geraldine both now knew that the case had gone cold, but still he hoped.

It came as quite a surprise to see a cheap old white Ford van pull up on the driveway and the bulking Detective in an old black leather jacket, brushing off what appeared to be grass seed and bramble, walk up the driveway towards the mansion. Simon, waiting on the doorstep, really didn't know what to make of him.

When Harris introduced himself, he wasn't inspired when he then let out a yawn. He was unshaven and his clothes and boots were muddied and dirty.

How the officer spoke! With the roughest of East London accents, a voice made from gravel, 'probably thrown in one's face,' he thought with disdain, but Simon offered entry and to make him a classic Earl Grey tea, but the Detective replied. "Black instant coffee, no sugar," definitely quite crass.

The Detective asked. "Where can I smoke?" Simon showed him the rear kitchen door that led to the garden and Simon stared out of the bay window overlooking the garden and watched, over kettle vapour, at Harris, who still stood yawning.

'The Detective looks more like a gangster,' Simon believed, perhaps more attuned to burying bodies than discovering who had put them there, his mind questioned.

But Simon took the officer's coffee into his father's study and called for the Detective and, on either side of the desk, they sat. For the next twenty minutes Harris explained why there had been such urgency to meet.

Simon listened to the officer explain how he knew his father through 'work' and how it had been his grim task to deal with his parents' bodies when they were found murdered. Harris then remarked and congratulated Simon on having tidied up his parents' home, as he explained it was him who had come to search their already ransacked home.

In frustration Simon could contain himself no further and began asking question after question.

Were the police any further forward in their investigations?

What progress had been made?

Why was this dishevelled Detective here?

And so, Harris began, though he was a little uneasy as he explained the degree of wounds and his removal of the bloodied corpse of his mother from the car. A body that was scalped of its skin, with the thin lengths of flesh flapping from various limbs, a slicing from neck to foot, this was this young man's mother after all, so he didn't go into too much detail.

Harris told of finding the folded train ticket on the ground, when he lifted Sophie from the family car and that Harris now surmised that there could have only been one or two orifices where the ticket had fallen from. The son's face turned ashen grey.

"You mean?" Simon spoke as he gulped.

"I mean whoever murdered your mother," Harris interjected, "had pushed a train ticket into her body as if sending her on a journey."

"My God." the young man whispered, transfixed to the Detective's words and the room fell silent as Harris waited for Simon to look at him. Harris waited for Simon to compose himself; there was no way he was going to continue until he knew Simon was going to be able to comprehend what he would be asking next.

It took time, a long time, as he watched Simon weep tears, where his hands covered his face. Patiently Harris waited.

Harris stood to stretch his legs and stepped away from the desk. Simon didn't notice, he was still in his own world of grief and horror as Harris became curious as to the array of awards and certificates that adorned the study walls. Then there were the framed photographs in the display cabinet, 'barrister gatherings,' Harris assumed and it was the cough that turned Harris' focus back towards Simon, who was now staring at him through watered eyes to continue.

Harris took a deep breath. "I believe the evil bastard that murdered your mother has killed others, but I need your help to prove this." He announced, to Simon's amazement.

"What, what, what do you mean?" Simon stuttered.

So, Harris told him of the link between the various train tickets that he had found. Simon was astounded by this latest revelation, but was pleased that at least, there was someone discovering new leads, even if he could pass as a bedraggled, nightclub doorman.

What Harris asked next though, was something he asked Simon to pass onto his sister, he asked him to explain to Geraldine why Harris would be requesting an exhumation of their mother's grave to seek further evidence. This was a sickening and heart-wrenching call. "But necessary." Harris told him.

The detective gulped the last of his coffee and explained that he had things to do on his day off and shaking Simon's hand, both were in gratitude.

On leaving the study Harris walked slowly, again glancing at the array of photographs that adorned the walls. Many of the pictures showed Simon's father dressed in various fineries at numerous events and as he pointed his finger towards one picture that showed Rupert standing within a group of men, Simon explained to the Detective. "They are friends of my father, they all studied law together."

Chapter 58

Noticing that there were three cars parked on Maya's driveway, Harris braked slowly in his battered old van and passed the house at a crawl to peer in. He saw that the front door was wide open and filling the gap was a young man who had obviously spent his youth taking steroids. He wasn't tall, just wide, with biceps pulling at the fabric of his tracksuit top, blonde cropped hair, flat faced as if a shovel had hit it and Harris knew straight away by these features that he was Russian.

Harris drove on to the top of the road and, parking several hundred yards away, he sat in contemplation. He was running the twists and turns of his mind through the various scenarios that in reality he now faced and would have to face, whatever the outcome.

Harris locked his van and placed the ignition key on top of the offside front wheel and walked towards the house, he didn't want his van to be known and he didn't want to be found with the keys on him either.

With every step Harris could feel his body twitch with nerves, his sweat began to rise, as did the bright sunshine. He so wanted to remove his leather jacket, but he knew it could offer him at least some protection against the blows his mind now imagined.

The last time he was around Russians, they had toyed brutally with his private parts as he had stared death in the face and here he was walking back towards them, but he wasn't prepared for any confrontation and he certainly wasn't ready to fight for his life.

However, the Detective turned onto the driveway that led to the house and in that instant the Russian at the door, who was watching Harris intently, suddenly called out in his native language to someone behind him. Harris stopped and stared at the henchman knowing that he would come out of a fight with this beast perhaps third if not second best, but he pulled his shoulders back and stood tall, staring through him, as he continued to walk to the doorway.

'Fuck he's a lump.' Harris thought as he got closer taking his final strides before stopping directly in front of that garlic breathed strongman. The Russian called out again behind him to which this time there was an answer and the man stood sideways allowing Harris a chance to squeeze by the gap that had opened for him.

Harris entered the hallway and turned to his right towards the living room where he heard a number of men speaking in Russian. It was far from what Harris had imagined in his mind.

For there, in front of him, was a line of men, but none faced him, each stood looking down towards the grizzled voice that was barking orders in front of them, it was a voice Harris recognised, a voice he dreaded, a voice from the bear of a man that he knew he'd have to face, it was Yuri.

Harris kept his distance, he wasn't that keen to edge forward and say, "Hello." However, he was pleasantly relieved that he hadn't yet been dragged off and murdered. So, he bided his time and waited, observing the various nodding heads of agreement that stood in front of him answering their boss in the affirmative.

Harris wished he knew more Russian than that word and the answer for, "cheers for health," Mind you that one word, 'Zazdorovje,' had always served him well in the past.

Another minute and more orders, then another and another and still Harris stood there shifting from one foot to another. Harris was thinking he must have looked like a naughty schoolboy who was going to blame the classroom smashed window onto another child. At last, with one last bark, the wall of giants parted before him and each brushed past the Detective as they made their way out into the hallway behind him and out of sight.

Yuri almost filled two parts of the three seater Chesterfield sofa, on the other part was another Russian that Harris recognised from the racing night that he had attended. It was a man wearing thick rimmed glasses, quite gaunt compared to most of Yuri's men. A silent man, as silent as he had been when he last saw him, but he was studious as he looked Harris up and down.

Yuri lent back and looked up, staring at the Detective in front of him. Harris stared back as if a stand-off had begun. Neither man spoke, Harris daren't, he believed he could still feel Yuri searching for answers and it was only when Harris looked down at the fledgling regrowth of his fingernails on his right hand did Harris first speak.

"You had me tortured you cunt! Who the fuck do you think you are, you fuckwit?" Harris menaced as he thrust the back of his hand out forward for examination.

"How the fuck dare you! After all I've done for you, too!" Harris snarled.

"Do you actually know how painful it is to feel your bollocks boil between your legs?" Yuri just sat silent and the Detective would have continued his rage if not for the call, "Enough".

It was a voice loudly spoken and one that came from over Harris's left shoulder.

Harris turned and saw Ivan by the room doorway.

"Enough." Ivan repeated to the Detective as he walked past and took his place standing beside Yuri and then there was a hard silence as Harris did his very best to calm his anger.

He did his best, but couldn't contain himself; he tried, but failed. "What about my fucking house?" He suddenly screamed.

"Enough, no more!" Ivan shouted back once more and on that note Yuri raised his hand to signal a halt.

Harris stared down at the man who was built like two brick shit houses; the Russian powerhouse who could crush a skull between two hands, a man who now pushed himself upright to stand beyond the leather-bound furniture that creaked under the strain.

This ogre, muscle mountain, who could no doubt snap Harris in half, he had heard enough and now toe to toe with each other Harris actually realised that he had forgotten how immense this animal was.

Even at his age, Yuri's body was sheer blocks of muscle on solid steel bone and he stood inches taller and at least a foot wider than the detective in front of him.

"I will not repeat this, so listen well my friend." Yuri spoke with authority.

'Friend, thank God he used the word friend.' Harris thought, had he done enough to convince this monster of his innocence.

"I am sorry." The Russian hushed his gritted whisper.

"I order what I order because I can, I ordered what I ordered because I wanted it so." Yuri weirdly philosophised.

"Now, you and I will be friends again," he told Harris.

There was no option in that statement, it was an order more than anything else.

"This is your new home, this is my thank you, my apology, you understand?" he asked Harris.

"Thank you." Harris uttered. He had survived.

"Yes my friend, your idea about the sweets, worked, how you say, fantastic!" Yuri announced and Harris saw Yuri's gold teeth in the broadest of smiles as waves of relief hit him.

Yuri and Ivan explained in their best broken English how Harris' simplistic idea had worked so well against the crumbling French criminal case.

What with Gregor dead and therefore unable to substantiate those spurious allegations, how easy it was to find witnesses to Yuri's charitable offerings.

All came forward, men of 'honour,' judges, policeman, politicians, not forgetting the numerous businessmen that included a local town mayor, each bore witness to Yuri handing out bags of sweets to the unfortunate children of East London.

Many spoke of how they witnessed Gregor helping Yuri with this charitable work and some even saw Gregor greedily keeping bags for himself. Then there were a few stories and allegations, all signed acknowledgement in court that related to this Gregor being involved in crime, a man with no scruples, who was having a secret affair with Yuri's wife Maya.

Perhaps circumstantial, but including this in an alleged plot against the unsuspecting, revered Yuri, the French judiciary had no option but to 'drop its case' and offer apologies to the Russian who was now suing the French Government for being shot.

So, it was that afternoon, awash with vodka, the four men sat in Maya's living room, Harris' new home, chatting, laughing and rekindling friendships and still the bespectacled man never spoke.

"How's your manhood?" Yuri asked pointing and laughing towards Harris' genital area.

"To be honest I really don't know." Harris replied still reeling with relief from not being found out.

"Well, no doubt you will find out soon enough." Yuri laughed at Harris who then spoke loudly in his native tongue, gaining the attention of Ivan and interrupting one of his numerous phone calls.

"Ivan and I have business to complete and I must see to some people." Yuri explained. "Some of my people need reminding who is in charge, some haven't worked as hard as they should have, and all need taking care of."

Harris knew exactly what that might mean, but cared not to comment.

"You will now work for me, no?" Yuri asked looking for Harris' agreement.

But Harris shook his head, "sorry no, you have enough policemen working for you, I work for myself, but, and this is a big but, you have my loyalty," and offered his hand in friendship which Yuri took and shook, nodding on this settlement.

"You are good man Harris, a good man." Yuri slurred raising his glass to yet another toast.

Harris took this opportunity and announced. "Yuri, I have something important to tell you about your daughter's kidnapping."

This immediately gained the Russians attention. "Your daughter was kidnapped by a man, a child molester, a rapist, you understand that right?" and the crime lord nodded anger in recollection.

"What of it? He's dead, he did not touch my child." Yuri retorted, hatred recalling this recent past.

Harris continued with his story. "He was just part of a group of men and women that prey on young children, they may even be targeting your other children," he said.

"I now know who they are, but I ask for your help." And with no hesitation Yuri agreed.

Harris talked at length about a proposition involving pain and payment. Both Yuri and Ivan sat forward, somewhat eager, when they realised the earning potential and influence to be gained by Harris' proposal and again all three of them settled agreement on handshakes and smiles as the doorbell rang suddenly.

Somewhat startled, Harris had never heard the doorbell ring before, the loud repeating chime caught him by surprise.

"Calm." Yuri uttered. "Ivan and I have to go. Is there anything else before we leave?"

"Yes, there is one more thing." Harris asked, confident that trust had returned.

"When Rupert Forrester and his wife were murdered, their home was ransacked. I believe that Mrs Forrester was targeted by a mad man, someone deranged, someone with hate and the answer to her murder may lay in correspondence and/or their computers that were stolen from their house. I need these please." he asked.

"How far will you look?" Yuri warily questioned.

Harris knew he was on 'dodgy ground,' the Russian pistol that took Rupert's life, told him so.

"I only want to find the person who murdered Mrs Forrester." Harris reiterated. "They may have murdered before and they will murder again."

"We will see." Yuri spoke carefully, no admittance or denial. "We will see."

Harris stood with the three Russians as they walked towards the hallway, but in an instant Yuri turned sideways towards Harris and opening both arms he embraced him tightly, clenching, clamping the Detective he announced. "We will meet again soon my friend." On that Harris found himself standing alone, stunned by his good fortune, his mind told him, 'Shit creek looked like it had been paddled.'

Turning to the front door he waved goodbye to Yuri, Ivan and the other Russian. Outwardly Harris was smiling, inwardly he whooped only one word, 'Yes!'

Chapter 59

It was a minute or two after the Russians' car had turned the corner and still Harris stood in the doorway breathing that sweet, afternoon, fresh air. He was brazen, alive, so very much alive, perhaps even born again and if Maya was gone for good, he had every chance of staying that way.

The relief was immediate to the officer, a tidal wave of realisation that made his legs jelly and Harris found himself leaning, edging, grabbing the door frame, pushed back by the sun's rays that shone upon his face, he gently lowered himself down, until he finally found cold solace in the shade of that marbled hall floor.

Harris sat silent, listening to the very breath of his own chest's rise and fall. He became oblivious to the world outside him. He had always believed in standing firm, only this time he was finding it hard just to know where exactly he should plant his feet.

He never heard the car pull up, nor did he hear the closing of its door, nor did he pick up on the high-heeled footsteps that clicked onto the driveway, but it was just the soft tone of a female Russian with the words. "Arris, you are Arris?" And he stirred.

Harris looked up and, to his surprise, standing in the doorway before him was a vision of sheer beauty. Long dark hair that swept her shoulders and standing at almost 6 feet of long legged loveliness, the green eyed young girl of around twenty, waving a mobile phone in her hand again asked. "Arris, you are Arris?"

Harris looked up and simply nodded, he was transfixed by the translucent outline of a sun-kissed body, and a body he could see through the thin cotton of a skimpy white dress. Harris didn't think this day could get any better, but it was about to and he quickly found his strength to stand up to her.

He was just about to question her presence, but as soon as he stood, the mysterious dark-haired beauty lent her head forward and began to kiss the officer's neck. Then her hands caressed Harris' chest and, ever so slowly, as still she kissed, gently her nails dug into his T-shirt sweeping the leather jacket off his shoulders and onto the floor. Feverishly she continued her open mouth kisses around each side of his neck towards his cheeks. Intermittent nibbles on his earlobes and Harris felt both breaths quicken. Her legs, oh those legs, that quick glimpse he recalled as both his eyes had closed, each smooth and supple in turn writhed high up and down on Harris' jeans as he held the oiled perfection of her thighs.

"Make love to me," she whispered as she pulled her head back from his face and Harris looked into two stunning emerald pools of want.

Half want, half desire and on full payment from her employer.

Harris had absolutely no objection as she closed the front door behind her, nor when she pulled her dress up and over her shoulders and apart from her white five-inch high heels she was naked, no panties or bra. Just the smooth tight tanned skin of her nubile young body as she climbed the stairs before him.

There were no words as they entered the main bedroom, somehow, she knew the way and she said nothing as she undressed the man in front of her. Finally, there was no explanation as she pulled him onto the bed, no words were needed.

The girl covered Harris as she pushed him onto his back and again, she kissed and sucked at his body. Their lips never met, Harris tried, boy did he try, but each time he neared, she pulled away.

Harris could feel her moist heat as she enwrapped his hard body and Harris was blessed that his entire body now stiffened for her. As the young girl writhed, moaning ever so gently, Harris could feel the moistened wet heat, leave their trail all over his thighs and midriff and although it felt forever, the moment soon arrived as she knelt between Harris' open thighs.

Then her hands were upon his manhood. Stroking, pulling, finger flicks and smooth caresses that held each inch and pumped with open palm and finger-tip grips, all this soon had Harris moaning as he looked down and watched her layered black hair gently sway from side to side as he felt the soft kisses and licks around the base and onto this hardness she still continued to stroke.

Closing his eyes once more Harris defaulted to the thoughts of stinking blue veined cheese, something he hated, something he needed to do to make this moment last forever. Then it was wrinkly old grandma's, pools of sick and buckets of faeces, anything to stop the build, the flow, that his body now yearned to shed.

He was as hard as granite, so hard it hurt and the girl was relentless, working his strain and opening her mouth to his length and rocking her head, she took him all in.

The girl pushed herself down, taking him as deep as she dare and then her throat pulled upward before plunging back down again.

She worked to Harris' urgings, increasing the suction and depth until there was no more to take and Harris, having placed his hands around the back of her head, now held her there, deep and perhaps longer than she liked, but he held her until he was ready to release.

Rapidly she rose, only to take Harris in for more repeated lengths until pulling off and exhaling high pitched gasps, joining his pleasure moan and each smiled at each other as throat saliva left her lips.

Coyly the girl waved her finger at Harris. "You not come yet." she said.

And Harris couldn't interpret if this was a question or request as she climbed up and sat astride his stomach teasing his manhood with the edge of her buttocks.

'She was clearly flushed,' Harris thought as she smiled, gently soaking her dampness back and forth along his midriff and still the Russian girl looked down on him and repeated. "You not come yet."

Harris shook his head and she nodded before slowly lowering herself down to envelope his hardness.

'Finally.' He thought.

'Finally, she is taking me,' his body sung out and she pushed down to just brushing his tip, then with a wide smile she slipped his length and pushed and pulled her body stroking his rigidity across her entrance.

The tension and frustration steamed in good measure as the boiling flames of pure lust held Harris at bay. But it was worth those moments, when at last she gyrated, pushing herself deep down and both hushed a moan of pure pleasure.

Then the girl held, held quite still as she worked her body to repeatedly grip and release from tiny muscles within. Harris was soon back to dark thoughts of being beheaded with a bread knife, stomach ripped open and entrails dispatched by a fork, anything, anything to avoid this inevitable climax.

"You not come yet?" The girl asked between licking each of his nipples and Harris concentrated to the core on his answer. "No, no way."

Slowly the Russian girl worked her trade, smiling sweetly, oh so sweetly, as she took his length up and down, time and again. Partly, halfway, all the way, each time she chose the length of their fulfilment. Then the tempo increased and so did her drive to have Harris every inch within her and Harris responded, he could bear no more as he gripped her skin to the thrusts. Time and again she cried out in pleasure and Harris knew it was pleasure, for she had soaked him in shudders crying out each time.

"You not come yet?" she screamed.

Harris couldn't, he had tensed to the extent that he had borderline cramp in both legs as his mind raced between past tortured pain and the imminent explosion to come.

"Come baby come!" She cried out.

Her sweat soaked face dripped as again she flooded upon Harris and then that was it.

There was the request, that plea; that want and Harris took less than an instant to respond to her urgings and amidst the screams of both consenting adults Harris filled her, creamed her, pulsation after painful pulsation until they lay exhausted.

Chapter 60

Reliving Saturday's pleasure brought Harris a smile, then remembering Sunday's journey to Kent that involved loading and unloading, it soon reminded him of why his back ached so much.

It was now Monday and he was wearing his only ill-fitting suit that he had rescued from his garage on the previous evening. A beige cotton ensemble enclosing a grubby white shirt and gold coffee stained tie, all of which had more creases than a well-read newspaper. He stood there anxiously, waiting on the fifth floor of New Scotland Yard.

Harris had sat there from 6 am that morning and now it was almost two hours later. He held a thick file in one hand whilst the other, clutching damp tissue, eased the painful nicks of that morning's head shave.

He didn't want to be there; he was an East End Detective normally surrounded by graffiti and he was ill at ease in that lift lobby area, as oil canvassed portraits of previous Police Commissioners looked down on him.

Then with a 'ping' the lift doors opened and out stepped the man Harris had waited for. However, the Commissioner with his entourage were somewhat taken aback by the fast approach of Harris, who spoke as roughly as he looked.

"Boss, boss, I really need a word." He asked and showing a 'flash' of his identification badge he was there directly in front of him.

Yes, even though he looked more like a thug than the usual 'Savile Row' clad Detective that the Commissioner would receive, he was asked. "What do you want?"

It was a Yorkshire accent, more akin to small villages than the bustling Metropolis as he reversed behind a two-man cloak of protection that stepped in before Harris.

"Five minutes of your time, in private Sir. I need your help. You alone can help me solve a series of multiple murders." Harris explained.

The group of five, all smartly dressed, looked confused at Harris in some amazement and Harris could hear the thoughts, 'Who was this upstart?' That was his perception of the scene. But nevertheless, Harris asked again and although he wasn't given the private audience that he had requested, he found himself sitting opposite the Commissioner and a uniformed commander who sat quietly taking notes.

Granted the initial five minutes, it soon turned into ten, then fifteen and half an hour as Harris captivated his audience with an explanation of his linked theory behind the murders of Nikki, Fiona Grant-Smith and Mrs Forrester.

"So, you believe that there is a man in prison who is innocent?" The Commissioner was intent on asking about Ralph.

"Unfortunately, yes sir." Harris replied. Going on to explain. "I haven't even had time to check the Police National database for any linked murders outside the Met."

The Commissioner glared incredulously when Harris told him of his belief that there had also been police collusion and perhaps even a perverting of the course of justice in the prosecution of Ralph.

"My God, do you honestly think there are any other murders that are linked?" he asked.

Harris had no option but to hypothesise. "I believe so sir, but, I've only recently started looking." To which the Commissioner breathed deeply, shaking his head in dismay.

The Commissioner, however, was sceptical when Harris explained the perceived thought process of being placed on restricted duties by Hutchings; but when Harris produced his 'trusty' pocket tape recorder and played his private recordings, the Commissioner's contempt was red-faced and obvious.

"How dare this man!" the Commissioner blustered.

"Who the hell does this man he think he is!" He bellowed and with an immediate phone call, there and then, Hutchings's fate was sealed.

Harris was soon to leave the Commissioner's office and he clutched a letter of authority signed and sealed by the Commissioner himself. A letter that certified Harris was now working for the Commissioner directly and on it, at the bottom of the page, was a telephone number that could be rung by anyone in opposition. Harris was more than grateful.

"Harris, you will have one boss in charge of you from now on and that will be me." He said. "And the Barking murder squad office will have a new Chief

Superintendent by tomorrow. You will report directly to him and he will report to me." On a final handshake Harris was gone.

His first stop was Empress State Building, but en-route Harris took great pleasure in receiving the next three phone calls. All were dispatch requests, from various murder teams, all of which he politely refused on behalf of the Commissioner's office and he quoted the 230-extension number.

In the lobby lift area, there was a directory that led him to his next port of call, the Department of Professional Standards (DPS).

They had recently moved offices from Tintagel house and Harris took no time at all in requesting access to one of their 'stand-alone' database computers and, although there was initial refusal, the letter saw Harris in front of a computer on which he began to seek out the full personal details of one D. Cooper.

His next stop was Mandela Way where, amongst smiles, he retrieved the two precious exhibits, the train tickets from both the Grant-Smith and Nikki deaths. Having made his way from there to Barking, he locked them securely away in the Barking exhibit store safe, along with the Sophie Forrester ticket.

Next Harris confirmed with the local Coroner's officer, the date and time for exhumation of Mrs Forrester and then he rang Ivan.

Chapter 61

Philip had the widest smile as he queued at his local 'Motor-Martini's' shop. His trolley was full to the brim with various accessories that would further 'spec up' his beloved Mitsubishi and, as he patiently waited in the queue, he looked down upon his trolley of JE pistons, a Kelford cam, Manley I-Beam rods and a new sub-woofer. Hidden beneath those were the upgraded valve springs with new head studs and below those was a new intercooler system that he was going to install and lastly, at the bottom, was the 800-horsepower fuel system.

Philip was indeed happy. He had cash to burn and his fingers were itching to work on his four-wheeled pride of joy.

Philip, once a refugee from Somalia, black as the night and standing as short as a winter's day, had arrived in the UK years ago, clutching a suitcase in one hand and a roll of suspicious diplomas in the other. It wasn't long before the benefits system had provided him with a nice flat in South West London, a security from where he quickly applied for a variety of jobs within the pensioner care service.

He already knew this was easy money, his visitors back home had told him so. Low wages of course, but the perks of Alzheimer's would always ensure that his wage would be well supplemented.

Employed as a care worker, washing, cleaning and occasionally slapping, he had worked in five homes, each with a slightly higher wage than before. That was until he applied to work as a shift supervisor at the local child care home where, only in that past month, he had been made manager. It was a position that he had worked hard towards over the last couple of years, no exams, just his latest spurious certificates, pure determination and a willingness to work those extra-long hours for better pay.

It was during those extra hours that he came to befriend his opposite shift supervisor, 'the old English gentleman,' he called him, Frank and it was Frank that had groomed him astray.

Frank had carefully watched Philip at work with the children and had soon realised that Philip cared little for the children in his charge, it was in fact as little as he did. But both men loved the money and it wasn't difficult for Frank to persuade Philip into selling the odd child for a night. Frank had all the connections and Philip had seen enough slavery in his life to think nothing of the consequences.

Both men worked as a team covering the twenty-four hour day, ensuring their commodities were well presented and silent to others. This partnership worked well, so well that, within a year, Frank had become a two-site manager promoting Philip as the sole supervisor to both twelve-hour shifts. The money flowed and both men grew rich, that was until three weeks prior, when old Frank fell ill, taking only three weeks to die from irreversible bowel cancer.

The health authority immediately asked Philip to take over Frank's position and, due to cuts in social service budgets, he was to oversee not only both sites, but a third, becoming the head for each venue.

Without hesitation Philip agreed, from now on only he would work towards earning from any child's misfortune and it would only be he who would provide the children for the drive-in customers and he alone, who would attend the monthly parties with a child or two.

Philip was indeed blessed and believed Frank was looking down at him, smiling from heaven, as Frank's gold and red stone signet ring that Philip had for so long admired, was bequeathed to him in his will.

Now as the site manager for three homes, he had an office in each that he could call his own. He had gained an extra week's paid holiday and was solely responsible for the budget in charge of supplies.

At a whim, he immediately overcharged prices and 'skimmed off' the profit, 'cooking the books' to show any council audit that the sites had unfortunately paid just a little more than what it actually meant to. With every penny or two on every single item from food supply to clothing, those pennies quickly turned to pounds.

Phillip wasn't a stickler for internal discipline, Philip, Phil, Prince P or Uncle P were the various names that his two-shift workforce of eight staff knew him by. They were more than happy to receive unofficial warnings as to their occasional, overzealous behaviour towards the children. However, it was those children in his homes that would call him, "The night beast."

As with any item that he entered in his note book, Philip knew exactly what he could withdraw each week in the form of a cash filled envelope and on party nights, as the man in the black suit would tell him, any "inconvenience money" was his to keep.

On the night when another of his girls was required for more than just that party in the field at Theydon Bois, Philip didn't hesitate, he really didn't care. He would just report them as missing, the same as he had done with other children on the previous occasions.

He recalled it was no odds to him when he drove back alone, the thirteen-year-old girl with a history of false allegations surrounding sexual exploitation would never be believed, no matter what story 'she made up.' In any case he might be lucky and, like some of the others, she would never return with any such allegation.

Philip left the store and smiled his smile with his bright yellow teeth and with no worries on his mind, he crossed the road walking back towards the West Barnes care home.

He never noticed the big man watching his every step as he carried his bags into the rear staff car park. Philip was more than a little taken aback when he realised that there was a man now standing behind him whilst loading the car boot with his recent purchases.

"Nice wheels, really nice, your car, is it?" The big man asked.

"Yes," Philip blurted in surprise when he turned and saw a man in a balaclava mask close by.

"Who are you?" He asked. Now frightened, as the big man took another step closer.

"This is private property, I am the owner, and you will have to leave." Philip felt threatened and fearful as he did his best to voice control at the big man standing directly in front, towering above him.

But the man didn't turn to leave and the only response Philip heard before being struck by leather gloved strikes, was the gritted growl of. "Feel the pain you bastard!"

Punch after punch rained down on the little Somalian with big attitude, but, begging for mercy didn't stop this big man, with hardened fists, rain the strikes to his face and body. Within minutes a mixture of choke holds, kicks, fist and elbow blows, saw Philip fully broken and semi-conscious.

Finally, the big man went to work on him with an open razor blade that he produced from an inside pocket of his leather jacket. Once the razor had scraped the flesh from Phillip's neck, the big man carefully wiped the flowing, Somali blood, soaking it up with a cloth.

The big man whispered. "No more monthly party nights, I know where you live. Do you understand?" And the petrified Phillip slowly nodded acceptance before the big man stood up from his onslaught and kicked him once more for, 'good measure.'

Later that evening, at home, Harris found himself in the garden, staring between the flames that engulfed his old clothes with an occasional glimpse at his bruised knuckles. It came as no surprise to him to receive a phone call from his landlord friend, Temptress Tina.

She was clearly in a state of distress as she sobbed down the phone and Harris imagined her tears as she explained that she was with the Police having recently finished her statement.

It had been a horrific discovery for her, of that open grave whilst walking her friend's dog in the Theydon Bois woodland.

"Innocence lies dead." Tina spoke between tears as she described how the poor girl's body was all smeared in blood as if she had fought back, vainly, at her attacker.

Harris had been waiting for the call and readily agreed. "Of course, I'll pick you up."

Chapter 62

It really wasn't how Harris had imagined an exhumation; it was his first and it was nothing like the movies. There was none of his preconceived scenes when, at the dead of night, amongst thunderclaps and heavy rainfall, the gravediggers would go to work in the splattered mud, on a burial, lit by an oil lamp or two. No, it was nothing like that at all. Instead it was early morning, the spring sun was shining and the mechanical digger made quick work of the hardened earth before a portable screen was erected.

Harris had arranged transport, so that Simon and Geraldine wouldn't have to witness the large digger and hand spades at work, but they would arrive and be present to stand at a respectful distance to ensure that their mother's dignity would be upheld.

Harris had promised them that he wouldn't take the body away for examination, only that he would open the coffin, examine, photograph and retrieve what he believed might be found.

Harris stood next to the 'on-call' Home Office Pathologist, Dr Haines, and found himself glancing between the screens towards the grieving adults. He noticed the flowers that Geraldine was holding and the Detective was pleased with the bouquet selection that he had ordered and paid for, white lilies and white roses with gyp and, between both, stood a local priest, whom Harris had also arranged, who uttered quiet words of condolence.

Harris' face soon took on a deep frown, as the delegated gravedigger/gardener struggled to open the expensive sealed casket. There was nothing dignified in using a mallet and a crowbar and the Detective felt anguish as the stench from within hit all close by as the lid was eventually prised open.

Harris held his position as the worker quickly scurried away, holding his nose. Harris stood firm and surveyed what body was left of Sophie Forester. She had been buried in a white dress, a white that was now ashen grey and had, in some parts, darkened black, sticking fast to the decomposing skin. Harris immediately knelt down at what was left of Sophie's feet and, holding his breath as best he could, he quickly took a number of photographs.

The plastic nail was plainly in sight, there in front of him, cherry red and cut to almost perfection. Dr Haines knelt beside him. Both conferred and made notes as they compared the false composite nail to her other toe nails and then under the direction of the pathologist and using his magnifying glass, scalpel and tweezers, Harris carefully made quick work in removing the false nail.

Only then did Harris and the doctor see the remnants of torn skin where her real nail had been ripped away from her toe, which was beginning to grow again. The pathologist was astonished, Harris was sated, as both now knelt in silence staring at dead feet.

The Detective lent forward and did his best in scraping into a glass jar, what was left of the glue-like substance that was attached to what remained of her toe skin. Then he went to work with a dry swab and a wet swab using distilled water and, wherever he could, he took yet even more photographs. At last the work was complete and once the pathologist's exhibits were packaged and sealed Harris replaced the lid.

Harris was conflicted between euphoria, professionalism and reverence. Inwardly he was jumping for joy and yes, perhaps he should have worn a paper mask, goggles and paper suit to avoid any potential cross contamination. However, he had waved away the potential health risk so that dignity remained with Sophie's children. Besides, Harris thought, he had at least double gloved.

Harris stood away, placing the seized exhibits in his briefcase he waved back the worker to re-secure the coffin.

The worker did this quickly and, once completed, Harris beckoned the priest and Sophie's children over. In silence and tears from both children, Geraldine laid the white bouquet on top of the lid among the airing of a few short words from the Bible.

--//--

Having returned to his storeroom office Harris finally completed the laboratory form and his wish list.

In respect of Mrs Forrester

1st Examination for DNA from the underside of the nail and the same examination from the various swab exhibits.

2nd Fingerprint the top of the nail, not much plastic to work with, but there may be a partial print as the murderer must have pushed the nail, hardening it into place.

3rd Chemical examination of the scrapings, the glue, what type and any potential purchasing outlets?

4th DNA, rather than fingerprint work, on her train ticket. Harris knew that latent fingerprinting using Ninhydrin would destroy any future possibility of further DNA work pending advancements. However, he could ask for oblique lighting and other light sourcing to search for fingerprints, at least that wouldn't damage the ticket.

5th DNA, the wet and dry swabs that Harris had taken when rubbing various parts of Mrs Forrester's body and hair and, along with them, a comparison with the higher and lower swabs that a Pathologist had previously inserted into her body's orifices.

In respect of Nikki

DNA work on her train ticket and due to forensic technology advancements further DNA work on her underwear.

In respect of Fiona Grant-Smith

DNA work on her train ticket

DNA work on the belt buckle

DNA and use of light source fingerprint work on the carrier bag that had smothered her head.

In respect of Ralph

His DNA elimination swabs were added.

Inevitably there was a short-lived battle with the Crime Scene Managers, budgets had long dictated that no more than 5 submissions at any one time could be made, but Harris had 'the' letter and a quick phone call saw them relent.

That very afternoon Harris was off to Lambeth with the submissions and a wry smile. Again, as he would always do, he took a ticket from the submission ticket machine and waited his turn.

He didn't mind it there, between staring out of the window at tourists and glancing at a large plasma television set to BBC News, he would lose himself in his thoughts. There he could look down from the second-floor window and, apart from those obviously on holiday, he'd watch normal people with normal lives going about their daily business. A part of him was jealous, they had normality. However, it was a glance back at the television that really caught his attention.

The story broke with the words, 'Murder Investigation,' and there on the screen was a photograph of the deceased, a man in his 40s who worked part time for the Foreign Office in diplomatic affairs. He'd been shot twice in the head at a small business address in a village. Kent police were heading the investigation.

The female reporter on scene, set in front of the dead man's home, told of local bewilderment, astonishment and fear. A quiet man; that no one knew, only that he visited there and worked away for long periods. The local postman had made the discovery.

None of the words were important to Harris, only the man's face in the top right corner of the screen, only the backdrop to where the female reporter flicked gusting hair away from her face. Harris recognised both and became anxious. For there was the man that Harris had seen at work using film footage in that backroom office, there on the driveway was the white van that the man drove and there was the cottage that Harris had burgled that past Sunday.

Harris gulped in surprise and took a seat to sit silently and, with his head in his hands, a professional hit, a 'double tap' as it's known and he didn't notice that he had missed his submission turn.

The detective was oblivious to all around him when he realised that the man was dead and most probably because of him. Whoever the man worked for, he, she, they, or them, were 'covering their tracks' destroying any possible link, perhaps a punishment, a warning to others, whatever the reason Harris knew they cared little for life.

After an hour of deep thought, he finally uttered the words. "Thank fuck."

Harris knew that there could be the possibility of CCTV, that's why he had worn a baseball cap low on his head and with all that had gone on in his recent life, he hadn't as yet registered or insured his van, so later that night in a quiet lane somewhere on the outskirts of Essex, it would receive a Viking burial.

Harris sighed with relief as he walked to the vending machine and took another ticket.

Chapter 63

The following morning the canteen at the Murder Squad offices in Barking was buzzing at the news that the Independent Police Complaints Commission (IPCC) was due to visit and investigate team 10.

Team 10, situated one flight of stairs and two corridors along from Harris' storeroom cupboard, were reeling from the effects of a mysterious death in custody.

Only the day before had they arrested a childcare manager called Phil, an immigrant, turned British Citizen who had been arrested on suspicion of the murder of a young care girl found half buried in Theydon Bois earlier that week. A young girl choked to death and smeared in blood.

Whose blood? Was the question, so various blood swabs and other retrieval work were immediately sent for DNA fast-tracking in search of a profile.

The site manager had been arrested because he refused to account for his recent injuries and, as a result, not only was the blood found to be Phillip's, but the best evidence was under the young girl's muddied fingernails, there the scientists discovered remnants of Phillip's skin particles.

These analysis findings, along with the fact that Philip was the one who had reported the girl missing were easily enough for a conviction and although the solicitor kept telling his client to remain silent, Philip was anything but.

Oh, how the Somalian claimed that he had been "set up," one of the interview team told Harris between sips of coffee in the bustling canteen.

A fanciful story about prostituting the girl to others in the woodland where she had been found, but he hadn't murdered her.

Could he describe those that had taken her? No, he could not.

Did he have a witness who could confirm these outrageous claims? No, he did not.

All Philip had was an animated solicitor who kept telling his client to, "be quiet and shut up!"

Harris was intrigued when the interviewing officer told him that Philip was also claiming that. "The fires of hell will kill me."

Intrigue it was, because it was that very morning at dawn when Philip had been discovered dead in his cell, as a result of an apparent heart attack, that indeed 'all hell had broken loose' at Tottenham police station, now besieged with another outcry that the police had killed yet another black man in custody.

--//--

Harris felt sorry for team 10 and all the troubles that the IPCC were bringing with them, but it was the quote, "The fires of hell will kill me." That dogged the detective's mind as he returned to his storeroom office, there was something in those words, something, but what? Harris shook his head, he couldn't fathom.

Whatever it was, that something had to wait, for in there, in his storeroom he received a phone call, "Chief Superintendent's office, ASAP."

Harris sighed, he didn't recognise the voice, but he knew his new boss was demanding an audience. A meeting that he could do without. It was time that he could best spend finishing his report to the CPS, rather than having to explain his findings all over again, but Harris had no option, the Commissioner had appointed Chief Superintendent C. Miller and it was Miller who wanted to see him.

By the time Harris returned to his storeroom office he was mentally shattered, he had just spent two hours explaining the evidence, the similarity, timelines and attainable goals.

Miller didn't want to go into Harris' storeroom where everything was filed and locked away. No, Harris had to return and take everything to him and, like a teacher with an ink marker and whiteboard, Harris penned bright red arrows between Nikki, Fiona and Sophie.

Then there was Ralph, an incarcerated innocent. Harris tried his best to convince Miller, but Miller wanted more. Miller wanted the full report presented to him within six weeks, a report that the Chief Supt would personally take to the CPS and Harris noticed the look in his new boss' eyes, a look that he had seen in other superiors throughout his career.

"Another fucking glory hunter." Harris murmured as he walked back to his storeroom. Miller was eager for the next rank up and Harris' investigation into a potential serial killer was merely another stepping stone towards hierarchy.

But what really upset Harris was Miller's mention of more staff for the investigation if Harris ever faltered. The Detective realised that he was starting to lose his grip on the case, something personal to him, an investigation where he had

no option but to share with the Commissioner and then there was Miller, who and
how many were next?

Chapter 64

Little old Ethel once again struggled with her national health, aluminium, notched, walking stick as the eighty-year-old descended the one, brick built step from her front door in Bessy Street, Tower Hamlets, London.

It was only a small step, but any step up or down caused the arthritis in her right hip to immediately 'flare up' causing a 'merry hell' of pain to her joints. However, Ethel was a proud woman, she didn't want Social Services in her life, and she didn't want to be placed in a care home. No, all she wanted, was to be left alone to enjoy her thrice weekly visit to Mecca.

Mecca, not the birthplace of Mohammed, the holiest city in the religion of Islam, a city that was built 900 feet above the Red Sea, but the bingo hall on the Hackney Road, 12 feet above the sewers.

She, as always, had her purse tucked in her knickers, something she had done since she had been robbed at knifepoint eight years ago. That fateful night, when she swung her handbag at the 'bastard,' only for the man to duck down and grab the leather from her frail arms, pulling her over and leaving her flat on the pavement, suffering two weeks in hospital.

Ethel had learnt her lesson, "never again." She vowed. And from that day on her purse was in her knickers and there it would stay. She didn't care about the looks she got from the bus drivers or shop owners when she dug deep down to pay, it was her money, no one else's and she hadn't missed a bingo session since the attack.

There wasn't a great deal to Ethel, she was small and thin and walked with a limp. Long gone were her swinging sixty days when she worked as a nurse by day and partied all night. But, she still had all her own hair and some of her teeth and, instead of a man, it was a nightly sherry that would send her to sleep.

However, today it was bingo that drew her to the streets and with only a short hobble down to the main road, up and down, left and right, her head would turn in every direction. She never forgot a face and eight years on she still looked out for that robber that she wished dead.

After five minutes or so Ethel got to her bus stop, she was waiting for either the number 26 or 48 and she settled herself on the red plastic seat attached to the shelter. She smiled as the sun warmed her, how she detested anything but summer and, as she sneezed at the pollen, she noticed a man walking along the pavement towards her.

Not the robber, but a tall and handsome white man. Her diminishing eyesight noticed that he carried a small brown paper package. How she wished she was fifty years younger and this brought about a little giggle, but what happened next left her more than a little surprised as the man stopped and stood directly in front of her.

"Hello lady, would you do me a favour please?" The man asked in a heavy foreign accent.

"What is it dearie?" she asked.

Then pulling out a large wad of folded £20 pounds notes, the man held them out towards her in a fan.

"Here is some money for you." He stated. "Please would you take this to the police station over there?" and in one hand he held out the money whilst the other held the brown paper package. He nodded towards nearby Bethnal Green Police Station, just a hundred yards away.

"Why me, why can't you?" Ethel questioned, suspicious as she took hold of the money.

The man answered quickly. "I can't, it is stolen and it needs to be returned to the owner, the Detective's name is on the package."

Ethel looked down to where she saw 'DC Harris, Murder squad,' had been written. Quickly she counted the money.

£200, 'oh joy!' she thought, it was only a short hobble and her arthritis was suddenly forgotten about.

When she looked up from the brown paper package and notes, she suddenly realised the man had gone, so quickly she pushed the cold cash into her knickers and rose.

Chapter 65

Yuri was satisfied that those immediate to him had been hard at work, reinforcing how truly evil Yuri and his men were. Those that had wavered or 'gone solo' thinking that Yuri had gone for good when arrested, these were beaten in the vilest of circumstance and all were left under no illusion as to who was their boss.

Beatings, slicing's and finger snaps, were minimal compared to the heavy mallets and baseball bats that struck various body parts. These were rife and then there was an occasional shooting, all stark reminders that Yuri was back in East London. The Homerton, Queens and Royal London hospitals bore the brunt of Yuri's exertions and the interpreter services was exhausted explaining away the 'trips and falls' that many a Russian came in with.

It was Yuri's catchment of crime that he again consolidated. It took a mere week of screams and sobs to re-establish himself. Further to this and no wasting time, he decided to expand his various 'business interests' to all points of the compass.

The East End was no longer enough for him. He had sat back too long whilst others had prospered. He had shown weakness by being arrested and again he needed to prove that he was a force to be reckoned with. Yuri found that he craved more power, it was an empire that he'd built and although wealthy he wanted more than East London to make him his fortune.

Suddenly many a known villain had vanished from their usual haunts, black and Asian gangs appeared to quieten as local Police took credit as most crime was hidden, driven far underground.

Yuri now held sessions where he would hear their pleas. "Emotion is turmoil," he told them.

Some would also plead for the families that he held to ransom. "Sentiment is weakness," derided the bullish Yuri.

Those that stood against him and failed to submit would simply hear his philosophical tone. "Death is the only true freedom." Yuri's English was improving.

Soon he had run out of the original, circular maggot discs that was his symbol of power, but he had other bodies that he could slice open to fester. He truly was a busy man.

In the weeks to come, it was the Land registry department that failed to register the curious new trend. The name Lord Yuri Yazov appeared on increasing applications, as he swept from East to West, South to North, across the capital, as he took over even more brothels, pubs and drug dens.

Yuri knew property was power and he was going to spend every resource to grow his portfolio. He would be just like the wealthy Asians, the professional footballers and MPs who knew there was wealth in run down parts of London. Yuri would purchase as many of these properties as he could afford. Usually a first pick of the ex-council properties, heavily 'discounted' through fear or fire damage.

Yuri even began to set up a number of property letting agencies, initially covering the East End of London, where only Russians or Eastern Europeans that he controlled would find tenancy. Almost all were either prostitutes or drug dealers, or both. As they sought immigration status in the UK, each would find sponsorship from a local MP or dignitary. It would be the local Borough Councils that would have to pay the extortionate rent on these properties that Yuri would lease back to them.

Within other properties, he stored the regular container loads of stolen goods and even his ever-increasing tactile army of ex-Russian soldiers had their own barracks in two small blocks of flats.

Yuri was indeed coming back with a vengeance, with an unnerving hatred of those that opposed him.

Chapter 66

Harris was still working hard on the potential CPS appeal; every sentence was re-read no less than five times to ensure its accuracy. His investigation had to be thorough and exact to each intricate detail. Not only did he get a 60-page statement from Ralph, but he even obtained a statement from a train station manager regarding the sale of the train tickets from a dispensing machine that no longer existed. Everything Harris believed could potentially provide either DNA or fingerprint evidence, the Detective had photographed and submitted.

Not the small brown paper packaging though, not the one that was addressed to him, nor the two hard drives that were held within. Harris knew these were 'a present' via an old lady, from a grateful Russian and Harris hoped to God that he was now in possession of the Forrester's computer hard drives when he submitted them to Newlands Park for examination.

To expedite a result, from the reluctant engineer, Harris requested that only the last month of data from each would suffice, the contents of 1. Documents, 2. Internet material and 3. Emails, all were to be downloaded.

The engineer told him it would take at least two months before the hard drives would even be looked at; however, with the Commissioner's letter and the prior pre-purchase of a bottle of finest malt whiskey from a nearby off-licence, it persuaded a 'stop' on all other work for the sole concentration on this submission.

In reality, it only took three weeks for the elated engineer to ring Harris and inform him that those files had been downloaded and were now available for examination on a readable disc format.

The Detective collected the discs that same day and, returning to his storeroom office, he immediately began working his way through them. First the documents discs and, to the detective's relief, he found a speech that Rupert Forrester had 'signed off' on. There were also items subject to legal privilege and various lists and ideas for a forthcoming party that the Foresters were never to host.

The next document disc was from Sophie's computer, these were mostly shopping lists, drafted letters and an occasional poem that she had randomly scripted. But best of all was a document that caught Harris' interest, a diary that she maintained until the day she died.

Harris was open-mouthed, laughing and occasionally staring in disbelief at the raunchy goings-on that Sophie had recently entertained. Middle aged sex, that only a short time before, had been a chore, a needless suffering between planned headaches. That was until Rupert had come alive with variables, now it was open air sex, public space sex, public participation sex, even Private party sex and all this had driven Sophie's body and mind to wanting more. The detective was gobsmacked by the pure wantonness of Sophie, she was losing all cares for self-regard, such was her want.

As for her dreams, well, whoever this Zodiac121 was, he was in for a treat, being licked all over, pinched, and caressed and the like. Wow he thought, wow indeed, but then suddenly, like a speed train, it hit Harris.

A screaming train of realisation struck him head on, Zodiac121, Z121, Nikki was Z121.

"Oh Christ" Harris whispered in disbelief, unable to keep his thoughts to himself, "Jesus H!" He now spoke as his thoughts erupted.

"I don't believe it!" He gasped.

He quickly read through the emails again and there, one of them confirmed, Zodiac121 had successfully made a bid for the couple on a group sex site that was littered with Russian bride adverts.

The Foresters were 'to be his' and this was just three days before their murdered bodies were discovered, this was going to be worth an extensive paragraph on his report to CPS.

Harris could finally put an identity on his serial killer, "Z121," he told himself.

He could have chosen the name Zodiac, as it sounded mysterious, adding kudos and status to the individual, who was driven by whatever, whoever and whichever, but Harris refused to glamorise this 'sick-fuck head,' the murderer that had thought absolutely nothing of his victims.

Yes, Harris was sure the press would make something out of the name Zodiac when it became known; star signs, mythology and 'all that crap' would be linked with no doubt quotes from the Bible. Harris found himself shuddering at the thought, "Z121 would do just fine." He reiterated.

So, was Rupert Forrester targeted by Z121? McDermott was the link.

'There may have been collusion.' Harris contemplated, he rarely believed in coincidence.

It was Rupert Forrester that had asked Harris to investigate the death of Fiona Grant-Smith on behalf of a client and the file that had been in possession of McDermott Harris now realised he was going to have to find time to travel north and speak with the poor girl's parents.

--//--

It was just over a week before Harris found himself driving a 'pool' car through affluent lanes on the outskirts of Leicester, he was in the middle of 'middle England' where large detached properties were found at the ends of long driveways on oak lined roads.

Large grandiose buildings, some vast, the size of mansions and each property with double, or even a treble sized garage, some that could be easily be mistaken for houses themselves.

Most of these properties he drove by were quite spectacular, 'far superior' to what the Detective had been used to, even the house that Yuri had given him was simply no match to this wealth. He had never seen 15-foot water fountains in real life, nor duck ponds with overhanging willow trees at the front of a house before, but he was seeing them now. One driveway even had a marble statue of an Athenian Goddess revealing one breast who offered out her fist sized grapes to no one in particular. 'Beautifully strange, strangely weird,' the Detective thought.

Eventually the satnav told him. "Turn right, you have reached your destination." An intercom and retractable gate by the roadside saw Harris pull onto the driveway.

Both parents were in and, just like Simon Forrester, they too looked the Detective up and down in disdain at his new leather jacket and faded blue jeans. Each carefully checked his identification card before they welcomed him in.

The front reception room was elegant and minimalistic in soft greens and brilliant white furnishings with only two paintings in a room the size of a small, studio flat. One was of a landscape, 6 feet across, with billowing clouds and the odd cow, the other had the same dimensions and portrayed the mansion he now stood in.

Harris wasn't offered a seat, so he stood as they sat and still they looked down on him. Harris spoke at length as they remained silent, he explained what he had uncovered from investigating the death of their daughter and that the parents were justified in calling for a murder investigation into the death. It was only then that the mother showed emotion and wept openly. Then, as the father spoke, there was an exchange of information, more detail, and more questions.

Harris became busy with his notebook scribbling keywords in readiness for a written statement that Mr Grant Smith, although hesitant, agreed to make.

It was going to be a further statement, not the long statement he remembered making to the local police many years before. Not when it was hour upon hour, amongst foul tasting police canteen coffee, where heartbroken he explained in detail his Russian origins, the family move to England and the short life of his daughter. This was going to be a short statement, to the point, but still his tears welled.

He told the detective that no leads had been uncovered and that there was no other official investigation, other than the presumed death by sexual misadventure. Only the private investigation, the one on which he had personally spent thousands and thousands of pounds on, the one that he had asked the barrister McDermott to look into his daughter's demise, only this was still active.

"What about Mr Forrester?" The Detective asked, "You asked Mr Forrester?" Harris sought clarification.

"No" came the reply.

"James McDermott, he was the only one." The father replied. "We paid him, for legal services, when we first come to this country."

"I didn't know the law in this country," he went onto explain "but my wife saw an advert in a magazine and after a phone call to his offices we met him and he arranged the buying of this property and others to let, he even changed our names."

Harris scribbled notes as the father continued.

"He even found accommodation for our Fiona in London and when she died we used him again." He sobbed.

"He told us that he had pushed hard to have his daughter's case re-examined, but he was unable to persuade the authorities," the father paused, "but, he took our money all the same."

Harris noted the legal change of names and the purchasing of property, but he was perplexed as to why he had sought out accommodation for the now dead daughter, as there didn't appear to be any great friendship between the parents and McDermott, only a business interest.

"Then we were put in touch with Mr Forrester, not long before he was murdered," the father went on.

"So, who put you in touch with Mr Forrester?" Harris scratched his head.

"Yuri Yazov." came the answer and Harris shuddered inwardly at the reply.

"He put me in touch with Mr Forrester, I needed help and I know he is a man who gets things done"

"And how did you come to know Yuri?" Harris dared to wonder.

"What Russian in England doesn't know Mr Yuri, Mr Lord Yuri," the father smirked. "Yuri told me that he trusts you to do your best."

Harris quickly crossed out any reference to Yuri, that name would definitely be omitted from the statement.

Chapter 67

Again, he was drinking yet another orange juice and lemonade that had been purchased from the local pub in the vicinity of New Scotland Yard whilst Harris carefully watched his prey.

'When is a man at his weakest?' He pondered. It could be claimed that it is when you are incapacitated through drink or drugs and Harris watched closely for the third consecutive evening.

Cooper was again drowning himself into a stupor before leaving for home.

That would-be Cooper's weakest point, but not when Harris needed him to talk, confess, and 'open up' to him.

Harris really needed to know what type of man he was dealing with, as he toyed with the thought of either including Cooper in his final reports or, deleting his very existence.

On one side he was deviant scum, a plague to children of a vulnerable age. On the other he was a Police officer, ex Special Branch/Counter Terrorism no less, a team focussed on counterterrorism, led by the espionage of spies within MI5 and the high ranking political puppets who pulled their strings.

Harris knew there had to be more to Cooper as he scoured the photocopied notebook on the table in front of him. He knew that Cooper, potentially, had so many secrets to tell.

Harris decided he wouldn't confront Cooper now, not whilst he openly drank his life away, sinking yet another double vodka and tonic, but he would wait until the following morning, bright and early, before Cooper had time to focus.

Harris left him alone with his thoughts and the occasional tear and drove his unmarked police car away to wait outside Cooper's home. It was only an hour before Cooper returned and staggered through his front door, Harris still waited till 'lights out' and, satisfied that he had put this man 'to bed,' the Detective set an early alarm and closed his eyes.

--//--

The birds were barely awake at 5 am, but Cooper was.

"Who is it and what the fuck do you want?" Came the voice from within, as Harris persisted in thumping the mock Georgian door.

"Police open up, open up now!" And Harris continued to hit the door with the base of his fist.

Harris could hear Cooper stumble his way towards the door as sounds of strewn objects and shouts of, "what the fuck?" came from within until all that stood between Harris and Cooper was the door that Harris still thumped.

"Show me identification." Cooper called out, so Harris held his badge to the door spy-hole and again announced. "Police, open up."

"What do you want?" Cooper screamed out for an answer, as he raised his .22 calibre West London gun club pistol up towards the spy-hole.

Harris lowered his voice knowing that half the street would possibly be awake by now, but he demanded. "I want answers into the murder of a girl called Nikki, you piece of shit." Then there was silence.

A silence that Harris deliberately toyed with, a silence that gripped Cooper to his core. That one word, 'Nikki' and Harris felt the jolt where he had speared realisation into Cooper's mind and a quiet when Harris inwardly warmed to the fact that he knew Cooper was looking out of his spy-hole, into the darkness that was his future.

There remained silence as Harris patiently stood knowing that Cooper was mentally 'dissolving' no less than 3 feet in front of him, a wooden door and a world of pain from him. There was silence as Cooper lowered his gun tucking it into the pocket of his pyjamas, wrapping his dressing gown around him, the door slowly opened.

Harris walked into the dimly lit hallway where both men exchanged quick glances at each other. Cooper saw a hard substantial man filling the doorway, worn, tired, but steadfast all the same. Harris saw Cooper as a mess.

Bedraggled un-ironed pyjamas wrapped in a potbellied, stained dressing gown of takeaway curries and the like. Harris even noticed that his slippers were on the wrong feet as Cooper waved him in, turning down the hallway, shuffling his feet towards the rear of the house, Harris closed the front door behind him.

"What's your name?" Cooper asked over his shoulder, "Miller," was Harris' thoughtful reply. "And from now on I'll ask the questions, starting with, where's your kitchen?" He asked.

"What?" Cooper replied, slightly bemused, did he hear right?

"Black coffee and no sugar for me." Harris was taking control of this situation and the sorry state of a man.

The kitchen was small, filth ridden and smelt of stale urine, just like its owner.

The various empty packets and boxes of food not only filled the bin, but overflowed amongst empty spirit bottles and, where other empty food containers were strewn across the work surfaces, the smell grew worse. Harris was pleased to see Cooper scrub two mugs clean as the kettle hissed, spat and boiled.

Harris sat at the old, blue, Formica table where new stains covered old, but at least the chairs were clean. By now Harris was convinced that he wasn't looking at Z121, believe me he had toyed with the idea, yes, he had thought of the possibility, but Harris was looking at a Copper, public paid and pub spent, in a house that hadn't been updated since the 80s. No way on God's earth could he have afforded to bid on Mr and Mrs Forrester, let alone mix in their circle of friends.

Having filled both mugs with hot instant coffee Cooper offered Harris a whiskey 'sweetener' but Harris declined as he watched Cooper 'crack' open a quarter bottle of Scotland's finest and pour two fingers worth into his mug.

Cooper sat in the chair opposite with both hands clasped around the mug as he drank away the uncomfortable silence in slurps.

Finally, Cooper uttered the word, "Nikki," as Harris quietly pressed down record button.

"Tell me about Nikki." Harris said.

Cooper shook his head, not in defiance, he was simply trying to form memories that he had tried to forget, a lost past that had cost him his marriage, children and almost his sanity. What were the words that would describe the one 'stray' from his wife, that girl that diseased his soul and ruined his liver?

"She was young, too young." Cooper opened. "In many ways, her nature was innocent and she was a breath of fresh air in my humdrum life." He pitted.

"She was pretty," he reflected, "she was impish, but she knew what men wanted and she could deliver."

"And she wanted you?" Harris asked incredulously.

"No, she needed me." Cooper shook his head. "It was me that wanted her." He admitted.

"And she deserved to die?" Harris persevered.

"No, she didn't, not at all!" Cooper drew a deep sigh.

"Yes, she used her body and her mind to look after herself, but doesn't any runaway around London?" He said, as his attempt to excuse himself.

"I wouldn't know mate, I don't think like you." Harris countered. "Tell me what made you so special?" Harris asked disdainfully.

"Nothing," came the curt reply. "I was just fortunate enough to come across her." Harris could visualise what Cooper implied.

"Tell me about the night she died, what happened when you were with her?" Harris needed answers and Cooper looked up from his steaming mug and glared directly at the officer.

"I didn't say I was with her, I knew a Nikki and now she's dead, that's all I know." He defended.

"And Ralph?" Harris whispered, imagining the noose tightening around Cooper's neck.

Cooper could barely hold himself together, let alone the mug he held, it shook as a wave of hot coffee spilled over the brim. Harris just sat there watching this opposite's implosion, calmly waiting for the next reaction.

"Ralph, I don't know anyone by that name." Cooper tried to convince.

"So, what about your black notebook where you keep names and dates and car registrations, the one on the hallway table I just passed. I guess you don't know anything about that either?" Harris spoke in contemptuous satisfaction, even a broad smile as he watched Cooper sit bolt upright then lean slightly over beyond the Detective's shoulder towards the hallway.

"Fist your right hand for me." Harris continued.

"Why?" Cooper shakenly asked.

"Appease me mate, do it." Harris asked and Cooper reluctantly complied.

Harris looked at the clenched fist and to the one thing that stood out from the near purple knuckles and said. "Your signet ring with the initials FOH, tell me about it?"

Cooper reached for a refill from the whiskey bottle.

"Explain to me how this ring can get you past a roadblock?" Harris was only too pleased to see Cooper visibly reeling from this verbal onslaught.

"I didn't kill her, I didn't kill her." Cooper muttered as he unwrapped his dressing gown.

Harris thought nothing of this loosening on such a cool morning, that was until Cooper reached down and pulled at his pyjama side pocket. Suddenly and to Harris' alarm Cooper pulled out and pointed the black metal pistol towards Harris who sat frozen to his seat.

Harris tried to gather his senses, he hadn't 'risk assessed' this scenario, he didn't think at 5 AM he would be staring down a fucking drunk with a gun.

'Fuck,' Harris thought, 'fuck,' wasn't going to be the last word Harris would utter, he told himself and a razor-sharp instinct forced mental momentum as he let out a sharp breath. "Calm down Cooper."

"Do you think I am alone?" Harris tried to convince, "There are three policemen outside, out front and the back and you and I have ten more minutes before they burst through your door."

"It's not for you." Cooper assured, but still he waved the gun in front of Harris' face.

"Who the fuck is it for then?" Harris asked in a mixture of indignation and fear.

"It's for them, them up there." And Cooper flicked his head skyward.

Harris immediately thought 'a nutter,' perhaps correct protocol should be mental impairment, but, a 'nut-job,' all the same.'

"I'll be ready for them," he said "when they come from me." Cooper announced loudly beyond Harris' hearing and Harris' mind readjusted from 'impairment to a complete loony tune.'

"I didn't kill her, I didn't kill her." Cooper spoke and again he waved the gun up and down between head and torso of Harris.

"And pointing a gun at me is meant to convince me?" argued the indignant Harris, unable to camouflage his poignant sarcasm.

"I'm a dead man, but I won't go quietly." Cooper continued. Harris was just grateful that the words weren't. "You're a dead man."

Harris tried to ease the situation. "Mate, calm down and give me that gun before you get as both killed," was the request. "I'm here to help Ralph, that's all," the Detective spoke softly and, slowly stretching out and opening his palm, Harris hoped he would be handed the gun. If not, Harris had decided, the table was going to at least visit Cooper's face.

"Give me the gun mate." Harris spoke with calm, "I am a friend, not an enemy, I just want to help Ralph," he disclosed.

All the time Harris was tensing himself in readiness for attack. How he hoped those last words would somehow penetrate Cooper's thoughts as Cooper looked on in silence and, for a few short seconds that felt like hours, Cooper complied.

"I want it back." Cooper said as he passed the automatic target pistol into the hands of Harris. "The gun, I need it, not right now though, you can have it and you can hold it for me." Cooper rambled whilst Harris removed the gun from view and held it at his side.

"Ralph." Cooper repeated.

'Clarity at last,' Harris thought.

"Yeah Ralph, that poor bastard who took the wrap for Nikki's murder." Harris said as he quickly pocketed the pistol into the side pocket of his coat. With hands shaking, he now sat on both, to stem the adrenaline that had filled his veins.

"What's Ralph to you?" Cooper wanted to know.

"He's fucking innocent for starters, that's what he is to me." The indignant Harris now took control.

"You know it, I know it, and Ralph fucking knows it and he has just spent around 30 years banged up for no fucking reason." Cooper nodded his agreement.

"Listen Cooper." Harris explained. "I have typed out two reports to the Crown Prosecution Service, both identical. However, the first report has your name plastered all over it, the other report doesn't mention you, not one word." He offered.

"Now it is decision time, what's it to be?" Harris invited, "Tell me about the night Nikki was murdered, or tell a jury."

Harris sat captivated, regularly checking that his tape recorder still whirred, recording, and capturing the Cooper confession.

Cooper told Harris about the monthly reports he would file after each 'party'; this vehicle, that vehicle, this dignitary, that celebrity, every detail went into his reports that he would hand over. Reports that Cooper could only assume were forwarded to the country's intelligence services.

Harris raised an eyebrow at Cooper's assumption and asked, "Intelligence Services?"

"Intelligence is MI5's currency." Cooper said. "They're the ones who collect and analyse any covert intelligence, these are the people who are critical to keeping the country safe."

"And?" Harris asked still quite puzzled.

"MI6 - their mission is to work secretly overseas, developing foreign contacts and gathering intelligence that helps to make the UK safe and more prosperous." Cooper was regurgitating a mental script.

Harris was in disbelief.

"What better way is there, than to have foreign dignitaries compromised, captured using and abusing young children." Cooper dared a grin.

"And the benefits are what exactly?" Harris needed clarity to the incredulous story being told.

"Practically the best intelligence in the world provides this country with the best domestic investments, even the best foreign investments, all of these contracts are achieved as cheaply and as quietly as possible." Cooper explained, "That's what we get out of it," he said, "that's the great, in Great Britain."

Harris was reeling, as was his tape recorder. His righteous world was collapsing around him at the thought that those barbaric acts were actually Government sanctioned.

But when he learnt it was an American Embassy car that had taken Nikki back to her squat on the night she was murdered, Harris slowly came to appreciate that Cooper may well be telling the truth.

"It was a pool car, a car used for regular 'run-arounds,' I checked with the embassy." Cooper revealed. "That week it had been signed out, one of their many cars, by the American Ambassador no less, signed out, for the use of one of his 'guests,' but they said they didn't have a name for me."

Cooper then told how he had tried to make discreet enquiries, but the Embassy had refused to proffer the 'guest list' and any further enquiries would have looked 'suspect,' he said. Cooper also doubted that any record of the guest list still remained after all those years and Harris nodded reluctantly.

"I am, however, responsible for Nikki and Ralph." Cooper admitted, cuffing what appeared to be a small tear using his dressing gown arm.

'To right you fucking are!' Harris thought, but stayed silent no less.

Silent as he was still in a state of shock realising that Cooper himself, among others, were working, actioned and state sanctioned by those in dark cloaks in the corridors of power.

"They know though, they do, you know." Cooper broadcast and again he offered his eyes to the ceiling.

'Rambling again.' Harris thought.

Cooper spoke out loud as if making an announcement. "They know I am spent, they know how I hate what I've done, I've told them so, they don't trust me."

Harris heard about all the boys and girls that Cooper had pimped and controlled on behalf of a recently retired and now dead Special Branch Superintendent and also, until his arrest, he had continued this work for a current Chief Inspector who had taken over the position, someone who also wore the same signet ring.

"What about the ring?" Harris asked, trying again to calm the flustered man opposite.

"Have you read any William Blake?" the Special Branch officer enquired.

Harris hadn't and was quite indignant that Cooper had suddenly become righteous, intimating a superior education, as it was with most Special Branch officers.

"Why?" Harris answered, keeping things simple.

Cooper then quoted. "As I was walking among the fires of hell, delighted with the enjoyments of genius which to angels look like torment and insanity."

"FOH on the ring, I walk among the fires of hell," and he fisted the ring towards Harris' face. "Fires of Hell, that's what it means."

Harris nodded, understanding all too clearly, it was a fucking pervert club, but Cooper continued. "Like the Catholic Guild and Masons have their rings to wear, the Fires of Hell have theirs.

Harris leant back and glanced again at the red signet ring and, tempering the rising anger, Harris gave his interpretation.

"So, it is a sick paedophile club run by some Government officials, safe in their ivory towers. Preying on little kids just for a few secrets, just for a few contracts, just for an investment or two." Harris offered across his condemnation.

Cooper refilled his coffee mug with yet another liquid chaser. "You seem surprised," as he quickly took another sip.

"Things like this have gone on for centuries." Cooper said, "You should read your history boy." Cooper was indeed becoming without sin.

"Hell Fires of West Wycombe were regularly attended by MPs, Lords and celebrities and, as for the Hell Fires in Dublin, the building was built by the speaker of the Irish House of Commons that was then turned into a Hell Fire club by a couple of Lords. One club survived on alcohol and debauchery, the other one added Satan worship." Cooper was in full flow.

"Although they were the first clubs to be formed in Great Britain and Ireland, they weren't the last." he said.

"A club like ours has just adapted with the times, a change of name, a change of priorities, but it is still, very much so, a controlling power of wealth." Cooper was beginning to enjoy the sound of his voice.

"It's the government who uses the vulnerable and weak and they do this to achieve more power, more wealth for themselves and our country." He continued.

Cooper lent forward and spoke further. "The present club continually relocates and adapts, it sets its targets to encourage foreign dignitaries into supplying information or gain favour, you know." Cooper looked for agreement, "contracts and influence." Cooper actually smiled at the Detective's disgust.

"Rather than it be run by and odd eccentric Lord, as in the past, the club is now run by one or two Government officials, ably assisted by the Intelligence services." Cooper chortled at the simplicity.

Harris was silent, he had come to Cooper looking for a perverted serial murderer, but now he stared into the abyss that was once his career, his life.

"Here we are at each end of the table, an angel and a demon." Cooper laughed.

Chapter 68

Later that morning Harris sat alone in his storeroom cupboard office, locking himself in from the outside world. He stared at the three items on his desk, and he desperately tried to think of a way forward, one that wouldn't involve his death.

The first book Harris picked up was the one he already knew of, it was the black notebook that he had previously photocopied, but the second book, a large green ledger this was the most intriguing. It was Cooper's private dossier, one that he had kept in his personal safe along with his pistol.

The green ledger contained a file on each of the paedophiles that Cooper had personally recognised whilst working with FOH. Years of names, reams of status and each with a photograph and last known location.

At the back, there was a file on each of those his Superintendent had either worked for, socialised with or was associated with. Names to faces Cooper had seen. Not only that, there were also places, buildings and the street corners where he had driven his dead Superintendent to.

It was a dossier filled of almost a 1000 pages, mostly fact, with very little assumption and, as he read, Harris recognised some and of those he did he realised that they were indeed powerful people. People that had influence and authority, people that no doubt could make one disappear.

Then there was the third book, a book of foreign nationals, mostly Government officials, who in their own right could buy and sell their country. But Harris also recognised that there were others with wealth. Those involved in diamond, gas, petrol, any and all raw material industry, owners, major shareholders that could and would be swayed.

At the rear of this third book were the celebrities and, according to Cooper's notes, these were actually held in low regard. Used as simple pawns, a welcoming party that by being there gave some form of glamour status to the parties, each one enticing 'Johnny Foreigner' into acts of deprivation.

After three hours of studying and marking an index of symbols, Harris closed the books and asked himself, 'what now?'

He actually asked himself, he sought clarity, just as he tried to earlier, when Cooper had also asked, "what now?" And these words pounded his thoughts.

Even Cooper's flippant remark of, "don't burn yourself," and "see you in hell," as he left, were quips Harris was quick to brush aside, but not now.

Harris lent over his desk seeking inspiration, but little came. However, he decided he would keep his word, Detective Sgt Dave Cooper of Special Branch would not be mentioned in Ralph's report to the CPS; his silence had been paid for in the three books that also made mention of the dates and locations of upcoming events.

Those thoughts aside Harris was conscious that the pistol now lay on his desk and he wondered just exactly what to do with it. Thank God, Cooper had forgotten to retrieve it, as he became embroiled whilst explaining almost every detail of the green ledger system. So, proud of his work, so proud of its accuracy, that for once Harris saw a clarity in Cooper, the sloth in a dressing gown could have once, in the dim distant past, actually passed for a decent Detective.

Harris looked closely at the pistol and noted it was called a 'Sport King,' it was made of black metal, perhaps as dark as Cooper's mind and Harris saw it was not too dissimilar to the German Luger pistol seen in many a World War II film.

Researching the Internet, Harris realised it was a .22 calibre, a pistol found in most British gun clubs and it was a gun specifically milled from a single block of steel. As he researched further he discovered that it was actually the preferred close quarter assassination handgun of the Office of Strategic Services (OSS) during World War II.

Harris sighed, he was right to have his arse twitch when he first saw it pointing at him.

He lay the pistol back on top of the books and just stared. He wondered at his future, or, of more concern, the potential the lack of it. If Harris was to report the green ledger, he knew, with the police officers named within, that it may well become 'lost' or 'accidentally shredded.' It was a dangerous book, far too dangerous for Harris.

Eventually he gathered the items together and, tucking the pistol in the inside pocket of his new black leather coat, he reached for his mobile phone and left his storeroom office.

Chapter 69

Elsewhere

The beast growled loudly as it struck the naked girl again, again it hit and again it kicked her after ripping the last toenail from her skin. The beast though wanted more, but she just had no more to give other than her whimpers of pain. She was all alone with the beast, the other girl had long gone and now, half-starved, she feared that she too would disappear.

A cowering wreck of rib cage, the beast deliberately stood on her torso and thighs against the muffled gags of agony.

The beast just stood there, saying nothing, instead it shuffled its steel boots up and down her frail body, riding the waves of her flesh, her body, with an ocean wave in its mind.

It stood silent as she lay there breathless and, reaching down, the beast's gloved hand pulled out from its overalls, a shiny pair of near glinting, new scissors. Then down it lent, pulling at the young girl's hair as it cut three lengths.

Standing back up, tall on her body, its arms widened to a crucifix pose it looked towards the ceiling and 'offered up' a murmured prayer to a portal of another realm and, in what was an eternity for the girl in pain, was a mere few seconds before the beast uttered its only audible word. Through the sackcloth mask it spoke. "Amen."

Chapter 70

The following day Harris' head was pounding from the vodka surge of the night before. He hadn't foreseen the night of celebration and he had forgotten how much Yuri could drink.

Wholegrain vodka, distilled in Russia, shipped through Europe, this is was what broke Harris, in that restaurant owned by the Crime Lord.

Harris tried to read over the forensic lab's final report that had been wedged under his storeroom door overnight, but all his mind could focus on was the previous day's events.

He recalled that he had left the office in Barking and walked to the local foot bridge, he was half tempted to throw the books into the creek below, but that would have been the coward's way out and, instead, he rang Ivan with an idea.

Harris explained that he had a proposition for Yuri and if the Crime Lord had time, could a meeting be arranged? Harris heard a bad attempt at the phone being muffled, he could hear Ivan's native tongue conversing with Yuri and then moments later Ivan was back on the phone with an appointment.

"An hour at Maya's place, perfect." Said Harris. "And just one more thing, can you bring a big van?"

That hour was long enough for Harris to return home, jumping on and off trains 'just to be sure' he told himself as paranoia took its hold. Harris had also watched the few passengers on that early afternoon train ride and walked from one carriage to the next looking for earpieces. Only once did he sit and that was simply because he noticed a discarded newspaper that he used to peer over. He never noticed the article that stated that the UK Government was pleased with its latest oil trade agreement with the representative Valentine Hill from the USA.

Harris travelled as far as Upminster Bridge Station, one stop further than needed, but it was an underground station that was so seldom used during the day. It also benefited from having a minicab office situated right next door.

He alighted the train alone, he was alone he was sure and then a £10 fare through the back lanes of Upminster, he was back in Emerson Park. Back to the house that Maya had lived in, a soon-to-be memory he hoped, as he tried to distance himself from his feelings, but it was still painful.

Once home he quickly removed the last pages of the ledger and carefully he folded them into a black bin liner. Following this he took a spade from the garage and buried his 'treasure.'

Ivan had arrived on time and in a big, white, Luton hire van. The Russian was all smiles. However, the other two Russians, who had been squeezed in the cab seat next to each other, just stared through their pursed lips.

Both men were just as well-built as near all of the Russian's henchmen Harris had seen working for Yuri. Nevertheless, Harris tried communicating with the two-shaven headed and heavily tattooed men, but he soon realised that they were freshly imported by Yuri, neither understood a word. Harris gave up trying and simply pointed out the various boxes that needed to be loaded.

Within 10 minutes the boxes were loaded and, knowing his place, Harris stepped into the back of the van, clutching the green ledger, as the shutter door was closed behind him.

"Don't worry Detective I will drive slowly." Ivan shouted through the thin corrugated frame and Harris resigned himself to the bumps and swerves as he sat on the floor cross-legged. With palms outstretched on either side to hold balance, he thought about a cigarette, but dared not, not at the speed Ivan had chosen, he needed both his hands out in an attempt to remain stable.

It had been an hour and Harris found the last 5 minutes were the worst. 'Pothole heaven.' Harris thought to himself and he hoped to dear God that nothing was broken within the boxes.

Finally, the van ground to a halt and Harris stood brushing himself down as the rear shutter lifted. Harris welcomed the bright daylight from the gloom in which he had travelled and Ivan was smiling again as Harris jumped down.

Ensuring the ledger stay tight to his side, Harris looked around and saw, parked nearby, a brand-new Bentley saloon. He admired its fine lines. Inside the car was a driver and next to him a front seat passenger, both men were muscle strewn ogres, but there was no Yuri in the car.

"Yuri is over there." Ivan pointed to the distance.

And indeed, there he was, across a dirt track and small field from where they had stopped, only some distance away, stood the big man.

Yuri was apparently distracted, looking away from Ivan's group, looking towards what appeared to be newly built footings.

There were numerous concrete spears that rose from the earth and two cement Lorries chugged and spun. Pumping more liquid strength into its hard-core base where Yuri was alone, alone in thought.

"What's he building?" Harris asked Ivan.

"More storage. I will wait now, he wants to talk to you on his own." he replied, ending the conversation.

Ivan shook Harris' hand, partly in friendship, but necessary to Harris, as he sought reassurance before walking across the field.

'Don't be stupid.' Harris told himself as he drew closer. 'You called for the meeting, not Yuri,' but Harris did wonder. Had Yuri found Maya, with her deceit and her lies, or had the Russian discovered the false trail of mooring fees that Harris had dumped on his men? The Detective hoped not.

"Yuri!" Harris shouted over the noise of the large diesel engines, "Yuri, Yuri." He yelled as he traipsed over the field ever closer, but still there was no response. 'He may be large, but he's bleeding deaf.' The Detective surmised and it was only a mere couple of yards before Yuri turned to the calls of his name and, seeing Harris, there was a nod of his head.

Harris couldn't help but notice that beyond Yuri there was a large pool of liquid concrete, many metres long and metres wide and, Harris assumed, metres deep. But it was what floated, half submerged on top, only a few feet away that caught Harris' attention.

It was bright white running shoe that lay half submerged on its side, he also noticed part of a fluorescent yellow sole. But where it was new, it was soiled by what appeared to be blood staining to the logo and most of the tongue.

Yuri followed Harris' gaze back to the trainer and after a moment, looking back at the officer, the Russian laughed. "I tried to tidy up before you came."

"I can see." Harris said and smiled with the Russian, but looking on in wonder he asked. "Another missing, London gangster wannabe that will remain missing?"

Yuri neither confirmed nor denied, he simply avoided Harris' remark and answered, "the shoemaker's logo, 'just do it,' so I did it." Again, he laughed, but this time alone.

Yuri walked the few steps towards Harris and bear hugged him as he always did, just as a long-lost friend. "Are you well?" He asked, leading Harris away from the concrete graveyard.

"Are you well?" he again asked.

"I'm fine." Harris finally responded, but the Detective was still trying to figure out if Yuri trusted him that much to show him what he had just seen. Did he trust him like a brother, or was it a test of loyalty? Harris knew, no matter what, the trainer would soon sink.

"I am at work my friend, what's so urgent for you wishing to see me?" Yuri questioned.

"A proposition Yuri." Harris replied.

"Ah, a proposal Officer Harris." And Yuri gripped his huge hands on either side of Harris' shoulders. "You are going to work for me now?" the Russian hoped.

"Sorry, no, I am not going to work for you." Harris replied. "This is a business proposition that I want little or no part of." He told him as he proffered the ledger.

"So, this that you are holding like a child is it a present?" Yuri asked.

"It's a business present to you Yuri." Harris answered. "A book that contains riches."

Yuri initially thanked Harris, but still he shrugged his huge shoulders. "It's a shame my friend, I still want you to work for me, however, business is business, I am hungry and you and I shall eat while we talk."

Chicken Kiev, fowl by name, foul by nature, an historic dish from the Ukraine where Russia once ruled. A garlic laden breast that was introduced into the UK in the late 1970s. They were indeed a cruel race to invent such a dish and Harris hated it as a child and as a man who still did, found himself sat in front of Yuri who was filling his face, there in his own restaurant in London's West End.

It was a restaurant recently rebuilt after a devastating fire had closed what was once an Italian pasta house.

"It is always good to have a fire, you can rebuild from the ground up." Yuri told him.

There were no other customers, just Yuri, Ivan and Harris; the restaurant would always close its doors to the public if Yuri was to order a table. Yuri had ordered a chicken Kiev for starter and chicken Kiev for the main, Ivan had cabbage soup and Harris sat wanting nothing, but fresh air, from the garlic stench.

Whilst they ate, they all drank vodka by the shot and, between shots, Harris explained the proposition. He told an incredible tale about wild sordid parties at which every dish was either a young boy or girl. Consenting adults, but scared vulnerable young children and Harris could see the anger rise.

Harris told of the abuse by celebrities and Government officials and, opening the ledger, he showed the detail.

Those Harris had marked with a circle were MPs or government officials both national and international, each with power and influence. These were the people to approach for contracts, payments for work without lifting a finger, he told them.

Harris even suggested perhaps a haulage contract and could see the irony that the British Government would be paying the costs for the illegal smuggling of Yuri's men and women into England. Harris also suggested that there would be fantastic deals in council housing for those that worked for him. He also announced. "You never know, they might even name a school after you." At this Harris laughed loudest.

Yuri was pleased, really pleased and eagerly nodded his approval, Ivan did likewise, as both visualised the £ signs floating around the empty restaurant.

Then, Harris showed those marked with a square. These were the powerful rich, Lord this, Baron that! Business directors, company executives, both British and foreign, it would be simple maths. They would become a little poorer, whilst Yuri would, each time, become a little richer.

Lastly, those Harris had marked with a star, these were the celebrities.

"Take what you can." Harris suggested. "Bleed their wealth dry and, once done, I ask you to see that most meet with an accident."

"An accident!" Yuri agreed. "I can arrange accidents, drug overdoses or heart failures, I have doctors that can administer a prescription or two."

Harris went on to explain the boxes full of electronic, visual and sound equipment. The files of discs, of pen and hard drives, Harris divulged, all were included in his pass on. Any combination of which would identify each individual in those sordid acts.

"All I ask are three things. Have your men's faces covered at all times and never have your men refer to each other by name." Yuri agreed.

"Secondly, with any banking transaction, Government or otherwise, make sure it is offshore and immediately diverted into other varied offshore accounts, could you do that?" Both Russians nodded without hesitation.

Harris then fell silent at the table.

"And the third?" Ivan asked.

"Make them suffer!" was his thoughtful reply.

Chapter 71

Harris' head was indeed pounding as he glanced again at the DNA results, he needed aspirin, and fresh air. So, deciding to leave his storeroom office, it was with a heavy head that he took the outside walkway and ventured to the canteen.

One black coffee, two bacon sandwiches and three headache tablets later, he returned and again tried to focus on the scientific report that he had taken with him. It was a report on the forensic submissions he had sent, one that was now partly smeared in English mustard, but it created an impact as he realised the wealth of the words that showed an 'identical match.'

He glanced again, he couldn't believe it, 'no don't glance, look.' He told himself and again he studied the pages.

There it was, a DNA profile was obtained from skin tissue left on the belt buckle that had strangled Fiona Grant-Smith and the same DNA profile was found on trace evidence on the lower stomach and lower vaginal swab from Mrs Forrester. Suddenly Harris visualised this evil beast standing above the poor woman and spreading himself across her in her last throes of life, perhaps as Sophie cried for mercy.

The report also highlighted that where not one bar of DNA coding matched Ralph's DNA. It was totally different and Harris was smiling as he danced lightly on heavy feet, spinning full circle towards the canteen counter where he ordered himself yet another strong coffee. He didn't care that the DNA profile could not be matched against anyone known on the DNA database, he just cared that there was a match and it wasn't Ralph's. Harris could not help but smile, he smiled at everything and everyone and was still grinning ear to ear when he turned to the last page of the report and saw two photographs developed through the fingerprint branch. The first showed the front of the train ticket found with Mrs Forrester and the second was a photograph of its reverse. Harris wasn't one for surprises, but that morning kept on giving, he couldn't believe what his eyes. There, on the back of the ticket, found through the use of UVA light sourcing, was a handwritten scribble, Z121.

'The fucker had actually signed off on the murder of Sophie using an Ultraviolet pen!' Harris thought and his head begun spinning presumptions.

Did Z121 want to be caught? Or was it just a taunt, a signature that might be jerked off too in some darkened room? Harris was in awe of the audacity, but he also realised its worth, he had handwritten scribble from the murderer.

It took the rest of the morning for the report to be complete and, on the last page, Harris left space for a signature.

Chapter 72

"Come in." Miller called out as Harris knocked on his door. As he entered Miller could see Harris' broad smile.

Miller wasn't smiling though, he hadn't asked to be at Barking, a crass, filthy place, full of crass filthy people and he especially resented being sent there at the request of the Commissioner all because of this badly dressed 'Arris' fellow.

"Is it complete?" Miller nodded towards the thick dossier Harris held in both hands.

"Yes, sir it is, do you have an hour to spare?" the Detective asked.

"No." Miller told him. "You have 10 minutes before I leave for New Scotland Yard."

"Oh, okay." Harris replied, somewhat deflated.

"It's quite simple Arris." Miller explained. "I am trying to move back as quickly as possible, every day that I am here is another day of missed opportunities in seeking 'fast track' promotion. Do you understand that?" Miller barked.

Harris understood all right. Although he didn't know the politics involved, mainly because he didn't have rank and nor did he want to, but he understood that being located in 'the big house' where the Commissioner sat, where all manner of senior staff were easily accessible, was a far easier place to gain the next rank, rather than working on the outskirts and invisible in the Borough.

"Well sir, I do have your ticket to help you get back there." Harris announced, wishing him gone too.

"Okay sit down and explain, 9 minutes." Miller told him curtly.

It was less than five minutes before Miller realised that Harris was indeed clutching a 'golden ticket' for promotion. A report that would prove the innocence of a man who had been jailed for over 30 years, not so much 'a Birmingham 6,' but 'an East London 1' and it was not so much the detailing of the report, but it was how Harris had repeatedly stated this was the investigation of Detective Chief Superintendent Hutchings and Miller. All that was left to do was fill in a blank space for the Investigating Officer to sign, the blank space just above the name that Harris had typed, Chief Superintendent Miller.

"Are you sure?" Asked the now smiling Miller, ready to seize this opportunity.

"Yes sir." Harris said, deliberately distancing himself. "You're the one that's going to sign off my overtime."

Chapter 73

The next few weeks saw both Harris and Yuri hard at work.

The file in respect of Ralph was 'fast tracked' to the Crown Prosecution Service (CPS) and, after a few phone calls to various executives in its hierarchy, a barrister was assigned. Then Harris took the file to the CPS offices at Tower Bridge where in one meeting he met Senior CPS executives, the barrister and a Home Office official.

Harris explained the details of the file that he was presenting on behalf of the Investigating Officers, Detective Superintendent Hutchings and Miller and he ran through the current evidence, to the dismay of those that were gathered. Although they were shocked, together they agreed that there was an insecure conviction and Ralph had been wrongly jailed.

Immediately a date was set for an appeal against conviction and the Home Office representative urged that the appeal should be accurate to the finite of detail and, for the following weeks, Harris was pulled left right and centre, an added statement here, an added statement there and always with the barrister calling after him, "paginate dear boy, paginate."

"Lengthen your report dear man." The barrister told him, "lengthen and paginate."

Harris knew only too well that the barrister's concern was that he was being paid by the page, rather than having sympathy for Ralph.

"Run along, achieve everything and by God don't forget to paginate." He would tell Harris.

So that was Harris, 16 hour days, with little thought of anything else but Ralph and numbering pages.

As for Yuri, this new venture that Harris had proposed had Yuri rubbing his hands with glee. The Detective had truly 'crossed the line' of conscience he thought and Yuri had welcomed him with open arms.

Yuri tasked Ivan to set up the 'torture' factory once more, but this time it was to be turned into something akin to a small cinema.

There were now two rows of three metal chairs and hanging from each armrest was a set of handcuffs. In front of them and beyond were vending machines that supplied free coffee and popcorn.

Against one of the walls Yuri had Russian engineers set up a newly purchased, massive projector screen and in front of this was a desk with a microphone on a small stand sitting in the middle.

Apart from the commode on wheels, there was an old, second hand, metal post-mortem table, one with drainage ports on each corner that had been converted by 'Soft shoe.' He had fastened thick, Velcro web strapping to hold limbs in place. In front of this, the commode and focusing on each of these were tripod cameras that had been primed to record every detail.

There were banks of computers, the visual and audio equipment that Harris had supplied. All wired and tested, so that visual images from the discs and drives could be screenshot and played onto the projector screen beyond.

"Perfect" Yuri told the small cluster of men that had worked so diligently, converting his warehouse.

Yuri had also organised a number of his men to work through the large ledger books of names and photographs, in order to 'marry' them to the various captured footage.

Not only was Yuri to rid the world of some evil paedophiles, but, having been given these gifts by the Detective, he would obtain riches in the process. It was not only the wealth he relished, he would now have the means to seek political influence amongst those that ruled the UK, a minister here an MP there, those that could sanitise him to 'untouchable.'

'Soft shoe,' as Harris had described him to Yuri, agreed that he would remain at the factory with his small team of experts, just to ensure any future 'guest' was made to feel just as 'uncomfortable' as Harris had been.

There was one small problem though, the date of the next party was soon approaching and, even though they had worked tirelessly, the Russians still had a mountain of files to check against the books they possessed.

It was a small problem that was overcome by a fire that could be seen for miles around the school building in Sussex that burnt to the ground on the very morning of the next party venue.

Chapter 74

Harris awoke, a bundle of nerves, the very next morning and he tingled with expectation all over as he awaited the Home Office meeting at 4 pm that day.

There was a brief exchange of pleasantries and a firm handshake between the two men before they were ushered through the visitors' reception area at Pentonville prison.

"So, Ralph, in four days you are going to go to court again." Harris spoke first in the consulting room.

"I am appealing your conviction." He told him. Ralph could only look back at him puzzled.

"You are innocent Ralph." Harris tried to simplify the terminology as he offered him a sweet.

"I know I am." replied Ralph still wondering why no one had believed him and Harris smiled at this announcement.

"I know you know you are." Harris agreed. "It is just that we have to tell some other people that you are innocent, so you're going to another building to tell those people that you're innocent, do you understand?" Harris was hopeful and, finally, Ralph nodded.

"And then I come back here Mr Harris?" Ralph asked.

Harris turned to the official who had positioned himself in one corner of the room, the Detective was looking for assistance, but was incensed when the man in the white metal framed glasses simply looked apathetic and shrugged his shoulders. Harris glared, he wasn't expecting silence, and he wasn't expecting such a dismissive response. That was until Harris offered, "don't worry, the Government will give you a house and if they don't you can sue them for one." With that the man suddenly coughed a response.

"There is a re-settlement team based in the prison. There are procedures to follow for when you leave and I will get the paperwork together for you Ralph."

"But I can't read and I like it here." Ralph urged as he turned to Harris.

Choking in frustration. "Please Mr Harris, you're my friend, tell him I'm coming back here, please Mr Harris, tell him." He pleaded.

Harris gulped deeply as he realised what an idiot he'd been.

Harris, on his vanquishing steed of justice, hadn't taken into account Ralph's feelings. No, he was simply bent on setting him free and now, sitting there in that cold room, Harris saw for himself, 'what a fool he had been.'

"Please Mr Harris, please tell him I'm coming back here." Ralph asked in fear, but Harris had nothing to offer and looked to the floor as he racked his brain for an answer, he was now only too aware that Ralph was openly crying.

"I don't want to go, please don't make me," he heard between the sobs.

"You're my friend Mr Harris, please tell him." Ralph wept as Harris remained silent.

Harris was now fully aware that Ralph had been institutionalised, a dreary routine, but a routine that Ralph had comfortably complied with and now here he was, tearing Ralph's world apart. Outside prison Ralph would be nothing, no job, no prospects and no danger to society, just a shell. A man that had been sentenced to life and his life had been taken.

Suddenly a thought, a flash of inspiration hit Harris who broadcast, "You are my friend Ralph and I have somewhere better for you to live, but please calm down before I tell you."

Slowly the inmate curbed his sniffling, and looked at Harris between eye rubs.

"Where?" He croaked with uneasiness.

"I would like you to help look after my sister." Harris divulged. "She is a nice, kind lady, who lives abroad, near the sea, where the sun is hot and you can look at the waves on the ocean," he told him.

Ralph looked interested.

"You will have a room of your own and three meals a day just like here." Harris continued. "My sister is disabled and she finds it hard to walk, as my friend, would you be kind enough to help her?"

At last Ralph smiled.

The official just looked at Harris with pure indignation. "So, what?" Harris replied to the stare.

"Well for one, it is against all protocols." The official said as Harris imagined his fist flying into the face of officialdom.

Harris just stood and walked over to the pen pusher, quietly whispering in his ear "You sort out a prisoner escort tomorrow and get his photograph taken, then FastTrack a 24-hour passport application or I will fast track my fucking fist into your face, do you understand?"

The man looked up at the hate filled face in front of him and nodded.

Chapter 75

Harris was expecting the usual overnight court warning that any serving police officer receives when due to appear in court, but he wasn't expecting the phone call issuing him two court warnings for the following day at the Central Criminal Court.

It was a Friday, a day where bad news could easily be hidden from the press, a day where no one cared for anything but the weekend in front of them and the Home Office had specified this date.

Although Harris was expecting the appeal warning for Ralph, he did not expect to be giving evidence at the trial of his former Inspector Pete Brown. That news came as quite a shock and Harris knew he would be torn between courts.

Harris had prepared for the appeal, he had dry-cleaned his suit, he had ironed his shirt and he had chosen the least stained tie. He had also persuaded 'Temptress Tina' to take a few days holiday with Harris' remaining safe money, so that she could escort Ralph over to Gibraltar. But he hadn't prepared himself to give evidence against his former boss, there had been no early court warning, and he wouldn't be able to study his notes until his appearance at court, the DPS had a lot answer for.

He had risen in a cold sweat as he relived that night's dream again. This time he visualised himself scaling the summit of dead bodies, bodies that quickly sank beneath his feet, only to be confronted with an axe wielding leather clad beast with blood dripping tusks. A beast that spat acid that corroded his feet, then the blackest of fur, the devil incarnate, striking out and blocking him from going forward to the light beyond.

"That's enough of that!" Harris said as a quick shiver ran down his spine. 'I've got work to do,' he told himself.

The journey on that damp miserable day was simply a blur as his mind ran through so many recent events and, many times, he asked himself, 'was I right to do what I've done?' Truthfully though, he knew the answer, it was the path he had chosen. One with Yuri that was against all his principles he had held when joining the Police. But, circumstance had backed him into a corner and, during the investigation into a serial murderer, never in his wildest dreams did he think he would uncover a plot so depraved, so sinister and so sickening.

"So be it," he said.

Chapter 76

Passing through the security entrance and walking down the marbled steps of the Old Bailey towards the gaoler's office Harris found his heart was pounding. There was no exertion, no sprint, no fight, but the adrenaline was flowing, it was anticipation, it was excitement. At last Ralph would have justice and it was all that squeezed him onward when he asked to see the prisoner.

Having been given permission, the gaoler's door was opened for him, but there was no joy when he stood there horrified, listening to the wince of pain that the cornered Ralph had uttered. Harris stared at a face that was black and blue from a beating Ralph had taken as 'a farewell present' from some of the inmates. However, even through the pain and two chipped teeth, Ralph still managed a smile.

"Are you okay?" The anxious Detective asked.

"Yeah, I'm a bit bruised." Ralph replied between dampened coughs. But, more interested in the weather than the usual beatings that he had suffered, he looked up and asked. "Is it still sunny at your sisters?"

Harris stood there smiling. "Yes, it is," he told him.

The appeal was due at 10 am, half an hour before the courts would normally 'open for business' and Harris waited outside Ralph's courtroom anticipating the tannoy announcement for Regina v Brown to send him elsewhere.

Harris heard nothing of the barrister's paginated speech, nor the announcement by the Home Office barrister who told the court that there was absolutely no objection to Ralph's release. He also missed out on the court commendations of Chief Superintendents Hutchings and Miller for their tenacity and professionalism, but the Detective was elated when he saw Ralph was free of handcuffs as he shuffled his way from the courtroom onto the concourse.

"They said sorry." Ralph said to Harris' smile.

The establishment had raised, ill-treated and forgotten this child of a man and only Harris was glad that Ralph had survived as he ushered his charge into the nearby Police waiting room a flight of stairs away.

Luckily there was no court press around, so no knocks on the police room door, no quotes, no kerfuffle, just Ralph sitting in a chair waiting for his friend who had left him there alone, as he had work to do before they left.

Harris now stood outside Court 3, there he recognised a couple of the DPS officers that he had worked with on Pete Brown's case.

"Is Hemmings coming?" Harris asked one of them.

"No, nor will he," came the curt reply.

"Apparently, he drowned a week ago, just off the shoreline and the Bermudan authorities have only just informed us," the man explained.

Harris had that sinking feeling himself, 'accident or Yuri?' he pondered.

Nevertheless, opening speeches, "these could possibly take the rest of the day," Harris was told. He'd have to wait until lunch to find out as to whether he was to be required that day.

So, he had little choice but to wander around the few display cabinets in nearby alcoves. There, his thoughts, trying to anticipate the questions he'd soon be asked, were interrupted by curiosity as he glanced at the displays that showed the buildings history. He stood in a building where thousands had met their end by hanging. A gruesome finale having taken a few steps, walking between ever diminishing white arches along the 'dead man's walk' just outside and Harris wondered to himself, if he was a 'dead man walking.'

Finally, the court rose and Harris was told he was, "free to go, but return first thing on Monday morning." That's all Harris needed to hear and he ran to collect Ralph.

Harris made sure that he and Ralph were allowed to exit the court via the Judges entrance, a rear door away from the press, away from the noise of potential well-wishers and it was just two men walking the pavement, side-by-side along the A40 in silence.

Chapter 77

Harris had a busy weekend, where he had booked the two flights to Morocco and then ferry tickets from Tangiers to Gibraltar.

'No way,' Harris had told himself, 'was anyone going to know where his sister lived,' especially the Home Office who could easily check the usage on Ralph's new passport.

It was sad saying goodbye to Ralph and Tina on the Sunday morning. Harris was tempted to get the flight himself, but, through tears from both travellers, he decided against it, realising that with these two gone it was less worry for the Detective.

From Monday until Wednesday Harris lived on his wits, he had returned to court as promised, where he spent the first day giving evidence on behalf of the prosecution. On every break Harris made notes to deliberate over, he knew the defence counsel would try their best in discrediting whatever he had said. He was always the guilty party; any copper is when giving evidence and the Brown defence team had intimated that the defendant had confessed under duress and now took verbal delight at Harris' muscular presence in the witness box.

The next two days were torrid. The defence team produced 'grey area' after 'grey area' and all the while ex-inspector Brown stared 'daggers' at Harris from 'the prisoner dock.' To add to that, ever so occasionally, Hutchins would make an appearance in the public gallery and glare at Harris with the same spite.

"Surely you would know officer?" Harris was asked time and time again.

"Not to my recollection Sir," was his standard reply.

It was two long days as if Harris was on trial, portrayed as an evil, sinister, vindictive Detective, not fit for the streets of London and, in respect of his recent past, Harris wryly thought. 'They weren't far off the mark.'

Mentally battered, Harris continued and was glad when he finally heard the words. "Just one final question officer."

Not much of a question though Harris realised. There was a five-minute summary of what Harris wouldn't or couldn't recall, as the barrister brandished him a liar to the jury at every opportunity. At the end of the small speech Harris was asked.

"Officer are there any recollections you think may help the court make clarity from the doldrums of your mind?"

To which he stood there silent, looking towards the jury awaiting the acknowledgement of all 12 jurors who, eventually stared back at him, that included the odd amateur sleuth or two, who had sat quietly making notes.

"Yes, your honour," and Harris paused again before turning to the judge. "I recall one fact." he stated clearly. "I'm not looking for anyone else."

So that was that, he had given his evidence and had been cross examined, he was finished. However, he had to acknowledge the fact that he may be recalled at any time to answer questions in R v Brown, but Harris was happy to leave the courtroom exhausted.

He fancied a beer, but he had a greater thirst for finding out where his future lay. He had been away from his storage room office for over three days. Three days in the knowledge that Miller wouldn't have waited for Harris' return but would have allocated either a full team or even a small group of Detectives to investigate the serial murderer that, up until now, no one even knew existed.

By the time he returned to Barking it was gone 7 o'clock and the Squad building was again likened to a ghost town with only one or two personnel remaining in the Team offices. Harris deliberately kept his distance from them. He wasn't up to talking, he was knackered and his brain was on overload as he walked the long corridor towards his storeroom.

However, when he reached his door, a huge dimpled smile lit up Harris' face. There in front of him was his storeroom cupboard and taped across the door frame were reams of, 'Police lines - do not enter,' along with, 'Crime scene,' tape and a banner that stated 'Congratulations.'

'That was nice,' he thought. His hard work had been recognised by some and he giggled as he tore away at the tape to get to his locked office.

On entering, everything was how he had left it, apart from a note on the floor from Chief Supt Miller asking him to phone on his 'personal' mobile number, privilege indeed and he did just that.

There were a few, "yes sir, yes sir," comments as Harris listened to what his boss had organised. Actually, there was far too much acceptance as Harris sat exhausted. However, he was relieved it was only a small investigating team that he was working with, one Detective Inspector, two sergeants and three other detectives, all like himself, who he knew were capable. Miller had chosen wisely from the influx of volunteers.

Harris was given that night, with what little was left of it, to prepare his notes of investigation for the first office meeting of operation, "Commute," that was to take place the next day and Miller ended the phone call giving Harris the Crime Reporting Information System allocated number.

CRIS, a system that was 'out dated' at its inception and now a 30+ year investigating tool held on its own computer was far too slow by any standards and had brought many a tear to a Detective who had tried to work their way through the repetition of boxes and multiple memos that had to be completed before, during and after each investigation. Now Harris had to face that 'devil' in grey screenshot.

Over the next couple of hours, Harris read what little notes he had 'two finger' typed onto the CRIS and still the victim's details were empty, but he was too frustrated to bother, there was something more important to deal with, a request to a research team based at his offices. A message request that was to be forwarded to the Police National Database that detailed the murders and 'train ticket insertions.' A request that was to be sent nationwide, including the home nations. Luckily, gone were the days when one Police County didn't talk to another. Harris sent a 'copy and pasted' Interpol message so that other countries in Europe and further afield could also research similar type deaths and insertions. Lastly, he sent a request to the Met Intelligence Bureau based in Central London, asking that they act as a point of contact.

Harris looked at the time and realised it was nearing midnight. As he yawned he decided on one last action, a search that almost every 'copper' would make during a normal work shift, it was a search of the human resources page showing 'reprimands, fines, sackings and death.' Just to lighten a dark moment in most 'coppers' black humour, just to find out who has suffered at the hands of the DPS and where the Grim Reaper had visited. Harris noted that DPS had been hard at work, saving the taxpayer from another pension. 'Nothing surprising there then,' he thought.

But, as he scoured the death page, the name Cooper sprang, a blazing bright blue from the screen.

There it was in a short-messaged announcement, the death of Detective Sergeant Dave Cooper of Special Branch. He had died two days previously on what was the day that Harris had first given evidence at the trial of Inspector Pete Brown. The short script didn't state the cause of death, nor was there mention of a murder enquiry. If the death had been suspicious, he thought, he would have heard about it. Yes, he would make discreet enquiries however. Right then he cared little, as he faced a much-needed sleep.

Chapter 78

Like most of Britain's coastline, where it could be cheaply afforded, a beach hut would be built. Originally used as a changing room for the beach these are still loved today. Rarely neglected these colourful builds flood memories for the masses, of saltwater air, funfairs, and bright pink candy floss.

Then came the caravan parks, private entrepreneurs building their mini villages close to the coast, but almost all were set apart by security gates and ticket only entry with exclusion to the general public. Now they struggle against cheap flight holidays.

Walton on Naze in Essex has both huts and caravans and is no exception to the downturn in trade. However, it is a town happily cocooned in the last century with little or insignificant modernisation.

Some claim that it is a seaside town caught in its own time bubble, a place where even the local Police Station, a neglected small terraced house, was only manned during summer weekends. It was here where Yuri, who had woken just before dawn, now stood outside and he noted the opening hours.

Yuri not only wrote notes, he made plans, he surveyed roadmaps, he had even studied the coastline when he first arrived on the East coast and it was from this Police Station he drove. Next on his list was the closed/abandoned caravan site which he realised had been a well-chosen venue for the forthcoming weekend 'Fires of Hell' party, a party he was now preparing for.

The site was situated on old farmland leading to what was once a distant shore, but due to sea erosion and a lack of funding it was a now close to a cliff edge where the few remaining static caravans and prefabs were in danger of collapsing into the North Sea, some fifty feet below. The caravan park was in an area rarely ventured, but only a mile and a half from the main town itself. It stood on its own at the end of a private road, 'An ideal location for isolation,' the Russian thought.

The main entrance itself was signposted some 12 feet high on a faded, white noticeboard and underneath was curtains of barbed wire fencing that surrounded the site. The signpost itself consisted of large wooden block letters all attached by hooks that had been shuffled and arranged by some anonymous 'wag' to title the site as 'WALTANNNE ZOO.'

The main gate was held closed by two steel bars and fortified with four heavy steel padlocks. Yuri explained to the two escort henchmen. "These won't be disturbed."

Yuri knew if he had removed these locks that no doubt someone would notice and he wanted to ensure that nothing looked like it had been disturbed.

"Come, we go for a walk," he told them and took the two men on a stroll of the perimeter. One carried bolt croppers and a reel of metal fence wire, lifted from the boot of Yuri's car.

Chapter 79

Harris had showered and shaved specifically for the 10am Thursday meeting and, over and over in his head, he rehearsed a short speech.

By 10:20am, the team that looked to him were suitably impressed and said so. Each took turns and introduced themselves. Harris saw intelligence and quality as each spoke about their various exploits, expertise and achievements. Harris was quietly satisfied when he realised that none were Exhibit Officer trained, he had his niche and knew, above everything else, he was required in that role.

It took three hours and one cigarette break for the team to 'thrash out' and formalise an investigation plan. The requests Harris had made both nationally and internationally the night before would be followed up by personal letters to the relevant Chief Constables and Heads of Authorities in the hope that a thorough search of all old murder and missing persons' files would be undertaken.

Both Ralph and Nikki were, at some point in their lives, under the care of Social Services, these too would be investigated and Harris found himself, sitting there, imagining Cooper's black book being handed into the Police as, 'property found in the street.' The black book where Nikki's name would be featured amongst the numerous other boys' and girls' names, their contact details and the names of the various children's care homes where those kids were supplied from. A book that would also show the names and telephone numbers of those that worked there and Harris was pleased as he envisaged plenty of prisoners and plenty of overtime.

There were two final announcements by the newly promoted Detective Inspector Jarvis. Firstly, Harris would receive a commendation for Detective ability and, secondly, the investigation into his house explosion had been concluded as an 'accident.' The fire investigation team were mystified that they could find no evidence of foul play. Harris smiled at the accolades of, "well done son," and the like, but he was more than elated that at long last his insurance company would be rebuilding his home.

"The pubs are open and Harris is buying." Jarvis announced.

"Too bleeding right." Harris agreed and they stood as one as they left the office.

Harris was supping into his third pint of Guinness before he suddenly realised that he had literally forgotten all about Cooper and was quietly cursing as the conversation around him became simply a blur.

Quickly he made 'his excuses' to pop back to the office on the pretence of something or other and the team were still happily drinking when he promised his prompt return.

It didn't take long; a short cab fare and Harris was soon pretending to be Hutchings again as he rang Special Branch from the canteen phone. He would have used Miller's phone, but he was in and the canteen phone was the next best, it was anonymous and it would have to do.

"Yes, an old friend." Harris lied.

"Suicide by hanging, poor chap." Harris was told.

"Cremation and when?" Harris asked.

Cooper would truly be welcomed into the fires of hell once more.

--//--

The following morning Harris was suffering from yet another hangover, mixing beer, wine and shots was never a sensible thing to do no matter what day of the week. It just seemed like a good idea at the time. His pounding brain struggled as he recalled celebrating his good fortune.

Like all good Detectives he dragged himself into work and, after a quick visit to the canteen for a 'fry up,' Harris was glad that he had done so. For, no sooner had Harris sat at his new desk than Chief Supt Miller walked in with a somewhat 'happy face,' well, it was his interpretation of someone who seemed happy. Both Miller's lips were curled up at the end as he walked straight over to Harris.

"Well done Arris," he said in his bastardised East End voice, "well done indeed," he said. Harris just stared, he had no idea what was going on and he hated smiling Guvnors, for it always meant someone was about to carry 'the shit end of the stick.' Miller was standing directly in front of him, but this time Harris was wrong.

"Morning Sir," he said, waiting for the bullshit bombshell.

"Good morning indeed," and Miller's smile widened. "Congratulations Detective, you're off to Scotland next week." And with instructions Miller placed a blue cardboard file on the desk in front of the officer.

"Very good sir, can I ask why?" Harris sighed in word and thought, 'Scotland, cold, miserable, damp, pints of 'heavy' and with its own statute laws to contend with, he was wishing it was Spain instead.

"You have another murder to add to the list." Miller told him.

"An unsolved missing person's case that they have had on their books for years," he announced.

"And?" Harris shivered, knowing he would soon be in lower temperatures.

"It's all in the file Detective, a dead girl who had been on the missing persons list back in the 1980s and she had remained so for five long years, that was until her skeletal remains were discovered. No cause of death though." Miller told him.

Harris was just a little bewildered and his puzzled face expressed this.

"Just read the file," Miller chirped, clearly happy. "Someone will go with you, so go pack a suitcase," and with those words Miller was off. As the office door swung closed behind him, so Harris began to read.

The report was just as Miller had described, a missing person's file on a pretty lass that on one Monday morning, many years ago, had failed to show up for work and, although she was over 18 and considered an adult to do as she liked, there were considerable efforts to find her. Her parents had been worried sick and fearing the worst they re-mortgaged their house and spent the money on numerous advertising billboards and newspaper appeals in order to find her.

But alas, there was nothing, not until her bones were found on some land due for an oil refinery, then her DNA was eventually matched to a hairbrush her mother had kept as a keepsake.

As news broke that the missing girl had been identified a fresh appeal was launched and it was the result of this appeal that froze Harris to his seat.

Like in all appeals, members of the public come forward and in those days, it was either in person, on the phone, or by letter. Mostly irrelevant or wrong information, but sometimes, just sometimes a golden nugget would shine. However, for the missing girl there was nothing but well-wishers and misdirection. At the time, nothing was thought of the envelope that was delivered, but it now transfixed Harris.

More than five and a half years since her disappearance and three weeks after the positive DNA identification, an envelope was received by Aberdeen police. It was typed and headed with a reference to the missing girl, posted from a local area of Scotland.

There was no accompanying letter, it was just a train ticket and initially thought to be the resulting act of a stupid prankster. In fact, it had almost been thrown in a bin, but for the simple fact that it was opened by a probationer police constable who was stationed at the front desk and, learning his trade, he was ordered by the Sergeant in charge to forward it to the missing person's bureau where it was then filed.

Harris stared at the scanned fax of the train ticket and there in front of him was an identical train ticket with a closely matched serial number, on the rear was a black ink squiggle which, under a magnifying glass, Harris could decipher as Z121.

Harris was dumbstruck, the murderer definitely wanted some form of acknowledgement for his work, 'the sick bastard!' Harris thought. Not only that, but 'the sicko' had chosen his name from the arm of Nikki. There was another thing he soon realised, the murderer travelled. He looked closely again at the scribbled letter and numbers and, quickly grabbing the photograph of Sophie's ticket, he looked for comparison.

Chapter 80

Friday night and Harris was packing for the forthcoming trip, he wasn't leaving until Wednesday but as he knew he could be busy over the weekend, he had nothing better to do than to iron a few shirts.

It was rather an anti-climax compared to the week that had just passed, but it gave him time to think, consider his options, value his survival and he was deep in thought when the front door bell rang.

Harris checked the spyhole and there stood Yuri and Ivan. A cold shudder entered his body for he knew he was still living day to day on, 'ifs, what's and buts?'

"Come in gents, how can I help?" Harris invited and quickly ushered both to the lounge.

'Phew,' Harris thought, 'they seem jovial enough,' and with a hand gesture all three sat.

"Firstly, I want to thank you Mr Harris." Yuri said.

"My men have studied the books, the discs and files and from documenting the people on them I am sure there will be vast profit to be made, both in money and influence. So, as a friend, and I call you my friend, I ask you what share would you like?"

Harris was a little taken aback as he looked at both Yuri and Ivan.

"I want your absolute trust," he said, "no money, nothing, but trust and just to let you know, I won't lie to you, but I've removed some pages from that ledger for personal reasons."

"I noticed that." Ivan interjected. "I saw some pages have been torn out, why?" He questioned.

"For the record gents, they mainly relate to police officers." Harris explained. "Those pages are for me to deal with, be okay with that," he nodded, "because you're not having them." And he looked for an agreement.

Both Ivan and Yuri looked towards each other then back at Harris and nodded.

"Now about the party this weekend." Yuri informed, "I have planned for it, are you coming?"

Harris shook his head. "No thank you, I am sure you have planned it well, but I will deal with the aftermath."

For the next 30 minutes Yuri and Ivan set out every detail and when concluding Yuri laughed out loud. "Yes, even down to the masks, it will be, how you say, eventful." and laughed again.

Harris smiled. "Have you enough men?" He asked.

"I have enough men, sometimes too many!" And Yuri bellowed further laughter.

Harris quickly excused himself to the kitchen returning with one of the torn pages from the ledger. He showed the page to both Yuri and Ivan and Harris asked. "Let me know if this person turns up and if so don't hurt him, treat him with kid gloves, Okay?"

Yuri looked puzzled but his answer was clear. "Okay Mr Harris, I trust you, but if you worked for me I would trust you as my brother Ivan, so I ask again, will you work for me?"

"Sadly no." Harris refused, "but I wish you good hunting," he said.

"Then take this." Yuri offered. "It would make me feel better." And with that his right hand reached down into his trouser pocket where he pulled out a small round resin disc with a maggot within.

"You don't work for me, but at least others will know you are in my favour," the Russian told him.

Harris took the warm disc in his open palm and clenching it tight he said. "Thank you." Harris was favoured, not dead!

"One last matter," the crime Lord stated, "I have found my Maya, she went home to Russia." Harris stifled his gasp.

"Apparently, she ran with my daughters when she saw that I had been shot, well that is what she is telling my men." Now Harris was stunned.

"They are being shipped back here to England as I speak. I don't want her damaged. That's why she's not going to the warehouse and I want you to question her."

Harris was speechless.

"What do you say?" Yuri asked. He waited, "what do you say?" He asked again.

Harris tried his best to gather his emotions and with turmoil erupting he nervously nodded an answer. "Gladly."

There was a bear hug from both, the one from Yuri almost squashed Harris' limp shocked body. He was again left with his ironing, left with the thought of Maya telling the Russians that he was in fact responsible for Yuri's arrest.

Maya was coming home, but was she coming home to him? Of course not! She had been found, she wasn't coming back on her own volition! What would she say? All these questions, his safety, when? How? What was he to do? Harris unplugged the iron, just as he tried to 'turn off' the thoughts of impending doom in his head.

Was it the right thing to stay? Should he flee? He asked repeatedly.

Was he right to remain or was he just trying to convince himself, was he falling into the cracks of sanity? 'So be it, so be it, whatever,' he told himself and, dismissing reality, he took himself to bed.

Chapter 81

It was Saturday and Ernie screamed, not a playful tummy rubbing 'tickle time' scream, but a scream of pure fear as he was frogmarched towards the cliff edge. He didn't care to look for the lights left at Harwich dock or to the right where Walton Pier stretched out into the sea. No, he just screamed as he struggled to release the grips on his arms.

He tried pleading again, but was punched to the floor, they didn't want to hear his speech; to them there was no closing argument. Reaching down one held his arms, whilst the other his legs and he cried for his life once more. They didn't listen, they didn't understand; they just acted on orders when picking him up, as they swung him back and forth. Again, the screams sliced the night air as he was finally released forward, outward, upward his arms swam, towards the silvery moon.

It was a violent front crawl in mid-air, but his efforts didn't support him and in that instant his body dropped from the cliff edge until his screams echoed with the screams of others who had witnessed his onset of freefall.

Many of the onlookers turned away shuddering. Some fell to their knees in prayer, others suffered body convulsions, but for every guest, each cable tied to another, it tore skin from their wrists and ankles as each shook with fear.

Ernie just vanished over the edge into the night and within that split second, none that had been gathered, had ever experienced such terror.

All thoughts from Ernie vanished, so far in life, his wife, his public office, there was no comprehension in those last two seconds, bewildering seconds that lasted no time, just a dire moment in time and his scream immediately silenced once he impacted onto the boulders below.

Just one twitch of nerve endings and then nothing as his body lay broken and dead on the deserted, rock laden beach. A sand dune serenity, broken only by the distant waves on the shoreline, that and various howls from above.

There was no quiet from the party goers above, not from those who were tied tight and had just witnessed the murder. Some tried to stand, to hop and to leap to the shadows of darkness that lay beyond the bright beam of portable arc light. How they urged themselves away to find safety, only to be beaten back down with the lathed wood of baseball bats and body blows. Some tried to wriggle away 'like worms' on the damp grass, only to be kicked from whence they came, many of them cried and each of them wondered who was next?

Yuri had just made an example of a man who had just lied to him about his true identity as he stood amongst the hundred or so of his men, all masked, armed and brutal.

Yuri had simply raised his arm above his head and clicked his fingers twice to the constant lies the man had spoken and it was on that signal, that two Russian ex-servicemen approached from behind where they cut the Member of Parliament's cable ties. Raising Ernie to his feet, they had dragged him some 20 yards, through consternation, complaint and argument they came closer to the backdrop of the caravan park and there they had swung and released him into the gloom.

Yuri had known who the man was, he had photocopies of the books that were now in his possession and his face was identified from one of the many photographs.

Ernie the MP was the first to lie, the first, of all those trussed up individuals who had been dragged to him for interrogation and, after that example, Yuri doubted that any more would lie.

Yuri's little operation was going to plan and he was quite satisfied that by daybreak, without hiccup, he would have achieved his goals.

--//--

It was earlier when Yuri and his entourage had arrived at that sleepy coastal town. A small convoy consisting of one heavy goods vehicle, two coaches, stolen, followed by ten hire vans and four hire cars, all obtained on false documentation.

After 'a scouting party' reported the 'all clear,' various bolt croppers made light work of the padlocks that secured the front gates. It was only then that the convoy entered the site and snapped open the padlocks which were quickly repositioned on the gate and 'cable tied' together to appear as if they were still secure. Within an hour the caravan park had settled into quiet, as the two coaches were positioned on the far side of the caravan park next to the disused social club, well away from the main car park. The Arctic lorry was opened revealing a multitude of portable floodlights and generators which were carried down. After the generators and lighting were checked over and found to be in good working order, each was turned off to await the arrival of dusk

The lorry was also emptied of wooden crates and boxes, each filled with various munitions, and then there was the odd baseball bat and a couple of garden rakes thrown in for good measure. Once emptied, the lorry was parked in the coach park along with every other vehicle, with the exception of two of the multi-seat hire vans. One of these 'people carriers' was to be used as an unnatural barrier across the one-way entrance to enclose the car park when needed, whilst the other was left alone, waiting dormant, at the far end of the car park which Yuri had decided was to be used as 'shuttle run' transportation.

Every number plate was covered in black plastic strips and duct tape, balaclava masks with openings for only eyes and mouth then covered the faces of those not dealing with children.

Those with masks quickly 'covered up' and entered each caravan where cameras and digital recording equipment were discovered and seized. Finally, there were those men who were specifically dressed in camouflage. These went to the main gate and hid amongst the hedgerows and bushes that grew on either side of the road. All others took their positions and laid in wait.

It was hours later when a white van was first seen approaching the main gates, within it was the gatekeeper and two visual recording technicians. They were arriving to prepare but as they halted in front of the gate they were quickly surrounded, each with a gun to their head. Then individually searched they were relayed passing from one masked man to another until finally they were led up the ramp into the rear hold of the lorry. There they were cable tied hand and foot and repeatedly kicked by steel boots and beaten with baseball bats. This was until they squeezed themselves into a corner of fear at the far end of the container.

It was the same scenario for the 'security' that turned up. One or two cars at a time, intermittent and relaxed in approach, where none queried the lack of salute to the fisted ring that they gave on approach to the gate. Only two men in black suits who simply waved them forward and then, to their total surprise, they were mesmerised and far outnumbered, as guns pointed towards them from every direction.

There was no resistance, even though one or two of them had been armed themselves, none were stupid enough to confront the overwhelming firepower that would have made 'Bonnie and Clyde' of their vehicles.

Again, they were searched and frogmarched towards the open lorry to await the same fate as the others. This was repeated, time and again; each man cable tied and bludgeoned towards the far end of the lorry and for those that shouted defiance, they suffered until bloodied, unconscious, or silent.

There was a couple of hours of nervous wait before the first of the care buses transporting the young arrived and like all those that followed, each was waived through by the men on the gates. Waved onward, towards the next men in black suits, then onto the next until they reached the tree lined car park where more men in black suits waited.

The children were already costumed as film action heroes, from Tarzans and Janes to Superman and Wonder Woman, that night's theme. As each clambered out they were gathered and ushered into the waiting people carrier which drove them around the site to the two waiting coaches.

As for the various drivers, well, once the people carrier was out of sight, pleasantries were dropped and they too were confronted with guns, searched and escorted to the lorry for their beating.

As for those that had dared ask for payment on receipt of the children, they beaten senseless, long before they made it to the confines of the lorry.

The night progressed, each vehicle was waived through one at a time, vehicles either filled with children or guests arrived and waited their turn in the queue to pass through the main gate and enter. It was a slow process, but no one suspected that this was to be the party that no one would ever forget.

Whilst the drivers and security filled the lorry, the guests had the long damp grass outside to sit or lie on. These were Yuri's reward, herded together, mostly men Again all were cable tied, illuminated by the portable lighting that encircled them as ex-Russian soldiers with guns dragged each, one by one, to the portable desk where they were searched for identity and questioned by Yuri.

Those that didn't have, dropped or secreted their identity in the grass were checked against the photocopies of the green ledger. Those that had been identified were taken to the lorry and those that remained unidentified were simply held in a smaller circle to one side. All bar Ernie, who had denied everything, demanding his release. For apparently, he had taken a 'wrong turn' and was simply lost.

It was a long night for everyone, including the children, but as the coaches filled and once Yuri was satisfied that there were no more late arrivals, these children were driven off in the two coaches, each filled to the brim with food, sweets and soft drinks, under guard, but happy, they set off watching the onscreen entertainment.

It was almost dawn before the last guest was dragged up towards Yuri. He in turn was searched, identified and then dragged up to the rear of the lorry. This left just seven, five men with no identification and two who Yuri had specifically chosen. All lay before him as he ordered them a beating.

Yuri turned and walked towards the lorry, in doing so he passed two compatriots who were already raking the long grass for any discarded trinkets or identification. Up the ramp he strode, he had a speech to make.

"Who I am is of no importance," he told them as the lorry quietened to a hush.

"What I am is though," he paused, trying and failing to disguise his strong accent.

"I'm your fucking nightmare!" He bellowed, hands on hips and postured like a great dictator to those that lay before him.

"I know where each of you live and work," he told them, "each of you will be contacted with the word Vortex."

"Vortex!" He yelled, ensuring those at the back heard every word, and everyone did.

"Pleasant journey," he abruptly finished his speech and with a flick of his dismissive wrist, he waved the mass goodbye. Down the ramp he turned, and the lorry's doors were closed and locked and only then the engine started.

Chapter 82

Sunday

It was God's day and at 6 am Harris wasn't best pleased that he had been woken up by a phone call from Ivan.

"The children." Harris confirmed. "How many?" He asked as he wiped his eyes, "How many?" He was astounded.

Ivan was clearly having difficulty hearing Harris above the vocal screams in the factory as 'soft shoe' went to work on his first captive with a pair of pliers.

"Let me think, I will give you a call back." Harris shouted, ending the call, trying to get the 'grey matter' between the ears to work.

Five minutes and a quick shower later, Harris had dressed and, with a coffee in hand, he returned the call. This time it was Yuri who had answered and agreed to the Detective's idea.

Chapter 83

Freshly brewed Brazilian coffee to wake the tired mind, an orange juice to clear the taste buds and local butter spread evenly on lightly toasted, crusty bread, followed by a small sliver of salmon pate, it looked like it was going to be a perfect sun-soaked Sunday morning for Mr Blue.

He had woken early as usual and tiptoed down from his marital bedroom, but not before he had checked on his sleeping children along the landing corridor. Only then he did he descend the stairs, in his dressing gown and slippers, to make himself his small breakfast. He had work to do, to prepare a sermon, as it was his turn in the local parish to take to the pulpit for Sunday morning service. So, carrying the small silver tray of mouth-watering delectable produce, he took it to the study and closed the door behind him.

It took him a good hour or so, flicking from one page to another in the family Bible and, having been set the title 'Protecting the children' it was passage in Galatians that caught his eye.

Verse 5:19-21 "Now the works of the flesh are evident: sexual immorality, impurity, sensuality, idolatry, sorcery, enmity, strife, jealousy, fits of anger, rivalries, dissensions, divisions, envy, drunkenness, orgies, and things like these. I warn you, as I warned you before, that those who do such things will not inherit the kingdom of God."

Mr Blue was indecisive as to such strong expression so he opted for Proverbs 22:6 "Train up a child in the way he should go; even when he is old he will not depart from it," and with a wry smile he began making notes of his past.

Mid-morning, he mounted the pulpit of St Jude's and stood in his Sunday, cotton rich, suit. There his Adam's apple wobbled as the congregation looked up in anticipation. There they saw him glow in a mixture of dust and smiles when the sunlight from the eastern window shone down on his stature.

His sermon was received in a mixture of silence, coughs and the occasional chuckle, as the parishioners listened in awe. He spoke about his household rules that kept his daughter's safe.

The only irritant was his mobile phone, set to silent vibrate, not once, twice, no thrice, he felt the tickle from his inside chest pocket. However, as any good Christian soldier, he worked through his notes, finally announcing to laughter the information he gave to the young boys in the audience, that he held a shotgun licence.

Returning to the family pew, there were smiles from his wife and his two loving daughters, but he was distracted from the congratulations as he looked downward at his phone, two missed calls and one text message. He read the latter quickly and became quite perturbed to the two words, 'Party crashed.'

He knew on his return home that Members of the FOH would be calling for a second meeting in as many weeks.

Was it obvious that he hadn't quite dealt with that troublesome Detective who had needed some 'adjustment' yes, he wondered, but another meeting?

The usual once a month meeting was long and arduous enough, but to throw in an emergency meeting and then another, this was becoming ridiculous.

As he looked up, the glare from his wife told him not to respond to the phone that now vibrated again, so he turned it off. It could wait, it had to wait; at least until after the service.

Chapter 84

East Ham Police Station, where opposite it on the same road is Newham Town Hall; that was where Harris was heading for. Saturday Harris had purchased another second-hand white Ford van, but this one had a refrigeration unit. That was where Harris headed having arranged with Ivan to meet the two coach loads of children.

Harris parked his van up in Wellington Road, a street just off the Barking Road junction, where the Town Hall and Police station meet.

He heard the fridge unit whirring away as he wrapped a West Ham football club scarf high around his face, put on a baseball cap that showed the same football club detail, ensuring that its peak was lowered to full depth so that between the cap and the high riding scarf, all that could be seen was his piercing blue eyes. He knew it would look a little weird on such a bright sunny day, but there was no way he was going to allow any street CCTV to capture his features or, for that matter, allow any passer-by to recognise his face.

Harris had specifically chosen East Ham Police Station, he knew it was due for sale and that it was currently being used as a substation. Minimal staff, perhaps one or two, one for the front desk and another in a quiet office away from the bustling street. He also knew that all that prevented the public from entering the rear yard was a single vehicle metal barrier that could be lifted, using the emergency button secreted on the wall nearby. He secretly congratulated himself on choosing this venue wisely.

As both coaches arrived he tapped on each door in turn and, when opened, he called the children out onto the pavement and, although it was now a massive gathering, he couldn't help but notice that some of the elder children were helping the younger ones to stand and a couple even piggybacked. It was then he realised that many were still recovering from the drugs their drivers or carers had obviously given them. Once satisfied that both coaches had been emptied he signalled the vehicles away and walked the children across the junction towards the barrier entrance of the Police station.

Though some of the children fled, not wanting to remain, perhaps fearful of the Police, many remained at his side and when the barrier was lifted, those that did entered.

Quickly the Detective gave out instructions as to exactly what to say when the adults came for them, some even waved him goodbye as he broke open and 'set off' the fire alarm.

Chapter 85

'At least they will be safer now,' Harris hoped as he imagined the scenes of bewildered Police and Firemen who were now looking after up to 80 children. There would be calls for assistance from other police stations, urgent calls to the child protection teams. There would be the call for ambulances to take those that were drugged and finally the taking of statements, each with the same story to tell. He smiled at, 'a job well done.'

He also caught himself smiling as he watched the evening local and national televised news in his lounge back in Emerson Park.

Though it wasn't in relation to a later news bulletin, informing that the Member of Parliament, Ernest Jones, had apparently committed suicide by throwing himself from a clifftop. A journalist had interviewed his distraught wife, caught unawares and totally shocked, as she thought he was in France at a conference representing the Government.

No, what made him smile was the big news item; the early-morning discovery of an abandoned lorry container found full of people in the departure lorry park of Dover's Ferry terminal.

Were there people actually trying to illegally leave the country? The commentator asked. Usually it was the other way around.

Chapter 86

Monday

It was a busy morning for the Detective. He moved the last of his possessions from the storeroom cupboard, from a solitude that had served him so well. He now sat at his desk in a new office, surrounded by a team where, for once, in a very long time, he didn't feel so alone.

Yes, although he had been followed for a number of weeks by a surveillance team attempting to watch his every move, it was still a loneliness that had haunted him. Now he was glad that he would no longer be left alone with his thoughts, where his only solace had been the company of a Russian that had crippled his sister; that was no friendship.

Now he had a team to work with, not just Detectives, but good Detectives who, on the face of it, seemed to understand his abilities and for once in a long time Harris felt appreciated.

Detective Inspector Jarvis also seemed a likeable boss, a fellow East Londoner whose work ethic was on the same lines as Harris. Single, 'job drunk' and just another local lad who was trying to rid the scum from London. Harris was quite happy that his office was next to where he now sat.

As soon as the meeting opened it was Jarvis at the helm and he made an announcement. He and Harris would soon be travelling up to Scotland and that the investigation files were to be scanned onto the team's new laptop for their use. Other than that, the team were allocated workloads, foreign enquiries to follow up and he included solved and unsolved cases from murders to disappearances along the British Railways.

After, each were asked individually, 'for any other business?' Harris went to work, scanning document after document; photograph after photograph and whilst it took him until mid-afternoon, he couldn't help but be curious as to the three ignored phone calls and a garbled message on his mobile from a barrister's secretary representing the honourable James McDermott and it was just before booking off that Harris rang back.

After apologies regarding the Detective's heavy workload, an appointment was made for Harris to attend the following morning.

'Plenty of time to prepare.' Harris told himself as he broke the seal of a new tape cassette and placed it into his mini tape recorder, that and a change to brand new batteries.

Chapter 87

Tuesday

The following morning McDermott called out to Harris' knock and the Detective entered slowly, deliberately and stared at his surroundings before looking towards the far end of the office where the barrister produced a smile.

"Come in officer, please come in and take a seat," Harris duly obliged.

"I can spare you half an hour Mr Harris, I'm sorry it's not longer, but the law waits for no man and I'm sure you'll understand." McDermott said whilst his arm gesture offered him a seat in front of him.

"Would you like a tea, or coffee perhaps?" And he lifted his phones receiver from its base.

"It's coffee, black, no sugar, thanks." Harris replied with a nod and checking his side pocket he felt the slightest vibration as the tape recorders wheels slowly turned.

Harris looked at this pompous little man and grimacing a smile to hide his disdain asked. "How can I help you? Your secretary told me it was quite urgent."

The barrister looked non-perplexed. "No not urgent officer, I just wanted to know what progress you've made in respect of Fiona's death."

This took Harris quite off guard, "I'm sorry but haven't you read the papers, my new boss Chief Superintendent Miller has recently proved that Fiona's death has been linked to the murders of two others."

"Linked murders eh, well I never." McDermott's attempt at surprise wasn't fooling, just misguided.

"Yes sir, he linked them, quite clever really and I'm really surprised that it has passed you by unnoticed." With that Harris watched as the little man clasped his left hand over his right fist to where he rubbed his thumb over his indented little finger.

"It won't go away." Harris announced, "not for a while, the ring mark will stay with you for quite some time, no matter how long you end up rubbing it."

McDermott didn't move, he just sat and lowered both hands under the desk and out of sight.

"I'm sorry officer, I don't know what you mean," that was the offering from the barrister.

"The red signet ring you were wearing the last time I saw you." The Detective offered. "The Fires of Hell club inscription, was it an oversight or did you wear it as a taunt? Perhaps a 'slight' towards Police incompetence or personally to me?"

"I'm sorry, you've lost me officer." McDermott qualified. "Yes, I did have a ring there." Offering the return of both hands from under the desk. "But I lost it and now I feel quite naked without it. But I really don't know what you're talking about, this, what did you say? Fires of Hell club?"

Harris offered sarcasm as his response. "Really?" He said. "So why did you want me here, last time you couldn't wait to get rid of me?"

"Professionalism, dear chap, we are both professionals and I'm simply keeping up with the Fiona's death," this was what he offered as the first beads of sweat hit his brow.

"Professionalism?" Harris repeated as he sat back to watch his prey squirm in the leather-bound chair.

"I'm professional enough to notice that you've removed the photograph of you and Mr Forrester from your wall where you can still see the dust marks." Harris said as he pointed back over his shoulder.

"And I bet another thing." Harris was on a roll. "I bet there are no other photographs in existence of you wearing your missing ring." And Harris watched with glee as McDermott's mouth slowly opened.

"Ah," McDermott slowly mumbled as he tried to form a sentence.

"I guess not." Harris retorted as he pushed his hand into the inside pocket of his jacket and pulled out a single page that once belonged in the Green Ledger. This he unfolded twice and began to read the notes.

"James McDermott, barrister, it has this chambers address and your home address in Middlesex. A wife, three children and your preference is little girls. The younger the better it notes and these you would regularly purchase during a Fires of Hell party, just so you could continue with them afterwards, you sick fucking bastard!"

Harris paused and looked towards the shrunken man. "It doesn't say sick fucking bastard, but I am sure you would agree with me." And Harris drew satisfaction that McDermott now edged away.

There was silence, Harris deliberately kept the silence flowing as he waited for the barrister to gather a reply and gather he did.

"It's lies officer, pure fabrication and slander and if you utter a word outside these walls I will sue you and the Metropolitan Police and you will have no future, do you understand?"

"Yes, sir I do." Harris said glibly, "but I don't want you, you 'fuckhead,' I want the murderer of Fiona, you know, the person you introduced Fiona Grant Smith to, the person you warned about Mr Forrester taking over the investigation, that's all I fucking want." And he took a breath.

"You're only the utter bastard that told the murderer that Mr Forrester was now in possession of the Grant-Smith file, so you know the murderer, and I want the name." Harris demanded.

McDermott laughed, it was a nervous laugh, but still a red-faced laugh of derision. "Pure conjecture and assumption, utter rubbish," he told Harris, "and if I knew the murderer, I am certain that under legal privilege that I certainly wouldn't be divulging anything to the likes of you."

"So, forget professionalism you piece of shit, why did you really invite me here?" Harris demanded.

The barrister leaned forward and offered his proposition, "Officer you can tell the world that it was Chief Superintendent Hutchings or Miller that led the enquiry, I don't care, but I know it was you all along." Harris silenced.

"I suggest you forget what you have seen and I, with due respect, will pretend this conversation never took place, otherwise you really wouldn't want me to tell my friends in high places that it was you all along, now would you?"

Harris suddenly jolted and stood. It was an electric shock of realism as he remembered Cooper's claims of the Government arm he worked for, knowing all too well their potential capabilities.

"Now kindly leave my office before I have you thrown out." McDermott dismissed and instead of repeatedly punching the little man full in the face, Harris did as he asked and turned.

"Thank you for your time." Harris said as he walked towards the door. Where in actual fact he really wanted to rip this man's throat out, but the Detective knew that there would be a time for him so thought better of it.

"One more thing." McDermott called out. "Be careful out there, you really don't want your fingers burnt."

Harris closed the door behind him and took the short flight of lush, carpet stairs down to the reception area. There he took his time ensuring that he said goodbye to both reception ladies and even waited whilst one ended a call on the telephone and, though strange, he also handed them his business card before he signed himself out.

Harris took a short walk to Embankment tube station and watched the Thames, but he wasn't leaving, not just yet, he had another appointment to keep at the Rawson Café in Villiers Street.

He sat down to make a table of three, as opposite was Yuri with yet another business partner, a Mr Grant Smith. Harris held out his tape recorder, that he rewound and pressed play.

Chapter 88

The girl was blindfolded and gagged, enclosed in a hessian sack that was tied tightly at one end and she shuddered in the darkness as she sobbed out loud. She no longer had nails to offer and her hair had been shaved off, she also knew the beast had tired of her when it had inspected her, squeezing her hands and toes as if pressing to produce instant growth!

Now there was that new girl who had arrived the day earlier, the beast had taken his first nail from her as she recalled those pitiful screams in that desolate building.

The girl had cried out, asking for her mother, her sister, anyone, how she cried, knowing that there was no one to help her. She cried from the pain of her tightly bound wrists and the pain of that first ripped nail. She remembered that girl had cried in desperation and had wet herself, just as she did now in that hessian sack.

There was a wince as the car hit yet another pothole, on what she could only assume was a dirt track, but she couldn't see out from her tear soaked blindfold, nor the thick sack, into the matt black of darkness surrounding her where she lay in the car's boot.

But she smelt the black oil surroundings, perhaps work clothes, perhaps cloth, perhaps just the boot mat, but there was also another smell, the musty aroma of damp, perhaps where other girls had wet themselves. She screamed her muffled screams trying to compete with the loud V8 engine and the Country and Western music from the stereo on full volume.

It was near the journey's end she assumed, the speed had slowed on an upward climb and it repeatedly manoeuvred left to right, then it slowed to a halt and the handbrake was fully applied.

Only then the boot was opened and she could feel the knife cutting sack, hands ripping at the cloth that she now curled in. The girl tried to offer up pleas, but these were indistinguishable as the gag restricted her voice.

Hands grabbed her, pulling her naked body out from what she had thought was her metal tomb and she fell into the sunlight. Then, with a rope tied round her waist, she was led.

Oh, how the weak form stumbled on such uneven earth, time and again she fell over clump, bracken and occasional rock, but relentlessly she was pulled until out of the sunshine, the shaded air cooled.

Chapter 89

The Penny hotel in Aberdeen had been welcoming guests since the mid-19th century, and, independently owned in the heart of the city, the flamed hearth warmed both Harris and Jarvis who stood nearby.

Both had just endured thirteen hours of delays and diversions when driving from fume filled London and, to make matters worse, the car's heater had stopped working at less than midway. It was gone 9pm and both relished a quick check-in and an even faster takeaway, followed by the bar.

At 8am the next morning Harris choked at the smell of 'heavy' on his breath and no amount of mints swallowed could hold the stench away. However, this was the least of his worries, he was already late for breakfast and he was starving.

A 'full Scottish' it was called and not in any way like a 'full English,' with its orange juice, coffee, porridge and toast. Then the usual breakfast meats, bacon and sausage and other accompaniments, but not a hash brown or chip in sight, instead it was 'tattie scone' and black pudding you could brick a house with. Harris couldn't move and he was stuffed until dinner.

It turned out to be quite a result really, as both Jarvis and Harris had spent the next ten hours in Aberdeen's City Divisional Headquarters in Queen Street. It was there Harris gave his presentation from the team laptop that linked their missing Claire to three London murders. From that point, they sat with the Scottish Detectives and went through all relevant statements. There were DNA findings and photographs, it had been long, long day.

Harris was feeling tired, he'd been tired from driving the day before and now he was tired of talking. He wanted to replenish, in reality he wanted a beer and after leaving his briefcase and team laptop in his room he headed with speed to the hotel bar to meet up with Jarvis.

"Excuse me Mr Harris, it is Mr Harris, room fourteen?" The hotel receptionist was heard to call out as he rushed past.

"Yes," he quickly stopped, "how can I help you?" He turned to the young lady.

"There is an envelope addressed to you," she told him and passed him a small brown envelope. The detective opened the envelope there and then and within it was a small computer pen drive.

"When did it arrive?" He asked curiously.

"Earlier, before my shift, I'm afraid," she told him.

Harris knew that Aberdeen CID were sharing information so he thanked her and pocketed the pen drive as he headed to the bar.

One pint in, Harris found himself continually reaching into his jacket where he held the pen drive, so he simply asked. "Boss are we expecting any deliveries whilst we are up here?"

Jarvis shook his head "No, why?"

"It's nothing boss," he lied, "I just wondered if we were expecting anything."

"Harris, you did a fine job, it was a good presentation and you've 'covered all bases,' even down to a copy of her train ticket to compare with Mrs Forrester's" Jarvis told him, "now let's get pissed and go for a curry," and Jarvis smiled as he palmed congratulations on Harris' broad shoulders. So, for the next couple of hours they did just that. Both agreed that the meal was superb and both were quite drunk and content with their day's work, that and each other's company.

Walking towards the hotel entrance both replied "Good night" to the posh voiced man that had called out "Twelve bells and good evening." It was a tall shadowy figure that quickly walked past and on passing both Jarvis and Harris in turn, turned to each other and improvised in their poshest voice a "Good evening" to each other, for it had been a bloody good night.

On entering the hotel Jarvis suggested 'one for the road' that turned into four before heading to their rooms and Harris had all but forgotten the pen drive in his pocket when he staggered through the door. That was, until emptying his jacket, where it fell out onto the floor along with his car keys.

"Ah, there you are," he slurred loudly and turning to the laptop on his bed he tried inserting it. He almost gave up after the third attempt, but with one eye shut he managed to focus and once in, he turned to the bathroom to run a shower whilst the wee machine 'booted up.'

Harris was desperate for the room to stop spinning before laying his head on a pillow and he thought a cold shower was just the solution.

He was only gone a short time before he returned clean and just a little refreshed, so pressing the settings and devices button he soon discovered that the drive contained a media video file of which he pressed 'play.'

Soon the silent flashing images pixelated across his blurring vision, he tried to focus on the four camera, quartered scenes. Top left, a pavement view of metal railings that lead to an entrance, top right, a back garden.

Harris had to guess the time by its darkness, either late night or early morning.

Bottom left a darkened hallway, leading from the street he presumed, then bottom right, a kitchen and apart from the glow of a cooker on/off light, it too was pitched in darkness.

The seconds passed, but nothing, no movement, nothing to stir his senses, just four untimed views and Harris yawned wondering what was on the hotel room's television instead, but as soon as he thought about searching for the TV remote, in the top left quarter he saw three men.

Well at least he thought it was three men by the size and stature of them, but each of their heads were blurred and distorted, a professional pixel edit and it now caught Harris' interest.

He watched as one of the men appeared to be fiddling with a door lock below the camera's angle. This was done whilst the other two flanked him on either side. Then a light was switched on, but where? Bottom left, presumably from a landing as it was a partial part of the stairs in the hallway that suddenly shone from above.

Harris' eyes opened wider as the central man now appeared to be working furiously, one second, two seconds, the detective counted and the men were in, each in turn ran up the hall stairs, upward and out of view.

Harris sat mesmerised and then it dawned on him, he was looking at Cooper's hallway table, his hallway stairs and it was now his light that swept from side to side.

An agonising slowness in time, nothing happened on all four views, but that was always the agony for Harris, the unknown.

Then at last he saw something, at least it was something in the upstairs shadows, fast waves of darkness back and forth they came, 'a struggle?' He wondered as he let his mind slowly realise what he was watching.

The Detective's jaw dropped at the same time as Cooper's body did and Harris felt sick to his stomach as he imagined the snapped jolt of the rope that hung Cooper by the neck. Feet kicking, body swinging, alone in that hallway.

There was shock, a total shock and it froze Harris through these images as he stared.

It was fear that hits once in a lifetime, a nerve ripping, chest pounding squeeze and Harris sat toward the screen, soul open and undone.

The End.

Printed in Great Britain
by Amazon

20824796R00212